Devil's Edge

B.K. Crawford

Edited by Mandy Cummins

Cover Design by *Jaqui Renee*
Photography by *Angie Crawford*

Published in the United States of America

Mind Key Publishing

ISBN 978-0-9912936-9-8
099129369X

Devil's Edge

This book is dedicated to Angie, my devoted soul mate who allowed me the love, freedom, and time to explore the depths of my imagination.

To my sons, Nick and Chris, around whose light and love my world revolves.

To my trusted friend and comrade, Mandy Cummins, without her devotion and editorial skills, this work would not be possible.

Special thanks to Lianne Anderson for her artwork contributions.

Devil's Edge

Contents

PART ONE

The Raid
1718

The scent of burning wood wound its way through the grove as Fujo Sinclair burst out the door of her hut, running with all the speed her legs could afford, weaving past blurring palms, intermittently pausing to cry out for her young sister, Catti.

The impact of thundering canon shots rocked Fujo from her feet. Knees buried in the sand, she pressed her hands over her ears and prayed for the safety of the village. Quickly regaining her composure, she stood to inhale a breath of air saturated with the horrifying rankness of expelled gunpowder, an odor seeming to waft from the annals of the not-so-distant past.

Spanish brigands had come to raid Jérémie three years earlier, mercilessly slaughtering anyone who stood in defense, torching half the village for folly. The stench of burnt wood and charred flesh lingered for months afterward. Although Fujo spent many a night praying this particular scent would never invade her nostrils again, it had returned.

Why didn't she show more concern when the bells of St. Marie sounded earlier? Had she placed too much trust in her second sight, not giving the alert the respect it deserved simply because she hadn't received a warning in a vision or a dream? There seemed no other explanation. How arrogant. How foolish.

She was still twenty minutes from the village and, without a miracle, the prospect of arriving on time did not seem promising.

Surely, Catti had taken refuge near the coastline. Veering right, Fujo searched as she approached the outskirts of the village. Previous raids on Jérémie taught her that those who came pillaging assigned guards on the lookout for strays, all the more reason for extreme caution.

Praying, she grasped her amulet. Coiled emerald, carved in intricate detail, the serpentine sculpture passed from priestess to priestess for the past two hundred years. It hung from a gold chain Fujo wore with pride and tempered humility; one day she would pass it on to her own daughter should Bondye find her worthy to bear children. The amulet had hammered against her breastbone as she battered through the palm grove, but now, as she cradled it, the powerful talisman seemed to assure her it would not abandon the hour.

As she ran, the dense foliage began to thin, freeing her to navigate the grove, and although this allowed for more speed, the sudden lack of adequate cover increased the possibility of detection by a hundredfold.

Her legs ached from the nearly inhuman sprint she maintained, both feet bleeding profusely, though she had no recollection of injuring them; sweat mixed with blood, causing crimson streaks to ooze from her arms and legs, her lungs begging for a reprieve she did not intend to provide.

She found her path suddenly blocked by a misshapen mound of sand rising up in a place where none had ever arisen before, and she had followed this path to the village enough times for accurate recollection. Was this a deception of the mind? *Bondye, pray thee, I have no time for tricks!* She slowed her pace as she approached the anomaly, supposing perhaps a tortoise had hunkered down against the mortar flying in off the sea. Attempting to leap over the blockade, her foot snagged on the rising clump of ground, sending her sprawling into the sand, face-first. To her surprise, the lump revealed itself as none other than Henri Vasquél's head as he chose the most inopportune time to lift it up in an attempt to have a look from his carefully camouflaged point of view.

"Henri! What are you doing? What's happening in the village? Where is your family?"

"*Shhhh*, Mambo. Dead...they're all dead...everyone's dead...no one lives...all dead. Save yourself...dig in...cover yourself carefully...they'll see."

"Henri! My Momma?"

Devil's Edge

"Donc désolé. Dead, I'm sure."

"*Momma!*"

"*Shhhhhhhhh!* Our heads will bob on the waves if they hear. Quiet, Mambo, or get on with you. I mean to live a long life."

Fujo's feet bore into the ground so quickly, so deeply, she left Henri sputtering out a mouth full of sand. He was wrong about Momma; a madman rambling on in shock with no concern for his words. Such things happen when chaos reigns, it is not unheard of. While it seemed true Fujo's second sight had abandoned her, she would sense it if Momma were dead, feel the weight of it on her soul, surely her heart would cease to beat and dissolve into the sands.

Drawing closer to the village, she heard the faint bark of men shouting, along with shrieks of rage and outrage. She shortened her stride, taking care to hide behind scattered palm trunks as she moved along. Clearly not everyone was dead: yet. Momma and Catti must be among the survivors. Fujo hoped for nothing else.

The whisper of a new prayer caught the wind as a strong pair of arms wrapped around her waist and a brisk leg swiped her feet from beneath her. She fell to the ground with such a blow she lost her breath. Captured.

In a moment, a swift hand would lift her face from the sand and rake a blade across her throat, sending her on to the spirit world.

She would spend her last moments wisely, listening to the wind as it tangled itself around palm fronds, coupled with the majestic roar of the surf as it broke against the coastline. She immersed herself in the sensation of the soft cushion of sand beneath her, tiny grains of crystal that would not amount to much without their stubborn unity. Of course, she thought of her betrothed, Bwanhe, painful as it was to know she would never again smell the musk of his skin, or hear his girlish laughter. She thought of the hundreds of villagers she had grown to love, souls gentle as newborn lambs and nearly as innocent, souls dying at the hands of strange men who knew nothing of them. Momma, stranded defenseless and alone while Père and Bwanhe sailed to Jamaica. Catti left in this violent world without comfort or care. A shrill shriek of angst escaped her throat.

"Quiet," urged a voice she knew intimately.

Rolling onto her back, Fujo swiped the sand from her eyes. The blurred vision of Catti's face came into view, rife with fear and smeared with soot, her long black hair tangled by the wind, both knees gouged and bleeding. Despite the look of her, Fujo had never been so happy to see her sister. Flinging her arms around Catti's shoulders, she pulled her into a tight embrace. "What's happening?"

"They sank the harbor guard...they're burning everything...killing those who cannot run."

"Who are they?"

Pressing her face into the nook of Fujo's neck, Catti spoke hastily, "Slave traders. They've taken some in chains. Dutchmen perhaps, I cannot be certain."

Fujo watched as clouds of churning black smoke rose over the treetops, billowing like hell's breath, toward the mountains behind. It would do no good to go to St. Marie's. The bells had grown silent; surely, the fire had already gutted the cathedral. Still, though time-consuming, they could use Tortue's path and approach the village from behind.

"Come, we must get to Momma."

"No, ma soeur," Catti shook her head with firm defiance, "They nearly had me. If I hadn't bitten one to the bone, I would be dead or in chains. We must go back to your hut and hope they don't follow."

Fujo pulled back to inspect Catti's eyes, "We can't leave Momma to face them alone."

"I love Momma as much as anyone and I am no coward, but neither a fool. We have no means to save her, no weapons between us. Are we to beat the brutes off with palm fronds and conk shells? We can only save ourselves and that we must do, as our Mother would wish."

Fujo gently kissed Catti's seared cheek. "You're right, of course. Go back into the grove and remain there until it's safe to return. I must press on until I know what has happened to Momma. Please understand."

"I understand only that you are a fool. First, to think you have any power over these cutthroats and, second, to think I would leave you to go on alone. If you're certain you wish to die today, we will do so together."

How had it come to this? The sun had risen peacefully that morning, with no hint of chaos on its face. Fujo began the day with an examination of Elana Louaine's protruding belly. Twins, definitely, but whether or not there were triplets, she could not say. Unwilling to utter words she could not speak with certainty, she had paused to carefully survey Elana's imploring eyes. The color of a cup of perfectly steeped tea, and soft in their expression, Elana's eyes seemed the same bright, loving orbs as always, although glassy and swollen with red trails of weariness. Fujo smiled then, remembering those same eyes once belonged to the fire-filled soul of a young girl with whom she'd mastered the art of crab and mollusk gathering, and to the same spirit caught in an unending giggling fit after seeing a boy naked for the first time when she and Fujo haphazardly stumbled upon Unmar Donuton as he frolicked in the lagoon beneath the Falls of Marchand. Had Elana's jubilant spirit somehow faded beneath the weight of her marriage to the hard-handed Gerard Louaine; a man who, at first glance, seemed temperate enough, but whose innards slowly rotted away over the loss of a promotion aboard the French schooner he had served for twenty years?

Since stepping inside her domestic roll, Elana's visits became altogether infrequent; not to hand Elana the entire blame for their neglected friendship, the vast responsibilities of a high priestess proved time-consuming as well, and the distance between the village and Fujo's hut also factored into the equation as it took more than an hour to walk the entire way. It came as a welcomed relief when Elana developed an over-estimated need for examination during the past few months; Fujo had missed her terribly. Now fate clasped Elana's safety, and that of her unborn children, in its hands.

Black smoke curled into the palm grove, putrid phantoms pressing Fujo for a decision. The desire to protect Catti raged strong, but no stronger than her desire to secure Momma's safety.

Tortue's Path

Ever notorious for its reptiles and insects; a body becomes a meal on Tortue's Path in a matter of hours if a swift pace is not employed. Fujo batted in vain at a cloud of mosquitoes. The more sweat she produced, the more ravenous the swarm. Dense, leafy foliage engulfed the path, serving as a heat and moisture trap. A mile long, the tract incubated some of nature's most vile creatures, a swamp worthy to challenge the bravest heart. Fujo followed the course only once in her lifetime and would have avoided that occurrence if her initiation as high priestess did not depend upon it; the soil beneath her feet felt solid then, as she had navigated the grounds during the dry season, now it oozed with a stubborn mud that clung to her ankles like demon claws. Catti fell four times since entering the forsaken jungle and began to curse like a seasoned sailor.

"Words such as those will not win Bondye's graces, Catti."

"If we stood anywhere near Bondye's graces we would have no need to battle through this stewing pit of lizard dung."

Bondye, shower your mercies upon Momma, Fujo prayed, *who could possibly deserve them more?* Reaching for the stem of a fern frond that stretched across the path she yanked it out of the way.

Countless villagers owed their very lives to the tenacity Momma displayed over the years, especially the year the winds of horror blew through Jérémie. Although the winds came during Fujo's youth, she never forgot the horrible storm.

A vision came to Momma a week before the tempest gathered; truly a gift sent from the protective spirits possessing her. In this vision, she saw all of Jérémie consumed by ravaging winds, along with a great wall of water sent to swallow all within its path. Without hesitation, she called for a gathering, conveying the horrendous accounts of all she had seen. Though many of the elders scoffed, claiming folly of the mind, she would hear no whisper of doubt, and insisted upon making immediate preparations for the evacuation of the village. This, she clearly stated, she would accomplish on her own, if no other would offer assistance, saying it is far better to live in the shadow of error than to misjudge the hands of fate.

In five days time, Momma's army of volunteers moved swads of emergency supplies to the highlands, Momma insisting, all the while, that Bondye had not placed a mountain range behind the village without reason. Still the elders scoffed. When a horde of angry clouds and tree bending gusts of wind moved over the village the following day, the elders were first to set a swift foot upon the path leading to the mountain.

The storm raged with the fierceness of a demon scorned. For days, predatory waters lapped at the foot of the mountain, threatening ascent, leaving waves of extended ocean where the village once stood. The elders spent the entire week boasting of the great wisdom they had shown in having supplies moved to higher ground.

As the storm's tantrum concluded, the skies cleared and the waters receded. Momma led the way as Jérémie's denizens followed her down the mountain and into the fields of sludge they once called home; not one soul lost to fate's fury.

The village, however, required reconstruction. The storm washed away hundreds of thatched homes and only the stone structures, few as they were, remained.

Because hers was one of the few stone homes built in Jérémie, (Père graced with the good fortune to afford such a luxury) Momma made it her first order of business to clear it of sludge and debris. The elders loudly proclaimed this a rather selfish thing to do, but Momma travailed until the house stood spotless and then insisted all of Jērémie's residents should reside as her guests while the rebuilding of the village commenced. For months, she arose before any other and set her head to pillow only after everyone else slept; elders included. Many were the days she returned home from a day of rebuilding soaked from head to toe and caked in layers of mud. Still she summoned the energy to spend half the night cooking. If a woman cannot offer what she has to give in a time of crisis, she said, no true worth resides within her.

Momma would readily sacrifice her life for another, her love was the cornerstone of Fujo's life, no jewel would ever shine brighter. Life without Momma would amount to no more than a dark abyss, merely an existence, no spice, no flavor.

The bleak smoke devouring Jērémie began to dissipate as Fujo and Catti reached the backside of the village, the pillaging complete. As Fujo feared, she and Catti arrived too late. She paused before leaving the security of Tortue's camouflage. Though the chaos in the village had subsided, and the smoke thinned, there could be stragglers, men left behind to waylay those fortunate enough to have escaped the initial onslaught. Although Fujo's heart called upon her to rush to Momma's aid, the house stood on the other side of the village, she could not risk detection.

The roof of Elana Louaine's hut, the first in Fujo's line of sight, smoldered in the sand as it coughed up its last testament. Whatever would the poor woman do with twins coming and no roof to shelter them? *A curse on the foul souls who have done this terrible thing.*

As she and Catti moved from one destroyed hut to another, Fujo ached with the desire to get close enough to the coast to see if Momma's home remained unscathed. She must also know if the attacking ship still lurked in the harbor. Scurrying from one hiding place to the next, she stopped only when a bellowing voice rode the wind. So far, she didn't see a single corpse, thanks be to the protecting spirits. Henri and Catti told her the assailants were killing anyone who couldn't run fast enough, yet she saw no bodies strewn about. Dare she hope no one actually perished in this assault? The prayer lingered as she and Catti made their way toward the sea.

The coast finally became visible, the sails of the invading ship an ominous sight. By far the largest ship in Fujo's recollection, it sported three main masts, its canvases breathing wind they had no right or claim to. Despite its exceptional size, the ship crept closer to shore than any other ever dared.

A commotion ensued on the beach near a line of dinghies shoving off to return to the flagship. An ocean of color rest at the soles of the intruders' feet and Fujo felt no desire to venture a guess as to what might cause such a bizarre sight. The attackers were rowing back to the ship, leaving Jerémie's shores. With the brutes gone, Fujo and Catti were free to run the rest of the way with abandon.

The house stood untouched by fire, as they hoped. Arriving at the back door, they found the kitchen in complete disarray. Pots lay smashed upon the floor, tables and chairs overturned, windows shattered, and a bag of flour left a telltale trail leading from the kitchen through the front door. The raiders took everything fit to eat and, of course, the silver. They ripped Père's meager art collection from the walls and removed every stitch of fine clothing.

Hearts heavy and jaws slackened, Fujo and Catti stared at one another in shocked silence until, suddenly, as if the thought crossed their minds in the same instant, they raced for the stairs, bellowing, "Momma!"

When no answer came, Catti dropped to her knees and slammed her fists into the floorboards. "They've killed her."

Fujo placed a hand on her sister's shoulder. "No. She's alive, I'm sure of it. We must get to the shore."

"What if pillagers remain? We'll be captured."

"Aye, that you will," interjected a gruff voice emanating from directly behind the startled women.

Fujo and Catti bolted for the stairs. Two men in leather armor lunged from the closet housing Père's most expensive whisky,

Devil's Edge

easily subduing their prey with little more than the surprise of their presence. The men immediately fit Fujo and Catti in rusted shackles and dragged them, kicking and screaming, to the edge of the sea.

The Devil Himself

It soon became clear what the ocean of color Fujo witnessed earlier consisted of. The marauders slew the villagers and left them to bleed into the sand, their colorful garments flapping in the wind. Fujo recognized them all and nearly lost her ground when she caught sight of Elana Louaine; lifeless, eyes aghast and opened wide, throat slashed from ear to ear, her abdomen hauntingly devoid of movement; the sea preparing to swallow her up.

Fujo and Catti's abductors put them under guard while they returned to finish plundering Père's whisky closet. Upon return, they uncovered a dinghy they took great pains to conceal, forced Catti and Fujo onboard, and shoved off for the flagship.

It is apparently possible for the soul to escape the body and yet leave the heart beating, as only this could account for the emptiness Fujo felt as she watched the mound of color on the shoreline recede, growing smaller until the gruesome sight disappeared altogether. Momma's demise seemed certain, although no one could say if she lie among those lining the shore. Without ample time for inspection, Fujo could not be certain, but believed she would have found more than one villager still breathing, which explained why they lay at the edge of the sea: those still alive would not have the strength to fight the incoming tide and would eventually drown. Fujo glared at the filth manning the dinghy: *murderous, thieving, black-souled vermin destined for the bowels of hell, may that journey commence swiftly.*

The sky grew devoid of its normal activity, not a single gull danced with the wind. A gray pallor stretched over the heavens, washing away what was, but a few hours ago, a bright and cheerful day. The water beat against the side of the small boat with a throbbing lament for the events transpired. No dolphins pranced through the surf, nor a kingfish or ray in sight. All of nature seemed aware Satan himself had come to plunder Jērémie.

Climbing the rope ladder leading onto the ship's deck proved a formidable task as sea slime coated the slippery hemp. Hands tangled in shackles, muscles fatigued from the trek to the village and the ensuing struggle against her captors, Fujo couldn't seem to find the strength to rise up. Despite a blade pressed firmly to her back, she faltered upon the ropes. If only she could give the rogue behind her a swift kick to the head. Tempting as this prospect seemed, Catti struggled in the middle of the procession and if the man prodding Fujo fell off the ropes, those behind him would tumble as well.

Arriving topside, Fujo met with an unfathomable sight. At the center of a heated quarrel, stood none other than Momma, shackled hand and foot, but breathing. *Glory to Bondye and the spirits of protection.*

Next to Momma stood a robust man who looked as though he ate enough for forty men, his pudgy cheeks red with too much sun or drink, and he spoke heatedly with another man whose garb matched those bequeathed to kings; golden threaded brass buttons and shining knee-high black boots, the long curls of his white wig insufficient to conceal his youth. Only the captain of a ship would wear such frocks. Here stood the man to blame for the evils inflicted upon Jērémie: the devil himself.

"Sir," the chubby fellow said, his voice rising for all on deck to hear, "She claims to fine cookery. The bloke hidden away in the galley merely burns rocks without spice." With a dramatic wave of the arm and a raised brow he bellowed, "Shouldn't we have a decent meal upon our journey now and again?"

The Captain spoke with distinct authority, "My instructions were specific, Donovan. Abandon the infirm and the elderly.

Devil's Edge

Correct me if ye find me in error, but this specimen is clearly elderly. However, as a matter of amusement, I shall give pause to the petition. I ask this, are ye truly willing to incite mutiny over culinary prowess?" Cocking his head off to the side, the Captain rest his hand upon the butt of a pistol nestled in a bandolier strapped across his chest.

Frightened by the Captain's words, Fujo shouted in rage, "Bondye, set your spirit upon this man's soul and move him to have mercy where he has shown none yet upon this day."

The Captain abruptly turned upon his heels, pointed a rigid finger toward Fujo, and barked, "What is this wretched creature daring to speak without invitation?"

One of Fujo's abductors promptly put a hand over her mouth and clamped her head tightly against his chest.

"That simply will not do," the Captain sneered. "Take it to the hold and put it in proper chains."

"But, we are her daughters," Catti screamed.

The Captain turned sharply to face Catti. "Is that so?" His voice lilted with amusement as he gave a furtive glance to each of the women, a coy grin playing at the corners of his mouth. "Forgive my ignorance," he said, bending forward in an exaggerated bow. "Ye shall remain."

"And now, sir," he said, replacing his hand upon his pistol. "I believe ye must answer my inquiry. Are we to have mutiny over a few burnt rocks?"

While Donovan held the Captain's attention, Momma made gestures in an awkward attempt to communicate. She lifted her knee, slightly but forcefully, then cocked her elbow and jabbed it downward, then raised her chin, tilted her head off to the side, and closed her eyes. Though crude, Fujo understood. She recognized the gestures as part of a defense exercise Père taught the village women. Momma had kneed one of her attackers in the groin and planted an elbow to the back of his head, just as Père instructed. If Fujo interpreted the last gestures correctly, one of the attackers had struck Momma, rendering her unconscious.

Blood smeared Momma's lips and locks of white hair fell loose from the tight wrap she kept it in, stray hairs clinging to trickles of blood dripping down the length of her dark face. The whites of her black licorice eyes appeared red and swollen. Her assailants stole her shoes, ripped her dress, and made her to look every bit the weak and unprofitable human being the Captain assumed her to be.

Momma gently placed her hand over her heart, bowed her head in the manner she practiced when expressing her love to her children, smiling with brave reassurance, and the world felt suddenly at peace, not because the spirits delivered a vision or a message, but because Momma's smile held a calming magic.

Wriggling on the edge of the Captain's inquiry, Donovan's face turned a brighter shade of red, though one would have thought such a thing quite impossible. Clearly at a loss for words, his reply consisted of no more than a slight turn of the lips, which seemed a bit of a mocking smirk. The Captain apparently drew the same conclusion, as he promptly broke his pistol free of its holster and fired. Donovan's body fell to the deck, a lead plug planted squarely between his eyes. Then, with the speed of a lightning bolt, the Captain returned his pistol to its proper place and unsheathed his cutlass. He took two steps toward Momma, spun upon his heels, returned the blade to its sheath, and chuckled as he glared at Fujo and Catti, both confounded by his actions, or what seemed a lack thereof.

The lines on the Captain's face furled into a grimace and, seemingly disappointed with the blank confusion washing over the faces of his observers, he took a determined step toward Momma, whose eyelids began to move in a wild flutter while her mouth opened and closed repeatedly without making the slightest sound, he curled his hand into a light fist and tapped the back of her head, which promptly fell from her shoulders and landed with a sickening thud at her feet.

Catti wailed like a Siren caught in a fisherman's net and although Fujo parted her lips with the same intention, she could not seem to raise more than a faint squeal.

Devil's Edge

The captain gave orders to throw Momma's body overboard, forcing Fujo and Catti to watch as her severed head battled to stay afloat. Leaning forward, Fujo fought to catapult herself over the rail—every instinct drawing her toward Momma—yet the men firmly held her back. Trapped, her ears gave reluctant audience to the Captain's laughter, which spewed forth with such merriment Fujo prayed he would die of his malefic mirth.

Once Momma's head submerged, the crew dragged Fujo and Catti off to the ship's underbelly and chained them to a long line of battered prisoners. Fujo spied Henri Vasquél muttering curses among the other captives; surely, he reconsidered his desire for a long life.

The Transfer

A week's worth of tide passed beneath the slave schooner when it met with a dire blow cunningly delivered by an undetected sloop. The devil Captain, clad in his fine frocks and pristine wig, stood precisely in the wrong spot as canon fire loosed a plank off starboard and sent it flying through the air with such velocity it promptly relieved him of the pompous weight resting so assuredly upon his shoulders. To Fujo's great satisfaction, the pirates who provided such relief saw fit to hang the bounder's severed head from the bowsprit of their sloop until, weeks later, nothing but bare skull remained. The pirates dismembered the schooner's crew, one by one; their innards used for fishing tackle, their meager wealth permanently transferred, most of them falling beneath the hand of a man who looked suspiciously pretty for a common sailor. Though one of the worst horrors Fujo ever witnessed, Momma's murder excepted, she thought it a fitting end for the devil and his minions, yet no less dangerous for prisoners shifted from the hands of one soulless crew to another.

The Merry Anne

The pungent odor of urine-soaked straw clawed at Fujo's nostrils as she awoke with a twist in her gut. Not a twist of hunger—many of those pangs she suffered as of late—but a much deeper braid, one causing the hair on her arms to stand at attention as her flesh grew unnaturally cold; a sensation she experienced far too many times over the course of her twenty-eight years. Pressing a hand to her stomach, she buckled forward as a shiver raced along her spine. Her vision blurred, though no tears obstructed her eyes, and the rhythm of a warring heart pounded within her ears, beating as if striking a battle drum. Breath abated, she slumped, unconscious, into a mound of straw.

As the bleary world slowly returned to view, she thought of the faint she suffered hours before her young nephew, Jacque, missed his dive off Hautes-chutes and shattered his head upon the merciless rocks: *may his peace last eternally*. Had this faint come bearing the same type of ill omen? Pray no, she thought, but yes. Something unspeakable approached.

Sails breathed bursts of tropical wind as the masthead of *The Merry Anne* groaned beneath the weight of its arduous burden. Weathered timbers moaned against the spanking waters, howling creaks and screeches, bellowing haunting trills. Scrawny rats dueled for rare morsels of food; demonized creatures gnashing at jugulars until the least fortunate became a sudden banquet.

A bell clanged on deck, its brattle sounding thrice before its harsh echo surrendered to the sea.

Fujo peered through the crisscrossed metal gate covering the mouth of the hold and observed as the dawn took its first breath. It would be wise, she thought, to walk gingerly today, keep the senses alert, and avoid contact—as much as possible—with the barbarous pirates holding Jérémie's remnants hostage. Such precautions held no hope to dissuade the spirits' omen but, with a token of good fortune, they chanced to buffer the impact of Hell's folly.

"Iwa be with us," she whispered, binding her long black hair with a ratty leather string. Slowly, she ran her fingertips over the soft fabric of her crimson dress, the one remaining possession the sea thieves had not confiscated. No longer the blazing red it once was, its rich threads faded from too much exposure to the Caribbean sun, the dress retained barely enough color to set off her bronze skin and dark eyes.

An urgent longing to caress Bwanhe's face overtook her. She had hoped for children of her own. She recalled praying for the grace of Bondye to permit Bwanhe to return from Jamaica in time for a summer wedding. She thought they might seize a few weeks of solitude before the whisper of the sea seduced him with its beguiling enticements. He made a vow to curtail his travels in the interest of raising a family, and although Fujo would have liked to believe his oath, she suspected Bwanhe did not know his own soul as well as she. How could he hope to constrain himself to a lizard nest like Jérémie? His was the spirit of an adventurer born to discovery and since he had turned over every rock in Haiti before his twentieth year, what choice did he have but to venture beyond her shores? For all his traveling, for all the wisdom acquired over the course of his thirty years, one thing he did not grasp, Fujo loved him as he was and would have him no other way. She would have given Bwanhe the freedom a wandering soul requires, and when she wasn't basking in the cradle of his arms, she would have happily remain behind to bear his children and kiss away their pain should they fall from a tree or swallow a bad fish. What part of her soul wouldn't she give for the sight of his reassuring eyes? Unheard prayers, hope shattered miserably at her feet, and the hour of her release reluctant, it did not seem as if she would ever see Bwanhe again.

Her throat constricted as she choked back a barrage of tears. Surely, she would never recover from the horrific memory of Momma's final moments. Nor would she ever forget the haunting memory of Elana Louiane's blood as the last of it spurt from her neck and seeped into the sand, her unborn legacies never to see the light of the sun.

Now more than ever, she needed Momma's strength and courage. Clinging to her amulet, Fujo prayed for Momma's guidance, purposefully neglecting to pray for her own forgiveness despite the fact hatred engulfed her, a rampant infection.

She watched Catti slumber amid a lump of straw and searched her soul for a parcel of gratitude; only by divine intervention did she and her sister live and breathe, but did survival come bearing a gift or a curse? Was there a cure for the dreadful void that stole the ground from beneath her feet when she thought of Momma and the others left cold at demon's whim? Would she ever again hear Bwanhe's soothing voice, ever again know the security of his embrace? Did a phantom time await, somewhere beyond the horizon, a glorious day designed specifically for the vanquishing of the soul's burdens, a healing hour, a moments' relief when vials of contentment might open once more? Perhaps not, but by the grace of Bondye, Fujo had one quest she meant to keep alive; she would not see shame come to her sister by way of the marauders.

She stroked Catti's brow until she began to awake.

"Arise," Fujo instructed with a whisper.

Catti grunted, sat up and rubbed her eyes, shaking bits of straw from her tattered clothes.

"Do not cleanse your face," Fujo instructed, "Do not tame your hair."

As Catti drew a breath rife with defiance, Fujo drew a rigid finger to her lips. "Do not argue," she said, fanning her finger as if a sword in play. She retrieved a small handful of dirt from beneath the straw, mixed it with saliva, and smeared the crude concoction over Catti's face.

Catti scowled. "My face will scar...I am becoming a gruesome abomination."

"Good," Fujo replied sternly, though she understood the protest. In a few years time, Catti's beauty would surpass her own. Cascading locks of dark hair glistened beneath the grime and straw pinned to it. Graced with large eyes, high cheekbones, and a rich caramel skin, her countenance reflected a dark mix of Momma's ebony air and Père's French vanilla ancestry, as held true for Fujo as well. Well-sculpted muscle, seemingly equine in strength and build, equipped Catti's tall, slender body. Surely it would go against all Bondye intended for her remarkable beauty to become permanently marred.

"Arise, Catti, we toil today."

"Let the vermin launder their own rags, I'll have no part of it."

"Would you prefer to dance with a school of sharks?"

Catti whimpered and rose to her feet.

If not for Catti, Fujo would have attempted escape immediately after the pirates snatched her from the slave traders. For, unlike the slave traders, the pirates chose not to keep their prisoners in chains as they were more concerned with how much labor a hand at large could perform in the course of a day so that their own hands might remain free to swill grog and grope unwilling women.

Escape, however, was not a viable option as, since witnessing Jacque's untimely death at Hautes-chutes, Catti developed a stuttering fear of water and never learned to swim.

Only sixteen, Catti was not yet a woman. Though the men aboard the sloop made no special effort to quell their interest in Catti, Fujo insisted they accept her instead. Thus far, she hadn't failed to protect Catti's maidenhood, but her allure would eventually fade. If she couldn't find a means of escape, Catti would lay prey, and Fujo may very well lose her life defending her sister's innocence.

The Omen

A rugged voice bellowed into the hold, "On deck, bloody wenches."

Fujo's eyes resisted the jeering rays of the rising sun as she climbed topside. She searched the horizon for signs of Père's flags at every opportunity, but months passed without sight of them. Did he assume his family had perished, or did he yet scour the seas?

A gaggle of snoring men lay scattered on deck, although a few rose and finished breakfast, leaving bits behind. Fujo reached for an unattended tin cup and, with dire anticipation, put it to her lips: barely a sip of watered-down rum. No one aboard the godforsaken tub drank fresh water. If not for stray grog, she and Catti would have died of thirst long ago. At least the rum no longer caused her head to swirl, or her stomach to boil, as it did at first. She hoped, for Catti's sake, there might be more scraps once other pirates arose.

The crew left their filthy sundries at the base of the mainsail, a pile of colorful garments reeking with an unsavory odor, barely less than the fuming stench of vomit and fish entrails baking in the scuppers. Tending to the wash looked a full day's work. So be it. It was better than digging dung out of the scuppers, an unbearable job the pirates wittingly reserved as a form of punishment among their own ranks.

Scrubbing a pair of one-legged breeches, Fujo thought to share a report of the oppressing omen with her sister. The child had a right to know. Then again, the news would only add another weight of burden. Perhaps it was best to keep foreboding omens locked behind clenched lips.

Calico Jack Rackham

The noon hour brought a cry from a young pirate dangling from the main crosstrees, "Sails aft!" Word bound quickly over the deck as each man lifted his voice to pass the message along. Fujo listened to the resound as it cast through the crowd and she watched, with intense scrutiny, as the Captain lumbered from below deck.

"What's the hoo-hah, Webster?" Rackham's gaze lifted to the crosstrees. Scratching his groin, he scowled, as if rudely awakened.

"Sails aft," answered a toothless, sun-whipped buccaneer who once introduced himself to Fujo as Richard Corner, despite the fact everyone else called him 'Tinclaw' due to a shoddy prosthetic devise attached to a stump on the end of his right arm. He was an excitable man and anxious to act as interpreter for young Webster who returned to his high post on the crosstrees. Raising his makeshift hook, Tinclaw pointed beyond the tail of the sloop.

"The tips of her sails are barely seen," Jack declared, "Be she a prize?"

"Can't rightly say as yet," the old man mumbled. With a flick of the tongue over dry lips, he jubilantly added, "With any luck, she's another ill-manned French strumpet filled to the brim with uncut rum."

Rackham cocked his head to the side, threw a clenched fist on his hip, and leered, his ostensive disapproval apparent.

"Aye and *gold*," Tinclaw added vigorously, as was plainly expected, "casks and casks of gold!"

"Ready the weapons," the Captain instructed, "be prepared to board. Let her approach until her flags be seen. Give us a shout once she shows herself."

"Aye."

A turbulent scramble erupted as half the crew readied the cannons while the other half dragged weapons and ammunition on deck. The men slapped one another on the back with anticipation and lifted their coarse, untrained voices in song:

"Be no road stretched beneath these feet
Me soul belongs to the sea
And if I chance to bite the bullet
I hope to do it with ye!
Hi dee hi dee hi dee hi
Hi dee hi dee hi dee ho...."

Had young Webster spotted one of Père's ships? *Bondye, full of grace and mercy, let it be.* Fujo's heart leapt with excitement as she allowed it to flood with hope. Père would come and, unlike the benevolent Bondye, he would show no mercy.

The crew continued to prepare for battle as the Captain retreated to the belly of the sloop.

Fujo breathed easier when Calico Jack was nowhere in sight as she thought him a treacherous man; none due to a ruthless spirit, for she never saw him do anyone bodily harm—contrarily, he seemed to avoid confrontation with great skill—but worse, there seemed a reckless abandon coursing through his veins. Men with thoughtless souls often proved most severe; perhaps not the kind to kill outright, but the kind by whose hand you lie dead nonetheless as they haven't the foresight to consider consequence. For all his show of pomp and bravado, Fujo believed Jack Rackham an ignorant man and feared nothing more than entrusting her life to a fool.

Scanning the deck, she spied Catti still scrubbing soiled linen, sweat streaking down her muddied face as she baked in the noonday sun. Half the wash, cleared away from the mainsail, flapped in the wind to dry. The ship running up behind *The Merry Anne* remained a speck on the horizon; it would take hours to approach. The pain in Fujo's stomach warned they would not escape harm's way until moonlight leaked upon the sea. This day had much misery left to bring.

Queen Anne's Revenge

Fujo and Catti had barely finished the wash when young Webster on the crosstrees dropped his looking glass to his hip and gave a bellowing shout, "*Queen Anne's Revenge*, starboard, ho!"

Upon hearing this, Fujo lowered her chin to her chest and cursed the powers of providence. The ship following behind *The Merry Anne* did not belong to Père's fleet after all.

She peered over the rails. Not merely one ship approached, but three, the late afternoon sun seeming to set fire to their sails.

Some members of the crew gasped and slunk away from the rails while others laughed and cheered. One man pronounced, "By fate, it's ole Blackbeard," while another scowled and grumbled, "He'll have everything we've prized for the last month."

Calico Jack emerged from below, briskly swiping Tinclaw's looking glass from his hand.

"READ!" He bellowed with a thread of desperation grating in his voice. "Fetch Mark Read!"

"Aye, Jack," Tinclaw said with a bob of the head he might have meant as a proper bow. The old sailor disappeared into the crowd of men leaning over the rails attempting to bag a look at *The Queen Anne's Revenge* and her entourage.

Rackham gave an order to fire a salute from the great guns and their explosive reverberations sent heaves and shivers throughout the sloop, causing it to rock like an oversized cradle.

Once the sloop settled from her convulsions, a small sailor, who could not have seen more than twenty years, as he had not yet achieved the frame of a full-grown man nor any facial hair to speak of, sauntered next to Calico Jack and said, "Aye, Sir?"

"Stop calling me 'sir' ye dullard. I've told ye time and again we don't go for that formal huck-a-rah on my ship. Fetch Annie straight away and hide her where no man will think to search. Stay with her until I call for ye."

"Aye, Sir."

The maddened fear playing in the Captain's eyes twisted the knot in Fujo's stomach ten turns tighter. Obviously, Rackham dreaded the approaching vessels enough to sequester his most precious cargo: Anne Bonny.

Fujo knew the Captain's 'Annie,' in fact, the suspiciously pretty sailor who laid waste to the slave schooner's crew was none other than she. The same varlet who pilfered Fujo's heirloom amulet and wore it upon an alabaster breast, which glowed beneath a glaring sun she took no measure to escape, her immunity to its burning rays evidenced in her skin's gypsum defiance. She sported a mane of golden locks muddied by a streak of red so dark, the thin line of mutated strands streaming from the center of her head made it seem as though she were bleeding out a mortal wound. Rarely were Anne Bonny's bright blue eyes plagued by weariness. Fujo never saw her with her eyes closed, not for so much as a catnap, a habit nearly all the other pirates incorporated into their daily routines. No, when Anne Bonny stood on deck, she remained ever on the prowl, searching for the slightest sign of trouble, thirsting for adventure. A redoubtable woman, yes, and crazed with the devil's blood; without conscience, and as treacherous as Calico Jack for the temperament of her foolhardy soul—though more fearsome than he, as anyone could see she had a thirst for blood her Captain did not share.

Anne Bonny dressed herself as a man with astonishing efficiency and, as such, readily boarded the vessels of the unfortunate souls she preyed upon. Time and again, Fujo overheard the Captain admonishing Anne for needlessly murdering innocents with the sour luck to squirm beneath the soles of her boots, to which the young woman would coolly reply, she had not come to sea to become an expert at needlework. By the weight of his brow, clearly Calico Jack thought himself beleaguered by his fractious companion. Beleaguered, perhaps, but beguiled as well. Not only a fool, but a fool in love; a combination bidding for disaster.

Rackham would be mad to think any man foolish enough to commandeer Anne Bonny's irrepressible insubordination as a prize. On the other hand, what could a woman from a simple village know of the marauder's ways? Clearly, if Fujo hoped to survive, she must learn. For now, she thought it best to borrow an idea from Jack Rackham, who seemed to have an intimate knowledge of the immediate enemy.

Calling Catti to her side, Fujo instructed her to get inside the hold, gather into a dark corner, cover herself with straw, and remain there until the loathsome Blackbeard took his leave. Once again, a look of defiance burned in Catti's eyes, but Fujo set her face so sternly Catti instantly withdrew all argument.

Field Mouse

Fujo felt a bit more at ease with Catti safely tucked away in the hold, but the moment the pirate known as Blackbeard set foot on *The Merry Anne*, the knot in her stomach ricked so tightly, she fought for air.

A tangled ebony, Blackbeard's hair fluttered in the wind, wayward locks loosed from the many braids he sported, his aphotic beard streaked with subtle strands of gray. His eyes, dark orbs devoid of soul, sank into deep gorges above the crest of his haughty cheekbones. A large man, his long-legged frame towered over Calico Jack's meager physique.

Blackbeard wore luxurious fabrics woven in Tyrian purple and black, his crisscrossed bandoliers made from the finest Spanish leather, his brace of pistols gleaming with young steel and adorned with exquisite mother-of-pearl gunstocks. Perhaps, Fujo hoped, this man blessed with ample riches would require no ransom from *The Merry Anne*.

So it seemed, as he and a small band of men followed Calico Jack to the galley where they spent dusk's hours drinking, laughing, singing, and, in general, making merry. Still, the knot in Fujo's stomach refused to unwind.

She scrounged the deck for unfinished bits of food; Catti would be hungry after the long hours spent hidden in the hold. Among the leftover scraps were half-chewed strips of smoked lizard, a mango stone to suck on, a hog plum rind, a small handful of jackfruit seeds, and a splash of neglected grog.

"How long do you expect me to cower like a field mouse?" Catti spewed.

"Eat," Fujo gently replied, understanding her sister's pride bruised more deeply with each moment she lay concealed, but also keenly aware pride flounders useless in the midst of dire circumstance.

"How long?" Catti asked, determined to hear an answer.

"Until it's safe."

Catti attempted to rip a stubborn piece of smoked lizard in two with her teeth. "Must I remind you," she seethed, "we would not be here, fighting for our lives, if you had listened to me in the first place and gone back to the grove instead of searching for Momma?"

Fujo lifted her face to the red and orange sunset blazing over the mouth of the hold. With a hand clasped to her stomach and a note of frustration, she replied, "This, I know too well. Still, you will remain here until these by-blows have gone their way. With any luck, they will soon depart."

Catti had so little to eat, though Fujo gave her every scrap, withholding nothing for herself. Fujo would have liked to stay, perhaps search for some comfort she might find to offer, but instinct drew upon her to keep a watchful eye on deck. Instinct remained one of the greater powers in her arsenal; she wouldn't ignore it. As she left the hold, she implored Catti, once more, to remain concealed.

Blackbeard's Folly

The first stars of the evening revealed themselves as Blackbeard returned to the deck of *The Merry Anne* and announced his departure; words Calico Jack craved since Blackbeard's arrival. The dreaded villain had his fill of uncut rum, apparent as he swayed in a drunken stupor, a wide smile mounted upon his face.

Jack knew Blackbeard's contentment was a good thing, indeed, but his business with the bloodthirsty cutthroat was not yet finished; Blackbeard would not leave *The Merry Anne* without a considerable bounty. The only question remaining was how much loot it would take to satisfy the scurvy hound.

"James Dobbin! Bring our most esteemed guest our last two casks of fine rum," Jack ordered, taking special effort to don his most charming smile.

Blackbeard's lips spread in a slight grin, but he made no gesture to indicate he meant to be on his way.

"Harwood!" Jack barked. "Our blessed friend would enjoy the lot of our smoked goat, if you please." He turned to give Blackbeard an exaggerated bow and another gracious smile. At this, Blackbeard belched loudly and sniggered but did not offer his hand in adieu.

Only a foolhardy soul would think a splash of rum and a few pounds of old goat sufficient to please the infamous Blackbeard, despite how much the crew of *The Merry Anne* depended on these bounties for their very lives. Blackbeard could take anything he damn well pleased, *The Merry Anne* herself: who among her crew had jewels brass enough to stand up to the scoundrel? Yet again, was it not well known Blackbeard preferred to have his bounties freely offered rather than chance to plunder a ship belonging to one of the brethren of the coast? Aye. Though it wasn't likely the sod would attempt to commandeer *The Merry Anne*, it would take more to assure his satisfaction, much more. Best cut to the quick and put an end to the masquerade once and for all.

"Fetherston!" Jack bellowed. "Fetch us our chest of gold and silver. You shall find the mighty specimen in my quarters. Make haste."

Upon hearing this order, Blackbeard gestured with a courteous bow of gratitude, but withheld his hand.

Damnation to the bowels of Hades and back, what would it take to see this insufferable braggart off into the night? If the finest chest of gold Jack ever plundered wasn't enough, what else could he offer? Retreating two steps back, he drew a heavy breath.

As his shoulders sagged beneath his gray mood, a most useful memory crept to mind.

He had lounged at *The Hornswaggle Inn* in Nassau for far too long one evening, about to fall off his perch, when the doors flung open and a small crew of freebooters, fresh off the sea, came barreling into the establishment. A burst of adrenaline charged his senses back to full alert, for this sort of occurrence always brought with it an hour or two of highly entertaining tales. Of most interest, in the light of Jack's current situation, a narration orated by one Lockjaw Bane, who claimed himself present in Martinique when Blackbeard stole away with the French sloop, *La Concorde*, thereafter widely known as *The Queen Anne's Revenge*. Bane recounted, with great animation, how Blackbeard seemed immediately smitten with a young cabin boy from *La Concorde* and forcefully insisted the pup join his crew. In fact, Bane summated, youngsters under the age of sixteen accounted for more than half of Blackbeard's entourage.

Jack cast an inspecting glance at the men standing ready at Blackbeard's side. He recognized Garrat Gibbens the moment the rogue put foot to *The Merry Anne*. He and Gibbens once sailed under the command of Charles Vane and conspired together to roust Vane from his command, a coup they pulled off quite valiantly, if Jack could say so himself. Not long after the mutiny aboard Vane's brigantine, Gibbens returned to Port Royal intent to take advantage of His Majesty's pardon, but apparently thought better of it since. Thomas Miller stood next to Gibbens, a man Jack saw only once or twice at *The Hornswaggle*. Both of these

Devil's Edge

men were seasoned cutthroats long past their youth. Though there were three other men Jack did not recognize, clearly no young pups stood among them. Jack had absolutely no way of knowing if Bane's tale held any truth or merit, especially considering the criminal character of the source, but if he'd learned anything about life in his years at sea, he learned it was rich with fading cards and heavy dice.

Having made a decision, he called forth his quartermaster and whispered his directives into the remnant of Tinclaw's clubbed ear.

Moments later, Tinclaw returned, dragging 'cross deck what looked like a she-lion amply clad in chains, claws out in force, spitting and hissing as she approached.

"No!" A desperate cry howled from the starboard bow.

Blackbeard's face demonstrated a mild amusement as Calico Jack stood face-to-face with a straw-infested wench who bit and twisted against Tinclaw's firm grip. The slave woman then scrambled 'cross deck, prepared to plead for the young kitten.

"What do we have here, Rackham?" Blackbeard asked, his eyes flashing a sudden light of sobriety.

"A gift, for my most reputed friend. A virgin for your pleasure," Jack replied, grabbing the girl by the shoulders and pushing her forward until she fell prostrate at Blackbeard's feet.

Blackbeard cocked his head back and let out a howling laugh, rich, robust, and guttural.

"No!" the slave woman screamed, lowering herself until she perched upon her knees, her head hung low in reverence. "I beg of you, kind sir, she is my sister...all I have left..."

"Restrain this wench," Jack demanded, his hand gripping the crest of an ornate cutlass sheathed at his side. At his order, two men stepped forward to secure her.

"She is not a virgin!" The slave woman protested; her eyes locked in a searing glare that exposed the polite tone she attempted to convey for the hellish hatred it truly was. "Sir, one of your own crew has lain with her. She has, most regrettably, lost her treasure."

"What trickery is this?" Blackbeard snarled.

Jack smiled reassuringly, though his confidence waned with the unexpected accusation. Blackbeard would by no means take kindly to a perceived ruse, and Jack had no desire to view the sea from a headless point of view, hanging stark-eyed from *The Queen Anne's* bowsprit.

"It's a lie," he answered with a large measure of hope, quelling a sudden urge to pray to gods he hadn't addressed since his youth, "...constructed to manipulate...she'll say anything...not true...not true at all."

"Woman!" Blackbeard barked. "Who lay with this maid?"

Jack watched the slave's face distort with confusion as she carefully contemplated the question put to her, her fingers clawing at the fabric of her red dress.

Plenty bragged about the bedding of the older slave, but Jack never heard a word about the younger. Most of the crew wouldn't miss an opportunity to crow about such a noteworthy conquest. On the other hand, new members of the crew sometimes took the pirate's creed much too seriously and it strictly forbid mingling with women whilst at sea. Damnation, if one of those mud-dogs had bedded the girl, he would fear confession.

"If one of my crew has lain with the virgin, I shall have him flogged to the last drop and sent out for shark food!" Jack roared. Best to make a good show of it; if someone defiled the dark pearl, it would seem he knew nothing of the happenstance, so much the better to secure Blackbeard's mercies.

"Shut your gob," Blackbeard seethed. "Woman, answer!"

"The boy," she replied, a nervous quiver fluttering in her voice, "the one they call Read. He came again last night to lay with her. He has ravaged her, Sir. She is no longer pure."

Jack let loose a hearty belly laugh, cackling so hard he doubled over, a barrage of tears stinging at his eyes. He might have howled longer still, if Blackbeard hadn't lifted him by the hair of his head and slapped him smartly upon the cheek.

"What do ye play at, rogue?" Blackbeard spit, his cutlass unsheathed with such speed it seemed to appear from the tips of his fingers.

"My apologies," Jack blurted, the threat of a giggle still playing at the back of his throat, "Perhaps we might speak in private."

Blackbeard raised his sword and loosed an angry bellow, "Leave us!"

The sound of scuffling feet prevailed as the crowd receded.

"Make it good, or make it your last," Blackbeard growled, a scowl deeply imbedded in his forehead, his cheeks burning Hell's blaze, the tip of his sword pressed firmly to Jack's throat.

The stars twinkling in the night sky seemed to smile upon Calico Jack Rackham. How lucky can a man be in a single lifetime? One moment fate found his head dangling from an angry bowsprit, the next afforded more good fortune than he would dare to dream.

"Forgive my rude mirth," he said, whispering his explanation, "but the young sailor this strumpet claims lay with her sister is none other than the woman, Mary Read, who dresses herself as a man and..."

"Save breath," Blackbeard said, lowering his sword, a smile returning to his face. "Tales of Mary Read and Anne Bonny reach from Maine to Nassau. Legends from the lips of rapscallions...one knows not what to believe." He paused to scratch behind his ear. "The virgin is yet a virgin?"

"Aye," Jack said with a hearty slap, "pure as honey plucked from the comb."

Birthing Revenge

"To port in North Carolina," Blackbeard answered when Jack Rackham asked what destination lie ahead for *The Queen Anne's Revenge*. Those words haunted Fujo's mind since she last saw her sister two years ago. Each night brought visions of the mind's ghost, ghastly remembrances of Catti's silhouetted form, biting, kicking, and scratching at her captors as they forced her aboard their departing vessel. Sleep became an abominable enemy.

Fujo had long since given up her quest to see her father's ships upon the sea. Perhaps marauders assailed his fleet as well. Although she continued to pray against it, no other explanation sufficed. If Père hadn't come in two years time, it seemed obvious he had no means for rescue. All for the better, she supposed. She would never find the words to explain how she allowed Catti to slip so easily from her grasp.

Père, the only hope Fujo allowed herself to cling to, could not and would not pose her savior. If destiny determined an escape from *The Merry Anne*, Fujo must accomplish the task on her own.

By the grace of Bon Dieu, she would find her way to the Carolina coast where she would reclaim her sister, steal her away if need be...slice a few throats if necessary—*Bondye, forgive the trespass.*

She would break free of *The Merry Anne* at first opportunity; though her opportunities would come less and less as she attempted flight so many times during the past months the pirates took to chaining her to the helm. Still, she would find her escape, and once accomplished, she would beg passage to North Carolina onboard a respectable ship.

Thus were the thoughts consuming Fujo's mind even as the wily Captain Barnet, in service to the Chief Governor of the Bahamas, Woodes Rogers, stealthily maneuvered a government sloop out of sight of *The Merry Anne*, yet remained close enough to insure her heart would faint come morn.

Devil's Edge

Captured

On the morning of November the 17[th,] in the year of our Lord, 1720, most of the crew captured aboard *The Merry Anne* had already performed their final pirouettes off the gallows at Deadman's Cay near Port Royal, Jamaica. There came a sweet respite, followed by the warming embers of revenge, as Fujo watched her assailants fall to death's brawny grip, one after another.

Not for the slightest moment did she allow her intense glare to shift from the cowering faces of the defendants as their trials dragged on. She listened with great disappointment as the Captain General Sir Nicholas Lawes—an old Englishman she thought stuffy and unanimated—delayed the trials of Anne Bonny and Mary Read until the 18th. Unfortunately, she would not remain in Port Royal long enough to see them sentenced. No matter, she already visited Bridewell Prison and spoke with Anne Bonny and Mary Read to her content. If the ghostly white pallor of women already paled by lack of light and ample food held any indication, she had driven her point across.

Jack Rackham and Tinclaw Corner were the only male members of the crew yet to encounter the noose's embrace. Fujo had also been given the opportunity to address the men privately at the prison, now she would see them ascend the gallows, then she would prepare for her trip to North Carolina; her passage aboard a British man-o-war gratefully secured by the Governor, Woodes Rogers.

The morning sun rose over Port Royal with enough heat to burn off a dense fog that lingered throughout the night. The air waft thick with the delightful aroma of a fresh hog turning on a spit. Clumps of women tended to pots steaming with corn porridge and yellow yams while others slashed ripe mangos and melons, their chatter jovial and enthusiastic. Local men beat on drums and blew handcrafted bamboo flutes while children shook dried gourds to the jubilant rhythm and danced in the sand, their laughter carried gingerly by a slothful breeze. Visitors gathered in droves on the beach, coming from far and wide...New Providence, Cuba, and Jamaica...Spaniards, Brits, Frenchmen, and Dutch, all come to witness the hanging festivities.

The Merry Anne swayed woefully off the southeast coast, her hull blasted by Captain Barnet's adept canons, her deck and mast newly plagued with adventurous lads who thought to use her as an amusement for so long as the Governor allowed her battered spirit to tarry within sight.

If Barnet had hoped for a valiant battle from Rackham, he was sorely disappointed. Barnet's sloop, *Mermaid's Song*, caught *The Merry Anne* anchored off the western coast of Jamaica, at Point Negril, her crew soaked to the gills in the fresh rum they pilfered from a merchant ship the day before.

As suspected, Calico Jack Rackham didn't have an ounce of courage trickling in his veins. Once he realized the government sloop crept upon him, he cowered in the hold along with his men, leaving only the women and young Webster to fight the entire company of Barnet's raiding forces. While temptation might cause some to define their capture as effortless, the ten men skillfully slaughtered by Anne Bonny and Mary Read demanded testimony to the contrary.

Captain Barnet himself loosed Fujo from the chains binding her to the helm. Now he stood tall at the foot of the gallows, his intense shadow shading her from the morning sun, awaiting justice for the men he lost, his brow furled with impatience. Once the festivities concluded, he reminded her, he would gather his crew, take Fujo to New Providence where she would board *The Queen's Maid* and make the journey to North Carolina. She prayed she would arrive in time to reclaim her sister.

The Haitian Woman's Curse

It was the skillful, stealthy approach of *Mermaid's Song* Anne Bonny couldn't chase from her mind. How could they have missed sight of her? She'd haunted *The Merry Anne* for days on end without showing so much as the twinkle of a lamp.

The blasted rum had done them in, of that Anne harbored no doubt. Mind it, she loved her grog as much as anyone, but always kept her wits about her, knowing when enough was enough. A brigand must keep keen wit—this parcel of wisdom she preached to Rackham time and again. Still, the oaf said nothing as the men stationed at the crosstrees guzzled pint after pint, four sods in six months destined to fall to an early end.

Young Webster offered no answer when she asked why he didn't spot *Mermaid's Song* before the sloop came within firing range. He stood with a look of dumb abandon pasted upon his face, his lips moving but no acceptable account coming forth. The stewed belch he let pass through his gullet sealed his locker. Anne planted a plug of silver in his forehead and would do it again if given another chance to play at yesterday. By Zeus, she wished she had another shot at Rackham, too.

"Where are the law clods?" She begged, her patience wearing thin, "Aren't we to watch Jack swing?"

"Aye," Mary answered.

"What then? It's well past first light."

"Woodes Rogers, I suspect. He will make delay to give Jack spare time to consider his sins."

"Many are they! Always the clever one, Mary, that's what I love about ye. Ye haven't to wrinkle a brow before wisdom comes spewing over those lips. Always right, too," Anne gushed, smiling widely.

Mary Read harbored more wit than the British and Spanish fleets combined. That same wit saved *The Merry Anne* and her entire crew on more than one occasion. As Anne put a gentle hand to Mary's shoulder, she wondered if the brightest and bravest woman she ever knew had the means to unlock the gates now barring them from freedom. By the sword of Ares, Anne Bonny did not mean to die in a rat infested prison cell. There must be one more unsuspecting ship on the sea, one more insolent throat to cut... one more chest of gold to lift and squander: *one more.* Was it too much to ask?

Less than a few months after she took to the sea, Anne became legend. As fierce as any man, they said of her. She heard the tales from the lips of her own captives, men appalled to be disarmed and subdued by the likes of a mere woman. Mary, too, had become infamous. Great women such as they would not die in a fetid prison, nor would they swing from the noose. By the weight of Athena's heart, no. The resourcefulness of Mary Read was unbounded. In that, Anne could take faith and rest assured there would, indeed, be one more chance for freedom.

"What think ye, Mary, of the Haitian woman's curse?"

Mary laughed and spit into the straw beneath her feet. "Her blood boiled when Jack gifted her sister to Blackbeard. She is a woman scorned."

"Aye, but is it to be trusted? The curse?"

"It would not be trusted in England," Mary scoffed, her amusement apparent. "Would it be trusted in Ireland?"

"Nay," Anne chuckled. Mary stood on the proper side of logic, once again. They had nothing to fear from the dark woman's curse.

A deep cough accompanied Mary's guffaw. "Put a shiver in your blood, did she?"

"Nay."

"Nay? Pray thee, where is your precious amulet?"

Anne put a hand to the spot above her cleavage where the necklace once rested. It was the finest piece of jewelry she ever saw; an intricately carved viper curled into a perfect circle, handcrafted from a superior emerald, wrought to fit securely on a dazzling gold chain. She took it from the slave and wore it proudly. Clearly, its worth exceeded any riches ever to pass through Caribbean waters. The infamous Anne Bonny had never returned an ounce of booty before, and certainly nothing worth a king's ransom. Why did she give in to the Haitian woman's demand and return the amulet? Surely, it was the work of that cock-eyed curse.

Anne felt her face flush. "She said it was an heirloom. What use had I for it?"

Mary giggled and slapped Anne's arse so smartly it stung. "Aye, she put the shivers to your blood."

At last, a barrage of heavy footsteps approached the holding cell. In a few short moments, the guards put a key to the lock. Anne cursed and kicked as six of the Governor's soldiers escorted the women to Gallows Point. Once outside the musty jail, Anne made it a point to inhale a hearty breath of the salty air holding Jack Rackham's last hour: a sweet scent it was, the smell of a coward's adjourn.

The Hanging

Mary Read hadn't felt the need to primp in years but, as she tried to run her fingers through the four weeks of accrued grime matting her hair, she found herself wishing off a healthy ransom for a hairbrush and a basin of cool water. The jailers robbed her and Anne of their man-clothes and gave them plain brown tunics bearing too much resemblance to lady things. Not that Mary had never donned a dress, she had, and not so long ago. Though the days she spent as William's wife, and mistress of the *Three Trade Horses Inn*, seemed a lifetime ago, it had only been a few years. She didn't miss playing the part of a woman. But, for so long as she breathed, she would feel a desperate longing for her pretty William. He would take a sudden flight from the grave if he had sight of her now, clad in chains, bedraggled like a common pauper, and mocked by the crowd lining the path to the gallows.

At least she found pride in walking beside a woman as fine as Anne Bonny. A braver soul she never knew, nor a woman who wore more beauty. It was an honor to serve upon the sea with the likes of Anne Bonny. An entire fleet of ships would do well to bear her name, for to her the sea belonged; the lover who rocked her to sleep, bid her fair morn, and spurred her on to the heights of her excitement. Ne'er a sailor lived who worshipped the sea more than Anne Bonny.

'Twas the same Anne Bonny who now found manner to render crude hand gestures each time a youngster from the gathering crowd poked her with a stick or whipped her with a palm frond. Of course, this only set the children's mothers to cursing, kicking, spitting, and throwing stones. It would seem, even after spending a month in Bridewell prison, Anne still did not consider consequence. But, wasn't it this same fearlessness that drew Mary to Anne in the first place, and the reason she loved her so? Aye. Let them throw their stones, and Bonny be Bonny to the end.

Jack Rackham and Tinclaw Corner dug the soles of their boots deeply into the sand as they approached the gallows, not an ounce of bravery or pride to share between them. Mary laughed aloud when Tinclaw planted his feet with so much determination his boots remained embedded in the sand. From that moment on, he squirmed—barefoot—between two guards with the unfortunate charge of escorting the slippery old goat to the noose. Jack's pitiful performance threatened to match Tinclaw's until he saw Annie, at which sighting, he straightened himself and approached her with the last bit of dignity he could muster.

"I have loved ye like no other," he professed, his eyeballs protruding like a wildcat caught in irons. "Have ye a plan to stop this nonsense?"

"Nay," Annie spit, her face flushing as if suddenly sun burnt. "Were there means for escape, I would not waste them on a wench such as ye."

Jack whimpered and fell to his knees before her feet. "Oh, Annie...no. I'll do anything ye ask...pray thee, don't let me hang."

She bent down to cup his chin in the palm of her hand. As she lifted his face to meet her glare, she said, ever so sweetly, "If ye'd fought like a man, ye'd have no need to hang like a dog."

Devil's Edge

The guards promptly pulled Jack back as he reached for Anne.

"Tell her, Mary," he pleaded. "Tell her this is no time for folly. Tell her they mean to *hang* me. Dear Mary, I implore. Haven't ye enjoyed the full extent of my hospitalities? Isn't there something to do for me? Have ye men waiting in ambush? Say it's so."

Mary leaned over to whisper her response, "Nay. But all is not lost. No doubt I can convince the Governor to let ye go. I shall speak with him at dawn on the morrow, *Sir*."

Jack's stare was mute; the muscles in his face constricting with the horrible realization he was about dance the hempen jig.

Drums beat with frenzy as the crowd, eyes wide with expectation, screamed their bloodthirsty yearning, "Hang the dogs!" Only a select few, standing at the foot of the gallows, held their composure. The Governor Woodes Rogers, his guards and, who stood next to Barnet? Ah, the Haitian woman, patiently awaiting her just rewards.

The guards retrieved Jack from his position of supplication and dragged him along until he stood weak-kneed beneath the noose.

Though she long anticipated the grand event, Mary didn't have the heart to watch as the executioner slipped the world away from beneath Jack's feet and yet, she was well aware of the precise moment Jack Rackham imbued the last of his wit and charm upon the world, as Anne expelled the hyena titter she took great pains to conceal whenever she adorned herself as a man; an infectious, telltale soprano lilt that harbored no question of gender. As Mary opened her eyes, her reluctant gaze met with Anne's teary-eyed glee.

PART TWO

Doctor Dramatico

Jillian Miller wedged a fingernail into a crack in the naked plaster beside the window frame and caught a palm full of crumbled rot. She and her younger brother, Whitt, stood smack in the middle of their father's latest psychosis, in which, he'd spent his last brain cell, pawned his sanity, and foreclosed on all practicality.

Hairy mold bearding the baseboards held the first clue the house he'd rented would never grace the cover of *Better Homes and Gardens*. It crept halfway to the ceiling in some places, amassing in others like a burgeoning bruise and, *would you look at that*, a whole new purpose for disposable razors. The house smelled like an abandoned meatpacking plant, one foul odor mixing with another until they forced Jillian to bury her nostrils in a shirtsleeve to keep her eyes from watering. Her father's solution (a can of Lysol and a bag of mothballs) wouldn't work any better than sending a troop of Boy Scouts after Al Qaeda.

Jillian's assigned bedroom was, by far, the worst of the lot. No longer clothed in plaster, thin wooden slats poked from behind decayed gypsum like the exposed ribs of a long dead cadaver. Faded princesses waved to adoring subjects from scattered wallpaper remnants, and the lace curtains (grayed beneath the pressure of dust and time) clung to a slight pink pigment resting on the edges. Obviously, a young girl had once occupied the room, but Jillian found it difficult to imagine anyone ever spending a peaceful night inside this flesh-defying carcass.

For this, she had given up her shot at the National Dance Finals, her one chance at lasting fame and glory. Okay, so it's an annual competition, but a girl is only sixteen once, and this year promised to be Jillian's prime year. *Favored to win the Nationals*, the *South County Independent* article said, and after winning the state championship, no one expected her to lose. No one but her father who declared the trip to North Carolina mandatory.

After months of tiptoeing around one another's feelings, careful not to rupture the surface of the sensitivities gurgling beneath, emotional dams burst into a lung-splitting bout that lasted from the end of the driveway in Rhode Island all the way to the North Carolina shore. Her head still throbbed.

She grabbed an ankle, guided her foot over her head and clung to her knee as her toes reached for what little remained of the bedroom ceiling. The stretch still felt unbalanced; she would never master it if she didn't remain determined. When she finished with the right leg, she reached for the left; it too, would ultimately bend to her will, unlike her father.

Whitt suddenly burst into the room, arms flailing over his head, mouth wide open, eyes prepared to escape residence and roll over the floor, his chubsy-ubsy sneakers skidding across the ragged carpet with such ferocity a puff of carpet grime rose from beneath them. Dr. Dramatico had arrived. Latching onto her arm, he tugged and panted, "In my room...gotta see...horrible...*horrible*, Jillian."

She so wasn't in the mood for his juvenile pranks.

Releasing her arm, he moved behind her and pushed. Although Jillian knew it a mistake to entertain her brother's overactive imagination, she also knew he wouldn't let go of whatever had his underwear in a bunch until she thoroughly inspected the goblins creeping behind the closet doors.

A dingy yellow light bulb clung to a set of bare wires and dangled precariously from the ceiling in the hallway. The sight of Whitt's shadow cast against the walls significantly slowed Jillian's angry pace, his Medusa curls exaggerated, appearing like a nest of snakes slithering over the cracked surface. The entrance to his room, a dark orifice, opened like the mouth of an enraged demon, waiting to devour anyone foolish enough to step inside. How could their father subject his family to such horrors? Who, in his right mind...? But that was it, wasn't it? Their father lost his last thread of sanity over a year ago.

Whitt rushed past and reached for the light switch. Just as Jillian suspected, he pointed a rigid finger toward the closet.

"What?" She sneered, making no attempt to obscure her ridicule.

"Open it," he said. "Double dare."

She grabbed him by the neck of his ketchup stained red-and-white striped tee shirt and leaned in nose-to-nose.

"I do this, *just once*, and you bug off for the rest of the night, deal?"

"Deal."

Flinging the door open, she pulled the chain affixed to the light bulb and stepped inside the closet.

"Nothing, see?"

"Wait," he insisted. "Watch the wall under the shelf."

Jillian glared at Whitt and thought about the last American History lecture she attended.

Professor Bracca was, indisputably, a brilliant man. His lecture was a tirade on the subject of fidiots. Leaning casually with an elbow pasted atop his podium, he'd explained a fidiot isn't your regular, ordinary idiot, but a special breed, one reaching for a much higher level of moronic aspiration, one whose crackbrained antics incite a greater public reaction than those awarded to the mere dope. He said it's never difficult to spot a full-fledged fidiot as they inherently crave accolades for their bloopers, seeking praise by buying elections, or worming their way onto satellite radio and cable TV. Raising his palms, as if to punctuate a dire warning, he concluded by saying 21st century newspapers and magazines seethed with the antics of fidiots which, in turn, created a national contagion known as the 'dumbing-down' of America.

Whitt was so ripe with fidiocy he reeked of it. Jillian wouldn't stand guard inside his closet for another second. Anyone could see he feared spending the night alone in this soul-sucking mummy-hole. Too bad. He would have to throw a tantrum and get Merlin (his Irish setter pup, twin to Jillian's Ruby) to protect him for the evening.

Devil's Edge

"Touch it," Whitt said, an unusual quiver resounding in his voice.

Jillian pushed her hand firmly against the wall. Without warning, Whitt screamed loud enough to empty every crypt in the local cemetery and then some. Just as she opened her mouth to give him a good what-for, she felt a sticky fluid begin to slither between her fingers.

"I told you so," he shrieked. "The freaking walls *bleed*."

The Mermaid of Tipper's Cove

Bumblebee yellow with black stripes, Ted Teach's Jeep rumbled into the driveway at 1720 Billard Way. Dixie Teach peered through the kitchen window to watch her husband's boots split the gravel exactly four hours later than they should have. It wasn't as if she expected tonight to be different from any other night, but it would be nice if, just once, the man could find his way home on time.

"Out neckin' with your mermaid again?" Dixie cackled, relishing in the way her husband's face flushed when she mentioned the infamous mermaid of Tipper's Cove. There didn't seem much left in life capable of embarrassing her old man. Though he would never let it show, Dixie knew the mere mention of a mermaid rattled through his brain like a bull on steroids.

Born an explorer with a fathomless infatuation for the sea, Ted wasn't the cuddly lap-boy his mother hoped for. And so, frustrated with the amount of time her little Jacques Cousteau spent at the beach, she accused him (in front of his friends, no less) of having a crush on a mermaid. Kids being what they are, it wasn't a week before the whole town began to rib him about his mermaid and no one let up over the years.

"You know I can't resist her beauty," he said, donning a wry smile.

Twisting her dishtowel, Dixie let it snap two inches from a second circumcision.

"Supper's in the microwave...a couple minutes on high. Sometime you might think about coming home in time to have your dinner fresh."

"And leave my ladyfish lonely, never." Laughing, he opened the microwave and peeked in at a plate of sweet potato meatloaf, a Dixie Teach original the whole family went nuts for even though it didn't have a lick of meat in it.

Ted pushed the reheat button. "You won't believe this," he said. "Donny Baker rented the house next door to a fellow from Rhode Island coming to work on the excavation team. And, get this, he's got a *family*."

Dixie's chair screeched against the hardwood floor as she yanked it from beneath the table and plopped herself down. "Cripes, kids? I don't suppose Donny went out of his way to mention the place is full of demons."

Dixie paused to grasp the absurdity of what she just said. Of course he wouldn't mention it, and what would Donny Baker know anyway? He wasn't there when they wheeled Evelyn Carter out of that house on a stretcher; her body wrapped so tightly in her psychiatric cocoon she could barely breathe, her pinball eyes searching for the slightest clue as to where, exactly, she might have left her mind. Dixie never saw anything more frightening. Evelyn was the first and, *thank you Jesus*, last person to rent the house after the Ballencroft murder.

Ted shrugged, stood up, and tried to remove his plate from the microwave, burning his fingers in the attempt.

"Ain't that why God invented oven mitts?" Dixie snapped.

How could Donny even consider renting that snake pit? Evelyn Carter's probably still making potholders to pass the time between her medications, Lord ease her troubled soul.

Devil's Edge

"It ought to be against the law to rent that place," Dixie hissed. "What it needs is a good wreckin' ball."

Though Dixie believed her assessment one hundred percent correct, she also knew Donny Baker wouldn't pass up a dollar bill if he had to reach up a shark's ass to get it. Hard as it was to imagine new occupants in the house next door, it apparently already happened. And, who would be the one standing there when emergency vehicles pulled up to the door again? Not Donny Baker, that's for sure. No, Dixie would be the one left standing there, the lone witness to sanity's escape.

Cripes, didn't she have enough grief in her life competing with a mermaid for her man's affection? Didn't she have enough hours to put in at the flower shop, enough grocery shopping, laundry, cooking, sewing, and kid spying to keep her walking on the edge of exhaustion without having to keep an eye on a gaggle of Yankees?

Summers were already nearly impossible to survive with the kids on the loose. True enough, Maurine barely posed a bother when her Tourette's wasn't acting up; like most teenage girls, she spent her time cooped up in her bedroom, downloading music from the Internet. In fact, if someone invented a way to download food and fresh laundry, Dixie doubted she would ever see her daughter. But Teddy Jr. and Ozzie were like two G-men on the hunt for the next James Bond caper. Teddy already spent a night in jail for stealing his uncle's police cruiser, and Oz took to setting fires in the basement (three times in the last two years) each time blaming it on a chemistry set with a bad attitude. If trouble were contagious, Dixie's boys would be the end of the world as we all know it.

As if he could actually see the thoughts swirling through her head, Ted ruffled her hair, trying to get a rise out of her. "Look at the bright side, Honey. Maybe the Yankee has a young wife who can help keep an eye on the kids this summer."

"And if he don't," she ragged, "I'll lasso that mermaid of yours and put her in charge of the laundry."

Devil's Edge

That Bloody Closet

Yes, he'd heard his son scream, but Professor Brad Miller wasn't in the mood for petty arguments or practical jokes. The drive from Rhode Island was pure torture. Jillian hadn't let up on him the whole way and Whittaker never acquired the capacity to spend a moment in silence. What's more, it's impossible to close the car windows with an eleven-year-old boy in tow, no matter how much you crave air-conditioning. Each time Whitt put a french-fry in his mouth, it came bellowing out his backside; green clouds of noxious fumes choking like stink demons sent straight from the bowels of Hell.

Obviously, young boys are foul creatures—Brad Miller could almost remember being one himself—but his son took the matter over the top the day he christened his rectum, 'Manaray,' and proclaimed 'Ray' (the shortened version, apparently) spoke a long-lost ancient language known as, 'Buttamine.'

Ruby and Merlin spent the majority of the trip with their snouts pressed deep beneath the seat cushions and Jillian took to breathing into a brown paper bag. Naturally, Whitt thought it all oh-so-hilarious, and cracked up each time he charred a cheek. Brad Miller had never been so happy to escape a vehicle.

As if the trip through Dante's Inferno didn't inspire enough chaos, the house wasn't exactly the 'exotic escape' the real estate agent promised. You can always count on a realtor to describe a two-room shanty as 'cozy,' or earmark pitchforks and spades planted on half an acre of un-cleared land as a 'fixer upper.' Accordingly, this place looked more like the set of a John Carpenter horror film, smelled like a herd of cows died inside months ago, and sounded like a bad knee, every board a creaker, every window a howler. It came cheap, though. No wonder.

Sarah would have taken her crystal ball into all the rooms, held a séance for the souls that passed through, then burned some white sage to clear out unwanted spirits and all that ha-de-rah. Sarah...

Another bone-tingling scream wound its way down the stairs.

Devil's Edge

Brad ascended them two at a time. "Where's the fire?"

Jillian stood planted outside Whitt's closet, staring intently at the palms of her hands while Whitt mindlessly pissed himself, a small puddle growing at the soles of his sneakers.

"My *God*, what happened?" Whitt didn't have a weak bladder and Jillian was rarely dumbfounded, though she seemed completely baffled now as she rubbed her hands together and held them to the light, curiously scrutinizing them as if she expected a toothy parasite to pop out of her skin.

"The wall in the closet," she mumbled.

"What about it?" He snatched up one of Whitt's baseball bats and pushed past her. The closet was empty.

Rubbing his temple with the tips of his fingers he begged, "Just tell me right now, because I have to say, I'm not in the mood for practical jokes."

Less than two weeks ago, Whitt put mustard in all the shampoo bottles. Yesterday, he stretched an invisible film of Saran Wrap over the toilet bowl at the Best Western. No telling what he might think to rig up inside a roach motel like this. Brad Miller winced, admonishing himself for believing the boy too tired from the trip to engage in any type of silliness tonight. He should have kept a closer eye on him, at least until the kid fell asleep. He had to hand it to the boy though; the puddle on the floor constituted an Oscar-winning detail. Was there no end to his creativity?

"Touch the wall under the shelf," Jillian whispered, still staring intensely at her hands.

"Touch it?"

"Touch it, Dad," Whitt urged, finally finding his voice.

Brad wiped a tuft of hair away from his eyes. "If that's what it takes to get a good night's sleep."

He rested his palm on a spot of battered plasterboard; until tonight, it probably hadn't seen the shadow of a human hand for a hundred years. The wall felt cold and clammy, as if the plaster itself shivered with anxiety.

Nothing happened. "Like this?"

"Push harder," Whitt insisted, his sweat-soaked curls glued to his eyebrows, his pudgy cheeks flushing as he caught sight of the puddle on the floor.

Absolutely nothing happened.

Another academy award performance, another humorless joke. "Is that it, then?" He barked, red faced. "We can all go to bed now?"

"Dad?" Whitt's puddle grew at once larger as he pointed at the closet ceiling.

A thick, sticky substance cascaded from between the ceiling tiles, bombarding Brad Miller's eyes as he lifted his face. For a moment he stood in shock, his hair glued to his face, his vision a blurred red hue, a salty transgression slipping between his lips.

Sweet Jesus, is that *blood*?

A Painful Remembrance

It took twenty minutes to wiggle into the attic and another eternity to root through the junk stored up there, but Brad didn't quit until he found what he went looking for. Tipped over the exact spot above Whitt's closet; an empty can of red paint. The only questions remaining were who put it there and why? If he ever found out, he would beat the living daylights out of the dirt-bag. He'd never seen Whitt so scared. Who knew the boy could scream like a girl, and who could blame him? The fluid leaking from the closet ceiling certainly looked like blood. Brad must have looked a gruesome sight when he stumbled out of the closet with that muck plastered all over his face. Any number of kids would have done more than fill their socks with pee.

Hopefully, the worst was over. Still, he wondered if he'd done the right thing by bringing the kids to North Carolina. Yes, an invitation to work on the excavation and restoration of *The Queen*

Anne's Revenge was a lifelong dream. After spending his childhood fantasizing about pirates and another lifetime studying marine archaeology, assignments didn't come any sweeter. Excellent pay too, and crucial if he hoped to send Whitt to college without a second income, a problem he wouldn't face if Sarah hadn't...

Here's the thing, people who say time heals are out-and-out liars, well-intended liars, but liars nonetheless. Anyone capable of spouting this type of useless rhetoric has obviously never known great loss. It takes personal experience to learn heartache is happiness crushed beneath the weight of a merciless asteroid. Not that it mattered in the greater scheme of things; Brad was on his own now and, for the thousandth time in a single day, he reminded himself it wouldn't do any good to rehash every 'if-only' fluttering through his mind. Today bore enough of a challenge without yesterday poking its head up every time he turned a corner. Didn't he just watch his son pee on the floor?

Though he could certainly understand how a house like this would scare the bejeezus out of anybody, he also knew he couldn't possibly turn his back on the opportunities at hand; the job paid four times as much as his gig at the University of Rhode Island. However, he could search for a different house. In the event he failed to find another rental, his work would only last through the summer, they would simply make do.

It took two hours to get Whitt into bed. Even after Brad patiently explained the goop on the walls was only paint, the boy seemed intent to head straight back to Narragansett. He shoved his jeans into the suitcase and Brad took them out. He stuffed a pile of his rusted underwear into the bag and Brad took them out. He loaded his X-Box into the gear bag and Brad took it out. They went around and around for half an hour before Whitt finally got it through his head they weren't going home. When Whitt finally conceded, Jillian stomped off to her room, returned with an American Express card (where in hell she got one of those, he couldn't guess) and insisted on paying for a motel.

His cheeks instantly flushed with indignation. Maybe she was right; maybe they should pack up and get out. Then again, maybe palm trees would sprout in Iceland before Bradford Miller would buckle under the pressure of a single can of red paint. Clearly, some malicious son-of-a-bitch terrorized his family in an attempt to force them out of the house. In fact, Brad could probably find the culprits hidden beneath the porch with a video camera and a microphone, itching for the Millers to come screaming out the door. Why? Maybe for the laughs, maybe for a shot at record hits on YouTube. Who knows why people do what they do? Damned if he would let the bastards win though; not a chance in hell he would tuck tail and run.

He vowed to keep a vigilant guard during the night. He'd sleep on the couch in the living room and keep Whitt's baseball bat by his side. Then he promised to look for another house first thing in the morning. What more could he do?

As he reached for the lamp on Jillian's bureau, he took one last look at her before toggling the switch. She didn't have Whitt's gift for theatrics and her attempt to feign sleep proved less than Oscar worthy. It didn't matter; let her fake it. He knew she was furious, but he was exhausted. Tomorrow posed another day; they would have a chance to work out their differences then.

A nauseous twist in the pit of his stomach gripped him as he took in his daughter's face. Was it any wonder? She was Sarah's clone; same big blue eyes, same red streak running through her short blonde hair, same athletic build, though an inch or two taller than Sarah.

Five foot ten at sixteen years of age truly was remarkable and, unfortunately, not the only sign of Jillian's premature development; he shuttered to think how tall she might stand once she reached her peak. She already knew the pain of being a social outcast—the kids at school razzed her mercilessly—and he knew how rough that sort of thing was on a kid. Sarah had the magic touch when it came to Jillian; caught her tears so delicately, assured her she was, by far, not a freak, but an exceptional beauty, and explained the others mocked her out of jealousy for her stature and grace. How many times over the past months did he wish he had the same delicate touch? He didn't have it, no use pretending. Truthfully, he felt like a behemoth stumbling through Lilliput when it came to his daughter.

When he looked at Jillian—really studied her—he often saw the subtle attributes of a child craving mischief and adventure, accolades and attention. And yet, there were other times when— no matter how frantically he searched for that child—he could only see a fully-grown woman, one who looked so much like Sarah, it seemed painfully impossible to keep the void from swallowing him whole.

He switched off the lamp and turned to leave the room, thanking God an exceptional mental capacity complimented Jillian's illusions of maturity; otherwise, he would fear trusting her to a world teeming with wolves eager to sink their fangs into the first morsel of vulnerability to happen by. Though he would never completely waylay his fear, he had done his very best to keep it in check, and he must have done something right because his pride and joy already had a two-year degree in liberal arts.

Okay, in all fairness, it was Sarah's idea to send their twelve-year-old to college, so Brad couldn't rightfully take credit. In fact, he actually protested with, 'A kid needs to be a kid.'

'There's nothing wrong with being a *smart* kid,' Sarah quickly retorted. 'I'm sure you'll keep an eye on her while she's on campus,' she'd said, and that was that. It took four years of extra study to earn a two-year degree, but it paid off. Jillian was an exceptional student. With a little luck, she would make it to graduate school and might even follow in her old man's shoes and become a professor, a doctor, or a lawyer, anything—if there's a God in heaven—*anything* but a professional dancer.

He crossed the hall to check on Whitt. His children both looked so angelic when they slept, albeit a very tall angel and a chubby cherub who rarely put a comb to his reptilian curls. "Like father, like son," he whispered, and quietly crept down the stairs to let the dogs in for the night. Tonight, especially, a little extra guardianship wouldn't hurt. Trying to keep those mutts outside always meant a losing battle anyway. Besides, the kids needed *something* to cling to, didn't they, now that Sarah was gone.

Hopefully, they were healing faster than he. It was time to get on with his life, he knew, but he hadn't quite figured out how a man can let go of his own soul.

Skulking Phantasms

Jillian watched obscure shadows slither over the ceiling and listened to the wind stalking the windowpanes. She didn't mention it, her father seemed so sure of his conclusions, but the can of paint he recovered from the attic went dry at least ten years ago. She explored every inch of the can and found nothing but cracked paint. Even if she found fresh paint, it wouldn't explain why the stuff completely disappeared from her hands and her father's face; vanished, like it was never there in the first place. Whatever leaked from Whitt's closet didn't have jack to do with Benjamin Moore.

Particles of dust, must, and mold scattered in the air as Jillian punched at the protruding springs in the thing beneath her pretending to be a mattress—*more like a freaking rock garden.* She rolled over, convinced her father lost more of his marbles than she originally suspected. How could he possibly condone spending another five minutes under this roof? When would he sense—as she had—that something dark, something sinister, something truly evil, lurked inside this house?

Every whisper of wind crossing the panes, every creak, every rattle, sent a flutter through her spine. How could her father be so unaffected? Did he really believe his lame paint theory? Surely, he couldn't be so dense. Even if he did suspect foul play, it still seemed as though it would take a strategically placed stick of dynamite to move him. She hoped she would never again meet anyone so downright pig-headed.

Pressing her pillow over her head, she tried to force herself to sleep. No use. Despite an overwhelming desire to escape, her racing heart would not allow her to sleep knowing the diabolic phantasms skulking in the closets would not—could not— slumber.

Whittaker H.G. Miller

The fuzzy red numbers on the clock beside Whitt's bed winked 1:40 am. Bleary-eyed, he sat up and stared until the numbers came into focus. He'd only slept for a few hours, what woke him? A large ball of orange dog slept soundly at the foot of the bed. Merlin hadn't done anything upsetting. What then? Baffled, he reached for a drink of water and knocked the glass off the nightstand. Lucky thing the glass didn't break, but now there were two wet spots saturating the old wooden floor. His cheeks burned.

Granted, it's not an everyday thing to see walls bleed, but how could he wet himself like a gutless infant? It would take an entire lifetime to live it down. Jillian didn't tease him about it right away but she wouldn't pass up the next opportunity. Was it his fault the house bled? His father's attempt to explain it with a dry can of empty paint was a good try: *not*. If his father had half a brain, he would have taken Whitt's suggestion and retreated.

Whitt flipped the light switch. His hippogriff slippers peeked out from beneath the bed where he left them. Hopefully, he could make a trip to the kitchen without disturbing the house demons.

Creeping slowly down the moaning stairs, he counted his biggest blessing: at least he was a world away from his buds. He couldn't bear it if they knew he'd wet himself, but it wasn't like the channel 10 news crew could pop out of the closet or anything, and his friends were back in Narragansett scrubbing up their boogie boards, tweaking their mountain bikes, and practicing the sensitive art of wedgie-twist. In general, those turdballs were probably getting on gloriously without Whittaker H. G. Miller.

Moonlight spilled onto the kitchen floor, mingling with the jagged shadows of torn linoleum tiles. As Whitt approached the sink, a beam of light flashed over tattered curtains. Just as he convinced himself what he saw was a bleary-eyed hallucination, another light flashed and the sound of metal scraping against metal came from beyond the back door. Someone prowled on the deck. Quietly setting the empty glass down, he stuffed his back against the wall, and crept toward the door. Unable to see anything through the filthy window, he gripped the doorknob and turned it as slowly as possible. The sound of his own rapid breathing monopolized his eardrums until the latch clicked. He pushed the door open an inch or two, just enough to see through.

Hunched about twelve feet from the kitchen door, a dark form hovered over a black metal box, screwdriver in one hand, a batch of twisted wires dangling from the other. Dark haired, the intruder wore a leather jacket and faded jeans. Whitt closed the door a crack and turned his face away, thinking maybe his father was right about that can of paint after all. Maybe the house wasn't haunted...maybe the guy on the deck came to hook up another blood-fest. Whitt cautiously clicked the door shut and tiptoed out of the kitchen.

Waking an over-tired parent is a dreadful event no child should ever have to endure. He thought to rouse Jillian instead, but she would only alert their father anyway, and then the old man would be upset Whitt hadn't come to him in the first place. There seemed no way around the dirty deed.

He poked his father's shoulder for the third time and said, as loudly as he could without breaking an urgent whisper, "*Dad!*"

Brad Miller's hair splayed over his forehead, looking every bit like someone poured a pail of black spaghetti over his head. His mouth hung wide open, a glistening line of drool slithered off his lower lip, and he snorted all Shrek-like.

Desperate measures were called for, since the poking obviously wasn't working. Pinching his father's over-sized nose between his thumb and finger, Whitt squeezed until he had the professor's wide-eyed attention.

Mr. Miller slapped Whitt's hands away. "My God, don't you ever get tired?"

"Shhh," Whitt warned, "There's somebody on the deck with a bomb. It's no joke, Dad. Keep quiet, he's right outside the door."

"There's really someone out there?"

"Yeah."

"Grab that bat, son. Hurry."

The intruder continued in his efforts to attach wires to his metal box as Whitt and his father returned to the kitchen. Once again, Whitt jarred the door open just enough to allow a good view of the vandal and his activities.

"That's probably the jerk making the walls bleed," Brad Miller whispered. His eyes narrowed and his lips went taut as he took a two-fisted grip on the bat and whispered, "Stay back, son. This won't be pretty."

It would have been awesome to see a good knockdown, drag-out fight, swords and pistols maybe...ninjas flying off the rooftop, or a swat team sneaking through the bushes: *Something*. But this confrontation ended before it started. Whitt's old man burst out the door, popped the guy upside the head with the baseball bat, and yelled, "Call 911." That's it—a total dramatic disappointment—until the police and ambulance came wailing into the driveway, then Whittaker H. G. Miller got more entertainment than he bargained for.

The Right to Remain Silent

The local sheriff looked into the face of the unconscious intruder and blurted, "Jesus Christ, it's Teddy."

Devil's Edge

As EMTs stuffed the gurney into the back of the ambulance, the sheriff turned to Brad and said, "You have the right to remain silent..."

"You've got this all wrong," he objected, a nervous twitch playing at the corners of his lips. "He was vandalizing *my* house, you see."

"Anything you say can and will be held against you..."

"You can't arrest *me*, I was protecting my family!"

"You have the right to speak to an attorney..."

"I *know* my rights..."

"Good, put your hands behind your back and spread your legs."

"You're joking, right?" Could they really arrest a man for protecting his family? He'd heard a lot of cock-eyed stories of justice gone wrong, burglars winning lawsuits for falling on skateboards located inside their victim's homes and that sort of thing, but this was ridiculous.

"Mr. Miller," the sheriff said sternly, "do as you're told or I'll charge you with resisting arrest."

The cold metal embraced his wrists and he flinched. "What about my kids? You can't expect me to leave them alone while you harass the wrong man."

Jillian and Whitt stood in the frame of the front door, watching wide-eyed as the sheriff frisked their father and pushed him into the backseat of a police cruiser.

The sheriff turned to his tall, scrawny, deputy and said, "Jared, go get Ted and Dixie." Then, he flicked a thumb toward the house, "Can't your wife look after your kids?"

"That's my *daughter*. She's only sixteen."

"Sixteen? You do know it's a criminal offense to lie to a law enforcement officer?"

"I'm not lying."

Skeptical, the sheriff cocked his head off to the side and raised an eyebrow. "Well then," he said, reluctant to concede the point, "I suppose we'll have to bring them along and sort this thing out at the hospital."

Devil's Edge

Jillian's glare seared as she and Whitt scrambled into the backseat of the cruiser. Brad knew the look well. If he accepted her offer to go to a hotel, none of this would have happened. Funny how women rarely have to speak to get a point across.

A migraine crept up the back of Brad Miller's skull and punched him full force in the temples. In town for less than one night and already on his way to the clink.

The deputy slammed the cruiser door and a middle-aged couple rushed across the lawn. A silver-haired fellow panted out of breath while the plump, weary-eyed woman running next to him suppressed whatever attempted to escape her throat with a hand pressed tightly over her mouth.

The woman climbed into the back of the ambulance and wailed, "Teddy!"

"What happened, Garrison?" The silver-haired fellow demanded, his hand maniacally twisting the brim of a ball cap he had jerked off of his head.

"Seems this fellow found Teddy messing with a bomb on his deck, or so he says."

"A *bomb*? Teddy would never do such a thing. Bring a girl home late from a date, definitely. Smoke a cigarette in the boy's room, probably. Steal a car, absolutely. A *bomb*? You know he wouldn't..."

"I know," the sheriff said, placing a hand of comfort on the fellow's shoulder. "That's why I'm retaining the Louisville Slugger here until we find out exactly what happened. Now, get in your Jeep and follow us to the hospital. I dare say our boy needs some attention."

The Elephant in the Room

They sat in the hospital waiting room for hours, Jillian's father looking as though he wanted nothing more than to inconspicuously ooze into the walls, Whitt failing miserably in his attempt to keep his eyelids open.

A nurse waltzed into the room to congratulate a Mr. and Mrs. Groton on becoming the proud grandparents to a set of twins. As the young woman turned to make her exit from the room, her eyes caught sight of Jillian sitting so stiffly in her chair she might have been part of the upholstery. Donning a deep scowl, the nurse mumbled, "You got to be kidding me," and promptly dropped her tray of medical supplies with an ear-splitting clatter. Flustered, she scurried to pick up her supplies and offered a timid apology. Unwilling to release Jillian's gaze as she moved to make her exit from the room, she craned her neck back so far she failed to notice an elderly gentleman blocking the doorway. Once again, the tray and its contents mercilessly clanged upon the floor.

Jillian had seen this type of reaction before, the last time it happened she was walking across campus when a passing gaggle of girls burst into a wild giggling session. Jillian felt a prickling heat flush into her face and, having had enough of this type of degradation, rushed into the center of their circle and, with all the patience of a monk allowed to speak for the first time in forty years, blurted, "What? You've never seen a giant before? You should meet the rest of my family...my brother's got two heads, my mother is a Cyclops, and my father is a freaking troll. Would you all like to come over for dinner tonight?" Pushing her way out of the group, she blubbered, "Did I mention we're cannibals?"

Hands down, one of the most embarrassing moments of her entire life. She felt the same indignation now, watching the nurse trip over her own feet, but this was neither the place nor the time for emotional outbursts. Enough hornets escaped their nests this evening.

"Mr. Miller," the sheriff shouted, "the boy you clubbed is my nephew, Teddy Teach, Jr. He's not a criminal, he wasn't setting a bomb, and he meant no harm to you or your family."

The sheriff's nephew, oh *shitski*. That meant jail for sure. Jillian vigorously ruffled her short, blonde hair with her fingertips; a nervous habit she inherited from her mother. God only knows what horrors lay inside backwoods southern lockups. Before Jillian could form a protest, Mr. Teach appeared in the doorway, his eyes slowly scanning the room, his trembling hands still trying to squeeze the sweat out of the brim of his ball cap. He spoke with a smaller man in a white lab coat who said Mr. Teach's son suffered a mild concussion and would spend a few hours for observation, but he expected a swift recovery.

Brad Miller let out a short sigh of relief and squirmed in his chair, his arms pinned behind his back, his bloodshot eyes darting side-to-side like a set of ping-pong balls maxed out on Red Bull. He wriggled against the handcuffs; his hands purple from the struggle. In his haste to confront the intruder on the deck, he donned a pair of mismatched socks, one white, one black, and though it wasn't the only fashion faux pas he had committed, it served to cement the impression of a raving lunatic lost to all sensibility.

Drops of sweat rained from beneath his disheveled black locks, trickling over the nape of his neck; the heat, the stress, or an eruptive culmination of both.

Whitt tapped his hippogriff slippers incessantly against the speckled white tile, arms tightly crossed, his chin pressed firmly to his chest, refusing to make eye contact with anyone, balled up in a fit of guilt or denial, Jillian couldn't tell which.

"Did you ask my boy why he was on your deck before you popped him in the head?" Mr. Teach lambasted.

Mr. Miller made no attempt to hide his sarcasm, "What was I supposed to say? 'Excuse me, is that a bomb you have there?'"

A stray voice approached from around the corner declaring, "It wasn't a bomb." Heads turned as Mrs. Teach entered the waiting room. "He had this in his pocket," she said, unfurling a long paper banner for everyone to see. Printed in a multi-colored font and decorated with splashes of bright graphics, the banner read: *WELCOME TO DEVIL'S EDGE.* "The box he hooked up was a confetti machine Ozzie invented a few years back. Apparently, Teddy got a good look at your daughter and meant to impress her with a warm welcome."

The sheriff jumped from his chair and took a stiff stance before his prisoner. "You're under arrest for assault and..."

Mr. Teach grabbed the sheriff by the arm, drawing him in close for a sidebar. "Wait a minute, Garrison. Is that right? How could he know what Teddy was foolin' with? For all he knew, it *was* a bomb. Wouldn't you do the same thing if somebody came messin' around your house? I ain't sure we should press charges. What do you think, Dixie?" Mrs. Teach glared at Jillian's father and shook her head. "I'm goin' to check on Teddy," she grumbled, storming out of the waiting room.

"Ted, this man damn near put your boy's lights out for good. Now, I understand what you're sayin', but I can still chain him up...give him a couple weeks to think about it."

"Oh hell, Garrison, you know Teddy could find trouble locked in a box on friggin' Mars."

The sheriff let out a loud guffaw. "Hell yes. I chased him all the way to Georgia to get my police cruiser back, remember? Kid's got dinosaur balls. Believe me, I know. But what happened here tonight wasn't his fault. That's what you've got to understand."

Jillian tried to get a fix on Mr. Teach's expression, searching for some telltale sign, but it was like trying to catch a spawning salmon with bare hands; one minute he seemed uber pissed and the next, meek and defeated, a virtual Dr. Jekyll and Mr. Hyde. His eyes flittered back and forth, as if they didn't know where to rest, and his cheeks burned red, his fingers kneading the brim of his ball cap. Jillian clung to a microscopic sliver of hope he might continue to consider her father's innocence.

"It's late, Garrison," Mr. Teach said, his voice dogged by weariness.

"Listen," the sheriff put a hand of support on Mr. Teach's shoulder. "No reason we have to sort this out now. I can slap this guy with a summons to appear before Judge Winthrop and let old Harry sort it out next week, if you're sure you don't want me to lock him up tonight."

Mr. Teach's face seemed all at once brighter. "That's a damn good idea. You do that. Meanwhile, I gotta say, Mr. Miller, you picked one hell of a way to impress your new boss."

Brad Miller slowly lifted his chin off his chest, his expression dire. "Excuse me?"

"Name's Theodore Teach, director of the UAB. I believe you were scheduled to join my excavation team."

Curing Giantism

The morning sun threatened to turn the sidewalks into molten lava as Jillian and Whitt leashed up the dogs. They barely stepped off the curb when the three children from next door bombarded them.

Jillian immediately took a defensive stance, convinced the neighbors meant to take issue over last night's fiasco.

"Those are Irish setters," said the smallest of the three, a fresh buzz cut calling the short blonde hairs on his head to attention. "Irish setters are known for their uncanny ability to unlock prison doors. Did you know that?"

Jillian never heard such a thing and immediately doubted it. The young boy squinted at her. A pair of thick eyeglasses rested inside his shirt pocket next to a pen leaking ink onto his oversized tie. The glasses would have been more helpful if put to proper use, and summer vacation started a week ago. What was with the tie?

Jillian relaxed slightly; relieved to find no need to testify in defense of her father's good character (if, in fact, he had one).

"It's a fact," the boy went on, the tempo of his speech so rapid it was difficult to keep up, "people who own dogs live longer than people who raise children…almost everyone lives longer than people who raise children. Our parents say trouble runs in our blood. As a matter of fact, if you look up our genealogy, you might find we could be related to Blackbeard, our names being Teach and all—I'm Ozzie, by the way—and while being related to Blackbeard might explain the occasional mishap, chances are just as good you'll find we're related to Grandma Moses instead, in which case, the mayhem would no longer compute. Follow?"

As if on cue, and in unison, the other two blurted, "Shut up, Oz."

The young boy blushed, stepped back, and stooped to pet Merlin and Ruby.

Oz. The same boy who invented the confetti box that caused so much trouble the night before? He looked small for a junior Einstein—no older than six or seven. His mother said he invented the contraption a few years ago; was he cutting teeth then, too? Jillian considered her own uncommon appearance, her own unusual accomplishments, and shrugged.

"Hi," the pretty girl said, reaching for Jillian's hand, "I'm Maurine. I expect you know my brother, Teddy. He ain't in the habit of givin' most people the time of day 'cause he's the oldest and way too cool for that. He's got himself a noggin' knocker today…a well-deserved headache, I mean. You've just met Oz. He's eleven and watches way too much Discovery Channel. There are only two words you need to know to get along with him, the ones we just used. And you are?"

"Jillian and Whittaker Miller," Jillian said stiffly. "And this is Ruby and Merlin."

"Merlin?" Teddy grunted. "Ya'll gonna *need* a dog with magical powers if you're gonna stay in that old dump. A fella once lived there, chopped his wife up into little pieces, shoved her in a cardboard box and parked her in the attic. By the time they found her, she was grade-A sirloin burger."

"That ain't true," Maurine cried, slapping Teddy sharply on the shoulder. "Why don't you go smoke a cigarette behind the soda shop and act all Johnny Depp for somebody who'll buy it?"

Jillian watched with amusement as Maurine chastised her brother. Thin and of average height, Maurine's stream of dark hair flowed nearly to her waist. Long lashes blinked over her explosive large brown eyes, her skin a toasty tan. Pretty as a doll on the shelf; a doll itching to give Ken a boot to the groin and a shiner, but a doll nonetheless. Her sleeveless, bright red shirt sparkled with a series of small silver sequins lining the pockets, the sort of shirt you might expect to buy at Dollywood, and she wore a pair of red sequined sandals to match. She'd fashioned her shorts from a pair of cutoff jeans. None of those things roused Jillian's interest the way the girl's commanding attitude did. Maurine Teach might walk on the southern side of the street (they all sported a thick drawl) but this little jalapeño firecracker displayed a spunk Jillian instantly admired. In fact, anyone willing to give Teddy Jr. a good tongue-lashing was A-okay.

Maurine whipped her long black hair over her shoulder with a casual twist of the neck, hooked her fingers into the loops of her shorts and said, "I'm fourteen, how old are you, twenty? Twenty-one?"

"She's only sixteen and dumb as a plug nickel," Whitt howled.

Jillian fixed Whitt with a burning glare.

"She is *not* sixteen. Any darn fool could see that," Teddy countered, and the smile he flashed was one Jillian immediately recognized: Elvis Presley. The cheeky squirrel probably practiced in front of a mirror twice a day, every day. Was this backwoods oaf seriously trying to make an impression even after he managed to drag Jillian's father through hell last night? Between the leather jacket (who wears a leather jacket in ninety degree weather?) pressed jeans, and the glittering smile, it wasn't difficult to mark him for a player, a player whose game had put her family in harm's way.

"I *am* sixteen," she said, happy to contradict Teddy's know-it-all tone, and she bent to unwrap the leash that had twisted around

Ruby's legs. "Whitt's eleven, going to pee…" she said, "I mean, going on three."

"Whoa, your momma lets you dye your hair?" Maurine exclaimed, her eyes wide with wonder.

Ozzie abandoned his bonding session with Merlin and jumped to his feet, delivering another rapid oratory. "Giantism originated with the over-consumption of pine nuts fallen from the great sequoia, it can only be cured by consuming a tea concocted from the nail clippings of miniature African toads combined with the budding leaves derived from dwarfed rose bushes indigenous only to the northern quarter of Greenland. Of course, you can also get some on E-Bay."

Whitt busted a gut and Jillian blushed.

Maurine kicked a cloud of dirt and sand in Ozzie's direction, "Shut up, Oz."

Tickled by Whitt's response, Ozzie invited him to the local soda shop. "I'll show you where Mr. Rittenhower spontaneously combusted," he said. "You can still see the outline of his body toasted in the floor. It's awesome."

Whitt tugged on Merlin's leash and replied with gusto, "Absolutely."

"Oh, no you don't," Jillian reprimanded. "I'm responsible for you. You aren't leaving my sight."

Whitt's face flushed red, his hands curled into fists, and he stomped his grayed sneaker six inches into the sand. "You can't tell me what to…"

Maurine quickly interrupted, "Ozzie's mostly harmless. We can walk your dog and meet them there, if you want. It's only five minutes up the road."

When Jillian offered a reluctant nod, Whitt and Ozzie took off like a pair of blow darts.

Jillian listened to the sound of Maurine's sandals scraping against the sidewalk pavement as they walked, unsure of what to say. Teddy Jr. offered no help, more concerned with perfecting his macho strut than making conversation. Jillian felt hopeless around strangers, nervous and awkward. Her father braining

Teddy Jr. with a baseball bat the night before certainly didn't help and Ozzie's comments on Giantism left her feeling exceptionally self-conscious. On the bright side, at least the Teach clan knew the way back to the house; Jillian could get lost in a GPS store, Maurine's guidance would prove invaluable.

Jillian cleared her throat, determined to break the ice. "Did someone really combust?"

"Oh yeah," Maurine said matter-of-factly. "Old Harry Rittenhower...went up like a moth caught in flame. My mother says he got what every married man sniffing at a young skirt deserves. Rittenhower had the hots for the local librarian." Maurine's cheeks flushed. "Don't get me wrong," she sputtered, "my mother isn't a bad person, she just has an opinion on absolutely everything."

Jillian nodded and pulled her cell phone from her pocket. As she flipped open the cover, Teddy let out an indignant grunt. "Unless you can afford to tie into a military satellite, that ain't gonna work. No bars. Welcome to Mayberry RFD." Amused with himself, he nonchalantly pulled a cigarette from the pocket of his leather jacket and sauntered off.

Jillian crinkled her lightly freckled button nose and whispered, "Disgusting."

"Oh, he don't smoke 'em," Maurine giggled. "He likes people to think he does, but he just lets 'em dangle on his lips; thinks it makes him look all Brad Pitt."

Jillian inspected the face of her cell phone, noted its lack of enthusiasm, and slipped it back into her pocket.

"I meant the lousy cell phone service."

"Oh."

Maurine stopped walking, donned a mischievous smile and turned to Jillian, "Teddy's probably gonna end up combusted too; he's got the hots for you."

"I couldn't care less," Jillian sharply quipped. And she meant it. She hadn't put swapping spit with rednecks on her to-do list, especially not *that* redneck. If it came down to the last thread in her life's tapestry, she would rather make out with a crocodile caught in the throngs of an epileptic fit. Teddy Jr. may yet succeed in having her father arrested and thrown in jail. He would never acquire her forgiveness.

As they rounded the corner and drew nearer to the business end of town, Jillian thought it time to clear up a misunderstanding. "I don't dye my hair," she confessed.

Maurine's eyes went wide. "Frog poop in vinegar, that red streak ain't dye?"

Jillian reached into her blue cotton button-down blouse, pulled out a gold locket, and carefully opened it. Inside was a picture of a very attractive woman with cropped, bright blonde hair, a thin red streak running up the center of her head.

"My mother," Jillian explained, though she knew she didn't have to.

"Lord, you look just like her. You're lucky. People say I look like my mother too, but I ain't so sure it's a compliment. Hey, I bet your momma's having tea with mine right now."

"My mother passed away last year."

Maurine's sun-tanned cheeks turned a deep cerise. "I'm so sorry. I didn't... Nobody told... Green bubbles in the bathtub, I am *so* sorry."

Spirit Rapper

"Just like he said," Whitt gushed, bending to pick up a stone nestled beneath the toe of his sneaker. "An outline on the floor so clear you could almost see the guy's face. The waitress said one minute she was pouring his coffee and the next minute the coroner was sweeping up a pile of ashes."

The stone sailed out of Whitt's hand and crashed through an unsuspecting window attached to the only house on Scabbard Street.

Devil's Edge

"What'd you do that for?" He wailed.

Jillian slapped him smartly on the back of the head. "You were aiming at a bird's nest, you heartless little rat."

"So you grab my arm and put a rock through a window? Brilliant."

Ozzie spoke slowly and stuttered, "That house belongs to the S-spirit Rapper. I-I-I've got homework, I-I'll s-see ya'll later." The sound of his shoes pattering against the sidewalk resounded long after he turned the corner.

"What's a spirit rapper?" Whitt asked.

Maurine gawked blank-faced at the shattered window. When she snapped out of her trance, it was sudden. "I gotta go make sure Ozzie's okay," she blabbered, and hightailed it around the corner.

Jillian felt the blood rush into her cheeks. "As if we don't have enough trouble already...you go around throwing stones. You've probably pissed off some wart-faced voodoo witch and who do you think should pay for that window?"

"You're the nature lover. If you hadn't..."

"Excuse me," said the singsong voice of a woman surprisingly calm considering Whitt probably just parked twenty pounds of shattered glass onto her sofa. "Was there a message on that stone? Lawdy be...I couldn't find a message. Ya'll didn't happen to see a skinny old fool whereabouts here, did ya? He's a little feller, wears suspenders...never could find a pair of pants to fit him right, and a white beard, kinda scraggly, and a black hat like them yodelers wear over in Dutch country, whatnot. Did you see him?"

Whitt and Jillian stood slack-jawed, shaking their heads negatively.

The woman stood an average height, if not a tad shorter, and filled her mud-smeared coveralls to their straining buttons. Her nose and cheeks were sun-toasted, splotches of red contrasted against the alabaster white adorning the rest of her wrinkled and aged face. A mischievous gust of coastal wind lifted the rim of her floppy straw hat and whipped thick strands of wild, white hair across her face. For the briefest moment, she appeared nearly mummified, tufts curling around her neck like ancient gossamers.

"You didn't see him? Who threw that stone, then? Lawdy, why would anyone throw a stone without a message?"

"It was an accident," Jillian confessed.

"Piddlepoop. Ain't no such thing as an accident, just one event stitched to another in ways we don't understand."

As the woman finished speaking, Jillian thought she recognized the faint scent of alcohol. Not nearly as strong an aroma as when, on too many occasions over the past year, her father came down with the Jack Daniel's flu, but the unmistakable scent of alcohol nonetheless.

The woman swiped her hair out of her face and adjusted her hat, twisting until the pink and yellow plastic flowers pinned to the bonnet faced front and center. Satisfied with the hat's security, she squeezed her hand into a large pocket in her coveralls and pulled out a pair of bifocals. Her eyes expanded ten times their normal size when she slipped the glasses on and stepped forward for a closer inspection. Her rapid examination of Whitt incited a "humph" and an "ah" but he didn't seem of great interest otherwise. Contrarily, when she lifted her over-emphasized silver eyes to meet Jillian's gaze, she gasped, raised her wiry eyebrows nearly to the top of her forehead, and fell backward, landing large-bottomed in the middle of a bay bush.

Merlin and Ruby let loose with an anxious barking tantrum as Whitt and Jillian clambered to help the flailing woman to her feet.

Once the lady righted herself and ventured to speak, her voice lost its calm demeanor. "Ya'll come inside," she insisted, hurriedly swiping leaves and twigs from the rear of her pants. "We need to have us a sitting."

A tall cast iron fence surrounded the property and encased a massive garden bursting with vivid colors and beguiling scents. Beyond the iron gate, a brick path wound its way to the front door. The house was a small English Tudor that resembled a medieval cottage, its tall, narrow windows peeking beneath a deeply pitched roof. Half-timbered in the traditional style, it looked as though it slipped off the pages of a classic fairytale.

Any minute now, Jillian thought, Hansel and Gretel would come lumbering out the front door and start dropping breadcrumbs. Except they didn't, and this strange—what did Ozzie call her— 'Spirit Rapper' expected them to follow her inside when they knew nothing of her, except they smashed her window to smithereens.

Already halfway to the front door, she hadn't looked back to see if Jillian and Whitt were following along.

"I'm not going anywhere with that crazy old bat," Whitt announced. "And you shouldn't either."

Jillian would have chalked Whitt's response up to the chicken pee staining his socks but Maurine and Ozzie's apparent fear weighed on her mind. Something about this woman scared them senseless. If the locals were afraid, chances were good Jillian and Whitt should be frightened, too. Or, was it entirely unfair to judge the woman based on the reactions of strangers?

Jillian hadn't quite made up her mind what she should do until, with a tone of urgency, the woman rushed back and professed, "I got a message from your momma."

Whitt pointed a rigid finger at the old woman and roared, "You *can't* have a message from our mother. She's *dead.*"

Leaning forward, the lady rested her hands on her knees, flashed a slightly gray smile, and said, "Lawd a' mighty, young man, a silly little thing like that ain't never stopped me before."

Revelations

"Allow me to introduce ma'self," the woman insisted. Reaching for Jillian's hand, she gave it a gentle squeeze. "The name's Agaritha Drummond. If that's a mouthful, you can call me Aggy."

"Jillian Miller. I'm sorry about your window... I'm sure my father will pay to have it replaced."

"No need to worry a t'all. My boy, Harold, owns the hardware store in the village; he'll fix it right up. Would you like a glass of iced tea? I make it with jasmine leaves...smooth and refreshing, if'n I dare boast. I take a little brandy with mine, care for a nip?"

Jillian accepted the tea, but declined the alcohol with a blush.

Mrs. Drummond shrugged her shoulders. "Have it your way," she said, sauntering off into the kitchen.

Shards of broken window lay scattered over a delicate Persian rug, the late morning sun twinkling off the edges of the jagged glass. The house, tastefully decorated with antiques, fluffy cushions, and easy chairs, seemed cozy enough—if one could ignore the disarray on the floor. A behemoth of a grandfather clock ticked away in a far corner but nothing else seemed out of the ordinary, until Jillian caught sight of the coffee table. A Ouija board sat idly on the center of the table, a ruffled set of tarot cards splayed next to it. A bag of runes spilled onto the fireplace mantle and incense burners lined up like ashen soldiers on the hearthstone. New Age. Paranormal. Much the same supernatural paraphernalia Sarah Miller always had on hand.

Did this woman possess psychic abilities? Did she really receive a message? If Whitt hadn't insisted on waiting outside in the garden, his curiosities would have peaked with the familiar sights and easy scent of sandalwood permeating the living room. Jillian took a deep breath, wishing for the millionth time in the course of a year she could retreat to her mother's protective embrace.

"I gotta confess, I was expectin' a much younger girl," Mrs. Drummond remarked as she handed a glass of iced tea to Jillian and plopped herself down on the divan. "Ain't the first time I got a message wrong...oh, and probably not the last," she said with a sigh. "I was under the impression you'd be no older than sixteen. I messed that one up but good."

"No, you didn't," Jillian retorted, inching forward in her chair, more interested in Mrs. Drummond than she expected. Most so-called psychics make a living parlaying obvious facts, or vague snippets; niceties like, 'You've had a really rough time of it, but your path is clearing now.' Or, 'The opportunities you have anticipated are upon you.' It was rare to find a psychic gifted enough to provide exact detail, but Jillian couldn't deny Mrs. Drummond just pinpointed her age, despite overwhelming evidence to the contrary. Jillian had known only one other woman capable of such precision: her mother.

She took a sip of the iced tea. It *was* smooth, its perfumed flavor lingered on the tip of the tongue like a gentle flower, a pleasant surprise. "I am sixteen."

Mrs. Drummond raised her eyebrows and smiled. "Dang, you're tall," she said. "Do people ask you all them dumb questions like, 'How's the air up there,' and all?"

Jillian lowered her chin and blushed. "Did you know my mother?"

"Sorry to say I didn't, but I do now. She tells me you're no stranger to second sight. Your momma's one of the most powerful spirits I've encountered. But don't let me ramble on. You must be anxious to hear her message."

A sudden onslaught of tears welled behind Jillian's eyes, but she strictly refused them release. No use getting into an emotional huff. For all she knew, this woman could be a retired carnival attraction with no more psychic skill than a box of rusted nails. Jillian swallowed hard and nodded, attempting to prepare her heart for what may, or may not, come.

Mrs. Drummond swilled her iced tea, hiccupped, closed her eyes, threw her head back, and inhaled deeply. "Your momma wants you to know she didn't suffer," she said, her tone breathy, "the blow to her head resulted in an instant passin', she felt no pain. As for your daddy, he's afraid of losin' you. Understand and forgive. Your time for fame and glory will come. Do you understand?"

Jillian paused to process the information. She'd been told her mother died instantly, but wondered if the claim was made to spare her grief. Her father had attended the performance and watched as the cruel events unfolded before his helpless eyes. If not for a late English final, Jillian would have attended as well. She still didn't know if fate spared or robbed her.

And then, as if someone suddenly replaced a burnt out light bulb, she understood. The non-stop bickering, her father's sudden immunity to her persuasive charms, his unwillingness to speak openly with her...he didn't want her to compete at the Nationals. Why didn't she see it before? Though she understood his fear, she found it far from acceptable. How could he expect Jillian to relinquish her dreams over a freak accident? After all, how many dancers actually die on stage? The odds are one in a kazillion. It wasn't so much Uri Brankov's inability to catch her mother when he should have-lots of dancers take a fall-it was the specific way her neck twisted when she hit the floor. As terrible as it had been, it was just a freak accident.

Jillian knew her mother wouldn't want her to give up dancing; they shared the passion long before Jillian learned to walk. In fact, her mother invested in a baby-sling shortly after giving birth and strapped the large pouch to her chest. With Jillian snuggled securely inside, the sling provided the freedom and mobility necessary for the two of them to dance together. To hear her mother tell the story, the pouch was the only pacifier Jillian ever needed.

And now, if Jillian could find her way to invest in just a few more years of sweat and pirouette, add just a few more inches of grime to the soles of her toe shoes, and cling to the memory of her mother's talent and grace, there might come a day when she would become half the dancer Sarah Miller had been, an accomplishment well worth striving for. There simply was no future without the stage and the challenge of the dance. Jillian would have to find a way to make her father understand...find a way to convince him to let her compete. Mrs. Drummond got one thing wrong, the time for Jillian's fame and glory wasn't waiting somewhere off in the distance; it was *now*.

With her attention settled back on the situation at hand, Jillian realized Mrs. Drummond had no carnival in her past; the woman proved highly skilled. She knew exactly how Sarah Miller died and absolutely nailed her father's fear. What else did she know?

Jillian forced a sip of tea past the lump in her throat. "Why would my mother come to you? I don't know you."

"She's a powerful mind, she knew you would come. I'd guess she has a history with all things psychic, ain't that right?"

"She knew stuff... Saw things before they happened... I don't know if she knew she was going to... to die, but yes, she had a gift."

Mrs. Drummond leaned closer and put a hand on Jillian's knee. "Your momma didn't see it comin' and she sure enough didn't die on purpose. She never would've left y'all if she had a choice. Do you understand?"

So often in the past year Jillian wondered why her mother hadn't foreseen the accident, why she didn't take the necessary steps to avoid it. She always seemed to know which planes to take, which trains would delay, which streets to cross, which people to avoid, even which days harbored sudden thunderstorms. Jillian learned to rely on her mother's instinct—as inconvenient as it often was—the comfort and security it created more than made up for the difficulties. How could her mother possibly not know? Was there no dream...no vision...no nagging notion? What good is a powerful gift if it isn't there to safeguard when it's needed most? The gift miserably failed the Millers. Jillian completely understood why her father smashed and trashed every paranormal trinket, every book, every reminder. How unfair to be blinded when vision is imperative.

Dealing with the anger was easy, it simply flowed unencumbered, but Jillian still felt at a total loss for processing the grief and sadness. She packed away the pain long ago, placing it inside an imaginary suitcase, vowing to open it one day when she might be better prepared to deal with it. Now, it seemed as though this strange woman sitting before her picked the lock and haphazardly spilled its contents. Facing her grief unprepared suddenly seemed too much like trying to move the African continent a few inches to the left using a hot air balloon and a pair of tweezers.

Jillian lost the battle against her tears and, though she tried to speak, her words stumbled over her tongue until she finally managed to say, "I should go."

Her expression aghast, Mrs. Drummond sprang to her feet and cried, "Heavens, no! You ain't got your message yet."

"But...I thought you already... Didn't you say...? What else could there be?"

"Miss Miller, you're in grave danger. There's things you need to learn, but fast. Things you need to accept, embrace, and master. Your survival depends on it. Remember now, truth is a huffy bridge, if you reject it, it'll dump you in the river. Don't be makin' that mistake...you won't survive it. Your momma's afeared for you and says she won't leave you for as long as you're in the thick of it. Don't doubt that."

"I'm afraid you don't understand," Jillian argued. "I'm not in danger. My father won't let me compete. I can't break my neck if I'm not allowed on stage."

"Ah, yes. Your mother was a dancer. I'm sure you'll do well to follow in her footsteps. Unfortunately, that ain't it. The danger I'm talkin' about is unfoldin' here and now."

What in the world was this woman rambling on about? If the danger wasn't in the dance, where was it? Here and now... Here, in Devil's Edge. Could this have something to do with the blood in Whitt's closet? Jillian almost forgotten about the closet, what with her father nearly arrested for knocking Teddy Teach senseless.

"Does this have anything to do with the house we're living in?"

"Best believe it," Mrs. Drummond said, her tone urgent, "and plenty more. You seen anything strange in that house, anything out of the ordinary?"

"You mean like blood dripping from the closet wall?"

"Lawd a' mighty!" Mrs. Drummond squealed. "Did anyone else see that?"

"We all saw it."

Mrs. Drummond cradled her head in her hands as if experiencing a terrible headache. "It's worse than I thought. You'll be needin' your power right away, child. Right away."

Jillian gasped. "Power? What power?"

"Don't you know? Of course, you wouldn't...you couldn't. You have a gift, Miss Miller, greater skill than anyone to ever come before you. If we can awaken your abilities, you might stand a chance against the terrible evils a knockin' at your door. If not...well...I'm afraid... But let's concentrate on the positive."

"Gift?"

As Jillian's mind played through a long list of things she may or may not have a talent for, she suffered the sinking feeling she was off track on all accounts. Surely, Mrs. Drummond didn't mean... No. She couldn't. She didn't. *Shitski.* She did.

"I don't want anything to do with the paranormal," Jillian shouted. "I am *not* psychic and I'll never *be* psychic. It's useless...ask my mother, I'm sure she'll agree." With that, she bolted out of her chair and charged for the door.

Mrs. Drummond called after her, "You ain't got time to play the mule! You come on back once you found the Ballencroft book."

Neptune's Grotto

Alexander Spotswood IV swayed his metal detector over the sand, to and fro, scouring the beach as he had every night for the past thirty years. The cumbersome apparatus promised a stiff neck and sore shoulders, but he would never allow a minor thing like pain to hinder his quest, even though he'd already developed a bit of a hunchback. It wasn't like he was a pretty man to begin with, never had much luck with the ladies, never took a wife, nor had any children—and just as well—they would only interfere with his objectives. Proud as he was of his dedication to the search, he admitted the grim bowing of his spine had, indeed, slowed him down some, and since those nosey mud-dogs from the UAB started sniffing around the harbor a few years ago it was more imperative than ever to remain diligent in the quest. No one deserved this discovery more than he, no one put as much time and effort into the endeavor than he, and what's more, he hadn't spent thirty years sifting through sand only to come up empty handed.

While nearly all the locals were familiar with the legends concerning Neptune's Grotto, most of them considered them old wives tales, pooh-poohing them as wishful thinking. That kind of doubt was Alexander's number one advantage. So far as he could tell, no one else visited the door and that, of course, meant no one else had found the key. He meant to keep it just so.

The sun snuggled onto the horizon as Alexander slipped inside the grotto. He reached for the flashlight he kept hidden behind a large rock and found it in its place, untouched. His hand trembled with nervous excitement as he clicked it on. Its thin beam of light shone dim: Blasted batteries. How many times did he replace them over the years? No matter, it would all be well worth it—wouldn't it—come that glorious day when he finally unearthed Blackbeard's jewels?

The cave was quiet, but for the occasional whoosh and splatter of water as it rained down through the blowhole (a circular hole carved into the rock high up in the ceiling; much too high for use as an entrance, but low enough to enable an especially vigorous thrust of surf to penetrate its vulnerability).

Alexander swept the floor of the cave with his beam of light, searching for telltale signs of rats. The beasts came this time every year, mating and nesting in the darkness, feeding on washed up crustaceans and injured seagulls; in short, they created an absolute nuisance. There's nothing like a swarming pack of rodents to give a man a solid sense of mortality—this he learned firsthand. So far, there seemed no sign of the insufferable vermin.

Immediately relieved of the weight of the cumbersome apparatus, he wedged his metal detector between two rocks, wrapped his long, braided, silver hair twice around his neck, tugged at his three-corner hat to secure it, and moved deeper into the cave. He retraced these steps so many times he could make his way with his eyes closed, if not for the layers of slime on the stones that made the way nearly as treacherous as a loaded minefield. Fifty paces past the large stalactite—turn right. Twenty-four paces past the gnarled lady (a bulbous group of melded rock slightly resembling the form of a hefty woman)—turn left. One hundred and ten more paces, including the stone bridge over the crystal pool, and there it was...the gate of water; not just a waterfall, but also a hidden threshold, something few ever realized.

The gateway would also remain a mystery to Alexander if he hadn't accidentally fallen through it some thirty years ago while exploring the grotto with his sadly departed comrade, Nicholas Targos.

Alexander pulled a fistful of crumpled rain gear from his pocket. Donning the gear, he braced himself for the impending onslaught and walked through the base of the waterfall. On the other side of the thundering wall of water, he immediately reached for the five-foot slab of wood he placed there earlier and began to wave the board through the air as if trying to ward off a swarm of bats or mosquitoes. In fact, he went through this ritual each time he came to the grotto, each time but the one time it really mattered.

Convinced nothing malefic meant to attack; he placed the board over a four-foot chasm and gingerly walked across. When he no longer required the makeshift bridge, he quickly picked the board up and slashed at empty air. At last satisfied with his safety, he stood glaring at his long despised nemesis, *La Porte de Ruine* (as indicated by the roughly crafted inscription chiseled into the stone above the door).

His feet stood upon the very spot where Nicholas fell victim to a centuries-old scheme. Would Alexander never banish the horrid memory? So many years had passed, and yet, without fail, each time he stood before this door, the same vision insulted his eyes— as if it happened only yesterday—the vivid remembrance of

Nicholas jumping over the chasm, eager to get closer to the door (after all, it was the first time either of them ever laid eyes upon it) when, seemingly out of nowhere, came a stone pendulum, archaic in its design, crashing into his skull, splattering his head as if popping a mere balloon, and sending him slinking to the ground, the lifeless mass of a foolhardy man whose greed outweighed his patience. Perhaps more horrible than the memory itself was Alexander's knowledge that he, too, was about to make the very same mistake and, had Nicholas not beaten him to the other side of the chasm by a fraction of a second, it would have been the death of him. This horrible acknowledgement sent him running from Neptune's Grotto, strictly traumatized and bereaved for the only true friend he had ever known.

Who knew if there were other booby traps waiting to assail?

The greatest shock of all came when Alexander returned to the grotto the following day and discovered his friend's body missing. A rather puzzling dilemma, as Alexander and Nicholas assumed no one else knew of the gateway. Apparently they were mistaken, for the only plausible explanation was a local came in the night, discovered Nicholas's body, and removed it. If that were the case, then it was possible someone else also knew about the parchment and the Cuffs of Gall.

It was highly unlikely anyone would haphazardly discover the grotto's secrets, no one besides Alexander had in hundreds of years. And so, in all likelihood, this 'someone' overheard an aroused conversation between himself and Nicholas. Maybe they spoke too excitedly after Nicholas returned from Ocracoke Island where, while on a private fishing expedition, he stumbled upon the foundation of an old abandoned house. As Nicholas curiously poked through the rubble, he happened upon a metal box containing the parchment and the bottom half of the Cuffs of Gall (antiquated slave irons). Time worn and barely legible, the inscription on the metal read, 'Permanezca Ponga,' a Spanish phrase appropriately meaning, 'Stay put.' Nicholas swore Alexander was the only person he'd shared the information with and vowed they would retrieve the treasure together for a fifty-fifty split.

However it happened, the mysterious someone must have followed Alexander and Nicholas to the grotto, must have seen what happened to Nicholas, and must have had designs on retrieving Blackbeard's jewels for himself. Hopefully, what this someone did not know was that in order to gain access to the treasure, The Door of Doom must first open and the door won't budge without The Emerald Viper. If Alexander properly understood the parchment's message, other relics were also required in order to make safe passageway to the hidden fortune, namely the second half of The Cuffs of Gall and The Sword of Woe.

If hindsight had any more worth than a glass penny, Alexander Spotswood would never again try to penetrate the grotto's secrets without the proper relics in hand, lest he end up side-by-side with Nicholas Targos.

He ran his hand over the wet edges of the boulder that comprised *La Porte de Ruine*. Somewhere on the other side of the stubborn portal lay a vast fortune rich in history, rich in worth, but more importantly, rich in redemption, for if he could acquire the prize Nicholas Targos set out to find some thirty years ago, then Alexander would know—once and for all—his friend had not died for naught.

He took out his flashlight and searched for evidence of intrusion: Nothing. Whoever that mysterious someone was all those years ago, he had yet to show a solitary sign of himself. Perhaps the coward, the fool, gave up the quest. It is true, though—isn't it—not every man has the steadfast determination Alexander Spotswood has.

Once again, he slowly traced his fingertips over the massive door, then rested his cheek against the cold stone and whispered, "Guard them heavily behind your stubborn spoil. Taunt me all you will. Your secrets are mine."

The Inheritance

"I told you she was a loony tune," Whitt gloated.

Jillian untied Ruby's leash from Mrs. Drummond's fence post, "You were listening? Ever consider joining a quilting bee?"

"Next time, I'll let Esmerelda cook you up in her weekly psychopath stew."

Starting for the end of the street, Jillian wondered which way to turn, "Take my American Express card," she jeered, "if you hurry, there may still be a life on sale at Sears."

Seemingly unaffected by the insult, Whitt yanked on Merlin's leash, as the pup had a nasty habit of licking his own jewels. "Which way is home?"

"Who knows?"

"Some psychic you are," Whitt sneered, promptly turning left.

"You're going the wrong way," Jillian called after him.

Whitt waved his hand in the air with a dismissive who-gives-a-shit flick of the wrist, "Ten bucks says I make it before you do."

Since Whitt took a left, Jillian wandered right and spent the next hour completely lost, wondering what the Ballencroft book was, and what it could possibly have to do with her. Worse, how horrid would it be to acquire the same curse that killed her mother? It did, didn't it? If not, it could have and should have saved her. Wasn't that the same thing as outright killing her?

What if Jillian did have some latent ability gurgling beneath the surface? Didn't it make sense? She had her mother's genes. Wasn't it possible for a psychic to pass that sort of thing on to her offspring? The answer boomed inside Jillian's head with a resounding 'yes,' but her stubborn heart clung to 'no,' or, more precisely, *'no freaking way.'*

A nagging feeling—not exactly déjà vu, but close enough—crept over her and she suddenly knew exactly what she needed to do: she needed to get out of this creep-show town, tuck-tail and head back to Narragansett. Unfortunate, not because she wasn't more than willing to follow the inclination, but because it wasn't her decision to make. Her father, his mind having jettisoned off the planet long ago, wasn't likely to take seriously what he would, no doubt, consider juvenile delirium. If the sight of blood seeping through walls didn't inspire him to leave North Carolina, Jillian's confrontation with Mrs. Drummond wouldn't dent his tin can either. No, she was stuck in Devil's Edge; sleeping in a house only a clan of vampires could admire, searching for a book she didn't want to find, and reluctantly awaiting evidence of an ability she wouldn't hesitate to trade for a case of leprosy. Didn't this summer promise to be the summer of all summers?

Pop's Soda Shop

Taking yet another wrong turn, Jillian ended up outside Pop's soda shop. Lost anyway, she decided to have a peek inside. A bell tinkled over the door as it opened. Jillian stepped inside the diner, its sock hop ambience a quality Arthur Fonzarelli and Richie Cunningham would readily admire. Fire engine red booths hugged the walls, stainless steel stools with red leather seats lined up in front of a lengthy white counter, framed memorabilia overcrowded the walls, and red and white checkered linen draped lazily over tabletops.

The haze of fried fat formed clouds so thick, breathing too deeply resulted in immediate heartburn. Tunes from the fifties and sixties repeatedly proclaimed their immortality as the jukebox housing them quivered in the corner. Pots and pans waged a cast iron war in the kitchen as waitresses struggled to squeeze their oversized bottoms into inadequate spaces between crowded booths.

Jillian attempted to convince herself this visit to the soda shop only involved thirst but it would take a certain amount of insanity she didn't possess to believe such a fabrication. She wanted to see the marks Mr. Rittenhower left on the floor when he combusted; not exactly an everyday sight. The black scourge on the floor truly looked impressive. No one occupied the four stools in the immediate area where their townsman met his demise, and Jillian assumed this was so because no one wanted to share in his fate; old town superstition. Jillian sat on the stool in the middle, throwing a shadow over the outline of Rittenhower's combusted chest. The waitress raised an eyebrow, but said nothing of it, merely taking Jillian's order for a root beer float and turning away with a shrug.

When she returned with the impressive beverage, Jillian took the opportunity to ask if she'd ever heard of the Ballencroft book, and did she know where to find a copy? The waitress gave her a curious look, then pressed two fingers between her lips and let loose with a spine-grating whistle. When every head in the place turned toward the counter, the waitress motioned to a thirty-something uniformed officer who just raised a two-pound cheeseburger to his lips. Clearly agitated, he grimaced and took a large bite of the sandwich, forcing it down his throat with an exaggerated gulp. Only then did he throw his napkin onto the table and saunter over to the counter.

"What?" He sniped.

"This 'un here wants to know where she can find the Ballencroft book," the waitress said, her amusement evidenced by a large, toothy grin.

"That right?" The officer asked, raking his hand through a full head of greasy black hair. The waitress nodded and turned away to serve a new customer.

Glancing over his shoulder at the burger he left behind, he reluctantly took a seat next to Jillian.

"Hot damn, lady, what do you know about the Ballencrofts?"

Jillian felt her cheeks flush, "Nothing, really. Someone told me to look for the Ballencroft book. I just wondered where I might find it."

"Who told you about this alleged book?"

"Agaritha Drummond."

He slipped a hand inside his shirt and nervously fondled a two-sided crucifix dangling from a thick chain.

"You a Yankee?" He asked, noting Jillian's accent.

She nodded.

With a grunt and a huff he stood to his feet.

"Tourists," he spat. "Ain't in town for five minutes and already poking your nose where it doesn't belong. You think you can crack a case no one's been able to solve for ten years? What's your name, Nancy Drew?" He reached for her face, his fingertips outstretched, but she backed away, refusing his touch. His gaze seemed to take her in all at once, resting, finally, on her chest. "You stick your neck out far enough someone's bound to take a swipe at it. So, forget whatever it is you think you know. Leave the law to the professionals." And with that, he headed back to his booth.

Jillian's head swarmed with confusion as she aimlessly wandered one street after the next, searching for the way back home (as if anyone would call that house a home). Apparently, the Ballencroft book had something to do with an unsolved police case. What exactly did Mrs. Drummond get Jillian involved in? Whatever it was, Jillian wanted no part of it. In fact, now more than ever, all that really interested her was finding a way to get her father to pack up his skivvies.

Say "Ah"

Though there are never more than seven pages to any given issue of *The Coastal Review*, Velma Sinclair always read the newspaper with the utmost care. Today's copy arrived bearing a gift that seemed designed especially for her; beneath a story on the casualties of the war and just left of the weather and tide charts, there loomed a large picture of Agaritha Drummond accepting an award from the mayor for best garden, an award the old bat seemed to win every year despite the fact Velma was the only gardener in Devil's Edge with the skill to grow wolf's bane. Granted, the plant is poisonous, but its delicate yellow flowers are but one of its redeeming qualities and it isn't exactly easy to grow and maintain, especially in clay-sodden coastal soils. Dog the mayor, a spit in the face for the Garden Club, and three cheers to Luke Meyers for printing such a large and clear picture of Aggy's face.

Velma carefully tore the panel of newspaper off at the seam and carried it to the birdcage. There, she removed yesterday's picture of Tom Flannery (*that's what he gets for not knowing who would've made the better wife*) and replaced his poop-laden portrait with a fresh Agaritha Drummond. Tapping her fingertips to Agaritha's unsuspecting lips, Velma let out a hearty cackle and said, "Open up and say 'ah.'" Then, because it was such a special celebrity gracing the bottom of their cage, she filled the cockatiels' food bowl with the nuts from the box marked, 'extra fiber.'

The clank of a key sounded as it turned in the back door, and Velma assumed her daughter, Lavender, had returned home after a late shift at the hospital. Well, it wasn't really much of an assumption. No one else had a key and rarely did anyone come to the cottage for a visit, so few in Devil's Edge appreciated the value of Velma's company. Besides, it was eleven thirty in the morning; precisely the time Lavender returned each day after pulling a twelve-hour shift at the hospital. Lavender always appreciated a nice hot cup of tea after a long night's work, so Velma put the kettle on the stove and ruffled through the kitchen drawer until she found an envelope of Earl Grey; her daughter liked that flavor best, while Velma strictly preferred the orange pekoe.

Most days, Lavender came home from work looking more haggard than a triple-pooped page of *The Coastal Review*. Today, her eyes seemed keen and sharp, her face drawn taut as a snare drum. It didn't take a genius to see something happened at work and she was itching to report.

"Sit ya'self down and have a sip of herb with me," Velma said, pointing to a cup steaming with thin, miniature clouds rising over its cracked and weathered brim. "That sorry excuse for a mayor gave the Best Garden award to Agaritha Drummond again," she moaned. "You think he's poking her pony while her husband's gone missin'? Don't answer. I suppose it's plain as day. Anyway, since Luke Meyers went to the trouble to print such a flattering photograph, I took it upon myself to invite the old bag over for lunch. The birds should be servin' up her entree any minute now."

Under normal circumstances, Lavender took just as much delight in Velma's birdcage antics as Velma did and didn't shy away from making her own suggestions as to whose photograph should end up as daily poop-catcher. This time, however, Lavender hadn't chimed in with Velma's long-winded guffaw, and the tone of her voice seethed with impatience, "Shut it, Momma."

As it was entirely uncharacteristic of Lavender to slight her momma in such a harsh way, Velma pursed her lips and waited for an explanation. Should that statement fall short of a satisfactory excuse for such a backwoods display of crudity, Velma had developed a sudden itch in the palm of her hand, which she would not hesitate to plant smartly on the back of her daughter's head.

"Listen here," Lavender said. "I saw Anne Bonny at the hospital last night."

A sharp breath of air passed through Velma's lips so quickly, she involuntarily whistled, "You saw who?"

"Anne Bonny, Momma. Clear as a mirror. She was sittin' in the waitin' room lookin' miserable as a mouse starin' at cat tonsils. I damn near tripped over myself makin' sure."

Velma slowly set her teacup on the table to avoid dropping it on the floor and took in a deep breath. News such as this demanded focus and concentration, else a body arrives carryin' all the wrong conclusions. After a few moments of careful introspection, Velma lifted her three chins high as they could go and laughed so hard she almost fell out of a chair far too small to support her hefty bottom in the first place.

Once she caught her breath, she said, "You got yourself stuck with another one of them hypodermies, didn't ya? I 'member the last time this happened, you had hallucynations for three days; cryin' on about cows skippin' rope under the bed and bats a playin' Canasta in the refrigerator. Weren't no picnic then and I don't suppose it'll be much of a ball this time neither. Get off to bed now. I'll call Doc Marlow and see if he ain't got something to help sort this out."

Lavender grabbed Velma's hand and, using her best I-ain't-insane voice, said, "I didn't get stuck with a needle and I ain't hallucinatin'. It was Anne Bonny sittin' in that waitin' room sure as I got a hold of the fat lady's hand."

"Dammit, how many times I gotta say I ain't fat? The family's big-boned and that's a fact."

Lavender deliberately glared at Velma's six-fold fat rolls, gestured to the double mousse cheesecake sitting on the table, and waved her hand over her own skinny frame.

Point taken, Velma swatted Lavender's shoulder, attempting to eclipse the insult with a scurrilous glare.

"There's only two ways to explain how Anne Bonny could be sittin' in that waitin' room tonight and, forgive me for sayin' so, Momma, but I don't imagine you're ready for either one of 'em." With that said, Lavender huffed out of the kitchen.

Velma didn't quite know how to react to the information her daughter so delicately passed on to her, but she knew this: Lavender was right...no matter how a body attempted to explain Anne Bonny's presence in Devil's Edge, there was absolutely no *good* way to look at it.

The Ballencroft Book

The Millers weren't leaving Devil's Edge anytime soon. Once the court summons arrived, Mr. Miller refused all arguments for skipping town. Since it looked as though Jillian would probably end up spending the better part of the summer in town anyway, and since she couldn't stop thinking about the Ballencroft book (though she made every effort to do so), she decided to at least try to locate the book, if for no other reason than to stop the mental nagging.

The last time she saw Maurine Teach, Maurine was running away from Scabbard Street as though her life depended on it. A little more than a week had passed since then. Since Jillian didn't have Maurine's phone number and, since a telephone directory hadn't arrived at the crypt yet, Jillian's only option was to knock on the door and hope a disgruntled parent didn't answer.

"Oh, it's you," Teddy Jr. said with a certain disappointment, and stepped aside to let Jillian pass into the foyer. Then he disappeared so fast it seemed as if his molecules had seeped into the carpet.

"What's with him?" Jillian asked.

Maurine blushed and admitted she told Teddy bout Jillian's disinterest. "He's playing hard to get."

"Who could ask for anything more?" Jillian said, smiling sincerely.

At the sound of Jillian's voice, Ozzie bounced into the hallway. In an exaggerated attempt to make eye contact, he raised his flyspeck face and spoke so rapidly his words were fired like bullets sprayed from a spunky Uzi, "Would you like to play a game of 30 Bones? It's an old pirate game originating in the Caribbean, though relentless rumors abound that they hijacked it from China. The pirates played for booty when they weren't blowing ships to smithereens or slicing someone's head off. Legend has it they used chicken bones, but I'm more and more convinced they used human bones. Did you know the hair and nails of a cadaver continue to grow for years after internment? Anyway, nowadays we use a more boring tackle: colored wooden bones. It's not like you can buy a set of human bones at the five-and-dime these days, though I don't imagine it'll be long before someone figures out there's a buck to be made. Once that happens, ladle and doorjamb manufacturers are bound to become interested, don't you think? Fact is I don't win the game as often as I should, what with the exceptional size of my brain and all, but, given the opportunity, I can probably kick your butt from here to the Taj Mahal."

"Shut up, Oz," Maurine said, and pulled Jillian into a spacious, well-maintained living room. Two side-by-side gaping bay windows allowed generous amounts of sunlight to spill into the room, the rigid rays resting on a massive entertainment center encased by a wall of bookshelves stuffed well beyond capacity. The house looked comfortable and lived in; the complete opposite of the dark disaster in which Jillian currently resided.

Ozzie plopped onto the plush rose-colored carpet and busied himself with the arrangement of a pile of multi-colored wooden pegs.

Jillian leaned over and whispered to Maurine, "Why's he talk so fast?"

Maurine giggled. "You've heard the hair-brained hokey he spouts. If he doesn't talk fast, there won't be an ear left in the room by the time he's finished. Besides that, a few years back he overheard a school nurse tellin' Momma he might be slightly retarded, he's been on a mission to prove her wrong ever since."

"Why would anyone say such a thing? He seems exceptionally bright."

"I imagine she freaked when she got a load of his toes."

"His toes?"

"They're webbed...you know, like a duck. He swims like a torpedo. Thing is, if you don't shut him up, he'll yack your ears off."

Jillian nodded. Pain-in-the-ass little brothers are a cruel universal requirement.

"Is *30 Bones* a real game, or did he invent that, too?"

"He found a reference on the web. It's real. But, far as I know, we have the only set in the country. Ozzie carved it himself and even sewed up the velvet satchels he uses to keep the bones in."

"Industrious little man, isn't he?"

"You have no idea." Maurine exaggerated a roll of her eyes and sighed. "It's a hoot to play, though, if you want to try sometime." She gently poked Jillian in the ribs with her elbow. "Ozzie says I'm the queen of *30 Bones*, I don't lose much."

In all painful honesty, Jillian sucked at board games. True enough, she was hell to beat at Scrabble, but most people her age didn't like to play and Whitt had learned long ago not to even try. She could work a mean crossword puzzle too, but had never considered crosswords a game, per se. Sadly, she couldn't remember ever winning a game of Monopoly, Risk, or Life. It would take a miracle to find a board game she had half a chance to win.

"I'd like to play," she politely lied. "But, I'm on a mission today."

"A secret mission? Like in the movies?" Maurine whispered, her eyebrows rising with intrigue.

Jillian laughed. "That would be fun but, unfortunately, no. I came to ask if you wouldn't mind showing me to the library. I've tried to find it three times on my own, but I keep going around in circles and ultimately end up on Scabbard Street."

"Scabbard Street? Whale pee in your soda, you gotta tell me what happened with the Spirit Rapper. Did she tell you how you're gonna die? She does that, you know. That's why everyone's skin shrivels at the sight of her. I'm here to ask ya, who wants to know somethin' gruesome as all that?"

Jillian heard the concern in Maurine's voice, but couldn't help but smile at the catch phrase she had used, '*whale pee in your soda;*' she'd made weird statements like that before and Jillian found it odd, in an interesting way. Teenagers were like that, either forcing themselves into square pegs in order to appear like everyone else, or going to extremes to come across as unique. Maurine either adopted the phrases from someone she knew, or invented them in an attempt to set herself apart.

Devil's Edge

"Mrs. Drummond mentioned a book and I'm hopelessly curious. I thought the library would be the best place to look."

"Chances are. What's it called?"

"The Ballencroft book."

Maurine jumped off the sofa so fast it seemed as if the cushion beneath her suddenly burst into flame. At the same time, Ozzie appeared in Jillian's lap with such speed it felt like he'd matrixed across the room.

"The Ballencrofts lived in the house you're renting," he sputtered, his eyes larger than plums, his face so close to Jillian's he zapped her with a bolt of carpet static when the tip of his nose touched hers. "Janice Ballencroft was hacked to pieces and found in the attic. Her husband, Marcus, and their daughter, Carla, simultaneously disappeared. They say the husband off-ed the wife and abducted the daughter...although most say he killed her, too. Everyone knows it's not difficult to hide a body in the marshes. Folks around here don't talk about the Ballencroft murder; it's a stain on the peaceful history of Devil's Edge. It's hard enough to live in a town that goes by the Devil's name, without people showing up hacked into a thousand pieces and gone missing. Keep your nose out of it, that's my professional opinion."

Maurine took Ozzie by the shoulder, peeled him off Jillian's lap and said, "That was rude, Oz. But listen, Jillian, maybe he's right. Maybe you shouldn't go lookin' for that book. Even if you found it, chances are it's nothin' but trouble."

"I doubt it's anything worth turning green over," Jillian said with a sigh. "Didn't you say that thing about the murdered woman wasn't true?"

"Sorry," Maurine lowered her voice along with her chin, "I didn't want you to worry."

"Well, maybe something in the book can tell me why the walls in the closet are bleeding."

The color in Maurine's face suddenly washed out. Falling back onto the sofa, she declared, "Rat turds on your keyboard! The walls do what?"

"They bleed," Jillian answered matter-of-factly. "I can't spend a whole summer in that house without getting to the bottom of it. Are you with me, or not?"

Maurine looked like she swallowed a rotten apple, worms and all, but agreed to show Jillian to the library. "After that," she said, her face set firmly, "you're on your own."

The First Resurrection

"Not much ever happens at the library," Maurine confided as she and Jillian walked toward the furthest edge of town. "It needs CPR."

Jillian chuckled. "A library is supposed to be quiet."

"Yeah. But last time I went, I half expected Jesus to poke his face in the door and yell, 'Arise and come forth!'"

The vigorous cronking of a flock of seagulls seemed to hitch a ride on the wind, an altogether aggravating sound, but one that reminded Jillian of a Chinese restaurant back in Narragansett, an establishment her family frequented despite the fact it was credited for single-handedly minimizing the seagull population (though you wouldn't think it minimized at all should you venture onto the beach with a Boston cream or a cruller in hand). Jillian's stomach growled; she left the house without breakfast in order to ensure Whitt's absence, an absolute must should she expect to remain sane for any practical amount of time. Thankfully, she had the presence of mind to drop a couple bottles of Evian and a breakfast bar into her backpack before she walked out the door. She would tend to food later; for now, she concentrated on memorizing the path to the library. If Maurine didn't plan to stick around, Jillian would have to navigate back to Billard Avenue on her own.

Maurine babbled on about Martian toes in your pockets—or something similar—but Jillian tuned her out in order to immerse herself in the sound of the rocking surf and the intoxicating scent of bay flowers; a sweet smell that might have induced a rather pleasant coma if it weren't ultimately followed by the fetid stench of charred kelp.

White sand blew in scattered patches onto the sidewalk and, though soft and warm beneath her sandals, Jillian wished she had had the presence of mind to wear a pair of sneakers; if there was one thing she couldn't stand, it was the abrasive grit of sand wedged between her toes. Born and raised less than a mile from the Atlantic, she'd never harbored an interest in becoming a beach bunny. While her friends dedicated their lives to sun worship, she diligently focused her energies on education and dance training. If the burning irritation currently attacking her feet held any indication of what she missed, three cheers for prudence.

"Nobody's got any proof, of course," Maurine professed, "but most everyone believes it's true."

The statement startled Jillian. She would like to ask what Maurine was going on about but would have to admit she wasn't listening in the first place, and since she had no desire to insult Maurine with such a rude confession, she simply didn't make the inquiry.

Maurine motioned to a dilapidated building fifty yards ahead. "That's the library."

As it turned out, the ramshackle remains of an old cathedral housed the Devil's Edge library; circa prehistoric, if Jillian could trust what she saw. Even if she managed to walk this far out of town, even if she stood square in front of this building, in all likelihood, she would have turned around and walked the other way without ever knowing she'd stumbled upon a library. Just looking at the monstrosity had much the same effect as a solid punch to the eye. It appeared a crossbred mangle of jumbled stone: half church, half castle, depending on which stones once existed. Piles of shattered rubble amassed at the foundation, restrained by a thick green moss and vigorous clusters of wild ivy.

The only indication a library existed on site was a timeworn wooden sign no larger than a loaf of bread hanging above an overgrown door made from heavy beams of worm-infested wood. The door depended upon rusted cast iron hardware for support and looked as though it might come crashing off its hinges any minute now.

Jillian was familiar with abandoned ruins (there still stands a roofless stone structure on Blackpoint near Scarborough State Beach back in Rhode Island) but the ruin that stood before her now had occupants and, what's worse, someone apparently considered it sufficient for housing invaluable books and documents. No wonder Maurine expected Jesus to make an appearance here—this place was in need of a serious resurrection.

Once Maurine helped drag open the cumbersome wooden door, she said her good-byes and, as promised, took immediate flight. Jillian stepped inside.

The interior of the library seemed all at once pitch-black, her pupils unprepared for subdued lighting. In the instant she expected to choke on the moldy smell of accrued rot, her nose caught the pleasant scent of cleaning oil. As her eyes adjusted, she stood in utter amazement. The library was, indeed, cathedral-like and stacked, shelf upon shelf, to the high-beamed ceiling with colorful texts. A massive chandelier burned a thousand candles high above her head, while electric lamps aplenty lounged upon the tabletops scattered about the gigantic hall. Not twenty steps ahead, a cloister of computer terminals seemed to introduce the 21st century to the middle ages, their redundant blue monitors patiently waiting for someone to put them to use.

If the stained-glass windows hadn't given the building's design away as a makeshift medieval castle, the suits of armor defending the front and rear of the library certainly offered a gainful hint. The interior of the library couldn't have been more contrary to its exterior; in fact, it looked glorious. A rich mahogany carved with intricate detail seemed to speak of a proud, majestic history, while luxurious tapestries and shadowed corners promised a well-guarded, undisturbed recluse.

Jillian suddenly felt both brave and adventurous, as if someone grabbed her by the shoulders and prodded, 'Gather strength and go forth.' A silly thought, but it put a smile on her face, and served to remind her of her mission.

She stepped up to the service counter and tapped the button on the silver bell perched next to a faded sign that read, 'Ring for Service.' A dark-haired woman popped up from behind the desk, quickly scanned Jillian's face, dropped the pile of books she had cradled in her arms and exclaimed, "It's true." Then, without so much as a how-do-you-do, she took immediate leave of her senses.

"What's with you people?" Jillian complained as she clambered over the counter. "I brushed my teeth this morning," she said, pulling a bottle of Evian from her backpack. "I showered," she said, removing the cap from the bottle of water. "I used deodorant," she said, pouring the water onto the woman's face, though most of it washed over the glasses she wore. "I took the wax from my ears," she said, gently slapping the woman's cheeks. "I'm not a freak."

"Where am I?" The woman whispered through pale lips when she came to. Raising herself onto her elbows, she gingerly tested her balance. As she stared directly into Jillian's concerned eyes, the woman's face all at once registered recognition. "I didn't think I'd live to see the day," she declared, and using the edge of her finger like a windshield wiper, she swiped drops of water from her spectacles.

Rising to her feet, she dusted off her bottom. "We've been expecting you for hundreds of years."

Forgetful Fools

Agaritha Drummond worried over a cup of brandy with a nip of tea. At times like these, she didn't mind the fact her ears were the only set available to hear the words she sputtered.

"The child's gonna need direction," she slurred. "A shove and a firm kick in the pants. Lawd, Lawd. One thing's for sure; this town will never be the same."

Devil's Edge

She pinned another Garden Club announcement to the corkboard in Ebbenwright's study. One of these days, she would have to discard the old fliers, the print on many of them already faded and the stack bulged so thick, it wouldn't be long before the pushpins no longer held their grip. It wasn't like she ever attended a Garden Club Tea; those socials had little to do with gardening and seemed more focused on measuring the worth of the human soul by how many stockbrokers a woman could stuff into her pockets. Why she had kept the fliers, she couldn't rightly say and it seemed well past time to put a stop to the practice. "One of these days," she murmured and bumbled into the living room until she stood swaying before the over-sized grandfather clock. It didn't matter where the clock's hands pointed, the time had come, and Agaritha realized it the moment she set eyes on the girl. Employing an awkward determination, she mounted a stepladder and peered intently into the clock's face. "You should be here for this, Ebby. We could use your help, ya know. You fool...you forgetful old fool!"

The Curse

Anne Bonny's voice held the slightest glint of sarcasm as she turned to Mary Read and asked, "What think ye now, Mary?"

"About what?" Mary Read sighed, knowing all too well what Anne would say.

"About the Haitian woman's curse."

Mary turned her back on Anne in disgust. "Are ye to go on with this for another two hundred years? Pray thee, have ye nothing better to do?"

"Aye. Troubled seas to sail, oceans everlasting...throats to cut, gold to seize, a seafarer's paradise waiting on the south side of the mere weeks ye professed to need to break this wretched curse.

Three weeks, two hundred and seventy-four years later, I still await thy blessed miracle."

"Need I remind ye, Anne Bonny, it wasn't I who put damnation upon your head...it wasn't I. While ye await a plan for escape, in all these years have ye offered a design of your own? Have ye? Nay. Not one. Stop harpin' on me, wench. I swear, if ye ask but once more, I shall..."

Anne laughed heartily. "Slice me throat from ear to ear, will ye?"

"I shall slap thine ethereal arse from here to the nether world. That I will. Don't ye tempt me."

By the weight of Thor's hammer, wouldn't that be something? If only Anne could feel the sting of Mary's hand upon her skin. Aye, she would trade a fleet of ships and seven lives to experience such a sensation, though the hand be thrust in wrath. Fate left no choice but to abandon embrace. What a cruel admonishment it was to learn they had become spirits quite incapable of physical interaction; bound to a miserable tomb already occupied with the obstinate spirits of Jack Rackham and Tinclaw Corner; two rogues with whom she and Mary had absolutely no desire for reunion. (Worthless as these men were in life, their paltry existence certainly proved of no good use now). Once and again Jack attempted entertainment with a jig he coyly referred to as the rat-head stomp (not that he could physically harm the rodents scampering beneath his feet, but that hadn't stopped him from pretending). Quite a show it was too, when first he performed it, but it had long since lost its pepper. Nowadays, he spent most of his time pretending to pee into a gurgling stream, while Tinclaw cursed at the stone door holding him hostage.

Though very much aware Mary made an oath she could not deliver, the promise of her touch was more temptation than Anne could bear. And so, without wasting another thought, she determined to test Mary's resolve.

"Mary?" she said, a sweet tone of apology resounding in her voice. "Tell us of the future man."

Mary coughed and sputtered at Anne's audacity. With furled brow, she turned to say, "And have ye scoff yet again?"

"I shan't scoff, ye have me oath."

"And thy oath is worth a chest of gold doubloons, is it?"

Using the honeyed tones of a skilled seductress, Anne insisted, "I beg of thee."

"Scoff and I shall speak with ye no more 'til the end of time." Mary pretended to rest her arse upon the crest of a stunted boulder and offered her story with whispered awe.

"Whilst the guard, Pennington, made merry with ye in his office," she said, "the future man appeared inside the cell at Bridewell; appeared like a phantom, yet solid as any living man, and carried in his withered hands the documents we used to secure our freedom. 'Don't be afraid,' said he, with a touch to the tips of me fingers, 'I have traveled from the future to aid in your release. Take these,' said he, and passed the roll of parchment into me hands. He then announced Sir Nicholas Lawes would grant our discharge in exchange for the documents. 'What's more,' said he, 'I have arranged a bribe with a local physician who will testify the two of you are with child. The court will stay your executions once you have made the claim. Show the first page of the document to Lawes and tell him he can have the remaining pages if he agrees to set you free. He will agree. Upon your release, the court will claim Anne's father paid a hefty ransom to redeem her sins and that you have succumbed to an unfortunate fever.'

Seeing I understood his directives, he departed in very much the same manner in which he arrived, which is to say, with a grin rife with mischief. In the wink of an eye, he seemed to melt into the straw at me feet. Ye know the story, thereafter. All came about as he predicted."

Anne raised her face until it met with a trickle of sun seeping through a small crack in the ceiling of the cave and roared like a buffoon caught in the throngs of hysteria. She had no restraint for it. Each time Mary told her story, she did so with such sincerity, it was almost as if she expected Anne to believe it. Of course, there wasn't a plank of truth to it. While she had no idea how Mary came into possession of the documents that had set them free, she was sure it was not by the means just described.

Anne allowed the bout of shrill laughter to play at her throat until her eyes had watered out, until her lungs no longer fought for air, until she could bray no more. Only then did she remember Mary's oath to speak with her no more, only then did she acknowledge she might have made more of an effort to understand Mary believed in her story, heart and soul, though her delusions were clearly a product of the prison fever she had, in fact, suffered during the last three weeks of their imprisonment.

As expected, Mary's boot passed through Anne's arse without a twitch of satisfaction.

Banished

"Are you all right?" Jillian asked.

The librarian adjusted her glasses. "Not at all, and unless you plan to leave Devil's Edge, no one else in this town will fare any better."

Taken aback by the woman's brash words, Jillian's face flushed with embarrassment. Speechless, she gawked at the curious woman who so brazenly asked her to leave town.

Bone thin and pale, the librarian stood a tad taller than Jillian and wore a pantsuit that was clearly a throwback to the seventies, all the rage these days, except it didn't look as if it came off the rack recently. Made of dark denim, embroidered flower petals adorned the blazer's lapel and the flare-bottomed pants were faded and stitched on a seam that had once ripped. The outfit seemed odd attire for a woman who didn't look as though she would approach her thirtieth birthday anytime soon. Long strands of brown hair, once pinned neatly to the top of her head, came loose when she tumbled to the floor and now draped over her shoulder, a stubborn hairpin dangling from a loose lock. One might consider the woman attractive, despite her disheveled appearance, if it were possible to ignore a large mound of duct tape glued to the nosepiece of her glasses. Unfortunately, the lump of silver glop demanded attention, snatching it away like purse straps at the mercy of an adept thief. In fact, the more Jillian tried to avoid focusing on the clump of tape, the more it seemed to shout, *'I'm an ugly pile of duct tape... don't you dare ignore me!'*

"What's your name?" Jillian asked.

"Candace Flute. Perhaps you should go now."

Jillian felt her cheeks burn. "My name is..."

"No, no," Candace interrupted, waving her hand as if Jillian's name wasn't at all important. "I know more about you than I care to know."

Suddenly uncomfortable with the claustrophobic space and the tension building behind the counter, Jillian slid to the other side. "What's that supposed to mean? And, what did you mean before when you said you've been expecting me for hundreds of years?"

Scurrying to pick up the books she dropped, the flustered librarian sputtered, "I really don't want to get involved. I would appreciate it if you left."

"And, I would appreciate an explanation."

Frustrated, Candace let out an elongated sigh. Once she placed the books on a tray, she gave her watch a nervous glance. A painful stretch of indecision—replete with mumbling, deep sighs, and an obvious unwillingness to meet Jillian's stubborn gaze—followed before she reluctantly spoke. "My assistant should arrive any moment now. If I cannot convince you to leave, perhaps it would be best if we spoke in private."

Jillian turned to survey the library. "There's no one else here."

Candace leaned over the counter and whispered, "One never knows what eyes turn corners, what ears lurk neglected."

"Whoa, how sinister-B is that?"

The librarian stared at Jillian, blank-faced and tight-lipped.

"Sinister-B, it means like from a B movie."

Unaffected, or insulted by the remark—Jillian couldn't tell which—Candace turned her back and clicked her tongue against her teeth, producing the "tsk, tsk" sound adults make when they want you to think they know something you don't know…something you will never, ever know until you, yourself, have mastered the art of 'tsk, tsk.'

Concerned she might create further frustration for the delicate woman, obviously aflutter long before Jillian had come through the door (as evidenced by her frayed fingertips and the tiny specks of rose-red nail polish glistening on her teeth), Jillian agreed to quell her curiosity until Ms. Flute's assistant arrived.

"While we wait," Jillian prodded, "could you help me find a text called The Ballencroft Book?"

"Sweet Jesus," the librarian squealed, falling once again to the floor where she convulsed, twitched, and fluttered like a Florida bass dropped into a pile of hot sand.

Snail Snot in your Root Beer

Maurine sat in front of her PC and clicked over to YouTube in search of more *Madness*. She downloaded the band's song, "Shame and Scandal," a couple weeks ago, laughed her butt off every time she replayed it, and had been on the prowl for a new release by the group ever since. She found no new *Madness* posted online today. Too bad, she could use a good belly twister. She checked her wall on Facebook and found nothing interesting there either, so she made a quick trip to the factory on YoWorld and logged off.

More than anything, she wanted to be with Jillian Miller at the library. More than anything, she wanted to know as much about Jillian as she possibly could. Maurine thought it simply stupendous Jillian looked so much older than sixteen. In fact, the only thing giving her youth away were the freckles on her nose and, for the love of turtle spit, Maurine knew hundreds of full-grown women with freckles. It had to be an absolute blast to go around looking so mature. To think of the line of boys Jillian must have knocking on her door...correction, the line of *men*, the parties she could get into, the things she could buy without being carded; dot your 'P's and cross your 'O's, she could probably even rent a car if she wanted to. Unbelievable.

More unbelievable than that, though, was the way Maurine snapped her head back into her shell at the first hint of trouble. Of all the people Jillian could have asked to show her to the library, she came to Maurine. What a colossal stroke of luck. On a scale of a million to a billion and one, just how unfair was it to feel the need to cower away from today's adventure? What if The Ballencroft Book really was at the library? What if Jillian Miller ended up solving the most gruesome murder case in the history of Devil's Edge while Maurine climbed under a rock just to avoid the stress? So what if her Tourette's got out of hand and she sputtered a few curses along the way, wouldn't it be worth it just to be Jillian Miller's sidekick?

She stared at the wallpaper on her desktop: a picture of Orlando Bloom in his Legalos gear from *The Lord of the Rings*—elephants doing the backstroke through the Lord's turkey gravy, boys don't come any more gorgeous than that.

Propping her feet on the edge of the desk, she leaned back, hands clasped behind her head, thinking sometimes there's no way around it, sometimes you just have to throw the dice. It was entirely possible nothing stressful happened at the library today. She should have at least tried. Now, Jillian must think of her as a coward, not the best of first impressions. Was she a coward? Or, was she simply trying to protect herself from the Tourette's? Wasn't it closer to the truth to say she tried to lock her disease away somewhere deep inside where no one would ever find it?

Hell's cockleshells, M&Ms do too melt in your hands, and nobody wants to admit they're not perfect, least of all when they're trying to make new friends.

Not so long ago, Maurine believed she had control of her Tourette's. Her therapist trained her to use catchphrases like 'snail snot in your root beer,' whenever she felt a bit of anxiety coming on. It worked like a charm, and what a relief to be symptom free. That is, until she got a failing mark in Mr. Finwicket's advanced English course last semester. The whole class got a mighty earful the moment she saw a bright red 'D-' scrawled over the top of her test paper. Worse, since Finwicket didn't know Maurine had Tourette's, he took a firm grip on her elbow and marched her down the center aisle of the main corridor. She dropped a trail of obscenities the entire way to the principal's office.

"Ms. Teach," Finwicket had said, his cheeks burning with old-fogey indignation, "I don't know who sabotaged your alphabet soup, but it would do you a world of good to learn some manners."

Maurine couldn't take her eyes off her shoelaces for the rest of the day. Everywhere she turned someone snickered and pointed at her. The only saving grace was when summer break came so quickly. The kids at school who wouldn't miss an opportunity to heckle her would have to wait until September to do it.

Something similar could happen again, she knew, so why couldn't she just stop beating herself up for not going with Jillian today?

She left her desk, crossed the room, sat down on the over-sized windowsill, and tried to imagine what was going on at the library. The building looked smaller than a drop of fly poop from her window. Even if an alien craft landed and the place swarmed with a herd of slimy-greens, she would never be able to see it from this far away.

Teddy cleared his throat, startling Maurine from her reverie.

"Why ain't you off with your new pal?" He asked.

She shrugged.

Leaning on the doorframe, he shoved his hands into his pockets, and said, "Best watch out for that one, anyway."

"Why?"

"She's a dullgern lesbian, that's why."

"Where in Satan's latrines did you come up with that?"

Devil's Edge

"Look at me, girl," he gloated. "Any woman who doesn't want a piece of this is a lesbo. Best believe it."

Maurine left her perch on the windowsill and, as she moved toward the door, her shoulders began to shrug uncontrollably. She poked herself in the arm, again and again, as her head jerked from side to side. "Dog farts in your...you son of a...get out of my...lemon boogers on pimple seeds..."

Her teeth bit into her lower lip as she forced herself to stop speaking. Hopping onto and then over the bed, she lost her balance on the carpet as her body continued to convulse. When she finally managed to stand less than six inches from her brother's lanky frame, she birded a lone finger in front of his nose.

Teddy giggled, backed into the hallway, leaned over the banister, and yelled, "Mom, Maurine's gone off her meds!"

Bullwinkle

Alexander Spotswood IV slowly ambled over a series of grayed wooden slats serving as a sidewalk and made his way toward a meager cottage that appeared more like an overgrown tool shed than a home. He fished for his house key as he approached the door, all the while supposing, in a year or two, the unnatural bowing of his spine would eventually enable him to enter his home without having to lower his head. Until that day came, he would have to tip his chin to his chest if he wished to pass through the door without whacking himself in the head; a simple maneuver too often forgotten when rushed, or when tightly caressed in the arms of inebriation.

It was still too early in the day for a nip, tempting as it was; he meant to scour the beach for a few hours before the sun abandoned the shore. A bite of Jack always seemed the best tonic to cure aching muscles after waving his spine-warping metal detector around. For now, a cup of tea would suffice. Coiling his braided silver mane around his neck, he pulled a box of matches from his pocket, lit the potbellied stove for a pan of hot water, then sifted through a pile of used tea bags resting on the counter, holding each one into a dim beam of light bleeding through the kitchen window, carefully inspecting each bag until he found one that seemed to hold more color.

While he waited for the water to boil, Alexander perched on a lobster trap serving as a makeshift chair and considered joining his glassy-eyed comrade, Bullwinkle, for a round of chess. Bullwinkle, however, wore a coy grin today, and that meant he'd probably calculated another winning game. Shifty character, that one, perfect poker face; keeps a fellow on his toes.

"Not today, you grimy flea bag," Alexander announced, completely ignoring Bullwinkle's apologetic gaze. When it seemed as though the great moose might actually drop a tear, Alexander scratched the beasts' head, immediately reminding himself to refrain from this practice; taxidermy being an imperfect art, Bullwinkle had already lost large patches of hair from behind his moldy ears. Poor mate would soon develop a shiver.

The water on the stove came to a boil and Alexander wasted no time in preparing his thin brew. Sifting through his pants pocket, he pulled out a white packet of sugar he'd pilfered from Pop's soda shop when he broke his last twenty on breakfast earlier in the day. Free is free. He ripped open the package, poured it into his cup, and used a knife to stir.

Satisfied with the tea, he turned to face Bullwinkle. *Prying gossipmonger; always wanting to know what's going on, speculations saturating his extorting eyes; scandalous inquiries resting on the tip of his calcified tongue.*

"I feel it in my soul," Alexander explained, "every time I walk through those wooden doors. They have something…a map, a letter, perhaps a book. I've searched high and low and cannot find it. Still, I know it's there and I have no doubt it will open *La Porte de Ruine*. They have guarded it well, the librarian and her assistant. But, they are mere women, my friend. Won't their hearts cry a little when I steal away with their spoil?"

Burping Through Time

Ebbenwright Drummond had never before battled a fire-breathing dragon, nor did he ever expect to quake before such an awesome creature. A seasoned archaeologist, Drummond, (along with every other scholar in his field) thought the asserted existence of dragons fodder for the over-imaginative, a choice ingredient for fairytales, nothing worth serious consideration. It was for this precise reason he ventured to approach the slumbering enigma. If it were at all possible to retrieve a scale or two, the smallest bit of DNA evidence for evaluation, it would constitute an unprecedented archeological find, something he lacked the power to resist. Thus, before him stood the insidious specimen—aroused by the pluck of a scale—reared on its fearsome haunches, ready to strike at the slightest misstep. Its mammoth nostrils flared a measured rhythm, its mosaic eyes scrutinizing, affixed with such absorption they left little doubt the full-metal firedrake meant to annihilate fear and enemy with one deliberate strike.

Without the aid of sword and shield, (or a bazooka, for that matter) this was one fight the little Dutchman had no hope to win. In fact, his only defense was no defense at all, but a fickle hope the creature would refrain from attack if Ebbenwright could maintain a motionless composure, a feat which may well prove far greater than any he achieved in the length of his lifetime, as the modified lizard surely meant to commence with an immediate barbeque and, quite frankly, the mere acknowledgement of this fact seemed more effective than a potent laxative.

As Ebbenwright conceded to the hopelessness of his situation, a sudden wind curled through the forest with a menacing snarl and burglarized his black fedora. As the hat flittered away, glancing off tree trunks like a nimble pinball, he instinctively surged after it, the mistake in taking such a foolish action instantly preying upon the weaker part of his bowels.

For a fraction of a second, the dragon seemed stunned by the temerity of its prey. However, it did not pause to dwell upon the matter, but inhaled a hearty breath of ammunition. A disturbing vision of the remains of a feeble old fool smoldering in deep-fried ruin presented itself to Ebbenwright, so sure he was of his immediate demise. Just as a ghastly stream of flame spewed forth, Ebbenwright felt a familiar tingle in the soles of his feet, a sensation he at once considered most welcome, despite the many recent occasions he perceived the same occurrence as an awkward annoyance.

He folded his arms about his head and ducked. Eyes clenched tighter than those of a toddler refusing pureed liver and peas, he hoped the opportunity to open them once again would arise.

A nose-crinkling stench overwhelmed Ebbenwright's olfactory nerves. Once convinced the smell was not the byproduct of sautéed human flesh, and with a careful amount of reluctance, he released the vise-grip his eyelids had employed, lowered his arms, and found himself standing upon shadowed cobblestone, thick tufts of fog slithering about his calves.

The wail of a distressed child pierced the night, striking an immediate chord of concern. Ebbenwright twisted toward the sound. It came from across the street, if he wasn't mistaken. As he stepped off the sidewalk, a horse and buggy burst through a cloud of dense fog and clattered over the cobblestone, sufficiently near enough to mash his potatoes if he hadn't quickly stepped back.

"Look there, Pearly," a boisterous voice screeched with a humored lilt, "the bloke's soiled 'imself."

"So, e 'as. Get a load of 'is costume... Takes all kinds, don't it, Martha?"

Ebbenwright turned to spy the silhouettes of two women bedimmed in the far corner of an alley. Since his trousers were, in fact, sufficiently soiled, and since no one else occupied the immediate vicinity, he presumed himself the subject of conversation.

Quickly advancing toward the women, Ebbenwright bowed courteously and inquired, "Excuse me, madams. What year is it?"

The robust woman, referred to as Martha, bellowed heartily, her cackles echoing off the alley walls, effectively smothered in the fog before they could turn the corner.

"Another escaped loon from the George Yard asylum...just our rotten luck, eh, Pearly?" She rubbed a stiff hand over her apron, clearly annoyed.

"I don't give a 'og's swallow where 'e comes from," Pearly grunted, "long as 'e's got silver enough to buy a bed. 'Ave ye silver in yer luggage, old crotch?"

Ebbenwright shifted the strap of his field bag so it slipped behind his back, shoved a hand into his pocket, and palmed a fistful of quarters. He nearly offered the silver to the women, but quickly remembered his coins were probably no older than 1970, potentially unacceptable, depending on what year he'd stumbled upon. That left only his watch and his wedding ring. As he wasn't willing to part with the wedding ring, he offered his watch.

"Shouldn't I sell a tumble for that worthless piece of junk?" Martha spewed. "Hitch yer smelly bum back to the asylum or I'll mop me shoes with yer noggin!"

"I fear you have misunderstood my intentions, madam. I simply want to know what year it is; I have no interest in a tumble."

Pearly snorted. "Not interested? Ain't a man lived what 'e weren't interested." She swiped the watch from Ebbenwright's hand and promptly shoved it into her apron pouch. "It's 1888, that's what year it is. Now off with ye, slimy dog."

"Wait, Pearly. See what 'e's got in 'is luggage first."

Pearly approached with apprehension. Ebbenwright whipped the bag around his shoulder and opened it wide so she could clearly see its contents.

"Old fool's got 'imself a pile 'o rocks," she sniggered. "Papers banded to 'em like they's belongin' to a bloody spy."

"Worthless loon," Martha scoffed.

Devil's Edge

So, the year was 1888. Ebbenwright considered the ankle-eating fog, the thick English accent, the horse and buggy, the cobblestone streets; each morsel giving his location away as Victorian London: the stench, the uncouth propositions, the wailing child...a slum, no doubt. What had Martha called it?

George Yard. And, why did that name put his toes in a curl? Indistinct facts railed through his mind but seemed slaughtered by passing trains before they could reach their final destination. He scratched at his beard and attempted to burrow through tunnels of memory. Frankly, it was a task no easier than trying to find a grain of sand in a vat of peanut butter. Once a man reaches a certain age, he has but a slight chance to access information stored away in those recesses and, if Ebbenwright could find room for a parcel of unashamed honesty, his *Age Of Precarious* dawned some forty years ago.

Then again, perhaps his uneasiness about George Yard wasn't of major concern. The pair of surly women staring him down seemed sufficient to put a man on edge. To that he conceded, took a deep breath, and turned to walk away.

Then, suddenly, as if a compassionate bystander put flame to a gas lamp, Ebbenwright's fact train pulled in to the station.

"Madam, your name is Martha Tabram, is it not? Your friend here is Mary Ann Connelly, better known as Pearly Poll?"

Martha gasped, apparently uncomfortable with Ebbenwright's accuracy.

"What of it, bloke? Mind yer business and get on yer way."

"I mean you no harm. But, if I recall correctly—and I believe I do—in August of this year, you are due to meet with a terrible scoundrel by the name of Jack the Ripper...right here in this alley. Madam, heed my warning, or I fear you will not live to regret it."

Martha's face turned a deep shade of purple and a large vein on the center of her forehead expanded until it looked as though it might burst. "Enough of yer shite. Get on or there's a constable with yer name tattooed on the tip of 'is night stick!"

Pearly picked up a brick and seemed prepared to plant it square on the side of Ebbenwright's head. He raised both palms in defense. "Forgive my intrusion, madams." Without lowering his hands, he bowed, took a few steps backward, vowing to be on his way.

He hadn't quite made it to the corner of the street when his feet began to tingle.

As it happened so many times before, the fragrant scent of peppermint preceded all other sensation and jarred Ebbenwright to full alert. He had a stone in hand long before he rematerialized.

Based on previous experience, he would have but a fraction of a second to accomplish his task. For some unknown reason, the time vortex would not allow him to remain in present day. Truth to fact, the reason was not a complete mystery, as he knew full well he broke protocol when he used the time clock without making the proper adjustments. What he didn't understand was why his visits to present day were so short-lived and, more importantly, why Aggy hadn't reset the clock as he instructed. He left a note on the corkboard where she could see it plainly, and threw at least two-dozen messages through the window since.

How long had he been missing? Burping through time bankrupted his internal clock and now that he no longer had a watch, maintaining a clear sense of time was simply a lost cause. If he had to guess, he would say he'd been away for a month or two, but this speculation—in and of itself—seemed worthless as a yodel in Tokyo. There were times when it seemed he'd been away for years on end. He barely had a chance to visit a restroom, God only knows when he took his last shower, and talk about eat and run. Nearly every era he visited negated the worth of what little money he had in his pockets. In fact, his only opportunity to obtain food was when he appeared close enough to swipe it. Ebbenwright Drummond was no thief, far from it, but when morality quarrels with the stomach, the stomach always wins.

He appeared alongside the dogwood, his feet immersed in Aggy's peppermint patch, a rather unaccommodating position for anyone requiring a clear view of the house. He hopped over the dahlia's, took a rose thorn to the left calf, squashed the heads of a group of under-developed strawberries, kissed the stone, hoisted it, and remained just long enough to see the windowpane shatter.

The Adventures of Eleanor Finwicket

Candace Flute lay sprawled on the floor behind the service counter at the Devil's Edge library. Jillian Miller was preparing to hop over the counter to revive the librarian with another splash of water, when an elderly woman wearing a droopy, oversized sun bonnet, white gloves, and an elaborate summer dress bursting with a purple orchid print, walked into the library and raised her leather-drawn face, her eyes briefly scanning the scene set before her. Without saying a single word, the over-dressed lady pulled a cell phone from her purse and dialed 911. Apparently, she had enough money to access those military satellites.

"Yes, this is Eleanor Finwicket. I'd like to report a murder at the library," she said, her demeanor as calm as if she'd asked a grocer in what aisle she might find the Preparation H. She inched her stout body—the shape of which resembled a squat pear—away from the counter, her eyes locked on the idle blue suede shoe sticking out from beneath it, and sidled toward a suit of armor no more capable of protecting her from harm than a bowl of rice pudding.

Jillian leaned forward, determined to make eye contact with the woman cowering toward the makeshift metal protector. "Excuse me, Ma'am?"

"Don't get huffy with me, Bridgett," Eleanor growled. "You know damn well I wouldn't bother to call if I wasn't staring at an actual body. Now, you best call Garrison and tell him to get over here before I get whacked, too."

As if she found her last statement particularly perturbing, Eleanor rushed to secure a position behind the suit of armor and intermittently peeked around its waist as she spoke to the operator. "Yes, the murderer is still here, and I haven't got the slightest clue how long I can hold the fort."

"Nothing serious happened here," Jillian politely insisted.

When Eleanor's telephone conversation suffered a long lull, Jillian dared to hope she had made her point. The woman, however, refused to abandon her hiding place, and when she finally spoke, she let loose a heavy sigh and said, "Hold on." Dropping her cell phone to her hip, she poked her face around Lancelot's derriere. "Lady, are you planning to run away?"

"No, ma'am," Jillian said, slipping her hand into her backpack, her fingers fumbling about until they wrapped around the neck of another bottle of Evian.

"She's got a gun! Oh God, Bridgett, tell Arnie I lied about having an affair with Tom Rogers and I only fibbed to save his feelings...it was so long ago, I didn't think it really mattered." Eleanor spoke the last of her sordid confession in a rush, clinging breathlessly to her knight in rusting armor.

The hand Jillian stuffed into her backpack remained idle as she took a moment to assess the situation. Apparently, the old lady was the Miss Marple drama queen type. Clearly, she wasn't in the frame of mind to listen to reason, and hell bent on making a fool out of herself. Some people require very little help along those lines—*fidiots*—but perhaps some aid was called for in this case. If she removed her hand from the backpack, the old biddy would know she didn't have a gun. And, if Candace Flute came to anytime soon, the tension in the air would simply shatter. Convinced she would derive a great deal of satisfaction from outwitting the snooty old broad, Jillian resolved to play along. Eleanor Finwicket probably had a few more choice morsels up her sleeve. What else might she confess?

If only the sheriff would arrive in time to see for himself what an assumptive little town Devil's Edge really was. Jillian could almost taste the sweet morsels of retribution; after what the police did to her father, a plentiful slice of humble pie seemed more than fitting.

Jillian peered over the edge of the service counter. Candace's glasses had taken leave of her face and slid across the floor when she collapsed. As suspected, she looked much more attractive without the duct tape bulging like a constipated gargoyle on the crest of her nose. Lying perfectly still, Candace gave no immediate sign of recovery. Jillian reveled in the smugness of what she knew to be a simple case of misguided assumption. She could already hear the old lady's apologies, could already see her face turn red with embarrassment. She would fall to her knees and grovel for forgiveness, beg for Jillian's discretion. It was all too sweet. That is, until a familiar thread of thought began to materialize at the forefront of Jillian's mind: *The odds are one in a kazillion...it was the specific way her neck twisted when she hit the floor.*

For the first time since she entered the library, Jillian thought to take flight. What if Candace Flute didn't come around? The Keystone cops were already on their way, Miss Marple saw to that.

To Jillian's knowledge, state penitentiaries don't have dance troupes. That's not to say they couldn't or wouldn't have them, if someone were to make the suggestion. Right? They do have the Internet. Hard to say how much time inmates are afforded for surfing, though. Jail cells are cleaner and better adorned than the room Jillian slept in now, though smaller. She might get lucky and find herself with a roommate as interesting as Martha Stewart, one never knows. They might release her in time to soak in a year or two of Florida rays before she croaked of old age.

Jillian quickly reprimanded herself. Her thoughts stampeded like a herd of wild horses, too quick to catch, scattered, and utterly useless in the face of the task at hand. She would simply do as before, throw some water on the librarian's face, and expose Mrs. Finwicket for a fool.

As Jillian drew the water bottle out of her backpack and began to twist the lid, a hunchback wearing excessively long silver braids beneath a three-corner black hat scuffled into the library. Baring a jagged lone tooth, his gaze met Jillian's. His speech carried a slight slur. "Aye, Anne Bonny, is it?"

Mrs. Finwicket promptly grabbed the old fellow by the sleeve of his scraggly shirt and pulled him behind the suit of armor. "Stay over here, Digger. That woman's murdered one of us already. If you're not careful, she'll have you, too."

As he prepared to make a reply, the old man's gnarled face turned to watch as the shadow of another visitor darkened the threshold. Framed in the doorway, jaw askance, there stood the very same nurse who had fallen over herself at the hospital. The dark haired, caramel skinned woman quickly scanned the room, her gaze resting on Candace's blue suede loafer.

"What's goin' on here?" She demanded.

Apparently, the 911 Operator asked the same question of Mrs. Finwicket.

"Digger and Lavender Sinclair, Bridgett. Is the sheriff on his way? Christ, we're about to have our heads blown off." Eleanor paused for the Operator's reply. "You know damn well he's at the donut shop. Where else would he be?"

No longer on the prowl for revenge, Jillian spoke up, directing her remarks to the newly arrived nurse. "She fainted. That's all."

"And, I'm Mary Poppins," Mrs. Finwicket boomed, her hand straining for, but unable to reach Lavender's sleeve, her feet unwilling to leave the spot they were anchored to.

Lavender raised her hand in a defensive gesture and employed an authoritative tone, "Step away from the counter, Miss."

Happy to oblige, and grateful a medical professional had arrived on scene (it wouldn't be long now before the truth set her free) Jillian clutched her backpack and put a healthy distance between herself and the counter.

Rushing to Candace's side, Lavender knelt down and began a rapid examination. Raising Candace's eyelids, she shined a small penlight into her pupils. Then, she checked for a pulse, following medical protocol like a seasoned pro.

Devil's Edge

When she finished, she stood to her feet, careful not to remove her concentrated gaze from Jillian, and declared, "She's dead all right."

Holding the Line

The voice echoing inside Aggy's head was one she had listened to for near on a month now: Sarah Miller's. An urgent message boomed inside Aggy's brain with such clarity, she almost fell off her stepladder. Without hesitation, Aggy stepped away from the grandfather clock and rushed into the kitchen. The satchels she prepared the night before were on the counter where she left them. She shoved them into her pocket and scrounged for two capsules of smelling salts from the cupboard beneath the sink. From the medicine cabinet, she took a tube of Aloe Vera, and from the mantle over the fireplace, she retrieved the stone the Miller boy threw through her window. How these things might come of use remained a mystery, but she learned long ago not to second-guess the departed. Chances are she forgot something—didn't she always? She paused for a brief moment, listening for the sound of Sarah Miller's voice. When no further instruction crossed her mind, Aggy got a move on. Time boasts no tolerance for waste.

Aggy cupped the doorknob in the palm of her hand and twisted. The faint squeal of a police siren whistled in the breeze. She didn't stop to reach for her hat and made no effort to close the door behind her. Hotfooting over the brick path, she listened to the wail of sirens as they drew nearer to Scabbard Street.

When a person lives as long as Agaritha Drummond, there's plenty of mischief to discover in the creases of the years and Aggy uncovered more than her share. Of course, there were times when she had no choice; times when all she could do was get out her shovel and dig up some trouble, times when all that mattered was fighting for what she believed in. Like the day the town announced their plans to cut down the oldest oak in town because some feared it might not withstand the next gale or hurricane to blow through Devil's Edge, which was pure blitherhucky. That tree faithfully guarded Sounder's Square for centuries without so much as a sniffle or a sneeze. What's more, it held more wisdom in one small branch than the yahoos on the town council could ever hope to hold. To think it would no longer provide shade for the town square if Aggy hadn't strapped herself to it, refusing to allow an axe or a saw anywhere near it. Though it took eight and a half days to make her point, she was determined to save the old oak and, at the same time, demonstrate that old age does not necessarily equate to weakness. And now, grim fate returned once again, demanding yet another dauntless demonstration.

Aggy turned the corner onto Sea View Avenue and planted her feet firmly on the double yellow lines. Either the sheriff would stop, or Agaritha would breathe her last whiff of bay berry.

The police cruiser flew around the bend faster than Aggy liked and, though this was by far the most cockle-brained thing she would ever do, she poised her hands on her hips and stood her ground. Tires screeched as they battled against the hot pavement. The driver tried to maneuver the car as it swayed off to the right, then veered left, the smoking rubber unable to grip the road, the car moaning and groaning its thunderous objections.

Aggy often wondered which thought might pass through her mind in the instant her soul reached for the great beyond. Now it seemed obvious. As the cruiser failed miserably in its attempt to defy the laws of physics, a single word assaulted Aggy's mind, a brazen ultimatum, an ugly directive scrawled across her mind in large, bright red letters, a word she repeated as if her tongue were a needle stuck in the groove of an old record album. *"Shit."*

The car skidded, passenger side forward, no choice but to exterminate anything foolish enough to remain in its path. Smoke curled from beneath the cruiser, producing a putrid stench Aggy would have been grateful to avoid entirely. She squeezed her eyes shut and braced for impact, that ugly little word pushing past her lips with increased volume and rapid repetition.

Chancing one last peek at the oncoming assault, she didn't see what she expected to see, and the impact seemed far less than she imagined as the passenger who rode shotgun with the sheriff chose the perfect moment to open his car door. Like a determined pinball plunger, the door slapped Aggy out of the way and bounced her into the ditch.

In the brief moment it took for her to realize she hadn't left the mortal plane, the sheriff flew around the side of the vehicle and stooped down to meet her flustered gaze. His entire body trembled as fear gave way to the nuclear rage contorting over his whitewashed face.

"What were you thinkin'?" His eyes darted over Aggy's crumpled form, searching for cuts and bruises he couldn't find. "What were you *thinkin'*?" He emphasized his last word loud and drawn out like, so it felt like a punch to the stomach.

"I needed a ride to the library," she mumbled.

"Did you, now? That's what I do, Agaritha, when I need a ride. I stand in the middle of the goddamn road and refuse to move even when oncomin' traffic is doin' eighty miles an hour. Yes, ma'am, that's how I git where I'm a goin'!"

"Pipe down and help me up. We all know I ain't no Einstein."

"Einstein? You'd have to dig through half a billion miles of solid granite at the speed of light just to escape stupid."

"Oh shush," she retorted expelling a muffled giggle, brushing debris out of her hair and picking small stones from the palms of her hands, some so deeply embedded they would require tweezers. "We got to get to the library right away."

Flabbergasted, the sheriff's jaw dropped and his fingers curled into a pale fist. "We do, do we? Exactly what makes you think I'd have you tag along on police business, especially after you saw fit to pull this crazy stunt?"

Aggy searched the corners of her memory, unsure if she'd ever seen a man's face turn such a foul shade of red.

Jared Duncan, the deputy sheriff who just managed to save her life, came alongside the cruiser, mumbling, "Hot damn," and swabbing a napkin over what looked like six ounces of perfectly fresh coffee splashed on the front of his uniform. Aggy hoped the coffee had a chance to cool before the sheriff slammed on the brakes, and yet she was sure she hadn't brought a tube of Aloe Vera along for nothing.

Garrison and Jared hauled Aggy out of the ditch, then briskly turned away and headed back toward the cruiser.

"I'm goin' to the library with ya, Garrison," she called out, her voice filled with the same stubborn tone one might use to say, 'I ain't letting go of this tree.'

"We're on police business. You ain't goin' anywhere near the library. Now git on home or I'll arrest ya for resistin' release."

Aggy paused for thought. There had to be a way to get Garrison to see things her way.

His hand pawed the car door when she called out to him.

"You'll take me along, or I'll have me a talk with Nelly Lockhart down at the coffee shop. Everyone knows that woman can spit like a camel and there ain't a thing she won't do for a dollar. You don't want to live the rest of your life wondering if old Nelly is harkin' in your cuppa."

A faint chuckle passed over her lips as she watched Garrison's shoulders droop in defeat. Refusing to turn around, he wiggled his fingers in a reluctant come-along motion.

You're the Man

There hasn't been any real excitement in Devil's Edge since Marcus Ballencroft turned his wife into a box of human mulch and pulled the perfect Houdini with his daughter back in the late nineties. Garrison wore a deputy's badge back then, still a little shiny around the edges and, because old Sheriff Rogers made it a point to hog all the media surrounding the case, Garrison's involvement amounted to stuffing a file or two into the mainframe computer which, when all was said and done, amounted to less than fifteen minutes of data entry. When the case went cold, the town slowly reverted to its tranquil ways, its denizens eager to put the spoilage behind them.

Since then, the smallest town on the coast hadn't gotten much attention, which was exactly the way Garrison liked it. He literally knew everyone there was to know: the women he grew up with, dated, married, and divorced, and the men he lost money to at Ricky Dunn's Friday night poker shootouts. People here minded their own business and, truth be told, there really wasn't much call for a police force, but for writing a few parking tickets and nabbing the occasional speedster. Crimes of a serious nature were about as common in Devil's Edge as the landing of alien aircraft on the Interstate, which only ever seemed to happen when Tommy Gilmore's moonshine still was in working order.

As far as Garrison was concerned, his was the sweetest job this side of a Hershey factory and he had become comfortable with the lazy arm of the law; maybe a little *too* comfortable in light of recent events.

Had a planet fallen out of orbit? Did someone shoot the key keeper guarding the gates of Hell? Or, was it just a ticklish moon? Whatever it was, something went off kilter and people were beginning to act like loons escaped from a nut house. Imaginary bombs and deadly baseball bats, an alleged murder at the library, and now Aggy Drummond nearly becoming the oldest poster child in history for safe crosswalk procedure; what in the name of the king of beers was going on?

Garrison put a heavy foot on the gas pedal and tore off toward the library. At least he could count on Jared Duncan to keep a level head. He'd used one hell of a maneuver to clear Aggy off the road. Garrison would hate to think what would have happened without Jared's keen wit and lightning reflexes. Garrison still couldn't believe Aggy had stood her ground. Something in old age must drain the brain like a vampire smoothie. Or, maybe she thought she'd seen too many sunrises already. Who could say? That's what makes the human race so doggone dangerous, you just

Devil's Edge

never know what kind of harebrained ideas people will come up with next. Garrison believed piss ants have more sense than human beings; they don't turn against one another and they rarely suffer through a day when one professes to know any more than the others.

Aggy put a hand on the back of Garrison's seat and leaned forward. "I had an ant farm once," she said.

"Get out of my head, Aggy, or I swear to God, I'll charge ya rent."

Garrison's knuckles went white as he strangled the steering wheel and made a right onto scenic 8A. Goddammit, he hated it when she did that. As a young boy, he considered Aggy Drummond an extreme form of entertainment—couldn't get enough of her magic, or her macaroni and cheese—but the older he got, the less he liked her ability to trespass on his private thoughts. After a while, she became a royal pain in the ass, her mental intrusions far too frequent.

Hell, he knew she meant no harm, she and Ebbenwright played a vital role in Garrison's early years, filling in whenever his alcoholic father and emotionally absent mother fell short, which was pretty much all the time. The Drummond's were eccentric in many ways, but they were family in Garrison's heart and soul, family he wasn't willing to lose; not today or any other day.

Frankly, sometimes Agaritha could be downright helpful. Nobody did a better job with locating a misplaced pet or relative. But, having a gift like that can backfire on a person, people were afraid of her and they whispered. If she had that kind of power, why couldn't she say what happened to the Ballencrofts back in the nineties? Most folks came to the conclusion that if she wasn't talking, then maybe she had something to hide. Garrison knew Aggy better than to believe that kind of bull, but damned if he could find an ounce of blame for the tidal wave of fright and suspicion lapping at her front door.

She sure was a lucky old broad. Or, did she simply know today wasn't the day the good Lord meant to cash her check?

Devil's Edge

A sand cloud rose high above the windows of the cruiser as Garrison pulled the car into the parking lot at the library.

"You'll stay here, Aggy, until we have us a look see."

"You're the man, Garrison, whatever you say."

He stepped out of the car, turned his hot face toward Aggy, and planted a rigid finger on the tip of her nose. "Don't you gimme lip. You stay put."

Busted

Mrs. Finwicket and the nearly toothless man cowered behind the suit of armor as the nurse stood guard over Candace Flute's body. Jillian's head began to swim and the floor beneath her feet felt like silly putty. These people had already wrongfully accused her father and now she, too, looked like a dot on one of their wet mount slides. Unbelievable. Seriously, how does a trip to the library end up on death row? She had her father to blame for this; if he let her stay in Rhode Island to prepare for the national dance competition none of this would have happened.

While she waited for the guillotine blade to fall, Jillian wondered why so many people in Devil's Edge seemed to recognize her. Was it a backwoods setup? Did they mean to pin their unsolved murders on the first stranger to step into their trap? She scratched her head. It didn't compute. She was only a kid when Mrs. Ballencroft got the axe; they couldn't possibly hope to lay the blame on a child. But, if that wasn't their motivation, what was?

Two police officers burst through the library door, their guns drawn and waving left to right, their sights resting on the center of Jillian's forehead.

"Drop the pack and hit the floor," the sheriff shouted.

Jillian complied. The deputy sheriff kicked the backpack away and knelt next to Jillian on one knee, handcuffs in hand.

"I didn't kill anybody," she shrieked. "She fainted. This isn't my fault."

"Save it for the judge," the sheriff barked. "What's your name?"

"Jillian Miller."

The sheriff's eyes squinted as he peered through the sights of his weapon. "Ain't you the daughter of the fellow who clocked Teddy, Jr. with the baseball bat the other night?"

"Unfortunately, yes."

"Looks like trouble runs in the family. You have the right to remain silent, anything you say can and will be used against you in a court of law..."

"Leave her alone, Garrison, she didn't do anythin'."

"Goddammit, Aggy, I told you to stay in the car."

"And I did, until now. You said you were gonna have a look see, but I don't think those eyeballs of yours are workin' one hundred percent."

"Oh, they're workin' all right. I got witnesses, I got a body, and I got a suspect. Open and shut case, and none of your business, I might add."

Mrs. Drummond shoved her hands into her pockets and flashed a wide, gray smile. Jillian didn't know what the old lady had up her sleeve, but she seemed calm, sure, and amused. Jillian struggled against the grip of the handcuffs and hoped Mrs. Drummond knew something no one else seemed to know, something to save an innocent person from spending the rest of her life in jail.

"Take this, Garrison." Mrs. Drummond handed a smelling salts capsule to the sheriff. "You're gonna need it in about thirty seconds."

"What is it?" He asked.

"Ammonia."

"What do I want with ammonia? Get back in the car, woman, this is a murder investigation."

Mrs. Drummond had no chance to reply, as an almost inhuman shriek pierced the room, followed by a series of high-pitched remarks.

"A murder investigation? In my library? Who's dead?"

Lavender nearly jumped out of her skin when she turned to find Candace Flute sitting erect and fumbling for her glasses. Mrs. Finwicket fainted straight away when the librarian suddenly jumped to her feet and demanded an explanation.

Jillian breathed a sigh of relief.

"But, I didn't find a pulse," Lavender complained. "She was dead, I swear it."

Mrs. Drummond grunted, "Well, she ain't no more."

The handcuffs didn't come off nearly fast enough and the apologies sounded weak and insincere. Although Mrs. Finwicket held sole responsibility for the entire fiasco, she didn't bother with an apology. Instead, she fixed Jillian with a scurrilous glare, like it was all her fault Candace Flute's untimely death would no longer serve as fodder for the daily gossip column. Jillian wondered if the old biddy knew she'd swallowed a bitch bug that had already consumed half her soul.

According to Mrs. Drummond, it was teatime. Candace's strength needed refreshing and everyone else's nerves needed calming. Pulling herbs from her satchels, she began to prepare her brew. Eleanor Finwicket bolted out the front door, the sheriff and his deputy followed in her footsteps, claiming they had another call to tend to—though their radios didn't make a peep—and Digger disappeared inside aisle five, apparently back on the hunt for whatever it was he came to search for in the first place. Although Candace insisted on getting back to work right away, Mrs. Drummond threatened her with a crippling hex if she couldn't find her way to sit down for five minutes. Still embarrassed, Lavender scuffled off to file a pile of books, leaving Jillian alone with the faint-hearted librarian and the precious old woman who saved Jillian's hide from fifty years of bitchology studies at the state penitentiary.

Devil's Edge

Mrs. Drummond stroked the back of Candace's pale hand. "The tea will put the color back in your face. Drink it. And you," she said to Jillian, "I hope you don't fancy this little misunderstanding the most difficult part of your day. Best drink up. You ain't seen nothin' yet."

The Hour of Demise

No one could possibly know everything there was to know about the legend of the chest of treasures, especially since *The Book of Trials* wouldn't open, but Candace knew more than most. An immediate exodus of the Miller family, Jillian in particular, would be the best thing to happen to Devil's Edge in centuries. From the instant Candace saw her face and eyes, she'd known exactly who Jillian was, and if those details didn't give up the fox, the red streak running over the crown of her head blazed like a modern-day billboard plastered on the hull of *The Merry Anne*.

Candace sipped her tea, studying the face of the young woman sitting on the other side of the table. It was a face she'd studied for a quarter century, a face she recognized as readily as her own. Like it or not, if Jillian Miller didn't get out of Devil's Edge, bodies would fall. The chest of treasures legend was powerful, and Candace knew as well as anyone there were those in Devil's Edge willing to give their lives to protect the legend and numerous others prepared to rob it of its substance. Candace belonged to neither group and had long ago determined not to take sides. And yet, here she was, up to her neck in the mire. As if her own feelings of impending catastrophe weren't enough, more evidence swirled like a cloud of doom over the glassy surface of Agaritha Drummond's eyes.

Candace firmly set down her teacup. "You have to get her out of town, Agaritha, for her own sake."

"That's a right nice idea, Candy. But, don't you think she's got a right to know why?"

Candace threw a sharp glare at Jillian. So that was it, Agaritha needed someone to give Miss Miller a quick history lesson, and who better than the foremost authority on the subject, Candace know-it-all Flute?

"You do it, Agaritha. I'll give you the keys. I'm a bona fide basket case today."

"Honored, I'm sure," Agaritha said. "Fact is nobody knows more than you do on this here subject. 'Sides, I got other emergencies to tend to."

Candace leaned close to Agaritha and hissed her words through clenched teeth, "She asked about a Ballencroft Book."

Mrs. Drummond donned a wily grin, pulled her chair away from the table, and stood up. Reaching into a deep pocket, she pulled out a small, black object and handed it to Jillian.

"It's the stone your brother used to break my window," she explained. "I expect you'll need it."

Brow furrowed with confusion, Jillian shrugged her shoulders and slipped the stone into her pocket.

"Candy, tell the girl everythin' she wants to know." Agaritha promptly made her way out the door.

Candace watched the light of the noon sun bounce off Agaritha's white coif, producing an eerie, almost ethereal glow around her head. That woman gave Candace the heebie-jeebies ever since the day she mistakenly confided in Agaritha about Harry Rittenhower's inappropriate behaviors, telling her how the old fool always hung around the library asking for a date, waiting for an opportunity to cop a feel, asking if Candace thought women were as randy as men. Agaritha had listened dutifully and when Candace finished complaining, the only thing she had to say was that on May 13th, at exactly 12:18 pm, Candace would no longer have to worry about old Harry Rittenhower. It wasn't much of a comfort at the time, and less of a comfort when, two weeks later, on Friday the 13th, just after noon, Candace heard sirens blaring from the north end of town. Not long after, Louise LaRouche, a waitress working at Pop's soda shop, called to say Harry Rittenhower self-combusted in front of her very own eyes.

Since then, Candace listened carefully to anything Agaritha Drummond had to say and took just as much care to avoid her. Along with every other child in town, Candace grew up with the rumors concerning the witch on Scabbard Street who could predict the hour of death. Every small town has its haunted house and (children being the cruel creatures they are) every town has a poor, misunderstood, soul marked as a source of terror...the proverbial boogey man, or woman, as it were. It takes but one dark summer night cramped around a campfire listening to some pimple-face teenager spouting ghost stories and the next thing you know, Dracula orders his Bloody Mary's from the third crypt on the northern corner at the local cemetery. Until Harry Rittenhower charbroiled himself, Candace wrote off the stories concerning Agaritha as urban legend and never believed a solitary word she heard. Things change.

Agaritha Drummond's power harvested goose bumps. People are wise to pay attention to the things that frighten them. Fear, after all, exists for a reason.

Candace vigilantly watched Mrs. Drummond waddle through the sand on her way back toward the edge of town. What was she up to? What good could come from arming Jillian Miller with information capable of opening Pandora's Box?

Candace thought to keep the keys locked in the safe where they belonged. She thought about home, the comfort of her old leather sofa, and the security of her feather-top bed. What would be the harm in taking the rest of the day off? She had fainted, not once, but twice. Didn't she deserve a few hours respite? The library was safe in Lavender's capable hands. She was a fine assistant, one with as much respect for the wealth lining the shelves as anyone could expect, and Candace would always be grateful to her for taking time from her busy schedule to volunteer at the library; without her, the days would stretch forty-six hours long. Candace supposed going home would undoubtedly be the wisest thing to do. And yet, she couldn't seem to find the heart to go. No use trying to throw a blanket over her own eyes, Agaritha Drummond made her expectations clear and Candace would comply. She had no wish to know the hour of her demise.

The Revealing

Although Mrs. Drummond's brew tasted especially sweet, Jillian assumed Candace Flute had other reasons for clinging so desperately to her teacup. Clearly, the librarian didn't want to disclose the secrets at her disposal, especially not to Jillian. While Candace coddled her teacup and stared blankly at the mahogany tabletop, Jillian contemplated an escape from the library, the bleeding house, the twisted town. Warp speed would do. Then again, she would still have the freedom to leave after the librarian spilled her beans.

Jillian snatched up her backpack and headed for the door. But, could she really leave without answers? She could and she would. As her fingers curled around the doorknob, she glanced back at the librarian's brightened countenance. Her shoulders no longer sagged beneath the weight and pressure Mrs. Drummond placed upon them, her eyes aglow with a look of intense relief. Something about it didn't sit right. Who did this woman think she was, telling the Millers to get out of town? They were American citizens with the right to go anywhere they damn well pleased, including Devil's Edge. What's more, Jillian had a right to know what kind of bees these people had stuck in their bonnets. If she left the library now, her family would never know why they were so mistreated.

Her backpack made a loud thud as she slammed it back onto the table.

"Hit me with your best shot," she said.

Candace raised her bloodshot brown eyes to meet with Jillian's determined glare and nodded in surrender.

The librarian reluctantly fit her key into a back office door and Jillian stepped inside. Looming before a large bookcase, Candace

stood seemingly transfixed as she mindlessly fondled an antique
skeleton key she took from a safe beneath the service counter, her
gaze locked on a copy of Moby Dick bulging from the top shelf of
the bookcase—a volume far too large for the perch it rested upon.
Breaking free of her trance, she placed a trembling hand on the
binding of Melville's epic tale and gave it a firm tug. The bookcase
groaned as it slid off to the right, exposing a hidden door.

Sinister B, Jillian thought, a scene sliced from a Sherlock
Holmes flick; cut and paste, add a touch of Technicolor. Any one
of her friends would absolutely kill to be in her shoes right now,
listening to the bookcase grind against the floor as it revealed a
passageway to God only knew where. How many opportunities in
life present a person with a chance to go through the mythic
hidden door?

Jillian distinctly felt her blood pressure rise as her heart raced.
A sudden voice boomed inside her head, urging her to take
immediate flight; a request she readily ignored.

Once the sliding bookcase stopped groaning, Candace inserted
her key into a small, average door, twisting until a loud metallic
click indicated the lock's yield. Stepping across the threshold, she
motioned for Jillian to come along. This was it: the crossroads.
Jillian could take a step and follow Candace Flute into the muck of
this town's darkest secrets, or she could leave the library, go back
to the house, and try to convince her father to get out of Dodge.
The clock on the office wall read quarter after twelve, but it
seemed of no consequence, what mattered was that Jillian stalled,
unsure.

Candace waved her hand impatiently. Jillian took a step
forward. She simply had to know who these people thought she
was, or spend a lifetime perplexed. She would follow the dizzy
librarian; listen as she exposed her secrets and then whatever
troubles this town had to iron out of its historical fabric, it would
have to accomplish on its own. Once Jillian quelled her curiosity,
she would have a talk with her father. By this time tomorrow, the
Miller family would be on their way back to Rhode Island.

Jillian fully expected the bookcase to slide back into its original position, permanently securing her to the hip of her decision to follow, but it did not. Candace reached to retrieve an oil lamp from above her head, struck a match, and put it to the wick. Although three more lamps rested on the ledge, she apparently thought one sufficient. The lamp shone dim, but cast enough light to navigate the narrow stairway. Weathered slat boards bowed and screeched as Jillian and Candace descended. The stone walls sweat a gray mold, the air thick with centuries-old moisture. As the stairs made a sharp turn to the left, Jillian reached for the banister, but found it dangerously wet with slime.

Dutifully following behind, she watched the back of Candace's head and imagined the many times in the past the librarian must have made this trek, treasures in hand, keys jingling mindlessly as she prepared to imprison a collection of Galileo's lost journals, or Plato's final platitudes; invaluable secrets buried away until such time as she saw fit to reveal them to the rest of the world. Jillian wondered why no one gave a second thought to bestowing such power and authority on the light-headed, feeble-hearted librarian.

The staircase led to a large supply room filled with old wooden furniture, boxes of tattered books; stacks of discarded clutter clearly of no use or value. Candace whisked past the jumbled rummage and turned left, her suede shoes softly scuffling against the floor, her lips muttering indecipherable complaints, until she arrived at a large, locked door. The iron keys clattered against one another as she searched the oversized key ring for the proper key.

"You mustn't tell anyone about these chambers, Miss Miller. Do you understand?"

Jillian nodded, mentally instructing the hairs on her arms to cease and desist their uprising.

As she stepped inside the chamber, Candace placed the oil lamp on a large, metallic table in the center of the room and pulled a modern, silver key from her pants pocket. She approached a column of steel file compartments resting against the wall; cases resembling safe deposit boxes, the type one can find in almost any bank. She inserted her key into the topmost center receptacle of the encasement and the clatter of snapping metal echoed from inside as each of the compartments unlocked simultaneously. The librarian ran her fingertips over three or four compartments until she found one of interest. She slid the drawer open and pulled out a small book bound in old leather, which she placed upon the table. Then, she tugged open a longer drawer and withdrew another book, this one broader than an opened newspaper, and she carefully placed the large volume on the table next to the first.

Drawing a chair from beneath the table, she sat down, motioning for Jillian to do the same.

"Explaining everything may take some time," Candace said. "And, I'm still not feeling one-hundred percent."

Unsure if she should feel guilty for taking the librarian's time when the woman didn't feel well, Jillian decided it okay to indulge in a bit of selfishness now and then. After all, she too had suffered through the same fiasco that put Candace in such a delicate state of mind. Besides, Candace Flute looked remarkably well for a woman pronounced dead less than twenty minutes ago.

Candace picked up the small leather book and gently fondled the binding, her fingertips coming to rest on a miniature rusted lock.

"This is the *Book of Trials*. No one knows for sure what it holds as we weren't able to open the lock. For fear of causing permanent damage to the text, we made no attempt to force it open. An anonymous donor gave the text to the library a number of years ago. It is believed only direct descendents can open this book. And this," Candace placed the small book back on the table and opened the cover of the larger book, "is a compilation of my own research concerning the legend of the chest of treasures. Please understand, Miss Miller, there are people in this town who would readily slice your throat for a mere peek at this material. Think twice before you carelessly wag your tongue."

Jillian swallowed hard and nodded. The librarian's hand trembled as she ran her fingertip over the headline of the first article pasted in her scrapbook.

"In the early 1700's, a young woman named Fujo Sinclair lived in a small village in Haiti, she was a voodoo priestess practicing the art of herbal healing. One day, Dutch slave traders pillaged and ransacked her village. Not uncommon, but an unfortunate event, as Fujo and her younger sister, Catti, were forced to watch as the captain of that ship mercilessly decapitated their mother. Some weeks later, a pirate vessel called *The Merry Anne* attacked the Dutch ship, plundering everything and everyone onboard. This is where you come into the story, Miss Miller. You see, that pirate ship was named for one of the rogues onboard, a treacherous woman known as Anne Bonny."

Candace tapped her finger on a hand-drawn photograph of a woman wearing cutlasses and pistols strapped to her britches. "Legend has it she was a robust, golden-haired woman with a vein of red hair running over the crown of her head, much like your own. She was widely known as a vile murderess who allowed no one to stand in the way of her folly. That is, until the day she met Fujo Sinclair. You see, Anne Bonny took a magnificent emerald viper from Fujo and claimed it as her own. Her ownership of that viper, however, was short-lived.

In November of 1720, a government sloop out of Virginia captured *The Merry Anne*. Most of the pirates hanged, with the exception of Anne Bonny and Mary Read, the only two female pirates onboard. As the story goes, Anne and Mary pleaded their bellies before the court in order to have their executions stayed. Neither of them ever saw the noose. Some say Anne's father bought her freedom and Mary died of a fever in prison, but I have reason to believe those stories were purposefully fabricated."

Jillian's jaw dropped. "Are you saying the people of this town are falling all over themselves because I resemble a woman who lived hundreds of years ago?"

Candace removed her fractured glasses and chewed on the edge of an earpiece. "Precisely," she said, and resumed her search through the pages of her scrapbook.

"You see, Fujo visited Anne Bonny and Mary Read while they were confined to Bridewell prison. There, she put a voodoo curse on them, a curse so powerful it frightened Anne Bonny into relinquishing the viper."

Jillian was perplexed. "This woman laid down a curse because someone stole her precious trinket?"

"Oh, no, no. She issued the curse because the crew of *The Merry Anne* allowed Blackbeard to steal away with her sister, Catti."

"You left that part out."

"My apologies," Candace blushed. "It's impossible to give you all the details at once, it's a complicated matter. The bottom line is, these sea rogues cost Fujo her family. They murdered her mother and gave her sister away. She never saw her fiancé or her father again and by the time she reached Catti, sadly, she found only a meager grave crudely marked, 'suicide.' She damned the entire crew of *The Merry Anne* for her losses."

Jillian's brow creased and she spoke solemnly, "It seems to me she cursed the wrong lot. Surely, Blackbeard was principally to blame for the suicide."

"Many agree with you, Miss Miller, Mrs. Drummond chief among them. But keep in mind Fujo didn't have direct access to Blackbeard, or she most certainly would have cursed him to the lowest level of hell. On the other hand, she did have the opportunity to address the crew of *The Merry Anne*.

Rumor has it Fujo may have second-guessed her actions many years later. They say she left a letter of instruction for breaking the curse on Ocracoke Island, where she spent the better part of her remaining years. There was talk, many years ago, that someone found such a letter and it contained a list of items required to open a portal called *The Door of Doom*, which they say is located in the grotto where Fujo died. I, myself, have never seen such a door, but I haven't spent more than ten minutes inside the grotto, it gives me the creeps."

"What, exactly, was this curse?"

"There is a great deal of speculation, but only you can say for sure. If, in fact, you wield the power I believe you may have."

"Me? How could I possibly know?"

"It's just a theory," a nervous excitement fluttered in Candace's voice, "but I'm willing to bet my career as a librarian you can open *The Book of Trials*, and the nature of the curse surely must be included in the text."

Jillian ran her fingers through her hair. "Why should I be able to open the book, I am definitely not a direct descendant of Fujo Sinclair."

"No, but you are Anne Bonny's descendant and I'll wager that's a better link."

Jillian took a deep breath and sat back in her chair, lost in thought. "Why would it matter if I were related to Anne Bonny?"

"A fair question. Speculation has it Blackbeard left a massive treasure behind when he died. A fortune in gold, the location of which he never revealed, not even to his most trusted comrades. Since no one has discovered this treasure over the course of hundreds of years, and not for the lack of trying, there are those who believe Fujo Sinclair might have found her way to it and may have put a curse on the treasure as well. She would have viewed it as blood money. Money used to buy, and ultimately end, her sister's life.

What's more, Voodoo priestesses believe strongly in the power of lineage, and are in the habit of calling upon their ancestors for help, seeing them as gods of a sort. And so, it stands to reason only direct descendants of those whom Fujo cursed could undo such a curse. That puts you right in the middle of the game. Miss Miller, you could be the one to finally unearth Blackbeard's treasure...or, just as likely, someone might bash your brains in before you can make the attempt."

Startled, Jillian protested, "There's no proof I'm an actual descendant. A streak of red hair is hardly enough evidence."

Candace seemed slightly amused. "Answer me this, what is your middle name?"

"Anne."

"Your mother's?"

"Anne."

"Your grandmother's?"

Jillian's mouth went slack. "Anne."

"And tell me, have any of the women in your lineage ever been born without that red streak of hair?"

Jillian lowered her chin, answering reluctantly, "No."

Candace nodded, allowing a smug grin to play at the corners of her mouth. "We will know for certain if you can unlock this book." She handed the text to Jillian.

The book felt small and light, its burden heavy. Just as Jillian reached for the lock, Candace sharply pulled her chair away from the table and remarked, "What's that smell?"

Jillian sniffed, abruptly declaring, "*Smoke.*"

"Quickly," Candace shouted, "get to the stairwell...it's the only way out."

Jillian stuffed the leather book into her backpack and bolted for the door.

Billowing puffs of stifling smoke already filled the corridor with a cloud so thick they could see no more than two feet ahead. Parking her nose in her shirt collar, Jillian pushed forward, attempting to keep her eyes on Candace's back as she searched frantically for the stairway. The fire snapped and cracked like a bullwhip and already engulfed enough old furniture and paperwork to throw off a searing heat. The ravenous blaze devoured everything in its path.

"The stairway's blocked," Candace wailed, "We're trapped."

Jillian peered at the base of the stairs and watched as the fire consumed what remained of the wooden slats: if that staircase really was the only way out...

"There's got to be another way," Jillian screamed, "a window?"

Candace nodded. "In the boiler room, but it's too high, we'll never reach it."

Pulling her nose from her collar, Jillian bellowed, "Would you prefer to take the stairs?"

A Social Leper

It took a good hour for Maurine to rustle up the nerve to head off toward the library; better late than never. She didn't know if Jillian was still there, but she was determined to find out. Super glue in your lipstick tube, the face of courage needs to see some daylight now and again.

Though she'd been to the library once already today, a second trip would be well worth the effort if she found Jillian still searching for the Ballencroft book. Wouldn't it be a hog-spittin' hoot if Maurine actually found the book? Imagine the headlines: *'Local Girl Locates Missing Evidence, Solves Age Old Mystery.'* That would put an end to the teasing at school; heck, even Teddy, Jr. wouldn't have anything mean to say for at least a month.

The constant cry of seagulls pierced the afternoon hour. The sea roiled, clawing at the shore in a manic fit, shredding mounds of sand and clumps of seaweed as if they were enemies rather than co-conspirators, regurgitating useless trinkets bequeathed by mindless tourists; plastic, metal, and Styrofoam.

What if Jillian had already left the library?

Maurine stopped walking, not because she wanted to go back home, and not because she felt a sudden tic coming on, but because a strange jolt of electricity surged through her whenever she thought of Jillian Miller.

You meet some people, smile, and say how honored you are to make their acquaintance, all the while thinking you'd rather drink a quart of snake venom than spend another minute in their presence. Sometimes, though, you look into a stranger's eyes and just know there's something special about them, something you absolutely must discover. All of a sudden, you're like an archaeologist with shovels for appendages. Some would attribute the attraction to pure chemistry, while others might lay a claim for kismet. All Maurine knew for sure was that she couldn't seem to rid her mind of Jillian's countenance; the Yankee accent, the preppy clothes, the punk haircut. Maybe meeting Jillian Miller was destiny, fate, or karma. Or, maybe Maurine was just staring into an empty flower basket filled to the brim with wishful thinking. Whatever it was, she couldn't help believing Jillian Miller held a key that might change Maurine's life forever; the kind of change a social leper prays for twenty-four-seven. Maurine felt as though she might begin her own lunar orbit if she had to wait much longer to find out exactly how those changes might come about. She began to walk again, her pace quickened.

The library came within sight. It wouldn't take long now to discover if her sudden burst of courage would shower her with reward or rain with disappointment.

A Bitter Pill

The boiler room in the library's dungeon barely had enough room to house the monstrous furnace parked inside, but it had a door that, for the moment, served to protect Candace and Jillian from the raging fire. There was a window, but not large enough for an adult to crawl through and, as Candace indicated earlier, it was located nine to ten feet off the floor. Worse, a bulbous metal vent protruding from the top of the furnace blocked most of the glass.

Candace pointed to a line of coveralls hanging on the wall. She suggested they use them for cover and get on the floor to avoid the smoke. Although Jillian knew this was the best advice given the situation, she would not submit just yet.

To the left of the furnace stood a small workbench housing a plethora of tools; large wrenches, hammers, and screwdrivers, implements Jillian deemed sufficient to break through the window. Her first attempt involved a rather large pipe wrench that proved too heavy; it clanged off the vent, nearly clocking her in the head as it descended, mission unaccomplished. Her second attempt went much like the first, the third like the second, and the fourth like the third. One after another, the tools on the table flew toward the window, hit the vent, and bounced back to the floor, each piece too large to make it past the cumbersome venting.

Jillian accepted defeat begrudgingly and punched her leg in frustration, her hand brushing against her pocket. Whitt's stone! She quickly withdrew the little missile from her pocket and took careful aim; she would only have one shot at it. The stone was small enough to avoid the vent, but if it missed the window, it might fall behind the furnace leaving Jillian with no hope to retrieve it. True to aim, the glass assassin flew past the venting and hit the windowpane square on, creating a rain of glass shards. The gaping hole in the window provided a small escape route for the smoke that welled thicker with the passing of each second.

No cure, the broken window would buy only a few minutes respite. Jillian took a pair of coveralls and placed herself on the floor next to Candace; there, she would most likely die, suffocated by the noxious breath of the flames licking at the door.

It no longer mattered if she bore a resemblance to Anne Bonny, no longer mattered if the people of Devil's Edge were right or wrong. All that mattered was the burning sensation in her chest and her lung's attempts to rid themselves of the fumes relentlessly assaulting them.

She never should have followed Candace Flute into this hellhole. Curiosity doesn't just kill the cat...it takes all nine lives at once. If only she had lent more credence to her instincts. She should have paid attention to what her gut told her and left the library when she had the chance. The fact she had ignored those instincts caused her to question her own judgment, made her feel as if she deserved what she'd stepped into. If she and the librarian were to die in this fire, she had no one but herself to blame.

She tugged at the coveralls, desperately trying to create a tighter seal against the floor, and thought of her father. What a bitter pill to hand to him, the loss of his daughter only a year after losing his best friend, his soul mate, his precious wife. There would be no consoling him. And what about Mrs. Drummond, the town's renowned *psychic*? Once again that terrible gift-curse would fail the Millers in the most god-awful way.

Why would Mrs. Drummond allow Jillian to remain at the library to suffer and die this way? Surely, she must have sensed the danger. In fact, Mrs. Drummond knew *exactly* what was about to happen. Hadn't she blatantly stated, 'You ain't seen nothin' yet,' and hadn't she purposefully given Jillian the notorious shattering stone? Suspiciously right about the danger being here and now, sadly wrong about Jillian's mother's promise to protect her while she wallowed in the thick of it. But, what reason could Mrs. Drummond possibly have for putting Jillian and Candace in harm's way?

The sound of Candace's violent attempt to bark up a lung interrupted Jillian's train of thought. Miraculously, the woman remained conscious. She turned toward Jillian and bravely managed to say,
"Smoke...ascends...Lavender...will...call...fire...department."

Though Jillian understood the need to cling to microscopic morsels of hope, she felt Candace's optimism was misplaced. The smoke grew heavier than ever and the heat broiled. In a matter of moments, the fire would conquer the door. Even if the fire department had deployed, it was already too late. As she struggled to breathe, failing miserably, Jillian felt her consciousness begin to slip away. The last thought to cross her mind was a useless, senseless—bordering on insane—mindless, trinket she held no hope to understand: *Super glue in your lipstick tube.*

Rehearsing Denial

"HONK! HONK! HONK! HONK!"

Maurine lay atop her bed, staining her white cotton pillowcase with wet splotches merging to form indistinct patterns, saline blending with what seemed like a never-ending supply of mucus. The universe doesn't play fair.

Yanking the phone from its cradle, she called the hospital and asked after Jillian. The nurse at the station uttered the same words she'd voiced eight times already this morning. "There's no improvement."

The more Maurine cried, the louder she honked. Lord, she hated this particular tic more than all the others combined; an ugly, guttural sound that shoved her into the same caste as a flock of constipated snow geese; unattractive, unfeminine, and downright inhuman.

"HONK!"

Often unaware, she would honk until someone piped up to say, "Where's the traffic jam?" The more upset she became, the worse the tic would get. Nothing about Tourette syndrome is pretty. She began many of her days begging for God's mercy, even tried blackmail once; promised the Lord she'd never speak to him again unless he immediately drummed up a cure. When it became apparent he didn't give a gopher hole one way or the other, she decided it best to withdraw the threat, he'd obviously deemed her unworthy. Stem cell research looked promising, but who could say when the government might allow it.

"HONK!"

No sense beating rocks with feathers; the universe doesn't even *try* to play fair.

Candace Flute and Jillian Miller had survived the fire, thanks, in part, to Maurine. She had arrived at the library to find smoke escaping from a small basement window and alerted the fire department. In the days that followed, the newspapers hailed her as a hero. The mayor planned parades and news crews expected interviews. Though she had set off for the library craving exactly this type of public adoration, she wanted nothing to do with it. Jillian hadn't regained consciousness, and less than a week after the fire, her condition took a turn for the worse as she spiraled into a coma. The doctors hooked her up to a respirator and whispered bleak words Maurine refused to believe.

Day after day, she camped beside Jillian's bed with its crisp, sterile sheets, and ignored the fact that Jillian looked pale and lifeless as a porcelain doll, her chest dutifully rising and falling in rhythm with the respirator. Someone needed to embrace blatant denial, someone needed to demand miracles; if no one else would volunteer, Maurine had at least rehearsed denial until she could play it like a piece of sheet music, upside down, inside out, and backward.

As for miracles, she knew better than to expect one for free. Apparently, you need to be on the same page with the likes of Mother Teresa to receive that kind of all-out mercy. As such, it seemed time for another dose of divine blackmail. If the Lord took Jillian Miller's life, Maurine would see it as a sign he didn't care more than a drop of grasshopper spit for the human race and she would live the rest of her life without his empty promises. This time, she most sincerely meant it.

She spent hour upon hour talking to Jillian. Ozzie wasn't the only one watching occasional episodes of the Discovery channel, and Maurine had seen enough to know holding lengthy conversations with comatose patients can aid in their recovery. If she had no other real talent, she was at least a professional chatterbox, not quite as advanced as Ozzie, but still in an Olympic class. The few times she caught herself snoozing in the chair beside Jillian's bed absolutely did not count.

Four days after Jillian slipped into a coma, the hospital staff called Maurine's parents to complain about her presence in the ICU, claiming she was in the way, an assertion so far from the truth it didn't even live in the same galaxy. The doctors and nurses only came to check vitals once every four hours or so. Everyone else visiting Jillian constituted family, or yet another flower delivery guy. In truth, Maurine's honking probably drove the staff bonkers, but she couldn't help it. Jillian looked so helpless with her blistered face barely flinching, her skin cold as a slab of salmon packed on ice.

Despite the lack of truth in the staff's assertions, Maurine agreed to spend the day at home, a decision she regretted more with each passing moment.

She walked to the window and stared at the small speck on the horizon that was the library. The fire department extinguished the fire before it fully ascended the stairs; most of the building and its contents remained unscathed. Miss Flute would be elated to hear the news, but would first have to overcome her drug-induced grog. According to the doctors, she'd taken in less smoke than Jillian and would make a slow but full recovery.

Remaining at home, drowning in a pool of misery, honking her heart out until she didn't have a solitary honk left, suddenly seemed no way to spend a perfectly bitchin' day. So what if she'd promised her parents she wouldn't bother the ICU staff today? Maybe the time had come to hoist a flag of rebellion. Hadn't she suffered through enough compliance to last a lifetime? The newspapers hailed her as a hero; well then, time to conjure up a little bravado. Maurine Teach (minus the cape and tights) would spend the afternoon at Jillian Miller's side, or rot in punishment for breaking her promise. Army ants playing Chinese checkers at the last picnic on earth, at least she wouldn't waste another minute blowing snot into her pillowcase.

Laments of the Cryptologist

Ozzie Teach tried to ignore the fact he was sitting on the Spirit Rapper's sofa. The hardest thing to comprehend was his willful agreement to follow her here, even if he had acquired her solemn promise to keep the time and method of his death a strict secret. What if her oath proved worthless, what if she just blurted out the dreadful facts? He would have no time for defense; the noxious information would take root in his brain like a fossil imbedded in stone. How can a man live knowing the hour of his expiration? He curled his quaking hands tightly round and round one another as he waited to inspect the cryptic messages that had drawn him so eagerly into the spider's web.

Merely an amateur cryptologist, Ozzie had never encountered the opportunity to take a crack at the real deal. Sure, there were codes posted on the Internet and plenty in books and magazines, but they were all insignificant and contrived. When Mrs. Drummond approached him at the soda shop to say she'd received shards of messages she couldn't understand, and that someone's life depended on his ability to decipher them, how could he possibly refuse?

Unfortunately, Mrs. Drummond's absence from the living room extended to a rather lengthy bit of time and, with every tick-tock of the amplified grandfather clock pulsating conspicuously in the corner of the room, Ozzie began to doubt his convictions. It wouldn't take much of an effort to make a clean escape; the front door stood less than ten feet away. As he contemplated the advantages of leaving, he recalled the recent photograph of Maurine's face plastered on the cover of *The Coastal Review* and thought of the many times Teddy Jr. found himself the subject of front page news, albeit for feats not quite so heroic as Maurine's. It seemed possible deciphering Mrs. Drummond's cryptic messages could finally bring about Ozzie's fifteen minutes of fame, thereby alerting the scientific community to his presence on the planet.

He ran his fingers through his buzz cut, poked at his glasses until they settled onto the bridge of his nose, and adjusted his tie. He couldn't leave, he wouldn't leave, though his bowels might fail at any moment, he would see it through. It had been ages since anyone asked for his expert advice; okay, in all honesty that never happened before, at all—*ever*—in real life. Still, he wouldn't shy away from the opportunity to share his vast knowledge just because the person asking for his help probably had Satan's phone number on speed dial.

Devil's Edge

The sun shone brightly through an oversized window. A pair of white lace drapes hung off to the side, completely insufficient to inhibit the golden beams of light that pierced the room and lit up the face of the systolic clock; a curious piece. Ozzie had never seen a residential clock built quite so large and had certainly never heard one beat so loud. He supposed if she wanted to, Mrs. Drummond could probably hide a body or two inside the belly of the engilded beast. As a series of gruesome images began to take form, he decided it best to focus his attention on the thin line of white smoke rising off the mantle. Emitted from an incense burner, the smoke carried the fragrant scent of sandalwood, an earthy smell, and quite soothing once he submitted to it.

Mrs. Drummond returned to the living room with a manila folder cradled gently between the palms of her hands. The edges of a hefty stack of crinkled papers dangled from the folder like pieces of lettuce attempting to escape a greasy burger. She handed the file to him. All at once, the hair on the back of his neck stood on guard. He held within his hands a bright and promising future. He would of course, accept the Nobel Peace Prize before the Pulitzer. After which, he would contact Stephen Hawking right away, they had much to discuss. Of course, he would no longer remain in Devil's Edge; a tiny, indistinct town that held no connection to mainstream science—Los Angeles seemed more probable, or Zurich. He would take his mother along, or, if she remained unimpressed—how very unlikely—he would buy her a summer home near one of his mansions. A new wardrobe was a must, but with no fashionista talent of his own, he would have to consult the Internet on the latest cuts and styles...Armani perhaps, but he could not say for certain without extensive research. Since the oval office no longer seemed out of the question, he would make it a point to erase presidential bloopers off his computer hard drive; no sense encouraging unnecessary enemies.

Mrs. Drummond cleared her throat. "Ain't ya gonna look at 'em?"

Ozzie turned his attention from the closed file and looked to Mrs. Drummond. Whose glasses were thicker, hers or his? A toss-up. Hers were definitely more stylish, though. There you have it; he really did need all the help he could get when it came to superficial social matters.

Opening the folder, he carefully inspected a singed piece of parchment. Most of the paper had been marred by fire, but a few imprints remained visible, unfortunately, they made no immediate sense; just the number '1' followed by a '3' and an exclamation point. He sifted through the remaining papers and found most of them in a similar state, each just as confusing when viewed apart from the others. Possibly, though, after some intense scrutiny, he might find a way to piece them together and, perhaps, discover something of value. One thing seemed sure; he wouldn't decode these messages quickly, or without a great deal of effort.

"Do you have copies of these?" He asked.

Seemingly perplexed, she replied, "Should I?"

"Well," he tapped his finger on the file cover, "Some paper is constructed out of papyrus—tree bark chewed and spit out by flatulent camels living in parts of the world where camels thrive, like Egypt, Tibet, and the Florida Everglades. While other papers are produced synthetically by manufacturing companies run by greed-driven heathens who only call their mothers once a year to see if they're still alive. Then you've got your average, everyday recycled paper made from used paper products. Did you ever stop to think it's possible we're all writing our grocery lists on the same paper Nostradamus used to foretell the fate of the world, or, just as ironically, on the same paper used by Howard Ashman for his first draft of *Little Shop of Horrors*? I'm not certain which type of paper these messages are, but my microscope won't fail to make the proper identification. The thing is, I may have to use harsh chemicals to get to the bottom of it all, and the paper could suffer permanent damage. I'll make a set of copies when I get home, just to make sure we have backups."

Mrs. Drummond's jaw had dropped so far Ozzie could no longer see the white whiskers on her chin; he must have seriously impressed her. She remained silent for a moment, but finally regained her composure. "Good thinkin', kiddo." She gave him an affectionate pat on the shoulder.

"You don't mind if I work on these at home, then?"

Mrs. Drummond leaned closer than Ozzie cared for, and chortled, "I'm in the habit of talkin' in my sleep...can't say what unfortunate facts might spill into those innocent ears a yours."

He released a faint squeal, stuffed the papers back into the file, and bolted for the door.

What a creepy old woman.

A Heartless Notion

A cold chill lingered in the air at Mercy General, as if this weak form of cryogenics would suffice to preserve patients until their physicians could clear the 18th hole.

Maurine stopped at the gift shop and bought a copy of Emily Bronte's *Wuthering Heights*, one of the few required reading assignments she enjoyed, then made her way through the corridors leading to the ICU. Obscure voices merged to form a garbled melody, its volume rising and falling like a Gregorian chant. Distressed patients wept in pain and cried out for attention. Heavy feet shuffled through hallways as medical professionals scurried off to reluctant places; blank expressions filling haunted eyes that have seen more than they could ever weep away.

The smell of rubbing alcohol and Lysol combined to produce the same nauseating stench that permeates funeral homes, the unmistakable scent of sanitized death. Maurine also detected the stink of overcooked broccoli, a hospital specialty that traditionally festers on neglected food trays until it's teeming with seven different strains of botulism, insuring repeat business.

She opened the brown paper bag in her hand, withdrew her newly purchased book, and tossed the bag into a nearby garbage can. She peeked at her watch and noted the time: twelve-thirty pm. She would read to Jillian until five o'clock, then run home for a quick bite and return afterward. Anyone who had a problem with her visit could park it where the sun can't see. Speak of the devil; two nurses stared intently and whispered to one another as Maurine passed them by.

She entered Jillian's room and slowed her pace, immediately aware that the hiss and grind of the respirator had grown silent. *Finally*. Jillian had come out of her coma and was breathing on her own. Maurine exhaled with relief. Smiling ear-to-ear, she eagerly pulled back the privacy curtain blocking her view of the hospital bed.

The bed lay barren. If the room felt cold before, it seemed arctic now. A crisp set of unfurled sheets awaited a new occupant, and the tangled wires and tubes of the life support system stood limply by in shameful defeat. The somber expressions on the faces of the staff as Maurine passed them in the corridor suddenly made sense.

"Honk, honk, honk, honk!"

Balling her hand into a fist, she cocked her arm back and punched the respirator square in the face. The sheer force of the blow caused the useless machine to collide with the wall and a nearby intravenous stand crashed to the floor. Maurine wailed as the skin covering her knuckles split open, the sting and burn much greater than she anticipated.

God is a heartless notion.

As she collapsed on the floor in pain, a nurse barged into the room, caught sight of the blood oozing from Maurine's knuckles, and reached to help her off the floor.

"Are you all right?"

"All right? My friend is *dead*."

As a stew of raw emotion broiled within her chest, Maurine glared at the plump middle-aged nurse and wondered if she'd attended the same school of stupid with the doctors who allowed Jillian Miller's life to slip between their bumbling fingers. A liquid tempest rushed to Maurine's face and the vein at the center of her brow began to swell the way it always did when the universe saw fit to slap her upside the head.

The nurse reached to take her by the shoulders. Maurine jerked away and began to mumble, "Cow pie pudding. Eyeball ice cubes." Once again, she turned to face the empty hospital bed. A sudden stream of unchecked tears singed her flushed cheeks as she screamed a long-winded, truck driver's repertoire of unchecked obscenities.

The Space-Time Continuum

There are two types of disbelief. First, the oil and vinegar things you refuse to believe. And second, the unicorn, puff-the-magic-dragon things you simply cannot believe. As Ozzie Teach examined the charred papers from Mrs. Drummond's file, he desperately wanted to embrace belief, but couldn't quite wrap his head around it. The baseline attributes of the papers Mrs. Drummond gave him were not only peculiar, but downright impossible. He hadn't made a mistake; every dime of his allowance for the past three years went in to making his lab every bit as good as a professional lab. The chemicals were fresh, and the microscope—an exceptional model—in perfect working condition. Everything seemed copasetic, except the results he had acquired, repeatedly. He twisted the tip of his finger into his ear to quell an itch, removed his eyeglasses, closed his eyes, and sat back in his chair to ponder the situation.

Time: the battle for the future. Those who manage to conquer time will conquer the universe. Ozzie understood this intricately, as he intended to be the one to break through the elusive barriers standing between physicists and the achievement of this ultimate quest.

It had been three days since Mrs. Drummond bestowed her curious jigsaw puzzle upon him and his around-the-clock focus had rested upon nothing else. Now that his results seemed definite, they presented more questions than answers. According to his calculations, each piece of paper in the file had a carbon date decades, centuries, and sometimes, millenniums apart from the others. No two pieces of parchment had come from the same era. Yet, the ink used to write each of the messages was circa 2007. Was this even remotely possible?

Ozzie found the handwriting analysis elementary. He simply crosschecked the scrawl against signature samples he obtained from the state university and found an exact match to Professor Drummond. Piece of cake.

As an archaeologist, Drummond would have access to such an array of time-dated material, but why would he put such valuable parchments in jeopardy by defacing them with modern ink and allowing them to become so irrevocably damaged? What's more, where was he? *The Coastal Review* had used Drummond's missing status as a sensationalized real-life soap opera for two years or more, even though most people in town had written him off for dead. Could it be Drummond wasn't dead or missing at all? At least, not in the way most people go missing. What if Drummond was traveling through time?

Ozzie pushed away from his desk, went to the drawing board, picked up a piece of chalk, and scribbled:

$E = mc^2$

"Energy equals mass times the speed of light squared," he mumbled.

$D^2 = x^2 + y^2 + z^2$

"The fixed difference in the co-ordinates of the three spatial directions..."

$D^2 = x^2 + y^2 + z^2 \ (1 - v^2/c^2)^{1/2}$

"...Contracted relative to the stationary observer."

$S^2 = x^2 + y^2 + z^2 - ct^2$

"...Plus the Lorentz transformation invariant for space-time. Hmmm."

Stepping back from the blackboard, he stared at the equations and considered the possibilities for time travel. Black holes might provide an answer. Or a fifth, sixth, perhaps even a tenth dimension. Ten dimensions would fit with super string theory, but you may not need ten dimensions in order to move through the second temporal dimension...you would, however, need at least five. If someone discovered a way to move faster than the speed of light, it's possible he could be flipping through time and returning without anyone ever being the wiser. In theory, a multitude of time travelers could already exist, refusing to reveal their methods simply because they need the universe to be intact when they return from their excursions. Was Professor Drummond among them?

If Ozzie's suspicions were anywhere near the truth, then Ebbenwright Drummond would have some serious explaining to do, and not just for Ozzie, but for the physicists around the globe who spent their days banging their heads against the proverbial wall.

Part of the answer lay concealed in the message Drummond had written, not a mysterious encrypted code after all, just a series of fractured sentences that proved far too easy to piece together. What the message meant, Ozzie could not say for sure, but there was little doubt Professor Drummond had asked his wife to set that old grandfather clock to thirteen and had shown more than a little bit of agitation with her for not having done so.

Upon deciphering the message, Ozzie racked his brains trying to recall the face of the clock but couldn't remember anything out of the ordinary. A person would remember seeing the number thirteen on the face of a clock; it would stick out like a polar bear roller-skating down the state highway: how could anyone miss such a thing? If Ozzie had seen a thirteen on the face of that clock, he wouldn't forget it. So, how could Drummond expect his wife to reset a traditionally faced clock to thirteen? More importantly, why?

Ozzie re-stuffed and banded the file, preparing to return it to the only person on the planet who could satisfy his curiosities. Like it or not, he would have to return to Scabbard Street and have another talk with the Spirit Rapper.

Jumpin' Jockstraps

Lepers eating finger food, who could blame Maurine for misconstruing the facts, what with the empty ICU bed and all? It was an honest mistake, and yet, her face flushed each time she saw the nurse who had bandaged her bleeding knuckles. The same nurse who calmly explained they had moved Jillian Miller out of ICU to bunk with Candace Flute in a regular room.

Over the course of the three days that passed since leaving the ICU, Jillian slowly recovered. Her throat began to heal from the singe of the fire and the intrusion of the respirator tubes, and although her voice had a bit of an ugly rasp, it was like soaking in the melodies of an angelic choir just to hear her speak.

Maurine had approached the central chapters of *Wuthering Heights*, the part where Cathy haunts Heathcliff (the best part of the story if anyone wanted to know) when Miss Flute sat up in her bed and took the oxygen tube out of her nose.

"Forgive me for interrupting, Miss Teach" she said, "but one of the nurses claims you saved our lives."

Maurine nodded and felt her cheeks flush.

"That has to count for something." The librarian said, struggling with a hairclip as she twisted her long brown hair into a makeshift bun and pinned it to the top of her head. "Can I swear you to secrecy?"

"Can you what?" Maurine said, sure she'd heard incorrectly.

"Will you promise to keep a secret, a very dangerous secret?"

A look of concern passed over Jillian's face as her gaze focused on Miss Flute and returned to Maurine. Maurine found Jillian's expression unnerving. Although she didn't know what secrets the librarian might expose, she certainly knew what the word dangerous meant. After the fire at the library, she didn't doubt for a solitary moment the risk of knowing too much could be very high. The fire department had released part of its findings after their initial investigation and announced the fire had been set intentionally. They had yet to find enough evidence to nab the responsible party, but it was shockingly apparent the arsonist who flipped the match meant to kill.

"Don't get her involved," Jillian fretted. "It's too dangerous. She's too young."

Miss Flute chuckled. "And you're not?"

"I didn't ask for any of this," Jillian replied sharply, "You're asking her to volunteer. It's not fair."

"I ain't too young for anythin'," Maurine snapped. "If you can almost die in a fire, I can at least keep a secret."

"You don't understand," Jillian rasped.

"I can't understand what I don't know."

Jillian fought through an extended bout of coughing. Once it subsided, she clasped her hand around Maurine's wrist and gave it a firm tug. "Keep it that way."

Refried vomit on Texas toast, what should she to do? She could decline the offer to become involved and suffer in the misery of not knowing what was going on, or she could accept the challenge and possibly lose her life. Her parents would definitely want her to stay out of it but, as adults, their answers were automatic. Teddy Jr. would say life's too short to live in fear, but he was so self-centered he probably drank a glass of his own piss on a daily basis. Oz would most likely cite a rapid series of equations representing survival statistics and the most probable outcomes, then throw in his suppressed theories on why the songs of the humpback whale seem so melancholy, none of which seemed helpful in any way.

"If we have any hope to succeed," Miss Flute said, "We will need all the help we can get."

"No one in this room is qualified to handle this," Jillian argued. "We've nearly lost our lives already. These things are best left to the authorities."

The librarian clicked her tongue against the back of her teeth, "Do you really think the Sheriff's department is adequately trained to chase ghosts? Or, that the FBI is any better suited?"

"You never said anything about ghosts," Jillian spurt, her voice crackling beneath the rasp, and a burst of violent coughing had her reaching for the bedside panic button before it passed.

Devil's Edge

"I didn't have ample time to explain everything to you. I thought we would have an opportunity to go over *The Book of Trials,* which would have revealed much...I never dreamed there would be a fire."

Maurine's eyebrows rose so high on her face it seemed as though they might curl over the back of her head. Jumpin' jockstraps. Ghosts? Were they real life, I'll-tap-on-your-windowpane-until-you-let-me-in-Heathcliff, ghosts? This changed everything. How could Maurine possibly justify spending the summer staring longingly out of her window while Jillian Miller and Candace Flute were off sniffing out honest-to-God ghosts?

"I can keep a secret," she blurted. "I swear."

"Don't do it," Jillian coughed.

Heart pounding, head spinning, Maurine blabbered, "I can help, I promise. Whatever y'all need me to do...just say the word."

"Jillian's book bag is in the closet over there, could you retrieve it for her?" Miss Flute pointed to the wall directly behind Maurine.

The so-called closet looked more like a glove compartment. She squeezed the charred backpack out of the miniature cubicle and gave it to Jillian.

"Please," Miss Flute pleaded with Jillian, "*The Book of Trials.* We need to know. At least see if you can open it."

Reluctantly unzipping the pack, Jillian reached inside and removed the aged black leather book, holding it in her quivering hand. As she stroked a small metal latch with her fingertip, it snapped open and the strap dangled free.

The librarian let out a delighted yelp. "After all these years!" Her face beamed. "Bless the Lord. I knew you were a descendant. Miss Teach, since my glasses were lost in the fire and Jillian can't stop coughing for more than a few minutes, would you mind reading for us?"

White-knuckled, Jillian clutched the book to her chest. "Don't do this, Maurine. There's no going back."

Fat-free bugaboos munching porcupine pop tarts, it didn't feel right going against Jillian Miller, but compliance would mean total exclusion from the adventure of a lifetime. She simply would not spend the summer blubbering into her pillowcase.

"I have to," she said apologetically, prying the book from Jillian's hands.

"Don't say you weren't warned," Jillian said.

"Gotcha."

Maurine settled back into her chair and slowly opened the cover of the book.

A Moonlight Cloak

"Right on time, kiddo." Mrs. Drummond grinned coyly as Ozzie stood on the threshold of her door with a bulging file tucked into his armpit, trickles of sweat creeping down the sides of his face and soaking into his collar.

Caught off guard by the unexpected greeting, Ozzie sputtered, "I didn't call to say I was coming over."

"All the same," Mrs. Drummond said, and stepped aside so he could slip past her rotund hips.

As she ushered him into the living room, he took cautious inventory of his surroundings. A lazy flame crackled in the fireplace, two oil lamps burned low on the hearth, and moonlight flittered through the large window, illuminating the clock face with an eerie glow. But for the throbbing beat of the gigantic timepiece, everything else seemed rather quiet and mundane.

Although the old woman kept her house in order, clean enough to indicate care, cluttered enough for evidence of occupation, her physical appearance did not seem quite so calculated. Black mud filled her fingernails to the brim, grimy wet puddles spread over the knees of her denim pants, and a splotch of caked soil streaked below her lower lip, blemishing her billy goat chin. It was impossible to imagine her countenance had ever approached commonplace, and now her wild, white hair seemed particularly disheveled as separate tufts stood erect on the crown of her head, the look of it vaguely reminiscent of Christopher Lloyd's interpretation of Dr. Emmett Brown, a brilliant, but eccentric character in one of Ozzie's favorite movies of all time: *Back to the Future.*

Did the Spirit Rapper have some scientific talent as well? Did a machine resembling the infamous flux capacitor reside somewhere inside her grandfather clock, or was she completely unaware her husband was most likely flipping through time like a disoriented butterfly fluttering from place to place, unable to return to the present?

As Ozzie stared at Mrs. Drummond's discombobulated hair, she raised her hands to her head, patted down the untamed hairs, and explained she'd been working in the garden prior to his arrival and hadn't thought to make herself presentable before opening the door; an explanation he may have readily accepted if the sun were still shining. What was she doing in her garden this time of night? Burying bodies? Or, worse, *re*burying them?

Granted, even Ozzie would recognize such an absurd thought as a paranoid suspicion under normal circumstances, but it suddenly occurred to him his mother had noted, on more than one occasion, that Janice Ballencroft had no love lost for Agaritha Drummond. As well as sharing an obvious terror with everyone else in town where the gifted Spirit Rapper was concerned, Mrs. Ballencroft had an apparent ongoing rivalry with Mrs. Drummond at the state fair, gardening competitions, or some such nonsense. What if the prevailing assumption that Marcus Ballencroft had committed his wife's murder wasn't true at all? What if someone else killed her, someone looking to win an unencumbered blue ribbon, someone unearthing god-knows-who in her garden beneath a moonlight cloak?

It wasn't entirely inconceivable to surmise the bodies of Marcus and Carla Ballencroft might be fertilizing an award-winning garden. This would certainly explain why Mrs. Drummond had never offered her psychic services to locate the missing members of the family. She knew exactly where they were.

Devil's Edge

A burst of cackled laughter broke the silence and Ozzie's face flushed. Had Mrs. Drummond read his mind, or was she laughing at something else? Perhaps she had simply reacted to his rude, wide-eyed interrogation of her unconventional appearance. With a terse shrug of the shoulders he decided it prudent to check back later with his thoughts on the Ballencroft murder. For now, he had other issues to deal with.

File in hand, he sat on a nearby divan and considered the gentlest way to explain his theory. Professor Drummond was alive, but trapped in another dimension, unable to return without help. Most likely, Mrs. Drummond would react with complete disbelief and, if not, she might feel shocked or hurt by the outlandish assertion. What if she misconstrued Ozzie's intentions and retaliated by reporting the hour of his death? Tugging at his wet collar, he wrestled with the dilemma.

Mrs. Drummond lowered herself into an oversized lounge chair next to the divan. "Have ya figured it all out?"

Opening his mouth to speak, he uttered a fractured bray, a sound normally issued from the mouth of a dying donkey. Clearing his throat, he struggled to collect his thoughts.

"I can put the kettle on for a nip a tea," she suggested, her gaze emanating concern.

Ozzie raised his hand in a manner meant to suggest it unnecessary. "No thank you."

"Mrs. Drummond," he started, determined to spit out what he needed to say before his last ounce of courage failed. "Scientists around the globe are racing to find a way to travel faster than the speed of light. Because, you see, if someone accomplishes this, we could travel back in time and tell nosy school nurses to keep their ugly comments to themselves, or rig up a confetti machine before a worried father tries to hit a home run with the head of a not-so-bright boy consumed by lust. We could make sure dastardly things like broccoli and asparagus are never invented." Strength returned to his voice, his excitement mounting like a gospel preacher caught in the heated throngs of a thrilling sermon, his tempo increasing with his passion for the possibilities. "We could speed up the progression of humanity by introducing the music of The Beatles to Attila the Hun's troops; get more Terminator movies on the market by ensuring a certain actor is never elected to office in California but sticks to what he does best. We could do away with all the great atrocities committed throughout history, and get front row tickets for Christina Aguilera concerts. You need to understand how important it is to win this race; it could mean the difference between eating chilidogs for dinner and staring at a plate of Duesseldorfer potato mushrooms. I don't know about you, but I can't stand mushrooms and the slightest attempt to speak the German language makes my throat raw."

Taking hold of the chair arms and shifting her weight, Mrs. Drummond reached to pat Ozzie on the knee. "A course. I ain't much on mushrooms, neither, but do ya know what those papers said?"

"That's what I'm getting at." He deliberately avoided eye contact, still unsure of how she might react. "Please don't tell me when I'm going to die, but I am relatively sure your husband is traveling through time."

She grabbed the bib of her overalls, her white eyebrows reached for the ceiling, her tense lips went slack, and she laughed until tears welled in her eyes. Once she had blown out her last grunt of laughter, she pulled a handkerchief from the pouch of her pants, removed her eyeglasses, dabbed at her eyes, and carefully explained she meant no disrespect.

"I know that part, kiddo. What I don't know is what those messages said. Did ya figure 'em out?"

Partly shocked, mostly relieved, Ozzie nodded. "Yeah, that part was easy."

Mrs. Drummond squealed with delight and leaned forward. "What'd they say?"

"They said you should set your grandfather clock to thirteen."

A look of befuddlement washed over her face, and she suddenly appeared as though she were standing beneath a particularly gloomy rain cloud. "I'm supposed to what?"

"Set the clock to thirteen."

Devil's Edge

"Did the message say how?"

Ozzie lowered his chin. "No ma'am, it didn't."

She angled closer. "Was there anything else?"

Ozzie scooted further back on the divan and mumbled, "One other thing."

"Well, don't hold back on me, kiddo. What'd it say?"

The look of shear worry surging from the old lady's eyes made it clear she had no more idea for setting the bizarre clock to thirteen than Ozzie had, which made relaying the rest of the message as uncomfortable as jumping barefoot on a bed of nails.

Ozzie fiddled with his glasses and tugged at his drenched collar. "It said, 'hurry.'"

The Book of Trials

'Once again I have spent an entire day with ears burning as each cutthroat makes his claim to innocence. All the while, I cannot cease my obsession with the time wasted in pursuing Catti's captors. Bondye spare the moments required to recover her.'

Maurine closed The Book of Trials and excused herself, claiming a need to use the bathroom. Truth was, Fujo's detailed account of having watched her mother's severed head submerge beneath the sea, and her desire to jump overboard, proved more than overwhelming. There wasn't a dry face in room 207 as Maurine read the vivid account for Miss Flute and Jillian. It was all so unimaginable, so horrible, so leaches-sucking-on-your-eardrums evil.

Though they say humans are the most rational creatures on the face of the earth, Maurine knew very well what absolute demons some people were. Reading through Fujo's story cemented the concept deep inside her soul and sent a shiver racing up the back of her neck. Truthfully, her bladder wasn't the major concern; she simply thought it common courtesy to puke in private.

She returned from the bathroom fifteen minutes later and found *The Book of Trials* still resting on the chair where she left it. Miss Flute and Jillian lay perched defiantly with their backs to one another, red-faced and tight-lipped.

"If you two are still fighting over whether or not I'm too young to chase ghosts, throw a blanket over it and tuck it in," Maurine said, "I'm here, and I ain't goin' nowhere."

With more than a hint of frustration, Jillian wrestled with a sheet coiled around her legs. "Actually, I inquired about the book I originally went to the library to find, but my esteemed roommate insists it doesn't exist," Jillian shot an over-the-shoulder glare at Miss Flute, "Which is pure bullshit."

"The Ballencroft Book?" Maurine said, directing the comment half to herself, half to Jillian.

"That's the one."

"Shouldn't we focus on *The Book of Trials* and the ghosts Miss Flute mentioned? I mean, the Ballencroft murders happened years and years ago, this here thing with Fujo and whatnot is sitting right in our laps. One thing at a time, right? Barbecued rat rumps, who gives a hoot about the Ballencroft murders?"

"I do," Miss Flute shouted, her face sharply twisting away from the wall. "Carla Ballencroft was my best friend and if I could do anything to shed light on her disappearance, I would not hesitate. If I say there is no such thing as a Ballencroft Book, then there is, absolutely, no such thing."

"Hold your panties," Maurine squealed. "You were friends with Carla Ballencroft?"

"We did everything together," the librarian said, a fresh batch of tears welling in her eyes, "studying, pajama parties, swimming, camping, horseback riding, hanging out at the soda shop, laughing, planning...we were going to become airline stewardesses. We even had matching diaries. I have never recovered from her loss." She planted her face in her pillow, her shoulders heaving as she blubbered and wailed, her fists driving into the mattress.

Stepping beside the librarian's bed, Maurine rubbed Candace's shoulder and patted her on the head. "I'm so sorry. If they gave out awards for saying the wrong thing at the wrong time, I suppose I'd have a date with a guy named Oscar every night for the rest of my life."

Seemingly startled, Jillian yelled, "Wait a minute," her voice suddenly sharp and clear. She had apparently intended to join Maurine at the side of Miss Flute's bed, but when her feet hit the floor, the tubes stuck in her nose worked like a well-tossed lasso, yanking her head back so forcefully it looked as though it might snap off. The oxygen tank parked behind the bed tipped forward, its nose clanging against the bedframe. Jillian sat back down, ripped the oxygen line from her face, and in the time it takes a cat to flick its tail, hovered over Miss Flute's lanky frame. "Did you just say Carla Ballencroft kept a diary?"

Wiping her nose with a loose sheet corner, the librarian sat up, "Y-you don't think..."

Caught in the throngs of her sudden revelation, Jillian insisted, "If there isn't a Ballencroft book at the library, what else could it be?"

The color in Miss Flute's cheeks bleached away, her expression pained by the prospect. "Who told you about this alleged book?" She asked, pressing her hand to her stomach; her cheeks bloated, her lips squeezed together like a stubborn vice. It looked as though her lunch had come dangerously close to losing residence.

The room grew silent enough to hear a flea burp as Jillian and Miss Flute stared at one another through anxious eyes.

Jillian's reluctant reply broke the silence. "Mrs. Drummond."

The librarian tightly embraced her waist as her head thumped back into the pillow, her eyes closing in slow motion, her words released in a hushed whisper, "Holy shit."

Growing a Fair Pair

Not for the slightest moment did Ozzie consider the possibility of saying no to Mrs. Drummond when she asked for help with setting the grandfather clock to thirteen. In a perfect world, the old woman never would have asked for his assistance in the first place. But, in the real world, gravity exists for no other reason than to prove the entire universe sucks.

It was late, half past ten. Listening to the rumble of passing traffic and the sound of his shoes scuffling over the sidewalk, Ozzie counted the cement blocks in cubic meters, simultaneously attempting to ascertain the solar caloric output (1.94 calories per square centimeter per minute), which approached zero since the sun had set more than two hours ago. Lifting his face to the sky, he searched for Ganymede, one of Jupiter's moons, but a thin strip of cloud cover obscured the area of the sky where the largest moon in the solar system could be found, and Ozzie suddenly realized that he, too, was not where he should be and would need a good excuse for being out so late. This constituted a major problem, as no one in Devil's Edge feared Mrs. Drummond more than his mother.

A few years back, the local radio station aired a program they called: *Delving into the Sixth Sense* and, as Ozzie's mother stood at the kitchen sink scrubbing a stubborn frying pan, she grunted her disapproval for the show's content by repeatedly stating, "That's what you think, Bucko." Her face flushed indignant, overwhelmed with the unmistakable fury that possessed her when she disagreed with what she heard. During a break in the show, a pair of tickets to an off Broadway production were offered to the tenth caller, and without stopping to rinse the soap suds off her hands, she swooped up the telephone and began punching the redial button. Once she had forced the call through, she courteously accepted the tickets and then, before the DJ knew what hit him, she blurted, "The Lord God Almighty will cast His fist and smite every living person in Devil's Edge with fire and brimstone, this whole town will turn into a pillar of salt if you don't stop this abomination. Psychic power can only come from deep within Satan's pockets."

Nope, no form of the truth would slip from Ozzie's lips when he walked through the front door tonight. Not only would he have to invent a story to account for his tardiness this evening, he might have to do so again when he returned to tinker with Mrs. Drummond's clock. Although he understood he would have to lie, the prospect did not sit lightly in his mind. No one on the face of the earth deserved his honesty more than his mother. So what if there was a nut or two in her box of crackers, she was a goddess, a pillar of strength and purity, a robust spirit full of love and support, an admirable monument to womanhood, but she would most likely implode before she exploded if he confessed to spending the last two hours anywhere near Scabbard Street. Still, lying to her seemed akin to thrusting a seppuku sword into his gut, its tip soaked in blasphemy.

How had he gotten himself into such a predicament?

A grown man would have stood his ground and said enough is enough; a grown man wouldn't hesitate to say no. Unfortunately, Ozzie couldn't see his impending manhood anywhere on the horizon. He stood still on the sidewalk, briefly pausing to wonder how long it would take to grow a fair pair.

No disrespect intended to the fellow currently occupying the throne, but if Ozzie were God, he would have designed the body to grow in concordance with the mind; the higher the IQ, the denser the muscle mass. No more multimillion-dollar sports contracts for guys who think the theory of relativity determines how many people show up at a family reunion.

If Professor Drummond had in fact created a portal for time travel, then Ozzie faced one of the greatest opportunities of his lifetime. The only way he could know for certain meant going back to Scabbard Street to have a look inside that clock, dissect it if need be. If setting the clock to thirteen somehow afforded a way for the Professor to return home, perhaps the old chap would show his gratitude by allowing Ozzie to take it for a spin. He could shoot the breeze with Albert Einstein on a lazy Sunday afternoon, or travel to Manhattan's Central Park West to remove the revolver in Mark David Chapman's raincoat pocket and replace it with an unloaded banana. More importantly, the Nobel Peace Prize loomed within sight.

First he would have to convince his parents he'd spent the last two hours studying Harry Rittenhower's embedded vestige in the floor tiles at Pop's soda shop and apologize for having lost track of the time.

Rounding the last corner toward home, he focused on a light flickering in the kitchen window and paused to consider the gravity of his situation. His parents were still awake, probably waiting with a swat team at the door, machine guns poised and ready to shoot him down for being an evil little twit. He deserved it; he was prepared to deliver an outright lie to the two people responsible for his very existence. The words resting upon his tongue tasted like betrayal sautéed with broccoli and asparagus.

Scheming

Bullwinkle had played yet another brilliant game of chess, leaving Alexander Spotswood IV to wonder why he bothered to move the first pawn; he hadn't won a game against the wily moose in months. There would come a day when Bullwinkle's faculties weren't quite so sharp—a sinus infection or a bothersome case of tick fever—and Alexander would be there with a tight rein on his knight, ready to disembowel the black king.

Alexander cuffed the beast smartly on the back of the head, took one last swig of his Jack, twisted the cap back on, and stuffed the bottle into the pocket of a ragged jacket hanging near the door. Only half a bottle remained and it would have to last another two weeks, perhaps more, depending on the government's unreliable schedule. His social security checks arrived later each month. Oh, he knew very well what the bureaucrats were up to with their calculated tardiness; the bastards were drawing interest on his money. Granted, they had allotted him only four hundred and fifty dollars per month, but multiply that number by the hundreds of thousands of people who draw social security and the profit-ridden picture begins to grow much larger. Those gadflies winning votes with their starched and pressed smiles might live like dignitaries, but they were lowlife pirates, every last one.

Stripping down to a pair of flannel shorts, he unfolded the sleeping bag that had served him for the past twelve years. Carefully inspecting the split seams near the zipper, he poked at the streams of escaping polyester until most of it returned to the cavities it had oozed from. No denying it, he would soon have to invest in new bedding. Then again, perhaps his days of sleeping on split wooden slats were nearly over.

Fate had donned a smug grin the day the library dungeon burst into flames, chasing the librarian from her overbearing roost, and Alexander had enjoyed a week's long search, unencumbered. Time was of the essence, what with the young Anne Bonny making an unfortunate appearance. Drat, the youngster and the librarian had survived the onslaught—a bucket of bad luck, that—but as long as he didn't have a set of prying eyes peering over his shoulder every thirty seconds, the sun would shine more brightly. Hopefully, the gangly inquisitor and the Bonny heir would spend a good amount of time in the hospital. In the librarian's absence, her secrets could not remain forever concealed and Blackbeard's booty would at last come to its rightful owner. He and Bullwinkle would purchase a new estate, complete with regal furniture, perhaps even hire a butler; wouldn't it be nice to have someone to fetch a pipe and slippers along with a chilled glass of high-end gin. He would sleep in a raised bed six mattresses high, his crooked bones singing with relief.

For now, he must retire promptly. Earlier that evening, he overheard a fellow on the arson squad say they were scheduled to finish their investigation in the morning; this would afford him his first opportunity to steal down the stairs into the dungeon where he was sure to locate whatever the librarian had been guarding so adamantly. She almost certainly possessed something connected to the treasure and, as such, never had a right to keep the information to herself in the first place. With any luck, her spoil would lead him to the artifacts. He had only to arrive bright and early, before the librarian's assistant showed up; no telling what might happen if she got in the way.

Backwoods Justice

Constipated gorillas in uniforms hoping to turn first offenders into lampshades guard the majority of the courtrooms in this country.

Brad Miller once had one of those apes literally breathing down his neck when he showed up at a Rhode Island court to protest a parking ticket. Apparently, he had transgressed when he whispered to his wife his hope that the proceedings wouldn't take long. No sooner had he breathed out the last word of his supplication than one of the lumbering oafs surged across the room and threatened to put him in jail for the night if he uttered one more sound. The testosterone-seething bailiff had managed to send Brad's liver sledging into his throat as he delivered the unexpected threat. Later (much later) it seemed to Brad the goon's dramatic overreaction had more to do with ego than anything else; some people crave the rush that comes with asserting power and control, harboring no concern for the toes they step on to achieve their emotional highs.

Brad had learned the lesson the hard way; a courtroom is like a minefield, it's best to walk gingerly and keep your thoughts to yourself.

Now, as he stood at the base of a marbled staircase leading to the miniature courthouse in Devil's Edge, he nervously glanced at his watch. They scheduled his case for eight-thirty a.m. and he arrived half an hour early, hoping to make a positive impression with his punctuality. He ascended the stairs, navigated a series of unmarked hallways, and stood before a large cumbersome door, marked 'Courtroom 1,' which incited a grunt of amusement. Clearly, the small building didn't have enough square footage for more than one courtroom. Taking a deep breath, he swung open the massive door, took one look at the Barnum and Bailey production staged inside, and immediately understood he'd stepped into a mound so deep only the presence of a twenty-ton dinosaur with a severe case of irritable bowel could fully explain it.

Naturally, he hoped the judicial system in Devil's Edge wouldn't turn out quite so bull and hammer as those up north, but the scene playing out before his eyes caused an instant regret for having hoped any such thing, and an obscure voice in the back of his mind taunted eerily: *Be careful what you wish for.*

A large walnut plaque hanging on the wall identified the presiding judge as one Harry Winthrop. The magistrate was an aged man who sat behind his bench wearing a scruffy white tee shirt with blue lettering that read, 'Myrtle Beach, S.C,' and he mindlessly toyed with a gavel constructed from the head of a shortened King Cobra golf driver. When he suddenly abandoned his chair, his expertly groomed salt and pepper head completely disappeared behind the massive oak bench, his stature akin to the scant frame of a horse jockey. The only evidence he hadn't taken complete leave of the courtroom came when a golf ball zipped past the corner of the bench, smacking into the jury box rail post.

"How much you pay for them golf lessons, Harry?" a bailiff sneered, his hands stuffed deep inside the pockets of his beige khakis, his flip-flops slapping against the floor as he sauntered around the official oak furnishings in search of the errant ball.

"Ain't you paid to mind your own business," the judge replied, his southern accent thicker than most, his high-pitched feminine voice lilted with lofty arrogance. Judging by the man's overall demeanor, Brad automatically assumed the moniker, 'Harry,' short for 'Harriet.'

"Crack open a box of them Callaways," the judge said, "they roll better on wood."

A middle-aged woman filing her nails at the court reporter's station raised her hand high into the air, the way an excited child eager for show-and-tell might. "Actually, Harry, Dunlop balls are much better for negotiating smooth surfaces. Donny Baker once made a three hundred yard putt with a Dunlop. He was shootin' the glossy floor down at the Stop and Save. That ball sailed clean from the deli all the way over to frozen food without so much as a hiccup...dropped in the cup like a gopher on his weddin' night."

The judge ambled out from behind the bench swinging the shaft of his putter as if he were twirling a baton and approached the stenographer. Using his club for a cane, he stood there, casually leaning, until he unexpectedly thrust his hips forward in an obscene gesture. "Pooh, pooh! Who asked for your opinion, Margie? What in hell do women know about golf?" He snickered and turned toward the gallery, suddenly aware Brad awaited the court's attention. Employing the delicate motion of a highfalutin woman hosting the annual fashion show, he flicked his wrist toward the only person in the room wearing a suit and tie; a fellow with his upper body slouched over the defendant's table looking as though he had an award-winning hangover.

"Counselor, is this your client?"

Without turning to make a proper identification, the woozy man nodded.

"What's he here for?" Winthrop asked, strolling back to his bench, his hips swaying a defined wiggle.

The counselor flipped open a file resting at his fingertips and cleared his throat, "Assault and battery, your honor."

"*Ooooh,* a hardened criminal. We don't get nearly enough of those. Spill the beans."

"Says here he attacked Teddy Teach, Jr. with a baseball bat...put his lights out."

Hopping up onto his chair, Judge Winthrop grabbed a swatch of black fabric from behind the bench and wrapped it around his shoulders, "Oh, yeah. If I remember right, Garrison was fit to be tied...called me personally to request the death penalty."

Sputtering a girlish giggle, he dropped his chin on the back of his unturned hands, his fingers interlaced, wriggling with excitement. Despite a dark tan, age spots, and deeply imbedded wrinkles, his demeanor resembled that of a tyke who had just spied his first dragonfly. He stared across the courtroom, his gleaming eyes relishing in the way he had shocked his prey.

Brad was horrified. Coming to Devil's Edge was like walking into a nest of army ants, nearly every encounter with a local resulting in another piercing bite in the ass. Even if the judge had issued a lighthearted joke at Brad's expense, the mere mention of the death penalty set him on edge. He squirmed in the gallery pew, his leg bobbing up and down in an attempt to churn through the wooden floor, wondering if his court appointed counsel, a man he had never seen before in his life, would offer some defense and at least provide two sides of the story. When the deadbeat counselor made no further remarks, Brad stood in protest.

"If I may, your honor..."

Outraged, the judge slammed his makeshift gavel and charged to his feet, red-faced, "No you may not. This is my court, Gomer, and if you don't sit yourself down, I'll cite you with contempt."

Sufficiently startled, Brad sulked back into his pew and began to fume, his mind wrapped around thoughts of gorillas, mine fields, and twenty-ton dinosaurs with oozing orifices. Didn't he have enough trouble with his daughter in the hospital—nearly having lost her life in a fire, his son screaming in his sleep every night, and his job at the UAB put on hold until the outcome of this trial was determined? If he had listened to his children when they begged him to return home after their very first night in this miserable little town, none of this would have happened.

Judge Winthrop remained silent as he played a game of stretch-and-twist-your-face, his lips protruding like a large carp fish, his eyes revolving in their sockets, crossing and uncrossing, his tongue darting in and out of his mouth: absolutely nerve-wracking, and too much like watching an old Jerry Lewis movie. Appalling really, to think a man's life rested in the hands of a nutter whose psychiatrist had clearly failed him.

The blades of an overhead ceiling fan whirred and clicked, whirred and clicked, a soft wheeze emanating from its asthmatic motor.

Finally, the judge's voice pierced the room with restored enthusiasm. "The defendant is sentenced to one hundred hours community service to be served as a costumed mascot at the Winthrop Wiener House. As long as he doesn't mind acting like a hotdog, it shouldn't hurt to look like one for a few hours. Case closed." He slammed his gavel with a dramatic flick of the wrist and picked up a fly reel, apparently intent on doing some indoor fishing.

Once Brad recovered from the surprise of receiving a light sentence, he reminded himself that when something seems too good to be true, it's usually toxic waste camouflaged in a bubble gum wrapper. All this talk about hardened criminals and the death penalty and then—*poof*—a slap on the wrist. Something was amiss; a piece of the puzzle hadn't slipped into place.

The judge mentioned he had spoken with the sheriff about the case; he must have known more than he let on. And, since it seemed obvious Winthrop was fully aware Brad had simply protected his family from potential intruders, he had no business imposing a sentence of any type. So, why hadn't he dismissed the case? Brad gasped when the striking realization suddenly arrived: *Winthrop's* Wiener House...Judge Harry *Winthrop*. The puzzle melded. The hotdog house must be a family owned business and Winthrop had just gained one hundred hours of free advertising at the height of tourist season. This was a classic case of bend over and insert shaft. Brad lurched for the gallery rail, his face burning with indignation. "I object, your honor!"

"Counselor," Winthrop admonished without taking his eyes off the fly he whipped across the room, his fishing pole whistling as it sliced through the air, "you ought to inform your client I like my wieners burnt to a southern fried crisp."

Devil's Edge

Half Baked

No one in Devil's Edge bakes a rhubarb pie to perfection the way Velma Sinclair does. Oh, plenty attempt, and plenty fail. For every blue ribbon Agaritha Drummond won at the state fair for gardening, Velma had two for baking. In fact, old Aggy-hag couldn't bake a pie to save her life. Amused, Velma chortled and lifted a hot cup of herb to her lips. She sipped, drawing in a long, satisfying breath of air filled to overflowing with the rich, sweet-and-sour scent of rhubarb. Glancing at the timer on the oven, she noted her masterpiece had five minutes left to bake.

The cockatiels busily preened one another and had already done an exceptional job of crapping on the large photograph that had, only a few hours before, donned the front page of *The Coastal Review*: a picture of Candace Flute and Jillian Miller recovering at Mercy General. Precisely the reason Velma had spent a large part of her morning preparing Wolf's Bane roots; she harvested them immediately after hearing about the fire at the library and had treated them more delicately than newborn children. They weren't completely dry, they could have stood another week or two, but once the roots spent a few hours in the oven, they were dry enough to grind into a fine powder and ready to make an interesting, although tasteless, addition to her rhubarb recipe. One pinch leaves a man paralyzed, double the dose and he stands face-to-face with St. Peter. Velma had dropped four tablespoons into the mix. Her plan was flawless, and to that she toasted, lifting her teacup to no one in particular, grinning like a mountain bear with fresh honey drizzling over its chin.

Once she finished her tea and took the pie out of the oven to cool, she carefully assembled the pastry box and reached for the black magic marker she used to write her inscription: *"To Candace Flute and Jillian Miller, with hopes for a full recovery. Love, Agaritha Drummond."*

Velma's daughter, Lavender, would take the special gift to the hospital and leave it at the nurse's station. Some unknowing fool would deliver it, and that meddling librarian and her Yankee sidekick would get just what they deserved.

Digger Spotswood was next on Velma's list if he didn't drop dead, a victim of his own body stench before she could get to him.

A woman makes certain sacrifices to protect her family name, ain't nothin' more important.

30 Bones

Ozzie arrived at the hospital bearing his box of *30 Bones* and, except for taking a lengthy amount of time to explain the rules of the game, he seemed unusually quiet and preoccupied. Jillian thought it odd the boy hadn't jumped into her lap, or attempted to drive her nuts with his motor-mouth tirades. She assumed he would have a million questions about the fire, or, at the very least, offer another neurotic platitude about giantism. He sat cupping his chin in the palm of his hand, the way young boys do when they're bored out of their minds, except this boy seemed extremely troubled. Jillian quickly surmised his silence was just as unnerving as his senseless chatter.

Later, when she asked about it, Maurine explained her mother had insisted Oz come along with her to the hospital, it was Mrs. Teach's way of dragging him away from whatever occupied him in the basement, if only for a few hours. Bringing *30 Bones* along was Maurine's idea and although it seemed to brighten Ozzie's demeanor slightly, it hadn't excited him quite as much as anticipated. Maurine couldn't really say what went on inside Ozzie's head, and with a giggle, she added, "We'd need a big ol' nutcracker to get an answer for that."

30 Bones was, more or less, a guessing game, but not as easy for Jillian as she had initially hoped. Each player held fifty colored pegs (called 'bones') to begin with and had a hiding-board called 'the gallows' with ten small hooks attached to the back, to which they affixed a number of colored pegs and kept them hidden until the other players guessed how many bones were lurking behind the board. The player hiding the bones was the dealer and each of the remaining players guessed, in succession, how many bones the dealer had hung. If any of the players guessed, within one, the number of bones the dealer had hidden, that player got to steal three of the dealer's bones. If a player guessed exactly how many bones the dealer had hidden, they got to steal that exact amount from the dealer's stash, three bones remaining the minimum spoil. Elimination occurred when players lost all their bones. The first player to stack thirty bones, without having them fall down, won the game. Not only was it a twisted guessing game, it also involved stacking skill, as the way the bones were shaped made it difficult to set them one on top of the other. A good sense of geometry played heavily; if a player's stack fell over, he or she must return the bones to their original owner (each player had a colored die sitting at the base of their gallows matching the color of their bones, eliminating any confusion as to what color belonged to whom).

Candace Flute kicked butt on the guessing, but couldn't keep her stack from falling over. Farsighted and at a loss without her glasses, (her appearance had improved dramatically), she simply couldn't see well enough to stack the bones properly. A frustrated grimace spread over her face as she watched Maurine expertly stack seven bones without so much as a flutter, and the librarian's sour demeanor didn't brighten any when Maurine quipped she and Ozzie had once spent nearly seven hours dueling through a single game of 30 Bones.

Jillian had little to worry about when it came to stacking bones as she had yet to win any. Her turn to deal, she took a lengthy amount of time to dangle bones on three of the hooks. Figuring if there were only three bones to lose, it wouldn't be so bad if someone guessed the right amount, and taking the extra time to set them up might cause the others to guess too high a number.

Having also noticed the vast improvement in the librarian's un-bespectacled appearance, Maurine piped up to say, "Miss Flute, now that you lost your glasses, maybe you want to think about gettin' some contact lenses."

Candace blushed slightly but retorted with a cutting tone, "Who wouldn't want to start their day by poking themselves in the eyeball?"

"Hmm," Maurine uttered, thinking it over, "Maybe laser surgery?"

Candace made no attempt to hide her sarcasm. "Marvelous idea, Miss Teach, and I will gladly comply once you've written a check for the proper amount."

While Jillian fumbled with her bones, Maurine apparently decided to drop the corrective lens issue and explained to the players, "If you can catch a peek at how many bones a player still has in their stash, it's easier to guess how many they're hidin'. It doesn't work so great at the beginning of the game, but toward the end, it comes in mighty handy." Candace nodded, but Jillian could tell by the empty look in the librarian's eyes she would rather read *The Book of Trials* than waste her time losing a game of *30 Bones*.

Ozzie had stitched together six brightly colored satchels for bone storage, but since there were only four players, he set the orange and yellow satchels aside. The youngest Teach pointed out that only the winner gets to keep their bones in the Golden Skull while everyone else must return their sets to the lowly satchels. He tapped his finger on the crest of a wooden skull he had carved and sprayed with gold leaf paint. Not the best sculpture Jillian had ever seen, but impressive for a boy his age. Finished with her extended time ruse, she indicated her readiness for the others to guess how much booty she had hidden. Ozzie guessed six, Maurine guessed seven, and Candace, barely paying attention, said, "Three." When Jillian turned her gallows around for the others to see, Ozzie and Maurine groaned and Candace sighed, apparently not at all confident in her ability to stack the three bones she had just pirated. This time, however, Candace's bones fell cleanly together and stayed where she had stacked them, extracting from her a slight, but satisfied grin.

Devil's Edge

They were a couple hours into the game when Jillian's brother, Whitt, traipsed into room 207 and said, "Hey, watcha doin'?" Ozzie waded through another slow explanation of the game, after which he offered Whitt the yellow satchel.

"No, no," Candace said. "Take my place. I'd like to rest a while."

Whitt, seeing that Candace had built up a slight edge in the game, didn't give it a second thought and slipped into her chair as she retired to her hospital bed.

Jillian watched from the corner of her eye as Candace carefully pulled *The Book of Trials* from beneath her sheets and covered it with the hospital's complimentary copy of the *Holy Bible*. She inched the imbedded book closer and closer to her nose, her eyes squinting so tightly, it became pitifully obvious she couldn't see a solitary letter looming less than a half-inch from her face.

Maurine had just guessed ten in a bid to win Whitt's hidden bones and Jillian guessed one, surmising Whitt would be too much of a coward to lose much more than that, and Ozzie took the middle road, guessing four. Whitt groaned and turned his board around. Maurine squealed. He had, in fact, hidden ten bones and Maurine had hit the mother lode.

Ultimately eliminated from the game, Jillian sat staring aimlessly out the window, wondering how long she would have to stay in the hospital. She was healing quickly and felt as though she couldn't stand another day cooped up inside, a prisoner of misfortune. Whitt, quickly eliminated from the game, joined Jillian at the window and showed her a nest of pictures stored on his dysfunctional cell phone, photographs of their father pouting in the street outside Winthrop's Wiener House, dressed like an honest-to-god hotdog, complete with relish, mustard, and ketchup. The images were hilarious, but just photographs. Jillian preferred to witness the spectacle in person. Perhaps, after his outright humiliation, her father would not be so stubbornly reluctant to pack up his pickles and get out of Deliverance. Jillian still had enough time to return to Rhode Island and prepare for the national dance competition. She couldn't say for sure if her scorched lungs would carry her through her routine, but she wanted to try.

"Has he said anything about going home?"

"Nope," Whitt muttered. "He's more stubborn than ever, if you ask me."

Jillian pounded a fist on the window sash and growled.

Whitt's face twisted into a map of frustration. "He starts work at the UAB on Monday. The freaking closet is still bleeding." His chubby cheeks washed white. "We're screwed."

Oh yes, they were nailed to the wood, cemented to the floor, squirming six feet under. Brad Miller still didn't have half an idea what was going on, and Jillian wasn't sure how much good it would do to fill him in. Half of what she would say, he wouldn't believe, and the other half, she wasn't sure *she* believed. If she couldn't convince her father to leave, she would have no choice but to attempt to exorcise the evils of Devil's Edge on her own. The very idea of it left an aching void inside her chest and a twist of nausea curling through her intestines. This town had nearly been the end of her once already, God only knew what would happen if it took another swing.

"How many hours are left on his community service?"

Whitt stuffed his cell phone into his pants pocket. "He's got, like, eighty more hours, but the Judge only wants him on the weekends. He's good to go for work on Monday." Leaning forward with an intensified glare, Whitt took on a stern tone, "You know I hate your guts to hell and back, but I would appreciate it if you didn't give Dad another reason to drink himself into oblivion. I still have a shot at a decent childhood if you stop trying to get yourself killed. Besides, you're hogging all the limelight."

Maurine let loose with an energetic yowl, and Jillian turned her head toward the small game table set up in the middle of the room. Maurine had confiscated all the bones and jumped to her feet, raising her hands to the ceiling until they indicated a touchdown, a triumphant look beaming over her face. She wasted no time in depositing her set of red bones into the Golden Skull.

Jillian released a heavy sigh. Once her father immersed himself in his work, getting his attention would be akin to sending a message to the end of the universe and waiting thirty billion years for the reply. She needed to consider the options outside her father's influence; he would never listen. It was time to form a strategy, get off defense and think about offense, time to own the advantages, if there were any.

Ozzie packed up his game gear and tucked the box beneath his armpit. He and Whitt promised Jillian they would walk the dogs, said good-bye, and took their leave.

Jillian pulled a chair to the side of Candace Flute's bed and demanded to know everything about the Ballencroft murder.

A Tempting Morsel

A perfectly baked rhubarb pie sat on the edge of the counter at the nurse's station at Mercy General. Doctors and nurses were all abuzz with the frantic activity involved in preparing for incoming patients: the surviving crew of a large fishing rig that had been lost at sea for several days. A medivac would fly in the six men who had washed up on the sands of Ocracoke Island.

Eleanor Finwicket tried to tie down one of the nurses long enough to ask which room her friend, Sally Dibble, had been assigned after suffering a mini-stroke the night before, but couldn't seem to get a word in edgewise. The pie on the counter caught Eleanor's attention. She shuffled closer to the edge of the counter, inhaling deeply as she drew near, and leaned in to read the inscription on the box. Funny, who would've thought Agaritha Drummond could bake such an enticing morsel? People knew the witch on Scabbard Street better for her gardening genius. Then again, hadn't she already signed one contract with the Devil in order to obtain the evil powers she currently possessed? Who's to say she hadn't signed another?

Eleanor traced her white-gloved fingers gently over the edges of the pastry box. What an absolute waste, delivering such a delectable treat to Jillian Miller, the very murderess who had avoided a life sentence simply because her victim wasn't quite dead. Why, the little trollop had probably set fire to the library as well, trying to eradicate evidence that would have most certainly convicted her, but not smart enough to get out of the library before she became trapped in her own ambush. Now, the law wouldn't hold her accountable, and worse, *The Coastal Review* hailed her survival as a miracle. What an outrage. God help those denizens of Devil's Edge who couldn't see the ocean for the sea. The irony and the absurdity!

Eleanor emptied a handful of magazines from her tote bag and surveyed the empty space inside; plenty enough room to hold the pie. As a twinge of guilt began to creep along her spine, she shooed it away as if it were an annoying fly. She simply couldn't think of anyone who deserved this scrumptious delectable less than *The Red Skunk*: a perfect title for the likes of Jillian Miller.

Since Candace Flute had the unfortunate disposition to share a room with an axe murderer, and probably wouldn't live past her next nap, why waste a perfectly good pie on the poor woman?

In fact, Eleanor's tea guests would appreciate a rhubarb pie more than anyone she could imagine. Since Sally Dibble could no longer host the social, what with being in the hospital and all, Mitzy Hammond had asked Eleanor if she wouldn't mind. The ladies would amass at the Finwicket estate in less than three hours and this pie would fit in with the menu rather nicely. Eleanor would simply say she had finagled the recipe from Velma Sinclair (everyone knows what a magnificent baker Velma is) and that would cause quite a buzz, as everyone would want to know how Eleanor had managed to secure one of Velma's prize-winning recipes in the first place. She would invent a story to dazzle them all.

The box was almost in Eleanor's grasp when one of the nurses slipped behind the counter. "Oh, what's this?" She said, turning the pastry parcel around to read the inscription. Lifting her face, she cooed, "What a nice thing for Aggy to do. I'll take this down to 207 right away, while it's still warm. Lordy be, who could resist such a heavenly smell?" The nurse whisked the box away and left Eleanor standing stiff and stunned, feeling rather stupid for having taken so long to decide to pilfer the pie, and still without a clue as to which room they'd stuffed old Sally in.

Chiming In

Ruby and Merlin seemed to appreciate the walk from Billard Way to the soda shop and back, tales wagging, tongues drooping beneath the weight of the heat, eyes gleaming with satisfied weariness. Ozzie handed Ruby's leash to Whitt, saying he had things to do and rushed off to Scabbard Street.

A pitcher of iced-tea sat on the table in Mrs. Drummond's living room and she'd set up a plate of pastries. Once again, she had anticipated Ozzie's visit, even though he hadn't called ahead.

"I'm sorry," he said, flustered, "Did I interrupt?"

Mrs. Drummond expelled an unchecked chortle. "Don't be so silly. Would ya like tea now, or later?"

Ozzie slipped his fingers nervously over his tie, thinking he probably should have anticipated Mrs. Drummond's keen sense of timing. Then again, he would probably never acclimate to the likes of Mrs. Drummond, no matter how many times this sort of thing might happen; the woman was a mind-bending freak of nature and nothing else.

Crossing the threshold, he moved immediately toward the clock and asked if he might inspect it more closely. Extending a hand to lead the way, Mrs. Drummond joined him beside the clock.

"Has Mr. Drummond ever been in the military?" Ozzie inquired.

"Dern tootin'. Long before I met him...did his time in Stuttgart, Germany."

Ozzie snapped his head sharply toward her, "Really? He speaks German, then?"

"That 'un and ten other befangled languages."

Ozzie blushed, "I apologize for mocking the German language last time we spoke."

"Oh, pay it no mind," Mrs. Drummond chuckled.

Reaching for the handle on the door covering the face of the clock, Ozzie found it locked.

"Is there a key?"

Without answering, Mrs. Drummond waddled off into the kitchen, brought back a stepladder, and ascended it, her hand groping over the clock's head until she retrieved a bright, golden key, which she handed to him.

Once they traded places on the ladder, Ozzie twisted the key and snapped open the small door, tracing the face of the clock with his fingertips, searching for oddities. He wondered what the exquisite timepiece was worth. Faced in pure gold, a nest of inset diamonds and rubies encircled each number from one to twelve. If the jewels were real, they were worth a hefty fortune.

Gently, he moved the delicate hands of the clock until they were set at 1 pm, and stood back, waiting for a reaction. He nervously explained that, being in the military, Mr. Drummond may have meant for Mrs. Drummond to set the clock to thirteen-hundred hours, which was 1 pm, as opposed to literally setting it to 13. Mrs. Drummond's eyes twitched with a brief look of confusion, but she scooted away from the clock and stood beside Ozzie, holding her breath, fingertips pressed to her lips.

When, after a few minutes, nothing happened, she turned to say, "Is that it?"

Gaze still transfixed on the clock, body rigid with anticipation, Ozzie muttered, "Is that what? Oh...wait...yeah... I think so... I mean...we should wait."

"All righty," Mrs. Drummond whispered, "If'n we have to wait anyway...might as well have us some tea." Without averting her focus from the clock, she backed away, stepping around furniture like a stealthy spy, and settled into her plush chair, squeezing her oversized bottom between the armrests, leaning forward to snag the pitcher of iced-tea.

"I'd like to continue inspecting the clock, if it's not a problem," Ozzie said, his hand already reaching for the stepladder.

"No problem t'all." Mrs. Drummond raised her glass to her lips and when she thought Ozzie wasn't looking, she pulled a silver flask from her apron pocket and poured a large portion of its contents into her tea.

At the very top of the clock face, there loomed a set of embossed numbers set in a golden arch: 1-5-10-15-20-25-29. Curious, but for the 1 and 29, the numbers were all groups of five. What purpose, then, had the 1 and 29? As this section of the clock existed high above the actual time face (too far away for the clock hands to reach) the arched numbers obviously had nothing to do with calculating the exact time. What were they for, then, and why were most of them odd numbers? It occurred to him that 13 was also an odd number, and a burst of adrenaline rushed through his head as he contemplated the possibilities. Could this curious archway of numbers have something to do with setting the clock for a time warp? A familiar voice inside his head began to sing the glories of winning the Nobel, while a miniscule, not so familiar voice emanating from the deeper halls of his mind began to warn: *not so fast, not so fast...*

He ran his fingertip over the arch. "Do you know what these numbers are for?"

"Mmm hmm," Mrs. Drummond gulped down a mouthful of tea, "They's the days of the month. And that big ol' circle underneath is the moon."

Ozzie sighed. A perfectly normal explanation, and one he would have derived had he not over-reacted but took the time to inspect the two half-moon orbs resting at the left and right side of the moon base. When the clock is set right, the large moon in the middle moves every twenty-four hours and each movement slowly obscures until the half circles begin to eclipse, allowing observers to note the current moon phase. Ozzie's cheeks burned: how simple.

Below the archway, the actual clock face lay set inside a squared frame, engilded with delicate detailing; shapes of plant leaves and curly-q lines, fashioned to make it look as though these intricate metal elements had grown forward in an effort to embrace the circle of time: left and right, two smaller, silver circles. The one on the left was marked, 'Silent, Strike, and Night Off,' which Ozzie assumed were the settings for the chimes. The one on the right marked, 'Western, Silent, St. Mich., and Whitt.' were tone settings that determined the way the chimes sounded when they gonged. So far, he'd discovered nothing out of the ordinary.

A sixty-second dial nestled beneath the large number '12' clicked off the seconds, its tiny black arm racing around the silver orb as if chasing its tail. Positioned below the numbers 9 and 3, and above the number 6, were holes fashioned for a key crank that raised the chains cradling the pendulum weights. The massive, golden weights dropped periodically throughout the day and if not reset regularly, the clock would simply stop working. These weights were located in front of an ornate pendulum, which swayed back and forth like a lone dancer entranced in an unending waltz. Housed inside the enormous belly of the clock was a compartment large enough to hold two grown men, the pendulum and weights posing no risk of obstruction if someone were to step inside. But for its over-sized midsection, the timepiece seemed rather run-of-the-mill. And, since Ozzie had found nothing out of the ordinary about the clock's face, he determined to have a closer look inside the monstrosity, asking Mrs. Drummond's permission to climb aboard. She responded with an aroused nod.

A curious thought sideswiped him before he stepped inside. "Have you ever seen your husband inside this clock?"

She nodded, "Seen him step in, seen him vanish, and before I could blink, seen him step back out. Got what he went in for, too."

"And, what was that?" Ozzie had one foot inside the clock, the other cemented to the Persian rug beneath it.

"The Book a' Trials, a' course. Wanted to make sure it didn't fall into the wrong hands, see? So, he donated it ta the library."

Ozzie pulled his foot out of the clock's belly and crossed the room. "What is this book, and why did he want it?"

"It's a firsthand account of a pirate trial commencin' hundreds a' years ago, and it tells about an awful curse. Ebby donated it b'cause some might a' used it ta condemn, and we feel it's put ta better use if'n it's used ta forgive."

By way of her fast growing slur and increased drawl, Ozzie assumed Mrs. Drummond's tea might well be flammable. What's more, she had begun to sway in her chair. Shoving his hands deep into his pockets, he rocked on the heels of his shoes, absorbing what she'd said. "Condemn or forgive who?"

"Never you mind," she blurted, staring at her glass of iced-tea with a scowl, seemingly aware its contents were to blame for causing her to say too much in the first place. "Jist tell me how to set that man-swallowin' genie to 13."

Reluctant to let the juicy conversation go, but seeing the scowl on Mrs. Drummond's face had grown deep enough to cast a shadow over her eyes, he dropped the subject. "Do you have a flashlight?"

She pointed to the fireplace mantle where a large yellow flashlight rested on the far end. Ozzie grabbed it and stepped inside the belly of the clock. High up in the corners, he could see tiny reflections of light bouncing off the protruding eyeballs of a gaggle of dead flies caught in a tangle of large cobwebs. He moved the light slowly, combing over every inch of dark mahogany, intent to find the slightest crack or stain, searching for evidence of tampering. Despite his scanning, probing, poking and prodding, the clock refused to reveal its closely guarded secrets.

As Ozzie exited the clock, a large window in the living room shattered, shards of glass spraying in every direction. He barely felt a thing, but couldn't help noticing the large piece of saber-shaped glass deeply imbedded in his gut. The gash began to leak red, blood pouring over the glass and dripping onto his shoes. Looking to Mrs. Drummond, whose eyes had grown nearly as wide as her bottom, he attempted to reach for her, then rolled his eyes into the back of his head and fell to the floor.

Unraveling

Maurine Teach peered out the window and watched a wailing ambulance skid into the emergency drive at Mercy General, unaware the cargo it transported was the body of her younger brother.

Miss Flute recounted the story of Janice Ballencroft's murder, concluding that when no one heard from Marcus Ballencroft or his daughter after the murder, the law named Marcus as the prime suspect.

"But, I knew him," Miss Flute's facial muscles stiffened with conviction as she spoke, "and, yes, he was a drunk, but a *happy* drunk. Mr. Ballencroft wouldn't hurt a fly, much less a member of his own family."

Jillian ruffled her fingers through her short hair, as was her habit when frustrated. "Are you sure?"

"Of course. I made the same statement to the police at the time, but they had no respect for a teenager's opinion."

Maurine knew what it was like to have her word discredited due to age, and the thought caused her cheeks to flush pink with a touch of persistent anger. Miss Flute's unfortunate experience with the police might well have swayed her decision to allow Maurine to help with *The Book of Trials*. If so, Maurine meant to offer her no excuse for regret.

Turning away from the window, she threw herself into a chair beside Jillian. She had always believed what people said about the Ballencroft murder, that Marcus Ballencroft went insane and killed his wife, but hearing a different version from the mouth of someone close to the Ballencroft family completely unraveled her convictions. "Boiled bat brains in combat helmets, who do you suppose did it?"

"What I wouldn't give to know," Miss Flute muttered. "One thing's for sure, a body cannot chop itself up and jump into a box. If Marcus didn't do it—and he *didn't*—it had to be someone else."

"Was anyone else hanging around at the time, someone the police might have overlooked?" Jillian prodded. "Did the daughter have any boyfriends, a secret admirer maybe?"

Choking on the junk still wallowing in her lungs, Miss Flute grabbed a tissue from a box resting on the bedside table and spit up some nasty, dark-colored phlegm. "Excuse me," she muttered, and with a more determined tone, requested her purse.

Maurine opened a drawer on the bedside table, withdrew the librarian's purse, and handed it to her. An odd grin spread over Candace's face as she shuffled through her bag searching for her wallet, and Maurine wondered what had tickled her so. Miss Flute flipped through her wallet, squinting at its contents until she located an old photograph. Yanking it from its plastic compartment, she handed it to Jillian, a look of pure satisfaction beaming in her eyes. Maurine leaned over Jillian's shoulder and gawked at the faded image. It was small and compact, like a photograph taken inside a carnival booth, and most likely cut from a longer strip of photos. It revealed the face of a much younger Candace Flute, her Bambi eyes full of mischief, her face glowing soft and strikingly free of the sadness and lines of worry that had invaded over the years. With her head poised on Miss Flute's shoulder, a blonde bombshell of a girl with a magnetic smile beamed at the camera.

"Boys buzzed over Carla like bees on honey. Everyone wanted her attention, but she went steady with a boy named Dale Archer, a freshman at the University of North Carolina over in Wilmington. He died in a car accident about a month before the murder. Carla was devastated." Miss Flute raised her hand in protest before anyone could utter a word, "I know what you might be thinking...I thought the same thing...but I was wrong. The officer who investigated the accident found a case of beer in the back seat and six or seven empties up front. Dale was a party magnet. An eyewitness claimed he saw Dale's car swerving down 8A, running seventy miles an hour in a thirty mile an hour zone, which was also consistent with Dale's character; a stick of dynamite looking for a place to explode, a thrill seeker through and through."

Maurine sighed with disappointment.

"Anyone else?" Jillian asked.

Miss Flute nodded. "The police interrogated Donny Baker because he was pestering Marcus to put the house on the market. That's what real estate agents do, but there was some heightened suspicion because Donny seemed relentless, knocking on the door two or three times a week. When they questioned Baker, he said he persisted because he thought Marcus was an easy target given that he was rarely sober."

Jillian shifted her weight in her chair, "The police bought that?"

Miss Flute grunted, "You would too, if you knew Donny Baker. He's a crafty moneygrubber. Everyone believes he was just after a quick buck. Besides, he was the one who made the initial call to the police when no one at the Ballencroft house answered the door for two weeks in a row. The sheriff concluded it would be rather bizarre for a murderer to report evidence linked to his own crime."

Intrigued, Maurine piped up, "But doesn't Mr. Baker own the house now?"

"He does, but he bought it for back taxes, years after the fact."

Jillian's brow furled, "Anyone else?"

"Just Mrs. Drummond," Miss Flute coughed, her eyes rolling in their sockets as if the idea was preposterous.

Startled, Jillian flinched and reached to steady herself by placing a hand on Miss Flute's bedrail, "Mrs. Drummond?"

"Urban legend," Miss Flute retorted, her tone incredulous. "Janice Ballencroft and Agaritha Drummond were highly competitive at the state fair and, because Mrs. Drummond has a propensity for finding misplaced people but never ventured to offer an explanation for the whereabouts of Marcus and Carla

Ballencroft, people assume she had something to do with Janice's murder. It's pure, unsubstantiated speculation."

Relentless, Jillian pressed on, "Was there anything else, anything out of the ordinary...something strange or unexplained?"

Miss Flute suddenly turned her face toward the wall, curled and twisted her lips, her eyes darting from side to side.

Insistent, Jillian tugged on her arm, "What is it?"

Miss Flute reluctantly turned away from the wall, "I reported this to the police as well, but as I mentioned, my input wasn't worth diddly squat. I told them Carla had been spooked by something, and even though she repeatedly insisted it was nothing, I knew better." A look of grave seriousness had befallen Miss Flute and the color in her face bleached away. She paused, as if summoning inner strength and then, as quickly as it had washed away, the color returned to her cheeks, burning bright red. "Let me tell you, Carla Ballencroft didn't scare easy. Like Dale, she was an incurable daredevil...always looking for another thrill. Despite my desperate pleas, she rode shotgun with him when he went drag racing. I hated it... thought for sure she would get herself killed, but trying to tame Carla was like asking Evel Knievel to take up the cello. I didn't have the slightest chance to change her mind. But, a few months before the murder, I saw Carla's eyes quiver with fear for the very first time. Believe me when I say the look of it shook me to the bone. When I asked her what was wrong, she shrugged it off and remained as tight lipped as a turkey in November." Miss Flute shuddered and her voice waned, "I never did find out what had frightened her so."

Jillian relaxed in her chair and remained silent, seemingly contemplating the information. When she finally spoke, it was with a note of urgency. "Carla's diary might say what she was afraid of. It's probably the only chance we have to find out what really happened, right? Especially if Mrs. Drummond thinks it's important."

Before anyone could respond, a flustered nurse rushed into the room frantically beckoning for Maurine. "You best follow me.

Your momma's fit to be tied. Sorry to say, your brother's been stabbed."

Feeling as though the nurse had delivered a punch to the midsection, Maurine stumbled to her feet and slowly moved toward the door, arms outstretched, fingertips desperately searching for solid objects to cling to—bedrails, chairs, tables, door knobs—anything to keep her steady as she approached the beckoning nurse. Just as Maurine approached the doorway, a second nurse arrived, and, in stark contrast to the first, whimsically waltzed into the room, her smile radiating over a white pastry box perfectly balanced within her extended hands.

Vexing Spotswood

The flagstone comprising the dungeon floor at the Devil's Edge library lay covered with a thick coat of slimy black soot. A swarm of fire department officials had left a plethora of boot imprints and, by the looks of it, not a single inch of the dungeon had gone un-inspected. Intrusive soot also infected the walls, rising as high as eight feet off the floor in some areas, its embedded shadow glued to the stone, the images it projected dispersing over the walls like a burgeoning black blaze.

Impressed by the devastation, Alexander Spotswood eagerly commanded his flashlight beam, twisting and turning, this way, and that. As his eyes absorbed the grim sights, he feigned a whistle (having lost the ability to produce the genuine article due to severe dental issues). Stepping off the last of the new pine slats the fire department had nailed into place on the staircase, he drew his attention toward a long, dark corridor on the left. If his suspicions were correct, he was only moments away from securing the librarian's hidden spoil. His heartbeat quickened as he rushed over the mired floor, the smell of roasted wood and moldy stone infiltrating his nostrils as his respiration increased, his mind reeling with the thrill of the hunt.

The first door on the left hung ajar, singed, its lower panels reduced to little more than brittle charcoal. Pushing past, he stepped inside a storage chamber cluttered with boxes piled high to the ceiling, many of them scorched by the fire, some completely consumed, all of them waterlogged, compliments of the Devil's Edge fire department. Completing a brief inspection, he found nothing of interest here; nothing locked, and no sign of a container worthy to guard hidden valuables. Grunting, he turned out of the supply room and rushed through the corridor, stopping before the next chamber. It, too, was fire-charred. Wrenching the doorknob, he met with immediate resistance. A wily grin played at the corners of his lips. Lifting a boot off the floor, he cocked his leg back and thrust it at the door. With a loud bang, the door opened, slamming into the wall and bouncing back to meet Alexander's insistent boot.

A metal table centered inside the chamber rested above two overturned chairs, and standing erect against the wall, column after column of strongboxes. Kicking away one of the toppled chairs, Alexander bullied his way to the far wall and stood to face the repository, feverishly tugging at the locked encasements. Waves of exhilaration and frustration washed over him. Surely, this chamber held what he sought, but each of the drawers beneath his probing fingers remained stiff and unmoving. Tormented, he slammed the butt of his flashlight into the face of the cabinet, the encasement objecting with a loud metal roar, the flashlight tumbling to the floor upon impact.

The twisting beam of light spiraled as the metallic tube first hit the toe of his boot then rolled beneath the table, the beam threatening to cut out as it twitched and fluttered before steadying once again. Mumbling a poorly formed curse and grunting from the awkward exertion, he secured his snake-like silver braid by wrapping it around his neck and stooped to retrieve the tube of light. As he stood, his right shoulder caught the edge of the table and lifted its legs off the floor. Table askew, something slid from its surface and hit the flagstone with a thud and, following that announcement, a faint metallic clink.

The flashlight beam revealed an over-sized, soot-ridden book, fallen spine up, its cover spread over the floor in a wide yawn. As a mere book could not explain the metallic sound Alexander heard, he pushed it aside and slowly scanned the chamber floor, inch by empty inch, until at last, he discovered a small key. Rising up, the glint of his newly retrieved prize reflected in his eyes, he expelled a somewhat girlish giggle.

He found his mirth short-lived as the key stubbornly refused to fit inside any of the keyholes on the first column and remained just as obstinate as the rest. Alexander frantically jabbed at keyholes, convinced—despite all evidence to the contrary—the key he held in his hand was not worthless. Breathing a heavy sigh, he scanned the steel vault and determined it held at least four hundred compartments, perhaps more. If it took all day, if he had to poke the key into every hole in the vault, he would not walk away empty...

But what is this? The flashlight beam came to rest on a small silver orb at the top center of the massive file system; a standalone keyhole, one that did not belong to a single box, but, rather, seemed to command the entire encasement. Lifting his quivering hand, he watched with sheer relief as the key slid into the hole and turned; an abrupt metallic click clearly indicating that each vault box had indeed opened. If he were twenty years younger, he might have danced a jig. Instead, he merely tipped his three-corner hat to the accommodating encasement and gave it a courteous bow.

He spent the next two hours emptying safe boxes, briefly examining their contents, haphazardly shoving objects back into them when he found nothing of interest. It was time ill spent. Was it possible none of the compartments contained the librarian's secret? The accrued frustration of thirty years of seeking without finding began to boil until he felt as though he might burst. Thrusting his fists on the table, he steadied himself, leaning full weight on his knuckles.

Scanning the dark room he, at last, conceded the barren chamber had cost him far too much time. But, was this truly the cliff's edge, or could there be another vault in one of the chambers further down the corridor?

Lunging toward the exit, he accidentally kicked the fallen, over-sized book. Having nearly lost his balance, he sought to punish the errant text, raising it over his head, prepared to fling it at the nearest wall, when a hand-written page bearing a familiar title fell from its folds and landed on the surface of the table. Stunned, he released the book and swiped up the escaped page. Slowly passing the beam of his flashlight over the written words, he read: *The Cuffs of Gall were the set of chains used to confine Fujo to the helm of The Merry Anne. The Sword of Woe, used to decapitate Fujo's mother, is also required, along with The Chain of Vengeance.*

A rattled gasp escaped his lips: the Chain of Vengeance? Apparently, the Door of Doom required more relics than he realized. What other choice pieces of information had the librarian hidden from him? Stuffing the sheet of paper into his pocket, he examined the rest of the scrapbook, ripping page after page from its binding, filling his pockets with a sense of renewed hope. The cunning prey had been under his nose from the moment he entered the chamber. Chuckling, he thrust the cover of the empty scrapbook back onto the table and left the ransacked chamber.

The librarian's assistant stood with her back pressed against the soot-stained wall as Alexander emerged from the corridor. She had apparently caught sight of the beam of light stretching out before him, thoroughly preparing her for his arrival as he turned the corner. Springing forward, she aimed a can of Mace squarely at his eyes.

"I knew it was you," her caramel colored face curled with an aggressive snarl, wisps of brown hair clinging to her sweat-ridden brow, "First you set the place on fire, then you come back to rob it. The nerve!"

Startled, Alexander took a cautious step backward, his hand brushing against the pants pocket into which he'd stuffed his precious pages.

"A man can not steal what belongs to the public in the first place, and the fire marshal knows where I live if he has collected evidence against me. Clearly, he has no clue, wouldn't you say?"

The faint hint of a curious smirk twitched at the corner of the assistant's mouth but her lips went taut and scarcely moved as her words hissed through her teeth, "We'll see what the sheriff has to say about breaking and entering. In the meantime," she snatched his shoulder, her nails digging into his flesh, "you're banned from the library for life."

With an indignant 'humph' he broke from her grip and pushed past her. Ascending the stairs, he looked back only when she planted a fist into the small of his back to punch him forward. Mace steady in hand, she escorted him through the library and might have slammed the door behind him as he left, if it weren't such a large and cumbersome structure.

Chuckling, he emerged into the bright sunlight. *Banned for life!* What did it matter now? He had confirmed his suspicions; the librarian had withheld information, and now he had her spoil tucked safely within his pocket. As for the assistant, let the sniveling wench call the sheriff, and anyone else she might think to call; a lot of good it would do her.

Unsuccessfully attempting to whistle a victorious tune, he set course for home.

Having returned to the seaside shack, he gently unraveled his booty and laid out the pilfered papers for Bullwinkle's inspection.

"We have other relics to locate, my friend. Look at this... The Cuffs of Gall, The Sword of Woe, The Emerald Viper, and it would seem the door also requires The Chain of Vengeance." Noting the quizzical look on Bullwinkle's face, Alexander rapped him on the side of the head. "Don't be an idiot. It's the chain they used to affix Blackbeard's severed head to the bowsprit of Maynard's sloop after they did him in."

Devil's Edge

Returning his attention to the librarian's list, he released a loud moan. "Drat. It wants *The Book of Trials*." He ingested the word 'book' like a potent poison and it clenched his intestines, squeezing until he could barely hold down his Jack. His blacklisting from the library hadn't been such a slight occurrence after all. He *must* have this book, and books—as any man can say—live inside libraries.

Pressing his nose to Bullwinkle's snout, he glared into the moose's eyes. "Things are becoming rather complicated, but Alexander Spotswood is not a man easily dissuaded, is he, my friend?"

Turning away, he curled his fingers into a fist and made a silent, red-faced vow. All opposition be damned, no mere wench would stand in his way, no matter how much Mace she carried. That book was already as good as his.

Removing his hat, he flung it at a hook near the door and missed. He allowed it to lie where it fell and unwrapped the snake-like coil of gray hair from around his neck, the braid falling loose at his back. It had been a difficult day thus far and another spot of Jack seemed in order. Never rude to a true friend, Alexander offered a jigger to Bullwinkle. Ill mannered as ever, the moose refused the cordial bid.

Relishing in the way the tonic burned as it slid down his throat, Alexander peered at the metal detector leaning against the wall in a corner behind the front door. He should take it up immediately and set out to find The Chain of Vengeance, but knowing he searched for something he hadn't hitherto sought did not change the fact that thirty years of digging had not yet produced this precious artifact. For the first time in as many years, he allowed himself to wonder where the relics might be if they had yet to wash up on shore. As the startling answer crept to the forefront of his mind, he nearly choked on the last of his whiskey.

The mud-dogs at the Underwater Archaeology Branch in Wilmington had been excavating *The Queen Anne's Revenge* for years now. Wasn't it possible they had these very artifacts already in their possession, perhaps without realizing what they were?

Bullwinkle winced at the sudden commotion when Alexander forcefully slammed his glass on the table and sprang to his feet, rushing to the nearest window. Wiping grime off the windowpane with his palm, he peered across the bay. A trip to Wilmington was in the offing, he needed to visit the museum to see what they had recovered. He would have to devise a plan to get his hands on the relics, undetected, even if they were already on public display. Amazed his deductive reasoning had been so long dull, he slapped himself on the forehead and turned back to face Bullwinkle, his face gleaming, "It won't be long now, dear friend, before a butler offers you slippers and a pipe."

A Twist in Time

A thin strip of early morning fog swirled over the sidewalk in the center of Sounder's Square. Ebbenwright Drummond stood before the majestic oak tree his wife rescued from the clutches of the town council only a few years ago, give or take the unknown amount of time he'd spent surfing through the eons.

He pulled a stone from his field bag, checked to ensure he banded the message securely, and wondered why the time portal left him here at town's square, rather than on Scabbard Street, as was the normal pattern. If, as before, he only had a few seconds to remain in present day, he wouldn't have sufficient time to make his way to Scabbard Street. His son, Harold, however, owned a hardware store less than three blocks away, and if Ebbenwright's aged legs did not fail him, he might arrive there in time to deliver a message. Perhaps this turn of events would prove fortunate, as Agaritha obviously hadn't understood his directives. Harold, on the other hand—dutiful and sober offspring that he was—wouldn't hesitate to institute Ebbenwright's every instruction.

Sprinting the entire way, Ebbenwright paid little attention to his immediate surroundings as he desperately tried to outrun the tingle that sent him hurling through the ages so many times before.

Passing Winthrop's Weiner House on the right and the police station on the left, he approached the corner of Ocean View and Langhorne, his arm cocked back, fully prepared to fire his missile. He would release the stone the moment he turned the corner onto Langhorne. When he felt the nerves on the soles of his feet begin to activate, he lunged the last few steps, sent the stone into motion, and gaped with astonishment as it sailed through a window painted with bright pink and yellow lettering loudly announcing: *Bonny's Baby Bay.*

A woman, who had been unfastening a howling child from the backseat of a car hovering near the curb, screamed, shoved her wailing legacy back into the vehicle, and thrust herself behind the wheel. The car lifted three hundred feet into the air before it jettisoned away at top speed, a blur of silver streaking against the skyline.

Glued to the sidewalk, Ebbenwright gawked as the sorcerized automobile became a small dot twinkling on the horizon. Lost in a trance of utter amazement, head tilted as far back as humanly possible, he became suddenly aware there were more automobiles littering the sky, many more. He stood there, slack-jawed, until four highly agitated women clambered out of the day care center; three clutched frightened toddlers to their chests, and one sporting an exceptionally high-lilted voice screeched to passersby, "Stop that man!"

Regaining his senses, Ebbenwright promptly set aside all thought of making apologies and dug his heels into the pavement, running as though chased by a horde of fire-breathing dragons.

Wrenching his gaze over the shoulder, he watched one of the women tap the right side of her jaw just below the ear, three times, and heard her yell, "911!" After a brief pause, she clamored, "Some son of a bitch threw a rock through the window at 4 Langhorne Avenue. Yes, Bonny's Baby Bay." Her voice dogged closely behind as Ebbenwright summoned his legs for all the speed they could muster.

Devil's Edge

The patter of high-heeled shoes clip-clopping on the sidewalk sounded like a group of rabid Clydesdales escaped from their cumbersome red and white wagon. How women managed to walk upright in those contraptions was a wonder that fascinated Ebbenwright, and those skilled enough to run full speed whilst suspended on miniature stilts...well, it simply boggles the mind. Suffering another glance over his shoulder, he watched the woman with the wicked-witch-of-the-west falsetto crank her left nipple as if it were a dial on an FM radio, and heard her bellow, "GPS on. We're right behind him. Hurry the hell up."

Was that a woman, or an android? Where was Harold's Hardware, and why hadn't the time portal whisked him away when he felt his feet activate? Ebbenwright cringed as a set of fingers slid down his back, the leader of the pack having nearly secured a fistful of his shirt. Darting sharply to the right, he picked up speed and set his questions aside. Not too far ahead, a sharp corner loomed. Once there, he might find a way to throw the high-heeled mob off his scent.

As if the powers of the universe had suddenly decided to take sides, one of the women stumbled and expelled a sharp yelp. Peering back, he watched her right herself, wobbling in an attempt to resume pursuit, the heel of her shoe fledging beneath her weight like a brittle bone snapped in two. The child she carried clung to strands of her hair as if clutching to the chords of a failing parachute, and she quickly lost ground. Two of the other women, still rattling the brains of the toddlers they had in tow, were also beginning to rethink the strength of their convictions and had begun to gasp for air. Only the woman with the miraculous nipple remained in prime position to continue the foot race.

Corbin's Fine Apparel, conducting another of their annual sidewalk sales, had a large rack of clothing parked outside the shop door. As he whooshed past, Ebbenwright grabbed the rack and sent it tumbling down behind him. Android woman fell into the mix and bellowed a mighty curse as Ebbenwright turned the corner and slipped into the alleyway between Pop's soda shop and the Devil's Edge theatre. A faint clip-clop shuffle sounded from behind; the woman had already regained her footing and would soon come barreling around the corner. Gazing back, staring intently at the entrance to the alleyway, Ebbenwright forcefully collided with a dumpster parked in the shadows.

Not one to turn his back on providence, he opened the dumpster lid and slipped inside, soundlessly lowering the lid. All at once unsure of his decision (the foul container reeked of decayed fish entrails and vomit soup) he slowly raised the lid and peered through a slim crack, calculating his chances for a successful escape. The shadow of his disheveled pursuer began to spread over the sidewalk and the sudden wail of piercing sirens woefully indicated law enforcement officials had arrived.

"What took you so long?" The woman screeched as two officers approached on foot.

The officer standing closest to her shrugged and said, "Your GPS is probably on the blink. Should I take a look at it for you?"

Flushed, she clopped past the dumpster and muttered, "I've heard more exciting pickup lines at the dry cleaners." Bolstering her determination, she blurted, "He definitely came this way. He's probably on Sycamore, by now, or hiding somewhere in the cemetery behind The First Baptist."

Ebbenwright listened as feet pattered by the dumpster, the sound quickly fading. Exhaling, he decided that despite its foul hospitality, he should remain inside the dumpster for a few more minutes so no one spied his escape.

Retail stores no longer located where they should be, women with electronic hardware implanted inside their faces and embedded in their breasts, cars taking to the skies like birds from a tree branch; obviously, the reason Ebbenwright remained in the present for so long was because he wasn't in present day at all, he had arrived in a future Devil's Edge, one existing without Drummond's Hardware Store. If this was the case, how long might he remain? The time portal had never jettisoned him forward before; he had spent all of his time perusing familiar annals of the past. The future was an unexplored area, one rife with serious possibilities. He peered through the crack. Just how far ahead on the time spectrum had he catapulted?

Tall and lanky with greased back black hair, a young boy donning a soiled white apron lumbered from the side door of Pop's soda shop carrying two large garbage bags and a stack of papers tucked beneath his arm. Ebbenwright ducked down, curled into a dark corner, and waited for the boy to lift the dumpster lid and dispose of his burden. Once the lad made his deposit and left, Ebbenwright reached for the newly arrived stack of papers.

A small crack in a rusted corner allowed a slight beam of shadowed light to infiltrate the dumpster, perhaps enough to read by if he employed a little patience. Banded batch of papers in hand, Ebbenwright dragged himself over heaps of discarded food, mangled bits of cardboard, and the fuming skeletal remains of fish, lobster, and clamshells.

Contorting in the tight space of the confine, he reached inside his pocket, withdrew a small, all-purpose knife, and used it to cut through the elasticized twine holding the stack of papers together. *Time* magazine was still in business, good to know, and a copy of *The Coastal Review* had been pressed between *Time* and a magazine called, *Taking Orbit*, an unfamiliar rag chock full of advertisements for various companies selling tickets for weekend space voyages. The largest ad, printed by Trump Enterprises, touted a vacation package to their newest getaway, the *Lunar Eclipse*, a satellite casino hotel orbiting the moon. The luxury package cost a mere twenty-two million for six nights and seven days. Clearly, Ebbenwright had jumped quite a distance into the future.

Nestled beneath the Lunar Eclipse ad, a smaller, less colorful, advertisement heralded the advantages of using a new and improved formula presented by *Salina's Surgical Suite*: buy one breast implant, get the second one free and, if the consumer mentioned the special coupon code printed in the ad, she became eligible for a free global positioning system chip implant. Grunting his disapproval, he flipped the magazine into a far corner of the trash bin and turned his attention to the newspaper.

Devil's Edge

Though partially obscured by a large splotch of ketchup, the pinkish date on the front page of *The Coastal Review* read July 22, 2030. Gasping with excitement, he rapped his head sharply on the dumpster lid.

Returning to the task at hand, he opened the mid-section of the newspaper and scanned another large advertisement, this one for the new Schick razor, touting twenty-five blades and a free precision laser used for fine trimming. As he perused the advertisement competing on the adjacent page, he chuckled; apparently, Gillette had had it up-to-here with the increasing number of blades race and had revealed its new single-bladed titanium razor which hailed, 'The Power of One.' The razor included a complimentary satellite FM tuner on one side of the handle and an HDSMX 1/16" TV screen on the opposing side. While it was difficult to imagine how anyone would engage a microscopic television screen while trying to shave, Ebbenwright gave kudos to Gillette for finally backing out of the blade race. He flipped through the pages of the rumpled paper, specifically avoiding the rest of the classified section, hoping to locate some sort of encouraging news.

On the third page of the section in hand, he read the remnant of an article continued from the missing front page that posed the question as to whether or not President Teach would make a re-bid for the Oval Office:

'When asked, the President donned the squirrelly smile the entire nation has come to know so well and quipped, "Maggots mixing margaritas on Cinco de Mayo, don't you people ever let up?"'

In the next column, he read another brief snippet of a continued story that merely noted:

'...an accomplishment nearly as notable as the solving of the Ballencroft murders earlier this century.'

Ebbenwright raised an eyebrow with heightened interest, he would definitely like to read the rest of that article, but if he had to take one more breath of air from inside the infernal dumpster, he would lose what little remained of his last meal; not that Tibetan llama cake harbored any sort of gourmet allure, but a kindly shepherd had given the loaf to Ebbenwright, saving him the grief of having to pilfer food from a nearby marketplace. Bland as the cake was, it at least filled his belly.

Having heard no noise in the alleyway for quite some time, he packed the newspaper into his field bag and slowly opened the dumpster lid, peering cautiously into the shadowed lane, his lungs feasting on fresh air. Convinced no one remained in the area, he slid from the dumpster and stealthily made his way toward Scabbard Street, ducking in and out of sight whenever passersby showed the slightest interest in his presence.

But for the raucous honking of a flock of seagulls scrounging for breakfast near the shoreline, Scabbard Street seemed devoid of activity. Ebbenwright approached the house from the north side, careful to lie low, lest someone spy his untimely visit. Creeping alongside the rusted iron fence, he inched toward the garden, peering through a hedge of overgrown foliage.

In the center of the garden stood a gray-haired man wearing a baby-blue polo with a black anchor stitched above the left pocket; the same type of shirt his son, Harold, had worn day in and day out since the fifth grade. As Ebbenwright concentrated his gaze, he realized that this man was indeed Harold, nonchalantly leaning on a spade, though bespectacled now, and hunched forward beneath the weight of old age. Harold engaged another fellow in conversation, a man whose tuft of white hair swayed before Harold's face, the rest of his small frame obscured by Ebbenwright's poor view. Parlaying for better position, Ebbenwright slowly stepped closer to the gate, his eyes affixed on Harold and his guest. Drawing closer, Ebbenwright recognized the dulcet tones of Harold's voice.

Speaking with a quiet sob, Harold dropped his chin, "I know, Dad. But, you have to admit, this is more than just weird, it's...*unnatural*."

The fellow speaking with Harold scratched behind his right ear, the way Ebbenwright always did when perplexed.

Devil's Edge

Clutching to the cast iron fence with both hands, his knuckles a blanched shade of white, Ebbenwright leaned forward, intent on hearing every word.

"Agreed, it is unnatural," the old man raised his hands in accord, "but I don't have any control over it, and I barely understand it myself. The past is much easier to grasp. Because all things are established, the line to the past is a linear one. But, the future seems a complexly different story. With all possibilities as yet undetermined, the paths to the future seem to branch off like the fanned blades of that lawn rake over there, each tine representing a plethora of possibility. Now, if the lines to the future are, in fact, split in such a way, then it makes an odd sort of sense that a time traveler might become split as well...traveling in many directions all at once, sampling each possibility as he continues on." Ebbenwright's carbon copy placed his hand upon Harold's shoulder in an effort to console him. "Though it's difficult to grasp the enormity of this, we have to reconcile ourselves to it. It's the only explanation we've got."

Harold nodded sorrowfully, "How do I reconcile myself to those?" He pointed to a pair of stones jutting up from the ground; white marble monuments Ebbenwright hadn't seen before. Scaling along the fence, he purchased a new position and strained for a clearer view of the monuments Harold's trembling finger indicated. The stone on the right read: *'Agaritha Drummond, Beloved Mother.'*

Ebbenwright squeezed his eyes shut and winced, feeling all at once faint and disoriented. Cleaving to the fence, he steadied himself, forcing himself to breathe deeply until he slowly regained his senses. Opening his eyes, he reluctantly scanned the words inscribed on the second stone: *'Ebbenwright Drummond, Fool For the Ages, his was an untimely death.'*

Slinking to the ground, Ebbenwright sat with his head planted between his knees and quietly mourned.

But, wait. Hadn't his carbon copy, clone, or counterpart—whatever he was—said the scenario playing out before them was only one of many possibilities? He had, he had. Regaining some semblance of control over his emotions, Ebbenwright raised his tear-stained face and returned his attention to the garden. Poor, poor Harold. Desperately trying to gain some sense of healing and closure, thwarted by the unexplained presence of the very man he grieved for.

If this was indeed the 'real' future, then it was starkly apparent Ebbenwright had expired before Agaritha, for only she would have thought to provide such a clever epitaph, and her choice of words made it seem as though his death had a direct connection to the time machine. Quite possibly he had never returned from the excursion he experienced now; which led him to the dire conclusion that either someone had permanently disabled the time machine, or Agaritha had never found a way to follow his instructions. Why either of these scenarios might have transpired, he could not say.

Was it his destiny to hurtle through multiple variations of the future, never to find his way back? How could anyone accept such a horrible fate?

He was at once struck by the simple genius of a catchphrase he had used throughout the course of his life: *'When you want something done right, do it yourself.'* Jumping to his feet, he lunged for the gate and burst into the garden. Startling his son and his carbon copy, he bolted toward the door, determined to get his hands on the grandfather clock.

"Grab him!" Harold screamed, ejecting the spade from his grip, his arms flailing after Ebbenwright, hands swiping frantically, his aim well off course.

Not to be outwitted, the carbon copy simply jutted his foot across the path, tripping Ebbenwright, who fell smack between the twin monuments.

Planting a heavy heel on Ebbenwright's throat, pinning him firmly to the ground, Harold turned to the carbon copy and growled, "Dammit, Dad, I thought you said this wouldn't happen again."

Devil's Edge

Face flushed, the duplicate stared down at his squirming twin, "I'm so sorry, Harold. It looks like there are more of them than I thought."

Harold turned his face away like a man who had seen more than he could ever bear. "I got rid of the last one," he mumbled, reaching into his pocket and withdrawing a small pistol, "It's your turn."

Hell Hath No Fury

The nurse wheeling Ozzie into emergency surgery received a lecture on binary kinetic inspissations from the heavily sedated junior genius. Maurine could tell the nurse had absolutely no idea what her brother meant, and it was just as well, no one else did either.

Sidling next to Dixie Teach, the surgeon asked if she wanted him to snip away the webs fusing Ozzie's toes together, it wouldn't pose a problem, he assured her, since the anesthesia wouldn't wear off for a few hours anyway. Maurine couldn't recall seeing her mother so on edge and she wasn't the least bit surprised when Dixie turned on the surgeon, "Don't you *dare* touch my son's toes."

Maurine and Dixie took turns kissing Ozzie's forehead while the surgical team assembled. When the doors to the operating room finally opened and they rolled Ozzie inside, Maurine stared blankly into her mother's emotionally charged face. Turning away, they walked without a word to the waiting room where they found Mrs. Drummond, sobbing over an untouched cup of tea.

Not one to pussyfoot, Dixie darted across the room to face off with the old woman, "What in God's name were you doing with my son? How could you let this happen? I'd like to slap you from here to hell's back door, Agaritha Drummond, you evil, *evil* witch."

"Mom." Maurine pled with her mother to control her temper, even though she knew there wasn't the slightest chance of compliance.

Dixie spoke with a baleful tone of admonishment, "Don't start, Maurine."

Fingernails digging into her hips and as red-faced as Maurine had ever seen her, Dixie glared at Mrs. Drummond. "I'll have you know I already contacted Garrison, he's chargin' you with child endangerment. Let's see if your voodoo can get you out of that one." Grabbing hold of Maurine's arm, she yanked. "Let's go. I will not sit next to this conjurin' hag. We'll wait in the cafeteria."

A Homeless Pie

"I don't like rhubarb pie," Candace confessed. "Do you?"

Jillian reread the inscription written on the pastry box, moved by the thoughtful gesture.

Unfortunately, the one and only time Jillian consumed rhubarb she enjoyed it so much she ate half the pie on her own and ended up with food poisoning. As much as she would like to forgive and forget, that battle would always be lost.

Jillian turned away from the box, "No."

"What are we going to do with it?" Candace's voice emanated with genuine concern. Apparently, Mrs. Drummond's angelic gesture touched her as well. It would be a shame to let the pie go to waste.

Ever since one of the nurses escorted Maurine from the room, Jillian's mind reeled around the glaring question: which of the Teach boys got stabbed? Try as she might, she couldn't stop herself from voting for Teddy, Jr. Ozzie was so small, so delicate, and so animated, while Teddy, Jr. went around just asking for it.

Based on Mrs. Teach's frenzied reaction when Jillian's father hit Teddy in the head with a baseball bat, she would be completely beside herself now that one of her sons had sustained a more serious injury.

"We can send the pie home with Maurine," Jillian suggested. "Someone in the family must like rhubarb; after today they might appreciate a little comfort food."

Candace thought about it for a moment but shook her head, "It's a good idea, but I doubt Maurine will be back anytime soon, and it's really not good to leave rhubarb sitting out for any length of time, it turns fast."

"Tell me about it," Jillian groaned.

"What about that nurse," Candace perked up, "the one who wears the traditional starched white cap. She's a hoot, isn't she? Always has a smile on her face, and doesn't she make you feel like you don't have a worry in the world? We could give it to her."

"That's a great idea." Jillian smiled. Not every nurse can make her patients feel like they'll leave Mercy General new and improved, but this one pulled if off seemingly without effort.

The nurse in question showed up ten minutes later with a blood pressure cuff in hand. Why, yes, she loved rhubarb, and were Jillian and Candace sure they didn't want the pie? Of course she would take it. As it so happens, her five grandchildren were due for a visit that very evening and they simply went insane for rhubarb pie. She left room 207 cradling the pastry box like a newborn infant, a wide smile spread over her face, an appreciative gleam in her eye.

Redeeming the Thief

Highly distraught, Eleanor Finwicket left Sally Dibble's hospital room vowing never to hold a conversation with anyone else who might have suffered a recent stroke. Her efforts to grasp Sally's slurred words proved excruciating and seemed too much like trying to understand a defunct form of ancient Aborigine, or a mangled sort of inside-out pig Latin. The only untangled words Sally could speak were cuss words. While Eleanor understood those perfectly, Sally's unbridled use of profanity shook her, as she'd never heard her friend utter such filth. She wouldn't have believed an upstanding woman like Sally Dibble capable of thinking such words, much less giving them voice.

The doctors said Sally would improve dramatically in the next twenty-four hours, having fortunately avoided a major stroke. Eleanor promised to return to the hospital once Sally replaced her colorful vocabulary with a more familiar repertoire.

Stepping into the hospital corridor, Eleanor pulled on her white gloves. Glancing briefly over her shoulder, she thought she saw Sally flipping the bird, but upon closer inspection, saw nothing but Sally's crooked smile and the flitter of her fingers as she waved good-bye.

In her rush to leave the hospital, Eleanor nearly passed the nurse's station without giving the counter a second look, but the white pastry box with Agaritha Drummond's scrawl on top now sat precisely in the same spot it had before. Quickly scanning the empty corridor, Eleanor shuffled through her tote bag to make room for the pie that had barely slipped through her fingers less than an hour ago.

With a Cheshire grin pasted on her face, Eleanor Finwicket stepped off the curb into Mercy General's parking lot. The sun shone brightly and a gentle breeze tickled the feathers in her bonnet. She couldn't ask for a better day to entertain the garden club.

Give Me a Hand

Though he rehearsed a number of excuses, Whitt knew his father would ultimately blame him for losing the dogs in the marsh. Dear old dad hadn't been in the best of moods lately, too many people had laughed and called him a wiener; morphing his ego into a giant sore gushing tons of green and yellow pus. Now was not the time to test his frustration level. After hours of fighting back the tall salt grass and slapping winds, Whitt forged on, keenly aware it was not in his best interest to return home without the wretched mutts.

Devil's Edge

Merlin's distinct howling grew louder; he and Ruby couldn't be too far away now. The setters were growing bigger and much stronger; it hadn't taken much of an effort for them to break free of Whitt's grip. They ran off, howling with glee at their newfound freedom. *We'll see how free they feel once they've eaten a pound of laxatives*, Whitt thought, squeezing between two bushes erupting with large pink flowers.

Thrashing through the stalks of hard grass ripped his legs raw and his tongue felt like a piece of sandpaper, swollen and desperate for a drop of fresh water.

He saw the signs posted on the edge of the marsh that warned anyone entering did so at their own risk, but had decided his father's wrath far outweighed any dangers he might encounter on the high marsh. That was, of course, before he disturbed the gigantic bird hidden in the grass, its wingspan large enough to classify the daunting creature as prehistoric, it's gray wings flapping defensively, the sharp point on its foot-long bill jutting at Whitt like a fencing sword, its maddened squawk demanding an immediate explanation. A thing like that would scare the ghost out of anybody. His only consolation was that no one had heard him scream, or saw him turn tail and run. What good was it to own a dog if Merlin wouldn't take up the fight when a freaking pterodactyl attacked his master?

There were other concealed creatures lurking in the mud, too. Incessant tiny crabs hooked their claws onto Whitt's shoestrings, clinging as if they'd won a free ride at a major amusement park, and a multitude of snails plagued the grass stalks like a serious wart infestation. Meadow mice scurried frantically as Whitt unintentionally trampled their nests, and a raccoon poked its head out of the grass, reared onto its hind legs, and seemed to enjoy a good belly laugh as Whitt rushed by.

He lost sight of Devil's Edge a long time ago; nothing seemed to exist beyond the expansive seas of brown grass swaying in the malicious wind. He dug deep into his pants pocket—there weren't any skittles left in there half an hour ago and there weren't any now. No telling how long it would take to get back to town.

When he finally caught up with the dogs, Ruby sat quietly panting, exhausted from the romp, while Merlin pranced in a circle, howling as if his jewels were caught in a bear trap. He didn't have a mark on him. Not willing to play the fool after such a long and arduous search, Whitt seized the leashes and wrapped the chords four times around each wrist.

He lunged for Merlin's collar, "What is your freaking problem?"

Merlin's head swerved low to avoid Whitt's grasp, and that's when he saw it lying there, partially covered by clumps of intertwined dead grass—the skeletal remains of a human arm, hand still attached, a dull band circling around one of its bony fingers. Whitt emptied his lungs with a piercing shriek and fell backward into a mound of mud. Merlin bound through the grass and lapped Whitt's face.

"Oh, *now* you care."

Gawking, jaw slack, Whitt's gaze fixated on the bones in the grass.

Terrified as he was to actually touch the remains, he realized he couldn't leave them behind. These bones had once belonged to an honest-to-god human being, a person who might have family still wondering where this arm had gotten off to. Besides, all gruesomeness aside, this was by far the coolest thing ever to happen to Whittaker H. G. Miller. Even Tommy Gordon, who spent his summers touring the globe with his parents, wouldn't have a better story to tell in the fall when school re-opened: no way, no how.

Hands trembling, Whitt carefully lifted the bones from the clutches of the meadow grass. His stomach retched and he gagged a series of dry heaves, but he stubbornly resisted the overwhelming impulse to drop the arm. Once his trembling abated and normal respiration resumed, he decided it best not to look at the bones.

Wrapping the dog's leashes around his left hand, he desperately tried to ignore the sensitive material dangling from his right.

Carrying the bones back to Devil's Edge put a sense of urgency in his quickened pace and the trek didn't take nearly as long as he imagined.

He considered taking his find directly to the police department, but the idea faded quickly. No, not only had he managed to corral the dogs after their inexcusable escapade, but he had also rescued a tombless treasure from the marsh grass. Treasure was an intricate part of his father's life and was, after all, the very reason the Millers were in North Carolina to begin with. The look of pride beaming over his father's face solidified in Whitt's imagination as he locked the dogs behind the backyard gate and crossed the porch to the front door.

I Went to a Garden Party

Corrine Brumbau has a pure white Shih-Tzu named Fancy. Around her neck, Fancy wears a platinum and diamond collar worth nearly four million dollars. She eats premium cuts of beef and laps at champagne served in engraved Waterford crystal. As she basks in the warm glow of Corrine's doting, Fancy doesn't know she isn't the first pooch to receive such exorbitant treatment, nor is she likely the last. In fact, Corrine has owned six Shih-Tzu breeds in the last ten years, each awarded the same name. Two of them bought it at the hands of negligent landscapers, subsequently dismissed chauffeurs did three others in, and the last of them actually managed to commit suicide by hanging itself with one of Corrine's Persian scarves. Not to be dissuaded, Corrine simply procures a new mutt, dubs it Fancy, bestows it with the multi-million dollar collar, and proceeds as if nothing ever happened, insisting the dog sitting on her lap is the same dog she had ten years ago.

What Corrine doesn't realize, of course, is her chambermaid has a terminal case of verbal diarrhea and carries on an illicit affair with Captain Morgan at Ishmael's Pub, entertaining a diversified audience every weekend. Word gets around, and those juicy morsels requiring the utmost discretion travel fast.

Eleanor Finwicket leered at Corrine who always sat in the seat of honor, without regard for the official host, and wished she had the fortitude to stand up to Corrine, put her in her place once and for all. But, in all the years Eleanor had attended the garden club, she'd only ever known one woman to stand up to Corrine and that was, unarguably, without favorable result. Not one to suffer social shenanigans, Mary Gladys Metzger had a spine made from petrified stone, and when it came time for Mary Gladys to host the tea at her elaborate home, she asked Corrine, in no uncertain terms, to kindly relinquish the chair of honor. Not two weeks later, Mary Gladys' husband, Vincent, a prominent stockbroker on Wall Street, went belly up, the victim of a fraudulent insider trading scandal. Penniless and on the verge of prosecution, Metzger and his wife made a run for the Mexican border. No one has asked Corrine to remove herself from the head of the table since.

Not in possession of a permanent service staff, Eleanor busied herself with instructing the antiquated butler she'd hired and strained to hear the idle chatter ensuing around her. Only six of the twenty-five garden club members bothered to attend, and this, too, set fire to Eleanor's collar. Because her house wasn't as large and expensive as the others, the teas she hosted always drew the lowest attendance. The message came across loud and clear, most of the members considered the Finwicket's beneath them. She once overheard Barbara Schwab say Eleanor's meager inheritance of three quarters of a million dollars did not qualify her to mingle with the likes of Corrine Brumbau, who inherited half the cotton mills in the south and owned controlling interest in Fruit of the Loom. Or, Tempest Moore who founded a prominent pharmaceutical company and had a strong hand in imported diamonds. It was one of the few times Eleanor took early leave of a tea social. She hadn't attended another for months afterward, until it occurred to her that Barbara Schwab had yet to gain the status of an immortal deity and, as such, her opinions were as worthless as anyone else's. Some club members considered Eleanor worthy: Cynthia Talbot always came to Eleanor's tea and so did Libby Jenkins, Amelia Piper, Cybil Sherman, and the Mayor's wife, Sally Dibble, although Sally wouldn't be attending today, obviously. So, to hell with Barbara Schwab.

While it was true one or two of the women did not agree with Eleanor's membership, it was also true no one in the club actually enjoyed Corrine Brumbau's company; they simply tolerated her, much like a temperamental mammogram machine. Suffice to say no one wasted any real fondness on Corrine, especially since she spent the majority of her time looking down her ski-slope nose at everyone she deemed beneath her, and no one Eleanor knew had ever escaped that unfortunate distinction.

The butler finished serving the appetizers and all but one or two of the guests had found their seats. Corrine's cloned pooch ate caviar from Eleanor's best china, while Amelia Piper put a serious dent in Cybil Sherman's ear recounting her most recent trip to Monaco.

Libby Jenkins asked Corrine why she wasn't fearful of losing the dog's collar and got a smug sneer in return. Corrine quipped that naturally she had insured the collar for more than it was worth and donned a lopsided expression meant to punctuate Libby's ignorance in asking such a stupid question. Libby's cheeks flushed beneath the weight of Corrine's condescension and she excused herself, stomping off to the ladies room where she would surely assault the mirror with quite an earful. Eleanor knew what it was like to be on the wrong end of Corrine's tongue-lashings, she knew how infuriating it was, and how much strength it took to keep from drowning the milked-out cow in her chowder bowl.

The sun was generous, the breeze kind, and the luncheon progressed without further discord. Eleanor remained anxious for dessert, for the words of praise she would surely receive once her guests had indulged in the glorious rhubarb pie. The butler's movements, however, were agonizingly slow and Eleanor made a mental note to specifically request a younger gentleman next time she called the staffing agency.

No sooner had the butler pulled the cover off the crystal pie plate than Corrine jubilantly clapped her hands and declared how very much Fancy enjoyed rhubarb.

Eleanor's face flushed as her tongue raced ahead of her better judgment, "I assure you, I have not gone to so much trouble to procure the recipe for this pie only to have it consumed by a *dog*."

Obviously taken aback by Eleanor's defiance, the deep lines in Corrine's face went momentarily taut. Then, a slight grin formed at the corners of her mouth, her composure regained, "You've gone to extra trouble, Eleanor?"

Unblinking, all eyes rested upon Eleanor. "Yes, I got the recipe from Velma Sinclair. It's an award winning pastry."

Gasps escaped and eyes went wide.

Corrine stroked Fancy with her diamond-ridden hands, the sun reflecting off the stones like harsh laser beams.

"Tell us," Corrine breathed, her voice heavy with intrigue, "how one persuades a commoner like Velma Sinclair."

Confidently adjusting her bonnet, Eleanor looked Corrine squarely in the face, "The same way anyone else is persuaded. I bought the recipe for twenty-five thousand dollars, a worthy investment."

"You mean to say Velma let her recipe go for a mere twenty-five thousand?" Corrine sniggered, her mouth agape with incredulity.

Eleanor held her chin high, "She did."

Corrine's raucous laughter resembled the clatter of a pair of cymbals crashing against the side of one's head and it seemed as though the audible assault would never fade.

Waving her hand, Corrine motioned for the butler to plate up the pie, "Let's see if you got your money's worth."

Naturally, the butler served Corrine first. Fancy got a good whiff of the delectable pastry and struggled to break free from her mistress's grasp. Grateful to see Corrine did not mean to allow the dog to indulge, Eleanor tipped her bonnet and smiled appreciatively. At that moment, Corrine leaned forward and released her grip, permitting Fancy to plow, muzzle first, at the plate. The slice of pie disappeared instantly, nothing left but a glop of pink goo matting the hair on the dog's alabaster chin. Fancy's smiling face seemed aglow with a look of sheer satisfaction, as did Corrine's. Then the dog passed gas like a hefty truck driver parked at a taco shop, belched, and curled into Corrine's lap, seemingly eager for a sudden nap.

A series of unpleasant squeals erupted from the guests and, red-faced, Eleanor slammed her fork down with such ferocity it embedded itself in the tabletop. No longer concerned with Corrine Brumbau's superior stature (it wouldn't matter if the old biddy held the kingdom of God in escrow) Eleanor would not allow such an outright insult to pass without defending her dignity.

Scrambling to her feet, she pointed a loaded finger at Corrine and drew her lips tighter than a Dolly Parton brassiere, "There will be no more..."

"Nonsense!" Corrine laughed, waving Eleanor off with a slight flick of the wrist, "There's plenty more. Henry, Harvey...whatever your name is," she gestured to the butler, "cut us another slice, won't you?"

Eleanor stood slack-jawed as the butler served Corrine another slice of pie.

Corrine lifted her fork to her lips, "Oh, sit down, dear. It's hardly the end of the world. Enjoy your investment."

Mouth locked open, Eleanor slowly returned to her seat and watched her guests chew and swallow, her appetite completely vanquished.

Amelia Piper declared the pie the best she ever had and stroked Eleanor's hand, a look of consolation exuding from her compassionate eyes. Smiling, Amelia delicately wiped the corner of her mouth with the tip of her napkin, then expelled an outrageous blast of air from beneath her; the horrendous emission loud enough to constitute an immediate escape from the earth's atmosphere.

With a look of pure shock washing over her face, Eleanor Finwicket felt like a wide-eyed child viewing a horror film at the cinema as each of the women first expelled boisterous flatulence, then toppled over, some landing with their expressionless faces pasted onto the table cloth, others tumbling from their chairs, sprawled out over the brick patio, unmoving.

Only Cybil Sherman remained conscious, the slice of pie on her plate untouched. Trembling, Cybil spoke as if lost in a dream, "I thought someone might whack Corrine someday, but why would you poison the rest of us?" Disengaging from her horrified inspection of the limp assemblage, Cybil rested her scurrilous gaze upon Eleanor.

"Poison?" Eleanor hadn't ruled a scream out of the question and pressed her fingertips against her lips in an effort to corral the broiling urge, "Are they...should we check...*my God...*"

"Shall I call the police, Madam?" The butler stared at the body-ridden patio as if he had a bothersome insect buzzing around his shoe, otherwise unmoved and emotionless.

"Yes!" Cybil slapped the butler as if he had asked the most ignorant question she had ever heard. Despite her numbness, Eleanor agreed, the man was a raging moron.

The senior EMT on scene stooped to examine the bodies littering the patio. After a series of pokes and prods, he turned to his partner and joked, "I ain't seen this many stiffs since last year's Viagra convention."

Half an hour later, five hearses cluttered the drive at the Finwicket estate. Deputy Sheriff Jared Duncan escorted Eleanor, handcuffed and shamefully trying to hide her face from photographers and curious neighbors, to his police cruiser.

Burning Bridges

When the call concerning the events at the Finwicket estate boomed over the radio, Sheriff Teach conceded that all hell had officially broken loose in his docile little town. Although things were happening faster than his mind could readily digest, his immediate priority was to bring Agaritha Drummond into the station; no one else on the force had the wit, gumption, or personal history necessary to deal with her. Jared Duncan could handle the situation at the north end of town; Garrison's hands would become soiled soon enough with the aftermath. For now, it was his duty to fetch Agaritha, despite his suspicion the child endangerment charges Dixie had pressed were seriously exaggerated and would never hold up in court.

Garrison entered the hospital waiting room just after Doc Ramirez arrived. Here was a man Garrison would never be able to look in the eye without experiencing an overwhelming desire to draw his pistol.

Ramirez was a Hispanic import, small, dark, and handsome, a jockey-sized Chihuahua with a suave accent. And that, apparently, fulfilled the prerequisites for seducing every woman in town, Garrison's ex-wife included. The little asshole had single-handedly driven the divorce rate in Devil's Edge to well over eighty percent. If not for his position as sheriff, Garrison would have repaid the bastard with interest a long time ago. Frankly, it still wasn't out of the question.

Agaritha was already up in the Doc's face, demanding an update on Ozzie's condition.

The surgeon tugged his mask down over his chin and asked Agaritha if she were immediate family, as if he didn't already know she wasn't. Refusing to answer, she drew in a breath of frustration. "Ain't you married?" She countered, glaring at a white band of skin circling the doc's finger, his wedding band recently removed.

With a start, Ramirez turned to leave, "That's none of your business."

"Then I'm guessin' you won't mind if I have a talk with your wife about the late nights you're spendin' with Larinda Talbot."

Face whitewashed, the doc turned back and spoke reluctantly, "There were unforeseen complications in the surgery."

When he didn't elaborate any further, Garrison prodded him with a poke to the shoulder, "What kind of complications? I'm family...spill it."

"Everything was going so well," Ramirez's dark face turned a gaudy shade of green, "then the kid flat-lined while we were sewing him up."

Without thinking, Garrison pulled his fist back and would have unloaded if Agaritha hadn't locked onto his arm.

"Ozzie ain't dead," she said, her tone certain.

Like any man with too much brain and not enough brawn, Ramirez flinched and lurched for the door, well out of Garrison's immediate reach. "That's right," he stammered. "We have one of our best cardiologists with him now. We've got a pulse, but it's weak and blood pressure is dangerously low. However, if anyone can stabilize the boy, it's Dr. Kim. Now, if you don't mind, I have to get back. I'll send a nurse to notify Dixie."

Garrison shooed the timid turd away with a flick of the wrist and turned to face Agaritha.

"Tell me what happened," he said, pointing to a chair with all the authority he could gather. Without question, Agaritha sat down and lowered her chin, her watered-down silver eyes blinking rapidly behind her bifocals.

"Another broken window," she mumbled.

Garrison felt his face flush. He had long ago determined to nail the bastard vandalizing the Drummond house but had never seen the slightest shadow of anyone lurking around the property. His intermittent stakeouts had all come up empty. It was frustrating as all hell, but the Devil's Edge police department didn't have the manpower or money to watch the house twenty-four seven. Agaritha wasn't to blame for Ozzie's injuries, Garrison was; he and every other officer who had failed in their oaths to serve and protect.

Tinkering nervously with the edges of his wide-brimmed hat, he felt his lip twitch. "I have to take you in, Aggy. Stupid as it might seem, it's the law."

"No sense sittin' around, then," she stood up, "Let's go."

Garrison dropped his hat and quickly bent to pick it up. He would not tempt good fortune. If Agaritha didn't intend to put up a fight, why should he argue? He would have enough weight on his shoulders once he returned to the station. Five bodies and a dead dog, the dispatcher had said. What in the name of the king of beers was going on?

He led her down the corridor, his grip light on her elbow. "Do you have to use your juju every time you're cornered?"

She grunted, "That little nugget of information came from Nelly Lockhart down at the coffee shop. Half the town knows about Ramirez and Larinda Talbot. It don't take no psychic to see a bullet planted between that man's eyes."

Garrison slipped his shades on as they approached the exit, "And what about Ozzie's future, does he have one?"

Agaritha curled her hand around Garrison's and squeezed.

Flicking Boogers

Alexander Spotswood stood in front of the ticket booth at the Greyhound station and begrudgingly paid fourteen dollars and fifty cents for a round trip ticket to Wilmington. A pimple-faced ticket agent slapped the money into his cash drawer, hunched forward, waved his arms about like an orangutan, and performed the worst Quasimodo imitation ever offered to a public audience. Alexander basked in a rare appreciation for his longevity; if it weren't for the senior citizen's discount, the ticket fare would have wiped him out completely. He stuffed the few bills left to his name back into his wallet, shoved a finger deep into his nostril and flicked an exceptionally ripe booger at the acne-scarred agent. Predictably, the startled smart ass sent a series of vehement expletives echoing throughout the station. Snickering, Alexander scuffled toward the departure gates.

The ride to Wilmington would take an hour to an hour and a half, depending on the size and general condition of the driver's bladder. Alexander should arrive at the Underwater Archaeology Branch with enough time to scout the premises. If destiny harbored any sense of fairness whatsoever, Alexander would return to Devil's Edge with the relics he needed to approach *La Porte de Ruine* with confidence and Blackbeard's legacy would finally become his. Bullwinkle will be so pleased.

The Awakening

Jillian sighed heavily when Candace asked her to read the same passage from *The Book of Trials* for the fifth time.

> *"Betwixt the muddy curtain*
> *Thy Spirit and Soul I bind*
> *All those searching eternity for thee*
> *Shall seek but never find*
> *Thine heart ensnared by dust and stone*
> *Thy voice a whisper unheard*
> *To linger where I breathe mine last*
> *'Til whence mine requirements are spurred:*
> *That a vestal heart, descended by thine blood in vein*
> *Shall provide reasonable sanity for thy sins' resolve*
> *In hand mine bidden tokens evolve*
> *These the blood-bourne grail*
> *Recovered to thine suffering site*
> *To set upon the balanced scale.*

I have cast upon them the earthbound curse and should they manage to outwit the noose, I pray their wombs are found barren."

Candace pointed excitedly at the book, "Repeat the part about the heir."

Jillian scanned the text, "Which part is that?"

Candace clicked her tongue against her teeth with impatience, "The vestal part."

"Okay. 'That a vestal heart, descended by thine blood in vein...'"

"Right!" Candace's eyes grew bright and a slight twitch toyed with the corners of her lips, "'With thine blood in vein.' It's exactly as I suspected. Only a direct descendent of Anne Bonny or Mary Read can undo the curse. But this passage leaves us with a rather...uh...*personal* question."

Jillian lowered the text to her lap, waiting for elaboration.

Candace poked at the bridge of her nose, attempting to adjust her phantom eyeglasses. Jillian had seen her do this repeatedly and wondered how long it would take the librarian to break herself of the senseless habit.

"The passage mentions a vestal heart. Taken literally, this would seem to require a virgin." Candace raised a finger on second thought, "Or, it could simply mean pure of heart. Either way, you're all we've got, right?"

Jillian felt her ears burn. Her virginity was her own business and—curse or no curse—she had absolutely no intention of sharing intimate information with Candace Flute.

"Someone thinks you're worthy, or they wouldn't have tried to kill you."

Suddenly chilled, Jillian pulled a blanket around her lap, "You're assuming they were after me."

Candace snickered, completely ignored the assertion, and poured herself a glass of water from the plastic pitcher perched on her bed tray, "Did you catch the part of the curse that said: To linger where I breathe my last? Have I mentioned Fujo died here, in Devil's Edge?"

"No, and I suspect there's a lot more you haven't mentioned." Jillian pulled the blanket to her chest and reached for another. She was sure Candace had yet to spill her last bean concerning *The Book of Trials*. Although they had read through Fujo's saga twice and again, with extensive discussions ensuing, questions remained.

Devil's Edge

Jillian understood Fujo's rage; the woman had lost her entire family to cutthroats, her life completely devastated, but it still seemed as though she had cursed the wrong lot. The crew of *The Merry Anne* hadn't ransacked Fujo's village, the Dutchmen did, nor had they done any direct harm to her sister, Catti, besides allowing Blackbeard to abduct her. It was long after the trials in Port Royal had concluded that Fujo arrived in North Carolina to find her sister dead and Blackbeard slain. In her subsequent search for answers, she discovered Blackbeard was a more vile character than she feared. He had not only raped Catti, but had invited others to do so as well; a sadistic voyeuristic amusement he frequently reveled in. No wonder Catti hanged herself.

Yes, Fujo had justified motive in issuing a curse, but her aim was off. The question burning at the forefront of Jillian's mind was who in Devil's Edge had reason to disagree? Why would anyone oppose the breaking of an errant curse?

Candace's voice was as enthused as her animated eyes, "She lived out her years on the south shore, alone and bereaved. They found her body inside Neptune's grotto, a large seaside cavern located a few blocks from Scabbard Street. You've probably seen the rock crest without realizing a vast cavern lies beneath. It's not too far from where you live."

"That's where the *Door of Doom* is?" Jillian asked.

"Most definitely," Candace nodded.

"How do we find the relics required to open the door?"

"I might know where to find one of them," Candace whispered, "as for the others, your guess is as good as mine."

A sudden frostiness swept through the room and Jillian began to shiver, goose bumps on her arms and legs, fingertips tingling, toes numb. No one had altered the air-conditioning and Candace showed no signs of discomfort. Jillian swiped a film of clammy sweat from her forehead. How was it possible to be so bitterly cold and still manage to break a sweat?

A nurse on the early morning shift had informed Jillian and Candace that their respective physicians would sign discharge papers in less than twenty-four hours. The sheer sense of elation

Jillian felt had been almost akin to winning the district dance title back in April. A sudden fever, however, would surely give the doctors reason to pause. Jillian wrestled with her blankets, wrapped them over her shoulders, and listened as Candace rambled on.

"It's said Fujo spent a great deal of time in the grotto, planning and scheming. Some say she died there on purpose; of course, the curse confirms this. She would have wanted a solid, long-lasting confinement for the spirits she cursed. The grotto provides the perfect environment. There are rumors she booby-trapped the caverns. I've never been past the entrance myself, so I couldn't say for sure, but I don't doubt she put all her energy into making sure those spirits are never set free. Unfortunately, if you want to break the curse, you'll have to do it in the grotto."

"Why do you suppose she went on with it, even after she realized Blackbeard was to blame?"

Pulling her bed tray closer, Candace lifted the covers off her lunch plates to inspect the torture hiding beneath them. "I don't know… I guess it was all she could do. Her thirst for revenge consumed her. That's more motive than most people require. At least she left a loophole: You."

"Remind me, one more time, how I got involved in of all of this?"

Tearing the lid off a cup of red Jell-O, Candace spoke matter-of-factly, "You were born into it." Her expression darkened, "With one attempt on your life already, it seems you have little choice in the matter. Unless you get out of Devil's Edge, you will either set the spirits free, or someone will set your spirit free."

A sharp pain pierced the back of Jillian's skull. Candace's concerned face became no more than a shadowed blur, her voice dimmed, and the room began to shrink. Jillian spewed a stream of vomit. Her heart slammed against her chest like a fist on prison bars and her head spun with the same intense dizziness she experienced as a child after too many turns on the merry-go-round. She dropped her chin to her chest and squeezed her eyes shut.

Devil's Edge

The sensation of a weighted cloud enveloped her and she tingled with wave after wave of the creepy-crawlies, her skin seemingly charged with an ultra awareness so intense she felt as though she must escape it, or succumb to the impending madness that would surely consume her should the onslaught continue. Suddenly, she knew—without understanding—that Mrs. Drummond was in danger. Unwilling to accept the idea, Jillian attempted to dismiss it, but found the more she resisted the impression the more pressing and uncomfortable the weight of it became. *Mrs. Drummond needs help...* As she accepted the disconcerting thought its immense burden began to lift.

Unable to open her eyes, she witnessed a series of fractured visions. The old man in the three-cornered hat stepped onto a Greyhound bus.

Her father and brother argued over an obscure object lying on the kitchen table.

Someone zipped a glassy-eyed white dog into a black bag.

Indistinct shadows fluttered against the glistening walls of a large, dark cave and, though Jillian could not see anyone, she sensed discord amongst the shadows. An argument ensued concerning cross-dressing.

Mrs. Finwicket wore handcuffs.

The vaguely familiar face of a young woman appeared to cower in a dark room, clutching a ragged teddy bear.

Then, Ozzie Teach's face materialized, a look of pure abandon glowing in his expression as he sang, "Should I stay, or should I go...?" Drawing near to Jillian's nose, he said, "Hey, Jilly. Tell my mother I won't be gone long."

The sheriff helped Mrs. Drummond from the backseat of his cruiser.

Jillian's mother stood beneath a budding willow. Dressed in her favorite pair of blue jeans, Sarah Miller held her arms out wide, beckoning with smiling eyes. Without hesitation, Jillian threw herself into her mother's arms and clung to her, allowing her soul to absorb her mother's presence like a thirsty sponge. Sarah drew

Jillian tight and lovingly whispered, "Don't fight it. The universe has trusted you with a valuable gift. It's not a curse."

Candace Flute frantically pushed the emergency call button, her eyes wide with fright. "Nurse! Nurse! Somebody...*help!*"

Jillian blinked rapidly, attempting to control the tidal wave of emotion overwhelming her, weeping like a small child lost in a vast crowd.

Candace bolted to Jillian's side and hovered over her. "Are you all right? You were going on about Mrs. Drummond needing help and spouted off something about cross-dressing teddy bears that didn't know if they should stay or go. I have never seen anyone sweat so hard and fast in all my life. We need to get someone in here to look at you."

"No, please don't...I just saw...they won't let me go home...did you see...*please*...I just n-n-need a minute."

Escaping the Desk Drawer

For all the value in lame reactions, Whitt should have taken the bones directly to the police station on his own. He spent a solid hour arguing that the arm might belong to the likes of Blackbeard or one of his notorious associates, and could be worth millions, but his father held his ground, insisting they had to turn the find over to the authorities. Authorities who, in Whitt's opinion, would most likely stuff the remains into a plastic bag and set them on a shelf to collect dust for the next fifty years. What a freaking waste. *Father: 10—Son: 0.*

The parking lot at the police station was a virtual anthill; cars pulling in and out, ambulances and hearses parked haphazardly, their drivers having lost all respect for the yellow lines denoting a common parking space, and large groups of people coagulated at the front doors of the building, coming and going in a frantic rush.

Whitt held the bones gingerly on his lap, his hands sweating inside the rubber gloves his father forced him to wear despite the fact he had already handled the remains with his bare hands after Merlin thoroughly covered them with a thick coat of dog slobber. Why bother to protect tainted evidence? The gloves were like rubber incubators steaming and suffocating his skin. Lifting the edges of the gloves away from his wrists, he blew inside; a crude form of air-conditioning, but slightly effective. *Father: 20—Son: 5.*

They found a parking spot at the end of the lot, a space so tight they both exited the vehicle on the passenger's side. Brad suggested it might be best if he carried the remains. Not to be undermined, Whitt insisted protective gear was a rigid requirement and since he was the one wearing the gloves, he would escort the bones into the station. *Father: 20—Son: 4,000,000.*

Drawing nearer to the crowd amassed outside the front doors, Whitt folded his oversized shirt around the bones in an attempt to hide his cargo from prying eyes. Uniformed police officers drew hard on their cigarettes, hands trembling, eyes batting anxious flutters. Emergency crewmembers feverishly whispered, some of them not trying hard enough to suppress bouts of laughter as others glared at them with contempt.

One woman, a brunette with fresh tears tracking over her cheeks, turned on two of her male associates and laid into them, "How can you morons stand there and laugh while a serial killer is on the loose?"

Apparently miffed at her choice of words, a fellow with a particularly gruff voice turned to argue, "She ain't on the loose...sheriff just brought her in."

"People died here today," the brunette lambasted, "Show some respect." Curling her trembling lips into a hateful snarl, she flicked her cigarette at his feet with deadly accuracy and jerked the station door open in a huff.

Devil's Edge

A serial killer? Whitt dropped his jaw and turned to face his father whose feet had become cemented to the ground they stood upon, his crinkled face revealing every second of his forty-two years.

"Maybe this isn't such a good time, Whitt."

Whitt shoved his way past the crowd and hollered over his shoulder, "There's no time like the present. Don't put off until tomorrow what you can do today!"

Plug that in your pipe, Pops, he mused, moving like a running back, forcing his way to the front desk where he demanded to see the sheriff.

Standing behind the counter, an officer with a thick, nasty, scar running from ear to chin raised his voice over the people who choked the lobby until it was standing room only, "This your kid?"

"He found a human arm on the high marsh this afternoon," Mr. Miller shouted. "He just wants to report it to the sheriff."

"Can't you see we're a little busy? Where is this arm?"

Whitt pulled the bones from his shirt and plopped them on the counter, "Right here."

The officer jumped back a step, gawked, and muttered, "Holy Jerusalem. Gerty," he yelled to a woman in plain clothes standing behind him, "Get me a zip-up would ya?"

Shoving and bumping her way to a shelf near the back of the room, Gerty returned with a large plastic bag and a pair of rubber gloves. The officer snapped the gloves on and gingerly stuffed the bones into the bag.

Whitt scowled. Just as he suspected, they would put the arm on a shelf in a dark room somewhere and leave it there to rot. He glared at the police officer, another freaking adult with absolutely no sense of adventure; all curiosity expiring on the same day the Easter Bunny and Santa Claus packed up and hit the road. Why does that happen to old farts? Is it because they stop reading comic books and watching cartoons? Or, because their hide-and-seek targets morph from groups of giggling friends to clumps of unanimated stocks and bonds? All life worth living ends after college: work and sleep, work and sleep...blah, blah, freaking, blah.

Whitt watched as the lady in plain-clothes carried the bones to a room at the back of the station, his frustration broiling. "Kiss my chocolate zero," he bellowed, wincing as his father's hand landed smartly on the back of his head.

"They're not going to do anything about it, Dad. Let's get the hell out of here."

"Watch your mouth..."

"You ain't goin' nowhere," the officer behind the counter scoffed. "Sheriff's gonna want to see you." He handed a clipboard to Mr. Miller. "Fill out these papers, take a seat, and wait it out."

They waited three-hours. Whitt used the time to siphon bits of scattered information from passing conversations, overhearing enough to formulate a basic idea of what had happened earlier in the day. Seems someone whacked five old ladies and a dog with a lethal pie. Now he understood why the EMTs outside were busting a gut. Seriously, what's not funny about a deadly pie? Predictably, his father didn't think it worth the air required to expel a chuckle.

The sheriff's face hung like a human punching bag, dark shadows encircling his bloated basset hound eyes. He sat behind his desk with slumped shoulders, attempting to shove his fingertips into his temporal lobes, which would have been kind of hilarious if he actually succeeded.

His voice sounded spent, "You said you found the bones out on the high marsh?"

Whitt nodded, somewhat relieved that someone was at least taking his discovery seriously, but cautious about how much hope he would invest on an actual investigation.

"Think you can find your way back?"

The question startled Whitt, it hadn't occurred to him he might have to relive his hellish trek through the pterodactyl-infested grass.

"I dunno... I guess so."

The sheriff pressed a button on the intercom and called for his deputy.

"Hot damn," the junior officer said, stumbling into the office, "that mob is worse than the year the mall ran out of Elmo dolls."

Devil's Edge

Flicking his wrist toward the door, the sheriff said, "You remember Jared Duncan, my deputy? Can you show him where you found that arm?"

Duncan's weary eyes brightened with a slight indication of interest, "What's this?"

"Boy found skeletal remains on the high marsh. Bright and early tomorrow mornin' you'll help him find his way back. I want the rest of this victim."

Whitt left the police station grinning. Devil's Edge has a sheriff who just might keep a Superman comic stuffed inside his desk drawer.

Untangling the Gnarly Truth

Garrison Teach listened patiently as Cybil Sherman explained she survived the onslaught at the Finwicket estate merely due to her abhorrence for rhubarb. She was a dainty woman, a L'Oreal brunette, thin, and well groomed, pretty in a plastic way, despite the half-century tucked beneath her Gucci belt. She seemed lucid, and unwaveringly convinced Eleanor Finwicket had suddenly become Lizzie Borden incarnate.

Placing a hand of comfort on Cybil's shoulder, Garrison made his way to the door and stepped out of interrogation room number one. He heard enough to believe a tainted pie was, in fact, the culprit, but it could be hours before the coroner officially verified the allegations.

Poised before the frosted glass door leading to interrogation room number two, he inhaled a deep breath and slowly twisted the doorknob.

Caught up in the craziness erupting at the station, no one thought to bring a box of tissues into interrogation two, so Eleanor had taken to blowing her nose into her white party gloves, which were soaked with tears and thick with snot. Garrison took a seat facing her, punched the intercom, and asked for a box of Kleenex.

He found it difficult to acknowledge the sniveling Grande dame seated before him was the same bulldozer of a woman who had pushed herself so far into everyone else's business she barely had a life of her own. Only one other woman in town had a better reputation for gossip mongering: Nelly Lockhart down at the coffee shop. Still, Eleanor was one bullheaded and determined old broad. Exactly what she meant to accomplish he never quite understood, but she always seemed to know where she wanted to go and how to get there. Never spent a day on the wrong side of the law, did her time at chapel every week, an all-around upstanding citizen. Until now.

Now she was up to her malfunctioning girdle in quicksand, slated to spend the rest of her life wearing a faded orange pantsuit, and a tight corridor on death row would become her modeling runway.

Garrison pressed the record button on the tape reel.

"Mind if I ask why you snuffed your garden club friends?"

Eleanor raised her reddened face. Garrison had never seen someone age five hundred years in the space of an hour, but she had somehow managed. The crevices lining her face had grown so deep and full of sweat a barge could float through them, her eyes bloodshot and swollen, her mascara pooling in Uncle Fester shadows, and her tidy bouffant hairdo, no longer tidy, no longer bouffant. Clearly, she had completely ignored the prospect of consequence while masterminding her muddled social-climbing coup.

Her voice sounded riddled with angst, "I didn't kill anybody."

"Well, now, here's the thing..." Garrison wished just once a perpetrator, caught red-handed, would buck up the nerve to confess. Confess, apologize, and do the time; that's what he would do if he tipped the scales of justice. Apparently, Eleanor Finwicket did not intend to appease his desire.

Stroking his forehead with the tips of his fingers, he wondered why people do the things they do—moronic things, idiotic things...cruel, unspeakable things. Why wasn't he waking from this nightmare playing out before him like a poorly staged Shakespearean tragedy? He wanted nothing more than to wake up, laugh at the strange workings of his slumbering subconscious mind and go on with a perfectly dull day in his perfectly dull town. The wrenching twist in his intestines testified as to how foolish a pipe dream that really was.

"We've got five bodies and a dead dog to account for. Thing is, Eleanor, they all arrived at your place in good health, but only one left with a pulse. You get my drift?"

Blanche Hathaway, Garrison's secretary, lifejacket, and anchor, opened the door to interrogation two and peeked around the door's edge.

"I've got the Kleenex you asked for."

Blanche wore her long burgundy hair pinned up. He liked it that way, it lent her that sexy schoolteacher look that mercilessly drove fifth grade boys to the brink of hormonal insanity. Her raw visual appeal never failed to provide him with a second wind, no matter how hectic life's onslaughts became.

He waved her in, wishing the world would go away and leave the two of them alone, just for five minutes. Another pipe dream.

"I've also got a preliminary tox report from the coroner." Blanche set the box of tissues on the table and raised an eyebrow as she pushed a file across the table's smooth, metal surface.

"What's it say?" He asked, not bothering to open the file.

A cat and mouse grin toyed with her lips, "I'm not authorized..."

"What's it say?"

"It says that pie had enough poison to lull half this town into an earthworm siesta."

Eleanor flinched, swiped a few tissues from the box, and began to blow her nose in earnest.

"Anything else?"

"There's a photograph in the file you'll want to see." Blanche's hypnotic hips swayed as she made her way to the door and Garrison imagined a pair of half-moon glasses resting on the tip of her perfectly formed nose.

Devil's Edge

The door clicked shut and he reached for the manila folder. Inside rested a photograph of a plain white pastry carton. The forensics photographer had snapped a close-up of the lid, which read: *'To Candace Flute and Jillian Miller, with hopes for a full recovery. Love, Agaritha Drummond.'*

"Aw, Christ." He slapped the folder closed and flung it on the table.

"Eleanor, you told Cybil Sherman you baked the pie you served at the tea party. That true?"

She puckered her lips the way people do when they can't decide between the truth and a lie, her eyes shifting like a mouse searching for the cheese at the end of a long maze. Slowly, she seemed to come to her senses and swayed her head negatively.

"Where'd you get that pie?"

Inhaling a deep breath, she bit her lower lip and squirmed, wrestling with her chair.

"I stole it from the nurse's station at the hospital."

"You stole it?"

Her chin fell to her chest and she expelled a short bout of hysterical sobbing, "I'm so sorry!"

Garrison turned the recorder off and laid into the intercom button.

"Blanche, bring Agaritha Drummond in here, please."

Always four steps ahead, Blanche stood outside the door with Agaritha already at her side.

The nightmare persisted. Not only did he have a fresh mass murder on his hands, but the past had also rushed back like a bull seeing cherry red. The arm the kid found out on the marsh wasn't just any old arm. Garrison didn't need DNA analysis to make a proper identification on those bones. He'd recognized the conundrum the second he laid eyes on the ring; a 1975 Penn State football trophy ring, the very one Marcus Ballencroft had bragged on for twenty years or more. The arm belonged to Marcus Ballencroft. What a stiff boot to the pants. If Marcus lay long dead out on the marsh, who killed his wife and where was his daughter: dead too, or somehow involved in her parents' slayings?

He instructed Blanche to take Eleanor to a holding cell and motioned for Agaritha to have a seat.

Eleanor sniped Agaritha on her way out, "*Murderer!*"

Garrison paused, waiting for the door to close behind Eleanor.

"You knew about this," he said matter-of-factly.

Agaritha nodded, "Saw it comin'."

"What's goin' on, Aggy?" He hoped she wouldn't answer. He hated doubting his integrity as a law enforcement officer, but this was definitely one of those times when he wished he could ignore the evidence.

Agaritha's tone was consoling, "You ain't got a choice. You have to charge me. But, far as I can tell, this here's a bid to make sure Jillian Miller doesn't break that curse. Some people, if you catch what I'm sayin', will do anythin' to preserve the past."

Scratching his head, Garrison spoke incredulously, "You mean to say this is about that old legend?"

Agaritha sighed and shook her head, "I don't know how many times I have to say it ain't no legend. I told you when you was a boy and I'm tellin' you now, they's cursed souls in that grotto."

"You don't really expect me..."

Clinging to the fabric of his shirt with a clenched fist, Agaritha looked him square in the eyes and glared like a bear with cubs in tow, "You only have to believe if you don't want no more bloodshed. Right now, there's somethin' I need you to do."

His jaw dropped, "Right now? Smack in the middle of all of this?"

Releasing her grip on his shirt, she nodded, "I need you to go over to the house and bring back them garden club fliers I stuck on the pin board in Ebby's study. There's information on 'em I'll need if I'm to get out of this mess. Don't send anybody else, that's important. Do it yourself. Just bring 'em all. We'll sort 'em out here."

It would seem more than a little strange for the head honcho to walk out of the station while all hell broke loose, but Garrison knew he had to do what Agaritha asked of him. He had no way of knowing exactly what she was thinking, but he'd never met a wiser soul than the one whose gaze currently burned through him, if her preferred methods for hitching a ride could be ignored.

"A couple questions before I go," he ventured, hoping he might get lucky and she might just answer. "Did you know Marcus Ballencroft was dead?"

She nodded.

He wouldn't bother to ask why she hadn't offered the information, her lips had tensed like vice grips.

"Do you know who killed Janice Ballencroft?"

She nodded, lips still glued.

"Is Carla Ballencroft dead?"

"No," she whispered, her expression pained.

"Did she kill her parents?"

Aggy shook her head, "No, Gary. And, I can't say anything else just yet. You ain't ready to hear it."

Agaritha's elusive responses had spawned more questions than answers, but the harder he pressed, the more stubborn she became. He crawled into the driver's seat of his cruiser sporting one hell of a headache.

Lunch with Albert

Ozzie Teach opened his eyes and scanned the recovery room. He found the gray and white walls depressing. Shadowed tones of black and gray swayed soulfully over the far wall, the silhouette of a willow tree waltzing outside the window. Stale, compared to the vivid landscape he savored only a moment ago. In that magical place, color could sing and reached out to tickle the soul. It loved, it blended, one color with the next, until every imaginable shade in the universe resonated like a symphony, creating a sound so joyful the only choice presented was complete immersion, or immediate escape.

Ozzie attempted to swallow, finding his throat raw. He winced, doubting his decision to return to the plane of pain. His soul would have made a strikingly beautiful midnight blue.

He knew now what few others ever come to know firsthand: the soul is a free agent independent of the body and unconfined by the limitations of the mind.

He began his celestial journey after rising above his body, which was still strapped to the operating table. Hovering near the ceiling, he listened to the surgical crew curse one another as they beat on the chest of the empty vessel they attempted to revive. Like a particularly saucy episode of the Three Stooges, nurses collided with one another, machines went berserk, surgeons fired insults and accusations and medical instruments bounced off the floor. Hysterical.

The light absorbed Ozzie like an unavoidable drawing salve, beckoning with an irresistible persuasion. On his way through the tunnel, approaching the light's apex, he'd stopped to chat briefly with Jillian Miller then moved on, drawing closer to the ecstasy inside the light.

He arrived in a place where the air smelled of chocolate-pizza-caramel-cookie-homemade bread sauce. A lush mound of purple grass sang a song glorifying each of his toes as it massaged his feet. He felt light as a feather, without a care, and content to be.

That's when Albert showed up and spoke to Ozzie as if he'd known him for all eternity. Einstein, walking with a youthful spring in his step, prepared to deliver an eye-popping lesson in metaphysics.

Retrieving the Flier

The inside of the old clock smelled like damp hours, moldy years, and decayed centuries, just as it always had. Garrison found the monstrosity with its door hanging ajar; shards of glass lay sprinkled on the floor, twinkling like fractured bits of ice laughing defiantly in the face of the late afternoon sun.

Unable to resist, he stepped inside the clock's abdomen and thought of the many times he hid there as a boy, convinced no one would ever find him, sorrowfully suspecting no one would make the effort. His concealments, however, never lasted for more than five minutes. Aggy had always come to patiently draw him out. She made no awkward inquiries, but treated him to pound after pound of Mrs. Fields chocolate chip cookies (his favorite) and gallons of iced-tea. She never asked why he felt the need to disappear inside the clock. The hour finally came when he found the courage to pose the soul-searching question himself, and after months of deep consideration, he decided his existence was not the least bit inconsequential. After which, his game of hide-and-seek the self-pitying-soul lost its allure.

Making his way to the kitchen, he shuffled through the cupboard nearest the fridge. Spying a red bag on the bottom shelf, he withdrew a chocolate chip cookie and clamped it between his teeth.

Ebbenwright's study was the last room on the right before the backdoor foyer, which led straight into the garden. A drawn shade prevented light from seeping through the lone window in the study and Garrison fumbled for the light switch.

The fluorescent lights flickered and steadied. His pupils struggled to make the necessary adjustments. Turning to give the room a good once-over, a sudden remorse tugged at his spirit. It had been two years since he last stood inside this den, two years since he had initially investigated the disappearance of the man who had gladly become his pseudo father. *How conveniently the busyness in our lives draws us away from those heartbreaking things we don't want to face.*

No time for philosophy now, Agaritha sat inside a jail cell awaiting Garrison's return. Pupils adjusted, he focused on the prehistoric raptor Ebbenwright spent the better part of his life collecting and reassembling until the bird's humungous skull

Devil's Edge

presented an ominous sight for those fortunate enough to pilfer a peek.

This room always held a certain fascination for Garrison, as well as for Harold, mostly because they were never allowed anywhere near the door unless Ebbenwright invited them in. Frankly, Garrison held a royal flush more often than he'd seen the inside of this study. He once suggested to Harold the two of them could probably gain unsuspected entry if they waited until three or four in the morning, but Harold merely gasped, slinking away into the nearest dark corner, apparently shocked and insulted by the suggestion.

Introverted and unadventurous, Harold Drummond wasn't overly thrilled with Garrison's presence in his life but, because he was perpetually friendless, he never complained about sharing his parents or his bedroom. And many were the nights Garrison spent on Scabbard Street, due mostly to his parents' habitual need to tenderize each other with stray shoes, heavy books, cast iron frying pans and anything else that might aid in their desperate attempts to pulverize one another.

The study looked tidy. Everything in its place, books sorted alphabetically, computer equipment in one corner, a makeshift lab in the other, microscopes on the left, cataloging materials on the right. Shoebox-sized containers lining the shelf over the lab counter held bone shards and pottery pieces. Larger specimens hung on hooks, identification tags dangling. Here, old science mingled with new technology, probably with the same reluctant tolerance Harold had displayed when Garrison hijacked his parents and made them his own.

Colorful garden club fliers burdened a pin board adorning the wall over the computer terminal, the pages fanning out eight inches or more. The pushpins holding the fliers to the board were less than an inch long. How they managed to stay affixed to the board would forever remain a mystery. And, how they could possibly help Agaritha angle off multiple murder charges was yet another enigma, but Garrison harbored no doubt they must play a large roll, or she wouldn't have asked for them. Removing them from the board, he folded them in half. A handwritten piece of parchment on the bottom of the pile caught his eye. Removing the odd page from the pile, he stuffed the garden club announcements into his pocket and shuffled to Ebbenwright's desk where he tugged the chain on the desk lamp and inspected the curious sheet of paper.

Addressed to Agaritha, the page bore Ebbenwright's scrawl: a simple directive complete with a small diagram. It read: *'If I don't return immediately, set the clock to thirteen.'* Ebbenwright had included one-two-three instructions for the accomplishment of this strange request. Leaning back in the chair, Garrison stared at the piece of parchment shivering in his hands.

How many years did Ebbenwright piss away tinkering with the old clock? He was obsessed with it, but refused to speak about the nature of his fixation. Only Agaritha knew what the old man was up to, and of course, she hadn't leaked a word, no matter how much Garrison badgered, even after Ebbenwright went missing. Surely she saw this note and already satisfied its requirement without favorable result. But, what if she hadn't, and what if it held major significance? Nearly everything Ebbenwright Drummond put his hand to held scientific significance. Why not the clock?

Garrison couldn't pretend to know the first thing about science and growing up under the roof of a renowned archaeologist hadn't helped. Ebbenwright made every effort to take Garrison under his wing, attempting to impart particles of scientific wisdom, and Garrison made a genuine effort to absorb, but it was like trying to force oil to mix with water. Ebbenwright had no better luck with Harold whose only real ambition involved reassembling small engines. Spending the weekend with a Brigg's and Stratton motor enticed Harold in the same way the prospect of a weekend jaunt with the likes of Blanche Hathaway seduced Garrison. Pity, but Ebbenwright's scientific endeavors proved ultimately un-inheritable.

The radio strapped to Garrison's utility belt let out a static cough and Bridgett Dunn's voice crackled over the air. "Your nephew's awake, thought you might want to know. Eleanor Finwicket lawyered up. She's lookin' for her walkin' papers, if you can find your way back to the station."

He groped for the radio, "Thanks, Bridgett. I'm on my way."

"Where to," she asked, "the station, or the hospital?"

"None of your bees wax," he snarled.

Bridgett's sarcasm oozed, "Yessa, Massa. Don't beat me, Massa."

"Bad news, dispatch," he sneered, "you ain't black."

"Bad news, Sheriff, you ain't Abe Lincoln, and you ain't never playin' cards at my house again."

Shit, shit, and double shit. He was in to Ricky Dunn for more than four hundred dollars, how could he recap his losses if Ricky's wife wouldn't let him past the front door?

"Sorry, Bridgett, I'm doggie paddlin' through a tsunami today, forgive me."

"Only if you buy the beer, I'm tired of payin' for those kegs."

"Did you know tomorrow's my birthday, Bridgett? Did I tell you that?"

"Lah tee dah," she said, "you're still payin' for those kegs."

"Deal," he groaned, and holstered the radio. Sighing heavily, he extinguished the lights in the study and sauntered toward the front door, pausing to stare at the face of the grandfather clock. "Oh, what the hell," he mumbled, crossing the threshold into the living room. Scanning the instructions once again, he reached for the stepladder resting beside the clock.

The glass door covering the clock face opened with a click. He gently moved both clock hands to rest on the six so they no longer obstructed the second-hand plate located just south of the number twelve. Slipping a fingernail beneath the circular plate, he coaxed until it, too, popped open with a click. There, beneath the plate, was a miniature clock face, unusual in only one way, instead of twelve numbers, there were thirteen. It currently read 3:45. Leaning in, he carefully persuaded the tiny hands until they both rested neatly on the thirteen.

Why would anyone rig a clock to include the number thirteen? Thirteen is notoriously unlucky. But, since Ebbenwright had rigged this particular clock, his reasons were most likely a galaxy too large for Garrison's pea-brain to comprehend. It wouldn't clarify the slightest thing if the damn clock grew a mouth and confessed all its secrets. Expelling a frustrated snort, Garrison closed the plate over the secret face and reset the clock's regular face to the current time.

Was it five thirty already? *My how time flies when the gates of hell are flung wide open.* Stepping off the ladder, he headed for the front door, deciding it best to make a quick stop at the hospital before returning to the station: family first. He had to see Ozzie for himself, had to know the kid would make a full recovery.

Come to think of it, why was Ozzie messing around with the Drummond's clock in the first place? More precisely, why hadn't Garrison thought to ask Agaritha what the boy was doing inside the clock? Unlike Garrison, Ozzie's mind was a scientific sponge oozing with factoids no one really needs to know, like why bubbles are always round and never square or triangle. Seriously, who gives a shit? But, if Agaritha asked Ozzie to tinker with the clock, there was definitely something shady going on. Once again, Garrison had asked all the wrong questions.

The front door had all but closed behind him with only half a crack to go when an ungodly crash emanated from inside the house. He held his firearm in hand without even realizing he'd reached for it. Jamming a shoulder into the door, he barged back inside. Hands planted firmly on the butt of his weapon, he waved it back and forth, eyes suddenly alert, scanning every inch of the floors and walls ahead. Safely inside the foyer, he turned left, his sights resting upon the clock's newly shattered belly, from which a crumpled human form had spewed, small and unmoving, lying face down in a sea of glass.

"Police! Don't move!"

That's exactly what it didn't do. Drawing nearer, Garrison discerned something familiar about the form on the floor. The more he scrutinized it, the more recognizable it became.

Devil's Edge

Approaching with extreme caution, he drew close enough to confirm what he saw was the last thing on earth his eyes wanted to see. Ebbenwright Drummond, field bag strapped over his shoulder, white hair glued to a bloodied neck someone had slashed from ear to ear, chest still and un-rising.

Holstering his pistol, Garrison lunged to the floor and grabbed the old man by the shoulders, flipping him over. Maybe he wasn't dead yet, maybe CPR could save him. Cringing, Garrison turned away from the sight of Ebbenwright's expressionless eyes, wide open and shadowed with the unfathomable emptiness only death can leave behind.

Cradling Ebbenwright in his arms, Garrison pressed the stiff, cold, flesh tight to his warring chest.

Anger, hatred, wrath, remorse, frustration...pure dread, a void like none other, sadness enveloping a deep despair. A hurricane of emotion tore at his being, guts squirming, chest imploding, pulse crashing against his eardrums like angry cymbals, the frail membrane of his soul ripping in half, tears racing, unrestrained, washing over his cheeks and filtering into his mouth where they tasted like blood, like a thirst for revenge, like helplessness, like hopelessness.

How could he possibly utter the words to Agaritha?

He rocked Ebbenwright like a newborn infant, determined to never let go, to hold on until the powers that be changed their minds, until they realized the tremendous mistake they'd made and gave Ebbenwright the boot, sending him back where he belonged, here with the people who loved him and depended on him to make the world a better place.

The clock startled Garrison with a sound resembling a gargantuan burp. That goddamn weird-ass clock was to blame, it had done something evil to Ebbenwright; it swallowed him up and spit him out like a meaningless tobacco cud. It deserved to die, no trial, no mercy. Garrison reached for his pistol and aimed the barrel at the clock face, his finger bearing down on the trigger. The clock responded by birthing another corpse, spitting it out so that it landed, with a sickening thud, in the same spot where the first one had fallen.

An unfathomable confusion wormed through Garrison's mind, his eyes unable to comprehend the sight set before them. The second corpse also belonged to Ebbenwright Drummond, complete with a menacing axe deeply imbedded in its trickling skull. Garrison scarcely had enough time to process the appearance of a second corpse when a third Ebbenwright arrived with a rope dangling from his severely bruised neck.

Shock struck Garrison with a force akin to a knee in the groin, and his headache morphed from migraine to an all-out nuclear explosion.

He fumbled for his radio and spat at the receiver, his voice urgent and nearly broken, "911, Bridgett. Send the coroner to Scabbard Street, like yesterday."

Contact

The night dragged on for Jillian Miller in anticipation of her release from Mercy General and morning came not a moment too soon.

Her father telephoned earlier to say he and Whitt would be out on the high marsh helping the police locate missing remains and, therefore, couldn't come to escort her home. Jillian made every effort to feign disappointment when, in fact, an empty house would insure her efforts to find Carla Ballencroft's diary went unencumbered; there would be no barrage of useless questions and she wouldn't risk tripping over fidiots as she scoured the house.

She said good-bye to Candace and enjoyed the walk home, relieved to breathe air uncluttered by antiseptics and human excrement.

Turning onto Billard Avenue, a police cruiser parked in front of the house caught Jillian's surprised attention. As she approached the driveway, a uniformed police officer came lumbering down the stairs off the front porch. The closer he came, the more readily she recognized him as the fellow with the two-pound cheeseburger at the diner; the oaf who told her to forget about The Ballencroft Book and leave police investigation to the professionals.

As Jillian peered over his shoulder to the front door, he tipped his hat in a nonchalant, gentlemanly way.

"What's going on?" she asked.

"Deputy Sheriff, Jared Duncan," he said, pointing to the shield pinned to his chest. "I received a report on a possible 10-31 at this address." Recognizing Jillian's confusion, he explained, "That's a break-in." Briefly glancing back at the door, he added, "A prank call by the looks of it. Nothing to worry about. All's clear." With another tip of the hat, he donned a wide smile and headed toward his cruiser.

Instantly uneasy, Jillian stared after the cruiser until the vehicle disappeared around the corner. She found the idea of a stranger rifling through her personal property disturbing, even if the officer did have an intent to protect said property.

Though it was difficult to imagine the house in any sorrier shape than the night she first gagged at the sight of it, the Miller men had somehow managed to worsen its appearance. Week after week, they had abandoned their dirty dishes in the kitchen sink and left piles of unwashed laundry to stew in dark corners like human entrails boiling in a cannibal's cauldron. The house reeked with the stench of over-cooked socks and hairy pizzas. A little antiseptic might help.

The search for the diary began in the most obvious place, Carla's old bedroom.

First on the list, the closet yielded nothing but a large dose of disappointment. Jillian would have bet her last dollar on finding Carla's diary hidden there, lying beneath a floorboard, or tucked into a hatbox on the top shelf. The last dollar is a hard one to lose.

An hour spent patting walls in search of weak boards that might indicate a secret hiding place yielded nothing. She tapped flimsy floorboards with the heels of her sandals, cursing empty drawers and boxes. Despite the excitement engulfed in the prospect of finding Carla's diary, Jillian's incompetent sleuthing resulted in nothing but a headache. Her efforts were too intense. If she could relax, regroup her thoughts, and formulate a new plan of attack, the search might flow with greater ease.

Lying on the bed, she allowed her throbbing mind to wander. The images were at first un-startling, the backside of a young hospital attendant who bent over to pick up a book that had fallen to the floor, Candace's face as she leaned out her car window to ask if Jillian wanted a ride home, sparkling sun rays dancing on the water's edge as the surf rolled in and the relentless image of the stack of grimy pots and pans waiting for rescue in the kitchen sink.

Uneventful visions gave way to shades of black and gray melding with streams of dim light, blurred and unrecognizable, until the face of a young girl began to assemble and solidify. The empty eyes staring back were those of an aged Carla Ballencroft, her expression drawn with exhaustion, her skin sallow and sagging, and her hair, no longer a silky golden blonde, appeared disheveled, frumpy, faded, and dreary, as if she hadn't shampooed for months. A cramped darkness made it seem as though she struggled inside the confines of a coffin. Had someone buried her alive? No, she sadly shook her head, the gesture apparently made in response to Jillian's unspoken inquiry.

Then Jillian heard a long, drawn-out belt of a scream, one that left little question as to its intended purpose. The mind automatically deciphers a scream's meaning, one scream indicating sheer delight, another, the product of bone-cold fear. Carla's was a wail of pure unadulterated frustration that left Jillian shocked and unthinking. Carla used this moment of shock, this brief expanse of barren mind, to invade Jillian's thoughts, directing her, with intense hand gestures, toward an antique bureau resting against the far wall; a bureau Jillian had already searched without favorable result.

Jillian formed her subsequent thought precisely: *The diary isn't there.* Carla screamed again, the annoyance in her falsetto starkly clear. Rising from the bed, Jillian approached the bureau with renewed determination. The drawers were still empty but for a dusty sack of mothballs.

Jillian concentrated on Carla.

Palms down, Carla bobbed her hands, indicating that Jillian should look lower. Scrambling to her knees, she peered beneath the bureau. There, collecting massive amounts of dust, a small book decorated with faded flowers hung from the bottom of the dresser, held in place by two rusted makeshift hinges: *The Ballencroft Book*.

Triumphantly snatching the diary from its hiding place, Jillian stood to her feet, immediately horrified by the sight of blood manifesting on the wall; trickling over faded wallpaper as it formed an eerily crafted message: *I'm alive.*

As if the apparition on the wall didn't upset her enough, a sudden stomach cramp sent Jillian reeling for the floor. Brief bursts of hot pain prickled through her head as though a thousand angry wasps mercilessly imbedded their stingers into her brain. The light filtering through the window in Carla's bedroom trickled away until nothing remained but the coffin-like darkness Jillian had sensed minutes before. A rank mustiness invaded her nostrils; festering mold, damp concrete, and sewer, mixed to form an unbearable stench that once again left her craving the scent of antiseptics she had so eagerly escaped when she left Mercy General.

Suddenly aware she clung to something soft and fuzzy, she tried to stand, but found herself hindered by unseen shackles, a searing pain pulsating through her ankles.

*Hot damn, hot damn, hot damn...*the words invaded her mind, cycling as if left on tumble dry, though she couldn't guess why, it wasn't a phrase Jillian ever thought to use. The figure of Jesus Christ hung on both sides of a golden cross, clinging to a hairy chest below the second button on a dark navy shirt. And Jillian Miller faded, minimized like a desktop icon, until her mind no longer remained her own.

The perpetual darkness drove her mad and she had once again chewed her fingernails until they bled. The silence didn't help. She hummed, but the melody always returned to *How Great Thou Art* and oh, how she hated that tune. It played in his car the night he whisked her away from a life of promise. The only song he ever listened to, he played it over and over again until she thought it might drive her into the halls of his insanity. Yes, she abhorred the song, but the humming served a small respite from the suffocating silence.

He'd forgotten to leave her a jug of water and her lips were cracked and dry from the oversight. He either left in a rush, or suffered another of his foul moods. She clung to the teddy bear he allowed her to keep, thinking what a wondrous thing it would be if the creature could tell a tale or two, it might keep her mind from slipping into the cracks it so often fell through; each fissure a dark, frightening episode she feared might one day engulf her completely, plucking reality from her once and for all.

She desperately tried to remember what it felt like to hope, how it felt to believe someone was searching for her. It seemed as if a lifetime had passed since she last saw a cloud scamper across the sky, watched the wind bend the branches of a tree, or listened to the rhythmic rumble of the sea. In the absence of these common events, all remembrance of hope had vanished.

If she had enough strength to yank on the chains binding her legs to the bed-frame, she wouldn't bother; the skin around her ankles had already swollen an angry purplish green, her blood pooling and drying into brown splotches on the bed sheets. Any effort to escape resulted in unbearable pain. It wasn't like she had the opportunity to grow stronger over time. Contrarily, she weakened into a mass of shriveled skin and bone. He was losing interest, of that she had no doubt. What he intended to do with her once he had enough of her whimpering and whining was a question only he could answer, a question she refused to entertain for any length of time.

In a few hours, he would return and mercifully spill a dingy light over her. He would complain she'd soiled the bed again, acting as though he gave her a choice in the matter. He would grope her, cursing her for his defilement, then leave her to the darkness that marked his shame as her own.

He would not release her. Once his interest waned, he would squeeze the life from her. Then, and only then, would she at last escape him.

Jillian awoke with a startle, clinging to Carla's diary. Carla Ballencroft was alive, enduring cruel conditions, and any hope for learning the identity of the monster holding Carla prisoner rested within the pages of her diary.

Dudley Too Tight

Guided by radiant rays of sun and a playful breeze, Whittaker H. G. Miller couldn't ask for a more perfect day to search for human remains.

The mission would go much smoother if the dull-brained deputy had allowed Merlin to come along. The mutt had, after all, sniffed out the arm in the first place. But, Dudley-too-tight would have none of it, saying he had enough to worry about without having to concern himself with a missing dog. Dumbest goddamn reasoning Whitt had ever heard, but he supposed it par for the course in places like Devil's Edge.

They traversed the high marsh for approximately the same amount of time it had taken Merlin to locate the arm initially and Whitt assumed they were zeroing in on x-marks-the-spot.

Like a blind man without a cane, the deputy continually veered off in the wrong direction, claiming nothing could survive so near the low marsh because the tide would eventually wash away anything not rooted down.

Whitt's father proved to be another pebble in the shoe. Taking stock in the cop's comments, he constantly stopped to ask if Whitt was certain they were going the right way. Without bothering to mask his sarcasm, Whitt asked why the tide hadn't washed away the arm suffocating in a zip lock at the police station. Still, he possessed no real certainty. Times such as these require a man to follow his gut; if he can't do that, he can at least follow the bay bushes. Though scant, the bushes seemed to thrive specifically between the high and low marsh. It was easy enough to follow them, not so simple to know when to stop.

The deputy seemed on edge and flighty; maybe the multiplying scuff marks on his shiny black shoes upset him, then again, maybe he wasn't the outdoor type. Whatever the problem, he repeatedly shoved a brick in the gears, questioning every move Whitt made, pointing out more likely places to search; hammering endlessly on sensitive nerves. At one point, he abandoned the search altogether and left the marshes for more than an hour, returning without an explanation.

It was Brad Miller who ultimately found the pair of bony feet protruding from beneath a tightly woven herring's nest. It became necessary to cut the grass away in order to reveal the rest of the skeleton, which remained intact but for the arm already recovered.

Once the deputy carefully placed the remains inside a black body bag, the triumphant trio made their way back toward town.

Nervous as a fly eyeballing a set of black widow fangs, the closer the deputy came to the edge of the marsh, the more strangely he reacted. The sun was hot, but insufficient to cause a man to soak the last inch of his shirt in sweat. Even Duncan's double-sided crucifix began to shed tears. He had carried the body bag the entire way, but it didn't seem as though the meager weight of a bag of dried up bones could explain the drenching. Maybe the dumb sap had a thyroid problem.

Finally arriving at the marsh edge where the deputy had parked the police cruiser, Duncan turned to the Millers, made a half-assed attempt to smile, and claimed he had other official business to tend to. He would appreciate it if they delivered the body bag to police headquarters, to which they eagerly agreed, glad to be free of the tension Duncan created.

The tires on the cruiser spun wildly, ejecting stones, and kicking up a miniature dust storm as the Deputy sped away.

Whitt rolled his eyes and twirled his finger around his right ear. Brad Miller hiked the body bag up on his shoulder and nodded.

"What a dope," Whitt grunted. "He could have dropped the bag in the trunk. It would have taken him less than five minutes to drive to the station."

Mr. Miller stopped walking and stared after the cruiser, watching as it became an eventual speck on the horizon.

Perplexed, Whitt yanked on the hem of his father's t-shirt, "What? What'd I say?"

Brad Miller spoke with a suspicious tone, "This body didn't get on the marsh all by itself. Someone put it there. Someone who might get a little nervous once it was recovered."

The Stalking

It didn't take long to discover what Jillian hoped to find inside The Ballencroft Book.

Carla first met Jared Duncan at Pop's soda shop where she and her friends hung out. Duncan had approached to ask if she would join him sometime for dinner. She politely declined, saying she already had a boyfriend and left the soda shop without giving Duncan a second thought. Page after page of Carla's diary documented the deputy's dogged persistence. On several occasions, she saw his police cruiser parked across the street and when they made eye contact, he would nonchalantly wave, as if his stalking shouldn't constitute alarm.

He proceeded to send flowers, left poorly written poetry in Carla's school locker, and invaded her home at will, leaving trinkets on her pillow to document his presence. Using his badge like a golden key, he persuaded others to perform unsuspecting deeds, coaxing them to open doors they would never open for a civilian, masking his motives like a seasoned spy. Jillian stopped reading as she realized Duncan had pulled the same stunt this very morning, standing on the porch in broad daylight, acting as if he had come to the house on official business. Clearly, his visit had nothing whatsoever to do with police business. He was searching for something; something Jillian had alerted him to, something she now held in her hands: Carla's diary.

Angry, Jillian turned a page using so much force she nearly ripped it from the binding.

Like a lion circling a stray gazelle, Duncan relentlessly stalked Carla until she found the nerve to approach him and demand that he stop. Angered, he threatened to put a nasty kink in Dale Archer's drag racing, insinuating Dale would make a nice cell wife at the state prison. That pissed Carla off. She promptly promised Duncan she would take the matter up with the sheriff if he ever approached her again.

Carla wrote her last diary entry the day after they unwrapped Dale Archer's firebird from the trunk of a tree, the ink on the page heavily splotched but decipherable. Dale, she wrote, never drove drunk and strictly refused to transport booze. Bells sounded when the cops claimed they found a case of beer inside the vehicle. Heartbroken and exploding with rage, Carla vowed to tie Duncan to the alleged accident. She wrote nothing further.

The mystery surrounding Carla Ballencroft's disappearance suddenly became clear. Mrs. Drummond had instructed Jillian to return to her once she located The Ballencroft Book and, since going to the police no longer seemed a viable option, that seemed like the best place to start. Diary clutched in hand, Jillian headed for Scabbard Street.

Devil's Edge

An Easy Heist

Alexander Spotswood stared at blurred coastline as the Greyhound bus made its way back to Devil's Edge, the sound of old metal intermittently clanking inside his jacket, the trip to Wilmington surprisingly productive. The second half of the Cuffs of Gall and the Chain of Vengeance were instantly recognizable. The museum crew at the Underwater Archaeology Branch had cataloged the relics and left them hanging on a wall behind a display case. Alexander simply waited for the room to empty, then snatched the booty off the wall and made a rush for the bus station.

Sadly, the museum was not in possession of the Sword of Woe, the Emerald Viper, or *The Book of Trials*. Still, he'd advanced further in his quest in the last few hours than he had over the course of thirty years.

Though he hadn't had much success at the Devil's Edge library, he strongly suspected he might find the remaining items housed there. If so, he would possess them by week's end. Silver hair snaked around his neck and a smile flirting with his lips, he caressed the newly recovered bounty. Arms wrapped tightly across his chest, he napped, certain the stars had finally lined up in his favor. Who knows, he might even win a chess match.

Slipping on the Peel

The things occurring in the living room on Scabbard Street were like scenes sliced from a 1950's sci-fi movie. The emergency crews had worked diligently through the night and now fought to keep Jillian from gaining a view of the living room floor, but ultimately failed. Thirteen bodies lined the carpet, each nearly identical in appearance.

The coroner stood scratching his head, mumbling incoherently, his face bleached to a ghostly pallor, generally looking as though he had slipped on a banana peel and skidded into The Twilight Zone.

Shuffling Jillian out the door, the sheriff offered her a ride to the station where she could speak with Mrs. Drummond.

Sliding into the front seat of the cruiser, Jillian clung to Carla Ballencroft's tattered diary. Sheriff Teach maintained a clamped jaw while Jillian read from the faded text. A purple rage ultimately replaced the initial white shock that had washed over his face. Planting his boot on the accelerator, he sent the car into a tailspin, choking the pavement with a burst of burnt rubber.

Ozzie's Near Death Experience

"It wasn't a dream," Ozzie insisted. Maurine nodded in surrender and relinquished the argument. She felt grateful her brother had survived his surgery, but the stories concerning his experiences on 'the other side' were truly unnerving.

"I saw you, Reeny," he persisted, "I saw you argue with Mom after she ripped into Mrs. Drummond. How could I know about it if I wasn't there? It happened exactly the same time the doctors said I flat lined. Explain that."

Maurine stared blankly into her brother's eyes and shook her head in defeat. She couldn't deny the fact Ozzie had died on the operating table any more than she could deny he somehow knew about the argument she had with their mother, but the bit about meeting and casually chatting it up with a renowned historical figure seemed harder to grasp than a handful of sand. How could she possibly believe Albert Einstein had shared world-altering information with an eleven-year-old boy? Too many were the times Ozzie voiced his desire to have an afternoon audience with Einstein. Surely, his experience was no more than a drug-induced hallucination. Still, there seemed no sense in pressing the argument; he obviously believed it and wouldn't back down from his convictions anytime soon.

Putting stock in Ozzie's account of his metaphysical meeting with Einstein was like hang gliding over the south side of impossible. Ozzie claimed the infamous scientist had revealed his knowledge of time travel but had warned him to keep the formulas a strict secret, just as Einstein had, due to the immaturity still prevalent in the human race. After the first nuclear bomb came into being, Einstein became convinced people were hell-bent on annihilating themselves and the planet. He'd put a tight lid on all subsequent discoveries. Frankly, that part of Ozzie's story wasn't so hard to believe.

Ultimately, Maurine could find no harm in allowing her brother his delusions. Whatever else may or may not have happened, Ozzie's near death experience had changed him profoundly. His speech was now slow and calm, he didn't seem to feel the need to invent facts like before, and he had reverted to calling her 'Reeny,' a nickname he bestowed upon her as a small boy but had since given up in the name of starched formality. What's more, he said he no longer had the desire to pursue science, but felt medicine might suit him better.

She agreed and spoke flippantly, "I don't suppose you came back with a cure for Tourette's?"

Birthday Bullets

Getting inside Duncan's place was like trying to penetrate Fort Knox with a toothpick. He must have installed thirty padlocks on the damn door. Garrison could hear the rat bastard scuttling around inside. He pounded at the barricade, first with his shoulders, then with a heavily booted foot. The door gave a little, but refused to open. Between beats, he listened to the sound of Duncan squirming inside, most likely scrambling for premium cover. Garrison backed up a few feet and came at the door with all he had, planting a foot squarely on its edge, encouraged when the wood cracked and the locks began to falter. The door gave way to a well-placed shoulder and Garrison stumbled inside.

Scanning the room, he peered over the tip of his pistol, straining to see in the darkness. Duncan had covered the windows with thick sheets of black plastic. Garrison gave himself a mental kick for neglect. If he'd visited Duncan at least once in the past ten years, he would have known something was off kilter.

A bullet discharged to his left. He lurched and rolled, landing behind a scruffy sofa parked outside the kitchen. The house was small and scantily furnished; he was lucky to find cover, insufficient or not. Inching the nose of his pistol over the top edge of the couch, he fired a blind round, his way of letting Duncan know he meant to put up a fight.

The moment they pulled into the driveway, the Miller girl began searching for hidden entrances and Garrison had let her go, thinking it best to keep her out of the line of fire. He heard her now, shuffling around the bushes outside, searching for a way into the basement. He assumed Duncan heard her as well when two more rounds came his way, one passing over the sofa, another buried inside its stuffing.

As well as Garrison could tell, Duncan hunkered down behind an island counter less than twenty feet away, its seasoned oak providing much better cover than a ratty sofa.

Outside, they heard the distinct sound of shattering glass, pissing Duncan off, and he started firing willy-nilly, a few bullets grazing off metal fixtures, others embedding in walls with dull thuds.

Staying low to the floor, Garrison inched his way to the left corner of the couch and listened as Duncan loaded a new magazine. Unless he'd scrounged up more ammo, there were only two magazines on his police-issue belt and he was already into the second. Another bullet pierced the sofa cushions less than six inches from Garrison's chest. Duncan zeroed in on his location and unloaded the second magazine like tomorrow held no clout, which meant he must have more ammo in stow. Unfortunate.

The sound of excited voices escaped the basement. The Miller girl must have found Carla.

Locked in position, Garrison struggled to think beyond the booming sound of Duncan's fire. He had to find a way to get a shot off without exposing himself. Closing his eyes, he listened, straining to hear anything that might give Duncan's position away. Duncan panted, scuffled his feet, and groaned...he was right of the island, firing low. Easing his pistol around the left corner of the sofa, Garrison fired—hoping Duncan would take the bait— then shifted quickly to the right, immediately spying Duncan's shadowed figure hunched to the floor behind the island. Garrison's next round hit home, how severely he couldn't say, but Duncan let out an encouraging yelp.

More chatter arose from the basement, along with the rattle of metal on concrete.

Crazed, Duncan began to fire into the floor.

"Die bitch," his voice strained in a maniacal tone, "I was done with you anyway."

Garrison hadn't quite settled in with the fact that his deputy was a nut-job. How could he work side-by-side with Duncan for so many years without knowing him at all? The pondering would have to wait; as long as Duncan pumped lead into the floor, Garrison's opportunity to stand and take a shot would never be better. Jumping to his feet, he let a round go and quickly retreated. The shot hit its mark. Again, Garrison didn't know where it hit, but it dropped Duncan to the floor with a full-body thump.

He wasn't dead. Garrison could hear him mumbling words no good Christian would ever utter.

"Give it up, Jared."

Duncan spewed a string of unholy words, and planted three more rounds in the sofa's midsection.

Two car doors slammed, one after another, just outside the front door. The Miller girl had gotten Carla to the cruiser.

"She's free, Jared. You can still leave here alive, just slide your gun over here."

Duncan fired. The slug hit a weak section of the sofa and came through, drilling into Garrison's flesh just above the belt, burning like a bee sting.

Ain't that one hell of a birthday present, he thought, pressing his hand against his gut, wondering how many people actually die on their birthdays. He was fifty-two today, and would need a solid plan if he wanted to see fifty-three. After this hellish week, he was prepared to make a swift change in careers; maybe Donny Baker could use a hand in the real estate business.

Duncan reloaded again, who knows how much ammo he had left...a lot more than Garrison, for sure. Garrison needed an edge, but even after his eyes had adjusted to the dark, he could find no better cover than the sofa. Maybe a mental edge would do.

"Backup will be here any second, Jared. Give it up and live to see another day." It was an outright bluff, but Duncan couldn't possibly know that.

Another bullet traveled beneath the sofa and passed to the left of Garrison's knee. The bastard was shooting low now. Garrison shoved his pistol under the couch and let a round go: two can play that game.

The sudden blare of police sirens began to wail despite the fact he hadn't called for backup, their shrill call the most angelic sound Garrison could have hoped for.

Duncan immediately fired another round, its path unclear. No thud in the walls, no thwapping of the sofa, nothing. All went silent.

Unwilling to fall for a ruse, Garrison waited it out. When he heard nothing more, he inched around the sofa and peeked into the kitchen. Duncan's head lay face down on the floor, swimming in a pool of blood. Had the sick bastard done himself in?

Garrison inched toward the body, reaching to check for a pulse. Duncan rolled onto his back and fired, hitting Garrison point-blank in the chest. *Happy birthday dear Garrison, happy birthday to you...*

Shifting Gears

Sensing the sheriff wasn't faring well inside, Jillian sat in the driver's seat of the police cruiser, trying to figure out how to the use the radio to call for help. She'd turned the engine over, in the event she might have to make an emergency exit, and flipped the switch for the siren. The radio receiver dropped to the floor and she winced as she bent to retrieve it; its coiled cable curled around her wrist like a boa on the prowl, but she had no idea how to power up the lifesaving gizmo.

Duncan staggered out the front door, an oozing heap of flesh, waving his gun at the cruiser, shrieking Carla's name.

Jillian screamed, dropped the radio receiver, and quickly shifted the car into gear. Suffering a moment's hesitation, she nearly stopped to reconsider what she was about to do, but the prominent picture of Carla's withered body chained to the bed in Duncan's basement spurred her on as she jammed the accelerator until her foot hit the floor. The last thing she remembered was the sound of spinning tires.

Devil's Edge

Mulching Bone

Garrison swaggered to the cruiser, its rear tires still spinning over Duncan's head—not much left but slime and shattered bone. The Miller girl slumped over the steering wheel, Carla Ballencroft lay unconscious in the backseat, and the siren blared. He reached in, cut off the engine and silenced the siren, then quickly withdrew. The inside of the cruiser smelled like a stewing sewer and it took a moment to identify the source of the foul stench as Carla's soiled nightgown.

Pressing a hand to his leaking wound, he inspected the Miller girl. She must have lost consciousness when the car slammed into a large boulder blocking the end of the driveway. A trickle of blood inched down the left side of her face, but one of Duncan's bullets had also drilled into her leg, the front seat saturated with blood. How she managed to remain conscious long enough to do Duncan in, he might never know.

Assembling the Pieces

"Lucky you were wearing a flak jacket," the emergency room physician mumbled as he stitched the hole in Garrison's gut. Didn't he know it.

Before he left the ER, he checked on Jillian Miller. The attending physician said her wound was superficial, but he planned to keep her for observation. From the look in Jillian's defiant eyes, Garrison doubted that very much. He would get back to her later.

Returning to the station, he sat down with Agaritha, who looked like she hadn't slept a wink all night, and was not the least bit surprised to hear Jared Duncan had kidnapped Carla Ballencroft after he'd murdered her boyfriend and her parents.

"If'n I'd said somethin' before Marcus was found, you wouldn't have believed me, and he wouldda killed again," she said, lowering her chin. "It wasn't an easy decision, but I couldn't see losin' more innocent people."

She was right. Everyone in town believed Marcus had killed his wife and that gave Duncan the freedom to dispose of anyone who got in his way without risking suspicion. Once it became clear Marcus hadn't done the deed, a new investigation would have surfaced. The biggest shame of all was Duncan didn't suffer nearly enough to pay for the horrific things he'd done.

Garrison looked into Aggy's eyes and thought of the other matters at hand. He had yet to tell her about the corpse-spitting clock. He delivered the news gently and left nothing out.

She would be the first to know if Ebby were truly dead and she wouldn't say another word about the matter, consoling Garrison with a pat on the back of the hand, saying how glad she was he was okay, asking if he hurt, wishing him a happy birthday. Then she inquired about the garden club flyers, pressing on as if nothing else had happened. Garrison pulled the flyers from his pocket and handed them over.

Agaritha inspected the flyers and asked for the coroner's photographs from the crime scene at the Finwicket estate. Garrison reached for the intercom and asked Blanche to retrieve the files. Once they arrived, Aggy's reason for requiring the garden club flyers became obvious.

Thanks to Cybil Sherman's distaste for rhubarb, a single slice of pie remained for the coroner's thorough inspection. Agaritha placed the forensic photographs next to a picture of the blue ribbon entry for the 2005 state fair pie-baking contest, a peach pie submitted by Velma Sinclair.

"Look at the rim of them pie crusts," Aggy said. "Only Velma Sinclair takes the time to weave a French twist into the pastry's edge. It's her trademark. I'll betcha a case of cookies she used Wolf's Bane, everybody knows she grows it."

Garrison leaned over the pictures and sighed with relief. If he could talk old Harry Winthrop into dropping those exaggerated child endangerment charges (a bottle of fifteen-year-old scotch should do the trick) Agaritha would spend the night in her own bed.

"Seems Velma don't want our girl Jillian breakin' that curse," she said. "Makes sense in a messy way, she's a descendant of the woman who breathed the curse in the first place. If'n I was you, sheriff," she poked him in the arm, "I'd have me another look at them notes on the library fire. If'n Velma feels strongly enough to commit murder, chances are her daughter's in cahoots."

A Race against Time

Jillian allowed the only words Carla Ballencroft had spoken to repeat inside her mind: *"I saw you in my dream."* Like it or not, some power, some freakish mind-melding ability, had awakened within her and had proven vital in Carla's rescue. As she watched the emergency tech pull a small silver fragment out of her leg with a pair of surgical tweezers, she reluctantly acknowledged how useful the psychic experience had been. She doubted her ability to pull the plug on these experiences, no matter how much she might want to. She wondered how readily her mother had accepted this terrible gift. Or, had she also rued its awakening? Whatever she felt about it in the beginning, Sarah Miller had ultimately come to terms with it. Perhaps, one day, Jillian would as well.

Concerned with her concussion, the doctor spoke of keeping her for observation. She emphatically refused to stay, insisting on leaving as soon as they bandaged her leg.

She caught a ride to the police station with an EMT, where she demanded to see the sheriff. A redheaded woman escorted her to the interrogation room where Mrs. Drummond and the sheriff leaned over a file of photographs scattered across the table. Though visibly exhausted, Mrs. Drummond didn't look half as weary and ragged as the sheriff.

He stood to his feet the moment Jillian entered the room and reached to help her into a chair, as if she were a delicate piece of china.

"You're a brave one, Miss Miller," he said matter-of-factly, his newfound respect evidenced in his softened gaze.

Jillian smiled weakly as she took the chair next to Mrs. Drummond. The old woman patted Jillian on the hand and said, "I hope you don't imagine this is over." Lowering her head, Jillian swallowed hard, acting as though the ominous words hadn't fazed her.

Toying with the bandage on the side of her head, she cleared her throat and asked if anyone had notified Candace Flute. "She'll want to know about Carla, they were best friends."

The sheriff raised an eyebrow. "If I recall, she was the only one in town who didn't believe Marcus killed his wife."

"Not the only one," Mrs. Drummond mumbled.

The sheriff waved at the redheaded woman and asked her to give Candace a call. The librarian would be overjoyed to learn her friend was alive, but seeing Carla in her current state—a breathing skeleton aged beyond her years by neglect and abuse—would not be easy. Jillian assumed Carla would need a miracle just to salvage some form of sanity.

Mrs. Drummond's face lit up as if she suddenly remembered something important. Clutching the sheriff's arm, she said, "Garrison, was there field bags on any of them cadavers that fell from the clock?"

He nodded, "On all of 'em."

Her words surfed over her lips as she exhaled, "Praise the powers." Lowering her voice to a near whisper, she leaned close to the sheriff. "Can you gather everything inside them? Can you do that now and bring everythin' here?"

"But Aggy..."

She said no more, certain her stern expression would make her case, which it did.

"Can I send someone..." the sheriff began.

"No, no, no, no, no..." she insisted. "If'n you send anybody else, they'll make off with what we need."

"I'll be back in ten minutes," he said hobbling toward the door, slumping as if a skillful boxer had beaten him to a pulp.

Mrs. Drummond's intense gaze locked on Jillian. "He's comin' back with an emerald viper, give or take twelve or thirteen," she whispered, "and you can get the book and the sword from Candace Flute. I believe our old friend Digger Spotswood has all the rest. You're gonna have to convince him to give you what he's got and that ain't gonna be easy, but do whatever it takes."

"You know about the relics?" Jillian felt her jaw go slack, flabbergasted.

"A course I know." Mrs. Drummond's facial expression seemed to say Jillian had just uttered the dumbest question under the sun.

"Why else would my Ebby run back and forth through time? To find them relics, a course."

Jillian's eyes went wide, "He what?"

"Never mind that. The faster you break the curse, the less chance anybody else has to take another swing at you. I suggest you go have yourself a talk with Digger, might take all day to persuade that old geezer, maybe longer."

Unexpected Visitors

A mischievous breeze taunted Alexander Spotswood's three-cornered hat, threatening to send it spiraling off into the sand, but not quite prepared, or willing, to do so. Steadying his hat, he swished a paintbrush into a rusted can filled with turpentine, watching as black paint swirled off the bristles, darkening the pungent liquid. Stepping back, he surveyed his masterpiece, a sign painted on a haggard wooden plaque, which simply read, *Bait*.

He didn't expect to get rich selling beetles and worms to tourists, though every man is wise to harbor hope. The cash-only transactions supplemented his meager income and sometimes meant the difference between one bottle of Jack per month, or two—a difference well worth a new coat of paint.

His errand complete, he stepped onto the planks leading to his front door. The bright afternoon sun momentarily blinded him, but as he twisted away from its searing beams he saw two figures approaching, at first no more than a speck of movement caught in his peripheral vision, then solidifying until he clearly saw a very tall young woman (he recognized her as the young Anne Bonny) and a much shorter girl (Blackbeard's alleged off spew). Their toes kicked up sand on the path leading to his house. Caught off guard, he scuttled inside and barred the door, frenzied and panting to catch his breath, trying to ascertain what this unannounced visit might mean.

He doubted, very much, they had come for bait. He had nothing else to offer but the relics and to those he would cling until the expiration of his last breath.

They'd probably seen him trip over himself to get into the house and would never fall prey to any ruse that he might not be home.

He scrambled from window to window, desperate to see past the grime, an impossible task. The girls rapped on the door. Leery, he pressed his nose to each successive pane, peering left then right, watching for the blurred figures of anyone who might have accompanied the two young women. It would seem they had come alone. Not an altogether wise decision.

Alexander's skills didn't include knowledge of the law, but he strongly suspected he had the right to slay intruders caught inside his own home. For that purpose, he kept a harpoon always at the ready. He moved it within reach. Swiping up a blade from the kitchen, he sheathed it inside a belt loop behind his back, and carefully wrapped his hair around his neck so it would not encumber.

"Prepared to die, are ye?" He bellowed through the unopened door.

Devil's Edge

"Cheeses H. and Mary's crackers, let's go!" He heard one of them say, and he doubted it was Anne Bonny's heir what said it, although he found it just as difficult to imagine Blackbeard's kin as the cowardly kind, no matter how distant. Just as his forefather, the governor of Virginia, had gained celebrity for putting an end to Blackbeard's antics, Alexander would do the world a favor by ridding it of these foul spews.

"We want to make a deal," a much steadier voice said.

"This ain't a used car lot. Alexander Spotswood does not make deals. Did ya hear? He does *not* make deals!"

"I have the emerald viper, the sword, and *The Book of Trials*," she insisted, "If you want to open the door of doom, you have no choice."

Alexander gasped and took a step back. They knew about *La Porte de Ruine*. Up until now, he assumed everyone had written the legend off as myth. This had to be the work of that meddlesome librarian, *Satan spit on her wretched soul!* Alexander paced. Now that the truth ran loose, the entire town and every treasure scavenger from the four corners of the globe would bear down on Devil's Edge until some greedy-eyed bugger walked away with the very treasure Alexander had devoted his entire life to. Not if he had anything to say about it, by Jack!

If these girls really knew where the relics were, he couldn't let them walk away without divulging their whereabouts.

"How do I know you're not lying?" He spat at the door.

The reply came without hesitation. "Would we be here if we were lying?"

"Maybe, maybe you just want the relics I have!"

"What good would they be if we didn't have the rest?" One of them exclaimed.

Oh, she had a point. Could it be? It must. They had the relics. Alexander scratched at his forehead, kneaded his gnarled fingers until they turned white, and paced circles trying to decide what to do. He wanted those relics more than a brigantine filled to the brim with Jack Daniel's. Now that they were within his reach, he couldn't let them slip through his grasp.

Negotiations

The house seemed more like an overgrown shed than a home and maybe the word 'overgrown' was far too generous but as Jillian scanned the room, her stomach turned and she wondered how anyone could live cowering in the shadows like a spider or a bat, amidst rotting wood and festering dust, ingesting the smell of time gone sour.

She sat on a lobster crate, engaged in a glare-down with one of the scariest men she ever laid eyes on. This was not her idea of an acceptable social outing, and yet, here she sat, trying to ignore a housefly busily digging its way in and out of the corner of a glass eye that belonged to a sadly deteriorated stuffed moose.

She had implemented Mrs. Drummond's sage advice and asked Maurine along for the nerve-wracking visit. She, too, sat atop a dilapidated lobster crate, her right shoulder twitching so badly it threatened an uppercut, her lips forming silent words that didn't make sense, her gaze failing in the attempt to remain glued to the toe of her sequined boot. She wore her fear like a gaudy feathered cap and it didn't seem as though she would be much help. God bless her racing heart, though, she had at least agreed to come along.

Despite the fact the afternoon sun had little chance to break through the grime on Digger's windows, shades of filtered light threw shadows over the old man. His braided hair encircled his neck like a boa constrictor; the lines on his rustic face lay grooved like the weathered bark on an old oak, and a lone tooth dug into his lower lip as he formed a maniacal grin. Was that a half-assed attempt at social etiquette, or was he still considering the prospect of inflicting bodily harm?

The knife hidden behind his back hadn't escaped Jillian's detection and a harpoon leaned against the wall behind the door, lurking in the darkest shadows. The faster this deal went down the better.

She suggested combining their respective relics and instituting a fifty-fifty split on whatever treasures the grotto might hold.

Hearing this, Digger pounded his fist on the table to accentuate the strength of his resolve, "Everything in the chest of treasures is *mine*."

"How selfish is that?" Jillian contested, hoping her quick-tongued assertion wouldn't ignite a loose fuse.

The old man's eyelids closed to thin slits and he reached behind his back, his reflexes quicker than expected. Maurine toppled off her lobster crate, expelling some god-awful sound—half scream, half belch. She, too, must have seen the weapon secured in Digger's belt loop.

The old man raised Maurine to her feet by the tip of his knife, its blade trembling beneath her chin. She went limp as a half-cooked noodle and released a string of expletives capable of slaying sensitive ears in one fell swoop. Jillian took a wide stance, bracing her knuckles on the tabletop, eyes scanning to-and-fro until her gaze came to rest on the harpoon.

"I'll slice her from ear to ear." Digger's baritone voice remained eerily calm and Jillian shuddered at the sound, not doubting his resolve for a second.

"Get those relics and meet me at the grotto. You've got one hour, or I'll cook me up some girlie stew. Aye?"

Ill-Fated Advice

Jillian left Digger's shack feeling like Alice in Blunderland. Her first hours in Devil's Edge had resulted in Teddy Teach's concussion and a few days later she nearly killed Candace Flute. She couldn't say for certain, but suspected she had some involvement in the deaths of the women at the Finwicket estate, and may very well have had an indirect hand in Ozzie's injuries as well. Now, because she didn't have the good sense to get out of town, Maurine quivered on the wrong end of a knife blade.

Damn it, what good is a psychic gift if it can't at least supply some kind of warning when all hell is breaking loose? Even if she could get the artifacts in time, even if she could make it back to the grotto, she had no guarantee Maurine hadn't already fallen victim to the sheer stupidity that left her at Digger's mercy in the first place. Though it's not entirely possible to fly through sand, Jillian made every effort to do so.

Okay, so this episode slipped by her psychic detection and had escaped Mrs. Drummond's senses as well. Or, had Mrs. Drummond known exactly what would transpire? Was that the reason she insisted Jillian bring Maurine along? The more she fumed, the more Jillian began to feel like a marionette attached to Mrs. Drummond's strings.

As Jillian's feet left the sand and bounded over solid sidewalk, she thought about each of Mrs. Drummond's directives. *'Listen to my message. Go to the library. Follow Candace into the dungeon. Find the Ballencroft book. Take Maurine to Digger's house.'* Every piece of advice had resulted in a major disaster. So the Spirit Rapper had a gift, that didn't necessarily mean she wasn't a loon, capable of putting anyone within her proximity in mortal danger.

Jillian checked her watch. Fifteen minutes had expired since she'd left Maurine at Digger's whim. Forty-five minutes to get the relics and return to the grotto. If she had any hope of accomplishing this task on time, she would need a vehicle. She ran both hands through her hair and leaned into the wind, heading for the police station. Someone would have to inform Mrs. Teach her daughter's life hung in the balance. Jillian decided that someone should be Mrs. Drummond.

No Ordinary Day

Anne Bonny willed herself off the floor and rose to the ceiling of her stone prison, aching to get as close as possible to the rays of sun filtering through a small hole. Ten feet from the top, she came to an abrupt stop, as if barred by an invisible arm. This unknown force had held her back for hundreds of years and, by the fists of Athena, she had had enough of its bullying. Concentrating with all her might, she pushed until every ounce of her energy expired, and yet, she remained precisely ten feet away from the only perspective inside the grotto that offered a view of the outside world. Shaking a fist at the unseen entity, she wailed, "Kiss me arse, ye blasted demon!"

A faint giggle emulated from below and Anne turned toward the sound, her eyes thin, her nose crinkled with disgust. "Tickled a funny bone, have I?"

Mary relaxed atop a large limestone slat, arms behind her head, ankles crossed. "Aye," she chuckled, "tis fair entertainment." With a quick shift, she sat up. "What insanity inspires ye to think ye can accomplish the impossible today?"

Anne slowly descended. "Laugh, wench. On my oath, today feels different than any ordinary day."

Mary stood to face Anne. "It does? Are ye to say it feels different in the same way ye first sensed our blessed Jack Rackham had no wits to speak of?"

"I heard that!" Jack's indignation echoed off the walls of the stone tomb.

"Or, in the way ye felt different when ye had no clue Captain Barnet's sloop had approached to deliver our demise?" Mary parked her hands firmly upon her hips.

Anne's expression softened as she offered herself to Mary, arms outstretched. "Don't chastise me, Mary Read. Today really is unusual. I tell ye, bizarre turns ride the wind." Grasping at her chest in an attempt to capture the emotions writhing within, she lowered her voice to a whisper. "It feels like Morgan."

"Morgan?" Mary scoffed. "Our children have been dead many a year. How can a day feel like your daughter?"

"I do not know how, Mary, I only know what I feel. She approaches." Anne wildly shook her hands in front of Mary's face, squelching any forthcoming comments before she could make them. "Aye, it reeks with insanity, but someone approaches."

Mary spoke abruptly and turned away, indicating the end of her participation in the conversation. "Aye," she said, "the loon who comes every fortnight to feast on fresh rat meat."

Anne disengaged, sensing she could say nothing more to convey the urgency spiraling through her mind. The sensation invaded at the rising of the sun and had not ceased since. She warred with it for hours, trying to convince herself wishful thinking had intoxicated her, but she lost the mighty battle.

Anne understood how it felt to know things normal people couldn't possibly know, as had her mother and grandmother before her. She had once overheard them confide in one another as to the unpredictability of their gift, and of the few truths her mother had ever uttered, this Anne could not deny, unpredictable it was.

Aye, as Mary inferred, Anne had not known Barnet's sloop had stolen upon *The Merry Anne*. But, she had sensed, on many other occasions, occurrences that would have done them all in had she not seen them beforehand. Mary had an exceptionally bright mind and Anne had a sixth sense with a mind of its own. Without these traits, they never would have survived the high seas, nor would they have escaped the noose in Port Royal.

Although Anne could not possibly know when the senses were failing to warn of some dire event, she certainly knew when she *did* feel something of immense importance. Today, she perceived adventure for the first time in nearly three hundred years and, by the weight of Thor's hammer, even if it be a ruse, she would feast upon it for as long as it lasted.

Collecting Relics

Jillian was six blocks from the police station when sirens began to blare in the distance. Three minutes later, Sheriff Teach's cruiser, packed to the brim with passengers, pulled over in front of her. Mrs. Drummond waved from the back seat, "Get a move on, girl. We've got relics to gather."

The car door slammed behind Jillian and she twisted into the backseat. "How could you let her go, knowing that lunatic would put a knife to her throat?"

"What's done is done." Mrs. Drummond's words sounded so harsh and heartless Jillian felt a sudden urge to slap the old woman.

"Take your best swing if'n it'll make you feel better. What matters now is getting Maurine back and breakin' that curse."

Candace Flute also sat in the backseat nervously chewing her nails. Beside her, Ozzie hunkered into what little remained of the passenger space.

Jillian poked the tip of her thumb in Ozzie's direction. "What's he doing here? Shouldn't he be in the hospital?"

"Gonna need him," Mrs. Drummond quipped, and Ozzie's face glowed in the way a young boy's face beams when he sees a brand-new bicycle parked under the Christmas tree.

"I don't suppose you bothered to inform Mrs. Teach her daughter is being held by a maniac, or that you've borrowed her son."

"No time to scrap. What Dixie don't know won't hurt her."

The police cruiser turned into the parking lot at the library. Everyone quickly abandoned the vehicle and ran for the building. Mrs. Drummond, wearing a bloodied field bag strapped around her neck, led the pack and stood at the door, waiting impatiently for Candace to insert her key. Jillian glanced at her watch. Thirty minutes to get to the grotto.

Amazingly, Candace had hidden the Sword of Woe in plain sight for all to see, sheathed in one of the coats of armor standing guard at the front door. It had been untouched for years and had settled firmly into the sheath. Though she made one admirable attempt after another, Candace had no hope to pull it free. Sheriff Teach stepped up to the task, tugging and twisting for the most anxiety filled twenty minutes Jillian had ever endured. Finally, Sir Rust-a-lot loosened his grip. Handing the sword over to Mrs. Drummond, the sheriff asked, "Have we got everything we need?"

Mrs. Drummond was already halfway out the door. "Everythin' but time."

Entering the Grotto

The late afternoon sun sparkled off the black surface of an SUV Jillian recognized as her father's. He'd parked near a stone path leading to the beach. Sheriff Teach pulled in next to the SUV and lifted a hand in salutation.

Four hundred yards past the pebble-riddled parking area, a massive mound of black rock rose out of the sand. On a foggy day this odd lump of molten earth might be mistaken for a beached whale, but crisp rays of light reflecting off the stone showed the crest of Neptune's grotto looming three or four times larger than the greatest sea beast.

The drive from the library took less than five minutes, but unless someone discovered a way to skate over sand, crossing the beach would take far too long. They were late.

The sheriff raised an arm, securing everyone's attention. Resting his hand on the butt of his pistol and incorporating an official tone, he said, "I'll be going in alone. No one is to go inside until I say so. Clear?"

Forcefully squeezing between Mrs. Drummond and Candace Flute, Jillian faced off with sheriff Teach. "No," she pushed her words past tense lips, "I left her alone with that whacko. I won't abandon her now." And, to ensure the sheriff didn't underestimate her resolve, she pointed to his pistol and said, "Shoot me now, if you have a problem with that."

"We're wastin' time," Mrs. Drummond insisted, nodding at the sheriff.

"All right, let's go, just remember, once we get to the entrance everyone waits outside 'cept me and Miss Miller."

Jillian stuffed her fingertips into her hair and raked them over the crown of her head, choking back a sudden flush of anxiety. She bolted forward and began to trudge through the sand, asking her father how he'd known where to find her. His lanky frame swayed as he navigated the deep sand, "Sheriff called." Jillian stayed close, grateful for the sense of security her father's presence provided.

Reaching to put an arm around her shoulder, he said, "I think you ought to wait outside with the rest of us until the sheriff takes care of that crazy old man."

"It's my fault she's in there."

Early signs of sunset began to appear as faint wisps of pink saturated the edges of scant clouds looming on the horizon. Seagulls rushed to secure their last meals of the day, their shrill calls battling over the rushing surf.

The bullet hole in Jillian's leg began to burn and her calves cramped. She forced her feet to move, her mind locked on the image of Maurine's horrified expression, her dark eyes pearls of desperation, begging Jillian not to leave her in the arms of a maniac.

By the time the entourage arrived at the grotto entrance, it was well past the hour.

Maurine's Fate

Mr. Miller squeezed Jillian's hand so tight her fingers turned beet red. "Don't be a hero. He's got the gun, let him lead. You stay out of the way."

A massive, gaping hole formed the mouth of Neptune's grotto. Jillian stepped inside the cavern and shivered at the sight of a giant, dangling stalactite. The exterior of the grotto masked its enormity. Sheriff Teach pulled a flashlight from his belt and began to scan the immediate area. Jillian anticipated meeting Maurine and Digger just inside, but they were nowhere in sight.

"Looks like trouble," the sheriff said, bending down to inspect the cave floor.

"What is it?"

Lifting two stained fingers, he spoke anxiously, "Blood. There's a trail."

Jillian's heart ceased to beat.

"Maurine!" She bellowed, employing all the volume her lungs would allow.

"Don't panic, this blood could belong to any number of things...bats, rats, seagulls, fish, you name it."

Jillian stared directly at the sheriff's face, but couldn't see him, couldn't hear him. "Maurine!"

The flashlight beam followed the blood trail. "It could be nothing," the sheriff mumbled, trying to convince himself as much as Jillian. As they moved forward through the darkness, the flashlight zeroed in on a small pool of blood. Panic radiated through Jillian's chest until it worked its way into a full-blown cranial explosion. "Maurine!"

A faint voice echoed in reply, "Over here."

Sheriff Teach stiff-armed Jillian, forcing her behind as they squirreled their way through a tunnel that veered off to the right and led to a small alcove. Turning the corner, they both stopped as if barred by an unseen wall, desperate to absorb the sight set before their eyes. Maurine stood in the darkness, her sequined boot pinned to the back of Digger's neck, a hefty rock poised to pummel his skull, a sheepish grin adorning her face.

The sheriff lunged forward, ripped his handcuffs from his belt clip, and gently guided Maurine's foot away from Digger's neck. "I've got him," he assured her, his voice radiating with sheer relief.

Jillian jerked Maurine away from the two men and, dumbfounded, demanded to know what happened.

"There was this rat, bigger than a Volkswagen, and when we came inside the cave, it went for his pant leg...latched on like a piranha invited to a smorgasbord. He pushed me in here, trying to get away from that nuclear freak, but it came back and attacked again; like there was a bull's eye painted on his ankle or somethin'. He starts to shake his leg, and the rat is like, whoohoo...a free roller-coaster ride, so I stuck my foot out and down they both went. I whacked Chernobyl Charlie a good one on the head. Swear to God, it just smiled at me, but seein' how I wasn't lettin' go of this rock, it finally turned tail. If that thing's got a daddy, we're all in deep doo-doo."

Thrusting herself at Maurine, Jillian threw her arms around her. "I'm so sorry I had to leave you."

"Yeah well, next time, leave me someplace where I can at least get a glass of champagne and a decent manicure."

A trickle of blood ran down the side of Digger's face where he smacked it when Maurine introduced him to the ground and his leg oozed around the ankle. "I wasn't going to hurt her, I swear."

The sheriff dragged Digger to his feet and, with more than a measure of disgust, snarled, "Save it."

Jillian stepped aside as Ozzie burrowed his head into Maurine's shoulder.

"What now, Aggy?" Sheriff Teach yanked on Digger's cuffs to keep him from sidling away.

"Now you have to let him go," she said.

The sheriff tilted his head, his expression incredulous. "Why?"

"'Cause he's the only one who knows how to find the door."

"You don't know?"

Agaritha expelled a chuckle. "Hell, if'n I knew, I'd a been in there years ago."

"I can't just let him go." Clearly, Sheriff Teach deemed Mrs. Drummond's request one of the most insane things she ever asked of him.

"I don't suppose you have to take the cuffs off, just let him lead the way."

Digger turned on Agaritha like a cobra no longer enchanted by the golden flute. "Find the door yourself."

Agaritha's cheeks flushed. "No reason to get snippy. Dare I say you made a deal with Miss Miller? The deal still stands."

Digger's eyes went wide. "It does?"

"A course it does. You get everythin' in the chest. If'n you can find it in your greedy little heart to lead us to the door."

Stealing Shadows

Dressed in black, face covered by a hooded sweatshirt, an obscure figure went unnoticed as it slipped inside the grotto behind the sheriff's entourage. Confined to the shadows and stealthy in its haunting, the figure followed closely behind.

Nice Day for a Swim

How much more could a guy hope for? Murder, skeletons, ghosts, pirates, treasure, curses; throw in a herd of rabid rats for good measure. Whitt observed the dire seriousness painted on the faces of those around him and desperately tried to keep from smiling. Difficult. Damn near impossible.

Here he stood, in the thick of it, at a time when his father would normally force him to stay at home alone, or worse, leave him under the rule of a lame babysitter. Oh, the damage parents inflict when they instill the idea children are not capable of caring for themselves. For shame. But not today. Today, Whitt gloated, his shadow would cast.

It was dark inside the grotto, not just for lack of light, but sinister too, in an intriguing way. The hair on Whitt's arms rose as if grazed by a balloon.

Stalactites grew from the cavern ceiling, protruding like venomous fangs. Echoes of dripping water resounded throughout the grotto—*plink, plunk, plop*—as drops of water slowly coursed down the stalactites, trickling to the floor, amassing into small pools that would eventually erode the stone beneath, forming larger pools and streams. Air collected in pockets of stale humidity, imprisoning the stench of expired rats and crustaceans carried in by high tides, the smell rank and unforgiving. Wisps of fog churned, clinging to the bases of the stalagmites jutting up from the cavern floor, and an occasional squeal and chitter served as a reminder of the bats infesting every nook and cranny.

Whitt covered his head with his hands and ducked, reminded of the time his grandfather tried to shoo away a bat trapped in his attic, only to have it end up tangled in his hair. Grams had to cut Gramps' hair to free him of the menace and the bat escaped without a scratch. Gramps never stopped complaining about the rabies shots.

Timid, everyone huddled close together as they moved deeper into the cavern, first past a mammoth stalactite, then turning right toward a clump of limestone that looked vaguely like a woman preparing to slaughter an audience with a powerful aria. Passing by Madame Butterfly, they turned left, entering a large alcove accentuated by a gushing waterfall that emptied into a body of water large enough to accommodate a yacht, so long as the boat didn't belong to some hotsy-totsy rich guy. A natural stone bridge stretched over the water's expanse, every inch covered in mossy slime, guaranteed to make navigation treacherous as all hell.

Forward progression came to a full stop. Digger warned of the nasty conditions on the bridge and insisted on having his handcuffs removed. It was impossible, he said, to get across without using his arms for balance. After some hesitation, the sheriff obliged. Digger then took the first steps across the bridge and turned to say what a shame it would be if anyone failed to make it across. Whitt tried, but couldn't perceive a sense of sincerity in the old man's tone.

Like a lion protecting a den of cubs, Mr. Miller insisted on holding his children's hands as they took their first steps onto the bridge. The word slippery didn't adequately define the condition of the stones. The moss grew thick and rotted beneath the intense heat and humidity. Stones lay at various angles, some higher than others, some steeper, some so sharply angled, one false move and sayonara. A hockey puck might have a fair chance to make it across in one piece, but a human being, not so much.

Because he seemed to know what he was doing, everyone focused on Digger's feet, eager to pick up the slightest hint for easing the all-around anxiety. Digger dug the toe of his shoe into the moss, twisting until clumps of slime let loose, baring the stone beneath. He then took another step forward and repeated. Each person took great pains to follow in his footsteps, not exactly the easiest maneuver when an overprotective buffoon is clinging to your hand. Twice Mr. Miller almost slipped off the bridge, nearly taking his precious seed with him.

Jillian piped up. "Let go, Dad. It's not safe."

The reply came back painfully predictable, "Not in a million years."

Whitt ascertained they'd managed to traverse nearly one quarter of the bridge's length and had begun to calculate the estimated amount of time it would take to complete the trek, when his father reared up and sneezed. Some people manage a gentle sneeze, others incorporate the hands, and still others will actually give a bit of a kick when they let one loose. Not Whitt's father—every muscle in his body goes into convulsions when he sneezes. Though the temperature in the grotto soared near a hundred and twenty degrees, Whitt found the water surprisingly cold.

Enter the Torpedo

"I got him," Ozzie yelled, handing his glasses to Maurine, stripping his shoes and socks off. His webbed toes slapped against slime and stone as he bent his knees and thrust himself into the water, performing a perfect dive, which, unlike Whitt's awkward entry, hadn't produced the slightest splash.

Jillian stared at the water's static surface, recalling the massive amount of time and money her parents spent at the YMCA trying to teach Whitt how to swim. After a years' worth of lessons, his cause remained pitifully lost as he repeatedly sank to the bottom of the pool with all the grace of a lead cannon ball. Instinct prodded Jillian to jump in after him; reason reminded her that she too lacked finesse in the water, as did her father. Her mother was the only member of the family who could tread water.

Jillian turned to Digger, who slowly swayed his head to and fro, scanning the water's surface for signs of movement. She didn't attempt to mask her fear. "How deep is it?"

"Dunno," he said, continuing to search. "No one's ever gone down far enough to measure."

Mr. Miller leaned over the edge, the desperation in his voice transparent. "What's under there?"

"Couldn't say," Digger mumbled, shaking his head. "Never fell in."

Mr. Miller dug his fingers into his scalp, forcefully pulling shafts of hair. "Somebody do something."

Sheriff Teach piped up, "If anyone can get that boy out of there, it's Ozzie. He swims like a dolphin and can hold his breath longer than a whale."

Brad Miller's face sagged like a skydiver who had pulled the ripcord too many times without result. Shoulders lurching forward, it looked as though he might catapult himself into the water, but he reluctantly pulled back, perhaps realizing his lack of swimming skills would do more harm than good.

Minutes passed and still the water's calm did not break.

Mrs. Drummond's suggestion came as casually as if she were ordering a glazed donut at Pop's soda shop. "Let's get a move on." Gasps and moans of horror issued all around and Jillian stiffened, her glare focused like a laser aimed squarely between Mrs. Drummond's eyes. Once again, the old witch had previous knowledge of an impending disaster and had done nothing to dissuade Whitt from entering the grotto. 'Gonna need him,' she'd said when Jillian asked why Ozzie came along, his purpose now evident.

Jillian scrambled for the composure she needed to keep from pushing Agaritha Drummond into the gloomy water below, expelling her words like bullets from the barrel of a high-powered rifle, "How could you let this happen?"

Mrs. Drummond suddenly took on the expression of a woman who had had it up to here. "What makes you think I couldda stopped it? Do you know anythin' about human nature? Do you know your brother? Ever heard the expression, you can lead a horse to water but you can't make him think?"

What was she saying, that had she warned Whitt he wouldn't have listened? That no one would have believed her? Jillian would have put stock in such a warning and would have prevented Whitt from tagging along.

Devil's Edge

"You don't have that power," Mrs. Drummond grunted. "Be grateful for Ozzie. We got to move on. If there's a strong current in that water, they mighta come up somewhere down the line."

"Drink," Candace muttered as she tore a fingernail off with her teeth, "You can lead a horse to water, but you can't make him *drink*."

Jillian rummaged through her mind, searching for an anchor of logic. The idea Whitt and Ozzie might have emerged somewhere else hadn't crossed her mind. She clung to the possibility.

"I'm staying here," Mr. Miller bent to his hands and knees, surveying the water for the slightest ripple, "Just in case."

"Won't do no good," Mrs. Drummond said, beginning to inch her way across the bridge. "Best stay together, Mr. Miller, we ain't alone."

"She's right, Dad. Whitt's not coming up here. We have to go find him."

"What's she mean, we're not alone?"

Jillian shrugged and took her father by the hand, pulling him away from the spot where Whitt and Ozzie disappeared into the water.

Maurine began a series of loud honking, a locating beacon perhaps, like a foghorn or a secret code previously established between herself and Ozzie. Jillian deemed it a good idea; if the boys were anywhere within earshot, they would surely hear Maurine's odd call.

Having successfully navigated the bridge, the entourage stood before a cascading wall of water. Issuing from approximately thirty feet above ground, the waterfall's width equaled the stretch of a dozen people standing fingertip to fingertip, arms extended. Its forceful spray, according to Digger, originated from the town drains and several wastewater reservoirs. Stone, sand, and limestone filtered the water as it made its way through underground tunnels and emptied into the grotto. The Door of Doom, Digger said, waited just beyond this fluid gateway. He pulled rain gear from his pocket and threw it over his head, but since no one else came prepared, they would arrive on the other side soaked to the gills.

The water felt frigid as Jillian burst through to the other side and she wondered if Whitt and Ozzie had felt the same icy chill. If they had, they could suffer from hypothermia. On the other hand, their suffering would not endure should they manage to resurface; the air temperature sizzled and absolutely stifled; it was like trying to breathe inside a plastic bag.

Unleashed from the remote recesses of the cavern, a bone-grinding scream pierced fragile sanities. High-pitched, the wail seemed to puncture Jillian's chest, threatening to withdraw with her fast-beating heart in hand.

The Stubborn Porte

Standing in vigilant silence before *La Porte de Ruine*, everyone watched as Digger ran his fingertips over the carved indents in the door, each groove shaped to fit its intended relic. Southernmost and central, a square awaited *The Book of Trials*, above that, a curved notch designed to receive the Sword of Woe, north of this, a place to hang the Chain of Vengeance, higher up and to the east and west, raised posts inviting the Cuffs of Gall, and northernmost, a crown for the emerald viper. Digger had attempted, three times already, to open the door by placing the relics in their intended sockets, but to no avail; the door simply refused to open.

Sweat dripped over Jillian's brow, not all of it the result of the overwhelming heat. Since hearing the spine-jarring scream, her thoughts had become a jumble of sheer worry. Was Whitt dead or alive? If he and Ozzie hadn't emerged from the water, who screamed? If the scream did come from one of the boys, what had caused them such terror?

"Try puttin' 'em on in a different order," Mrs. Drummond suggested.

Digger turned to give her a quizzical look, and then nodded. "Which way?"

"Heck if I know," she said. "Try going left to right."

Satisfied with her instruction, Digger took the relics off the door and began to reassemble them.

Mrs. Drummond reached into her pants pocket and withdrew a silver flask, drawing heavily on the liquid inside.

Candace Flute stopped biting her fingernails for the mere fraction of a second it took to say, "Happy hour?"

The Half-Headed Man

Whitt desperately tried to absorb the events of the past thirty minutes, but some things in life simply defy explanation.

He had wholeheartedly resigned himself to the fact that he would drown in the icy waters churning beneath the slimy bridge when a merman suddenly torpedoed through the water and raised him to the surface. His lungs, half a second from expiration, sucked in the most satisfying gulp of air they would probably ever experience. The merman turned out to be Ozzie Teach who, with an arm wrapped beneath Whitt's armpits, had paddled him to the safety of a ledge hanging a few feet over the frostbitten pool. The bridge was nowhere in sight. The water's bullyrag current had obviously swept them away. How far was anyone's guess.

Creeping along the ledge perimeter, Whitt and Ozzie attempted to get a solid sense of direction in hopes of locating an exit. Darkness hindered the trek, although intermittent streams of light emanated from a few cracks in the cavern ceiling and row upon row of silvery threads cascaded from above; threads glimmering like tiny white bulbs on a string of Christmas lights. An uncertain variety of glowworm created these lights, Ozzie explained.

Bioluminescent bugs, he called them, and though they aided somewhat in lighting the way, Whitt quivered at the sight.

"What if they've been hanging around for centuries just waiting for a human meal to come along?"

Ozzie laughed, saying it wasn't likely, but provided no scientific evidence to back up the claim, as was his norm. Whitt found the omission deeply disturbing.

Between nearly drowning and encountering the flesh-eating worms, Whitt's inner strength suddenly seemed mortally shattered. A bona fide testament to that fact solidified when a half-headed man with a rat's tail hanging from the corner of his mouth emerged from a nearby tunnel.

Two eyeballs rolled on the top edge of the man's left cheek. No way could either of the extracted orbs provide adequate vision. Right? By evidence of his lumbered gait and apprehensive movements, Whitt felt safe in assuming the man slightly blind, if not completely. Squashed or cut away, the right half of his head melded with the left side. He had squeezed through a ground level burrow and stood less than five feet away.

An automatic response, Whitt's scream left his throat before he realized it had been born, and upon hearing the labored wail, the half-headed man shuffled back into his dark lair, whimpering gasps of surprised dismay.

"What the hell was that?" Whitt squealed, looking for Ozzie and finding him hunkered behind an under-developed stalactite too small to conceal a rabbit. He looked as though someone had stapled his eyelids to the top of his head.

"I'm not sticking around to find out," he said, grabbing hold of Whitt's arm and dragging him away from the burrow, scuttling along the thin, stone ledge as quickly as his webbed feet could carry him.

Following along as closely as possible, Whitt briefly considered the brilliance of the young man who had saved him from the cavern's gullet: You gotta know when to hold 'em, and know when to run like hell; that is the true sum of wisdom.

Ten minutes later, they had turned and twisted through so many stone divides, the chances of finding their way back to the half-headed man's burrow were miniscule at best. As much relief as this thought provided, they were still lost, quarts of courage leaking from every orifice and sweat gland.

Arms folded in a tight clasp across his chest, Whitt leaned against a jutting stone and whimpered, "How can a place look so small on the outside and be so freaking big on the inside?"

"You haven't noticed the ground slants forward? Every step we take leads us deeper underground." The hint of a smile crept over Ozzie's face. "It's fascinating really."

Ozzie began studying the walls, noting the cracks in the ceiling, pointing out where the glowworms arranged themselves, and in which direction the bats had flown. Poking a finger into the air, he measured the direction of a draft, and lent his ear to the constant bat chitter, attempting to determine which direction led deeper into the cave and which would lead toward an exit. Whitt watched in awe, dazzled by sheer genius.

Ozzie's brilliant calculations ultimately led to a circular opening, no further tunnels or burrows evident, a small pool of stagnant water at its center; a dead end.

As Whitt waited for Ozzie to recalculate, he watched the edges of the shadows behind him contract and expand as if engaged in a waltz.

"There's something behind you," Whitt mumbled, not entirely convinced he'd spoken the truth.

Ozzie glanced over his shoulder. "I don't see anything." He shrugged and returned to his airflow measurements.

Whitt had all but given up on the matter when a figure leapt from the depths of the shadows; the half-headed man, a large rock in hand, poised to come down on the back of Ozzie's unsuspecting skull.

The Assembly

The flutter of bat wings overhead put everyone on edge. Candace Flute raised her shoulders like a tortoise trying to slip inside its shell. Jillian instinctively ducked as well, attempting to focus on a furtive shadow lurking beyond the waterfall, but it disappeared before she could identify it. It was the third time she noticed the same elusive shadow. 'We ain't alone,' Mrs. Drummond had noted. Had someone followed them to the grotto and, if so, why?

Digger spewed low-toned grumbles, his curses drowned out by the clatter of the chain of vengeance as he struggled to secure it to *La Porte de Ruine*. He had removed the relics and rearranged them on the door a dozen times, slapping his hands against the stone after each failed attempt, demanding it to open.

Jillian's patience had all but run out. "Why don't you just tell him the right way to put the relics on the door?" She huffed at Mrs. Drummond.

"B'cause I ain't got a clue," Agaritha replied matter-of-factly.

Raking her fingers through her hair, Jillian trembled with frustration. "You know everything else."

"Ain't my fault you were born with a gift. Best get used to it. It ain't likely to turn tail just b'cause it ain't welcome."

Insulted, Jillian raised her voice, "What's that got to do with the damn door?"

"Nothin', and everythin'," Mrs. Drummond said, her tone firm. "You look at me convinced you see your future. What you ain't took into account is this: You ain't me and I ain't you. Now, you can be mad at me for the rest of your life, or we can get on with what we're here to do. Choice is yours."

Jillian repressed the urge to reach out and slap someone. Seething, she retreated, stepping away from Mrs. Drummond, her attention immediately stolen by the sound of shuffling feet, once again originating from the other side of the waterfall. Maurine had apparently heard the shuffling as well, as her head twisted sharply toward the disturbance.

Candace suddenly gasped in the way people do when a particularly juicy revelation inspires a thought. "The curse," she said, closing her eyes for concentration. *'In hand mine bidden tokens evolve, these the blood-bourne grail...recovered to thine suffering site, to set upon the balance scale.'* What if," Candace said, reaching out to yank one of Digger's braids, her pitch escalating, "What if the relics have to be placed on the door by order of historical occurrence?"

Digger squinted, cocked his head to the side, and said, "Oh, go on, spit it out!"

Candace pumped her adrenaline-fired fists in quick bursts. "The balanced scale. Look at the door. Fujo carved those grooves in the order of historical occurrence. She had the viper before she left Haiti, so that would go on first. The Sword of Woe second, because they beheaded her mother on the day of her abduction. The Cuffs of Gall would go on third, because they were used to chain Fujo to the mast of *The Merry Anne* to keep her from jumping ship."

Without pause, Digger began to reassemble the relics in the order Candace suggested.

"The Chain of Vengeance would go on fourth because it was used to hang Blackbeard's severed head from the bowsprit of the ship come to slay him, and *The Book of Trials* would go on last because it wasn't written until all the other events transpired." Candace transferred the last of her information in such a rush she was panting for breath.

Digger scrambled to place the relics in their proper order, mumbling threats and tokens of encouragement directed at the door's stone face. When, at last, he had placed *The Book of Trials* in its place, the ground began to shiver as a sudden earthquake surged. *La Porte de Ruine* began to open without grace. Stone grated against stone, the sound exploding like a supersonic boom, the increased throbbing of the earth forcing Jillian to her knees. Stalactites severed from the ceiling, falling like sharpened spears, crashing to the cavern floor like impact grenades. Stone projectiles scattered in a maddened flurry, a rather large chunk striking

Maurine square on the head, rendering her unconscious. Jillian threw herself over Maurine to shield her from further assault. Stalactites exploded left and right in a deafening fury, barring escape. If it didn't stop soon, the raining rubble would bury them all alive.

Escaping the Bat Cave

Ozzie reached forward to retrieve a gold chain from a small pile of limestone dust and a searing pain exploded in the middle of his spine. He lurched and rolled, grasping at his back. Turning, he watched in horror as the half-headed man reached for another rock. Whitt began to throw a barrage of small stones at the disfigured creature, missing more often than not, but putting up enough of a fight to distract the ghoul from his task.

Planting his feet, Ozzie pushed, propelling himself into the pool of idle water located in the center of the hollow. Compared to the waters beneath the slimy bridge, this pool didn't amount to much more than a warm, overgrown puddle. He swam until he reached Whitt, who extended a hand, helping him out of the water and onto solid ground. Armed with fistfuls of small stones, the boys pummeled the half-headed man until he raised his head in frustration, clenched his fists, and opened his mouth to release a silent scream. At first, Ozzie assumed him mute as well as blind, but when a massive flock of bats entered the cavern like a swarm of bees protecting their nest from a misguided baseball bat, he immediately understood the half-headed man had hailed them. Whitt expelled a high-pitched girlie wail, pulled his t-shirt over his head for protection, and ran in circles. Determined to keep the enemy in sight, Ozzie searched for the half-headed man. The fluttering black wall created by the swarming bats made it nearly impossible to see.

The decision seemed obvious. They could stay here attempting to fend off the bats, hoping the half-headed man could see no better than they, or they could search for an escape route. "Follow my voice!" Ozzie bellowed, braying frantically until Whitt finally bumped into him. Ozzie grabbed him by the belt, pulling him toward what he hoped was the center of the cavern. When his foot detected the edge of the pool, he gave warning, "Take a deep breath," and lunged forward into the waiting water.

Warm water requires a source of heat. The most likely culprits here were geothermal emissions or direct exposure to the sun. This pool didn't seem deep enough for a geothermal effect and very little sun had filtered into the bat-filled cavern. If the pool connected with another body of water, it could lead outside, or perhaps to a different cavern with some sun exposure. It was worth the gamble.

Easy on the eyes, the water ran crystal clear. Diving straight down, Ozzie scanned until he spied the dark outline of a gaping maw a few feet beneath him. An underwater passageway, but was it a dead-end, or a way out? Propelling Whitt behind him, Ozzie finned toward the tubular cavity, praying they had enough air in their lungs to make it to the other side.

Twenty feet or so inside the waterway, an odd quiver forcefully rippled through the water. Ozzie stopped short, knowing only seismic activity could produce such a pronounced riffle. Alarmed, he tugged on Whitt's belt and raced ahead.

Darkness permeated the waterway but for a pale silver light emanating in the distance, close enough to ensure they had enough oxygen to reach it, but far enough away to cause concern should the passageway collapse. No sooner did this thought cross Ozzie's mind than a dark form slowly began to slip over the thread of silver light up ahead, leaving nothing but complete darkness in its wake.

Whitt's body began to wriggle in fits, his oxygen already in short supply. Ozzie turned to inspect the path behind them, aware the trip back would take more time than traversing the few feet required to arrive at the spot where the silver light had been only moments before. They had no choice but to try to push past the barrier ahead.

The half-headed man made an effective case for haste as his blurry form appeared in the water less than five feet behind Whitt's outstretched sneakers.

I Feel the Earth Move

"Get inside!" Candace howled, dodging falling debris as she hurdled toward *La Porte de Ruine*, which had finally opened enough to allow passage. Jillian watched as the librarian successfully shimmied through the door. Using Maurine's armpits for leverage, Sheriff Teach and Jillian lifted and dragged her toward the door. Any place was better than the meteor field exploding around her. Half way to the door a rock, propelled like shrapnel, grazed the side of Jillian's face, burning her skin and momentarily blinding her.

Digger crawled across the threshold proclaiming, "Your secrets are mine!" Mrs. Drummond followed closely behind, blood oozing from a gash on the crown of her head. Once safely inside, Jillian helped lay Maurine down, patting her face gently in hopes of bringing her around. Maurine responded with a faint grumble.

Light streamed into the grotto from a small blowhole in the ceiling, illuminating a thin stream of water running the length of the enclosed area. Thankfully, no stalactites hung here, but a group of large rocks lay strewn about as though Mother Nature had insisted on a bit of furniture for her cozy den.

The earth continued to tremble as the door persisted in sliding aside; opening wider with each passing second.

Candace spoke with utter relief, "We're safe."

Mrs. Drummond reached for her flask and unscrewed the lid. "I ain't convinced," she said, gulping down the last bit of courage left inside the gleaming container.

A Haunting Reunion

Anne Bonny cried with glee, her arms outstretched toward the bloodied group of mortals tumbling into the grotto. "As I vowed, Mary Read, a day such as none other. Deliverance, at long last!"

Jillian reeled, as if caught in the throngs of a vivid hallucination; voices issuing from solid limestone must certainly be the result of having been pummeled by one too many stalactite shards. Stepping in line with her suspicions of acute brain damage, an apparition appeared before her eyes, blurry at first, but solidifying until it formed the distinct outline of two women perched high atop a large boulder.

The taller of the two women looked like a striking image of Jillian's mother and she wore a pair of black pantaloons, puffy from hip to knee where they met the top edges of her dark leather boots. Bandoliers crossed her white, billowy shirt; two rustic pistols harnessed within their sheaths nestled beneath her breasts, and a cutlass dangled off her hip. Long locks of blonde hair coursed over her shoulders, a streak of fire-red screaming over her crown. *Anne Bonny.*

"Morgan!" Anne wailed, drawing nearer, her smile reaching ear to ear.

"Nay," the other woman said sharply. "Tis well past Morgan's day."

"Look at her, Mary," Anne insisted, "She is all of me."

Her toes dangling four feet off the ground, Mary drifted close, staring at Jillian with intense scrutiny. "Aye," she said, "but harbor your hope, Anne Bonny. Tis not Morgan. And I fear the lass does not see, nor hear us."

"You're wrong," Jillian sputtered.

Mary recoiled in shock.

Anne let loose a fiendish giggle, clapping her hands with uninhibited glee. Attempting a jubilant hug, Anne's arms passed through Jillian's flesh, leaving an icy shiver behind.

"Morgan!" She shouted.

"My name is Jillian," she said, unbuttoning the last button on her shirt and ripping a strip of the fabric away, "Jillian Miller."

Kneeling beside the stream, she wet the cloth and returned to Maurine. There, she placed the rag over Maurine's brow and gave her another gentle slap on the cheek. Maurine's eyes fluttered open, her lips moving without sound until she found her voice, "Where am I?"

Screaming from a short distance across the way, Digger exclaimed, "I found it. Step away wench, it's *mine*." Strong-arming Candace so she could come no closer, he stood before a large black chest nuzzled in a deep nook carved into the limestone wall. Reluctantly accepting her curiosity's defeat, Candace backed away as Digger threw a protective embrace over the treasure chest. His affection adequately bestowed, he set his sights upon a large rusted lock on the face of the chest, pounding away at it with an arsenal of stones, which continuously crumbled beneath the force of his blows. It didn't seem as though the tenacious lock would break anytime soon.

By this time, two male figures had come to stand at Anne Bonny's side, their expressions riddled with curiosity and excitement.

"As I live and breathe," the fellow dressed in brightly colored garments proclaimed. "But for the short locks, I would think myself in the company of Anne Bonny, youth and beauty fully restored."

Anne spat a mouthful of saliva in his direction and attempted to kick him in the groin, her boot passing clean through. "Dare ye say it again, Rackham?" He cringed and floated out of reach. "Hair of the dog, still a coward," she sniped.

" 'Ave they come to set us free?" The older of the two men inquired, a metal claw on his right hand pressed to his lips, his voice a whispered quiver, perhaps in fear of Anne's rebuke, perhaps in fear of hope.

"If me name be Anne Bonny. Aye."

At this, the man's face brightened and, for a moment, he looked as though he might try wrapping his arms around Anne's torso. "I shall split ye in half," she seethed. Threat accepted, he floated off to whisper excitedly with Jack Rackham.

"I don't have the first clue for setting you free," Jillian said so matter-of-factly Anne seemed taken aback.

"Who you talkin' to?" Maurine asked, her eyes flitting in a wild attempt to see what Jillian saw. "The ghosts? Are they here? What do they look like?" All at once, the gravity of the question took hold and Maurine erupted with exhilaration. "You can see them!"

Maurine's jubilant cry caught Mrs. Drummond's attention. She and Candace left Digger to his not-so-artful lock picking endeavor to join Jillian and Maurine.

"Do you?" Mrs. Drummond asked, placing her hand on Jillian's shoulder. "See them? I feel a strong presence and I'm picking up lots of chatter. But, I ain't never actually seen a spirit."

Jillian slipped her shoulder from beneath Mrs. Drummond's hand and gave her a reluctant nod.

She beamed, glowing with grandmotherly pride. "I said you was powerful."

Jillian's resentment broiled. Her brother and Ozzie were missing somewhere inside this underground crypt; dead or alive, no one knew, and all this woman could think to say was 'I told you so?'

"Can you really?" Candace squealed. "Oh, Miss Miller, please...I have so many questions for them. Would you mind?"

"Are you insane? This place is going to implode any minute now and you want a freaking interview?"

Candace looked hurt, but rebounded quickly. "The ground isn't shaking anymore. We're safe. Please, just ask them what happened after they left Bridewell prison. I simply must know."

"Who is this woman so keen to hear our story?" Mary asked, her tone so bland Jillian couldn't tell if Candace's inquiry had upset or intrigued her.

"The local librarian, she's spent the better part of her life studying your history and unearthing the curse."

"Our infamy lives on," Anne said with a wide smile.

Devil's Edge

Although it must have seemed as though Jillian was talking to herself, no one uttered the slightest word of disbelief; what's more, each onlooker directed a gaze in whatever direction Jillian turned her attention, as if hoping to catch an immortal glimpse, Maurine especially.

"She looks a frail, timid sort of creature," Anne observed. "Has she power to break a curse?"

Jillian shrugged. "I told you, I don't know how any of this works."

"What are they saying?" Candace's eyes were wide, her words spoken in breathy excitement, and she had, at least for the moment, given her incisors a break from their incessant nail trimming.

"They're asking if you know how to break the curse."

"Of course I know. What I don't know is what happened after Bridewell." The exasperated expression on Candace's face turned hard. "I will not give my aid in breaking the curse if I am to leave here without answers."

Jillian stood to go toe-to-toe with the obstinate librarian.

"I'm going to go find my brother. You ask them, and while you're at it, break the damn curse yourself."

Jillian sharply twisted away from Candace and Mrs. Drummond caught her by the wrist.

"Listen," she said, "I understand you wantin' to help your family. But I promise, if'n you go, you'll get lost. If'n you stay, them boys will meet you right where you're standin'."

At no time since Jillian's journey to the deranged south did she feel further away from her own sanity than in the space of this moment. A part of her wanted to choke Mrs. Drummond until the drunken old fool begged for mercy, while another part wanted so much to know that her family was safe, she embraced the desire to believe as if clinging to the Titanic's last rail.

Anne Bonny apparently felt she'd kept silent long enough. "Tell the librarian," she said, "we sailed to Fort Nassau in men's britches and took on jobs at the shipyards, building the finest schooners ever to set sail. Taking great care to conceal our bellies, we gave birth to children to ensure that our curse, were it true, might one day be broken. These we raised as men though they be not." Anne reached out to touch Jillian's face, retreating when her fingers left a frigid chill on Jillian's cheek. "We trusted few, nor did we give strangers pause for suspicion. We occupied our spare time compiling a journal we sold to a London publisher in 1724. 'A General History of the Robberies & Murders of the Most Notorious Pirates.' Aye, Mary's clever invention, published under the name of Captain Charles Johnson, so that none would know that the infamous Anne Bonny and Mary Read had escaped the hempen grip."

"Anne Bonny, ye make it sound as if ye abandoned the sea," Mary interrupted. "Nay, off ye sailed, for weeks on end, sometimes months, leaving me to tend the children so ye might seek another throat to cut."

Anne laughed heartily. "Tis true enough, but on with the tale. In 1732, the governor Woodes Rogers offered to pay handsomely for the finest ship builders to construct a sloop. Esteemed as the most skilled builders, the governor readily accepted us. Standing in his office, about to sign our contracts, the good governor spies a patch of blood soaking through me britches and, thinking me beguiled by some dreadful disease, offers his personal physician for examination. For fear of discovery, I decline, but the foolish governor insists." Anne sighed, engaging in a lengthy pause before going on to say, "Physicians carry with them lethal tinctures what should not be mixed. It was long whispered the governor and his physician died of a mysterious illness."

Mary nodded and interjected, "We could no longer remain in Fort Nassau. Packing up the children, we boarded the first ship to set sail."

Eager to reclaim the telling of the tale, Anne interrupted. "We knew not the tub be bound for the northern tip of America...east coast no less. I, unwilling to freeze me arse off, insisted on remaining in Caribbean waters. Now I look back on it, regret starts there. Mary and I took command of the ship with ease, twenty-seven rogues fed to grateful sharks. Afterwards we set sail for Great Abaco, a place of refuge we knew well. We sailed in a rush, for the ship we commanded had but two cannon and a handful of firearms. As I look back, this is the greatest regret. Pirates took us. By Athena's shield, the memory still stirs me sick," Anne lowered her chin and shook her head.

Mary picked up the oratory. "There's a true word. The scallywags meant to send the little ones to Davy Jones. Not without a fight, declared I. To the slaughter we sent those foolish enough to step in the bullet's path and sliced through many more. But, there came a two-fisted swordsman with wrists like lightning and blades of thunder."

"Aye," Anne said, her eyes glassing over as she relived the moment. "The last vision I saw as me throat opened from ear to ear was a pair of swollen breasts protruding from beneath the swordsman's coat." A long silence ensued as Anne and Mary looked to one another, engulfed in the irony of their horrid end.

"We could not know," Anne continued, "if our children survived, not until this very hour." Anne's smile seemed genuine, her countenance so much like Sarah Miller's, for the briefest moment, Jillian succumbed to her adoring gaze. "Go," Mary said, "Tell this tale to the librarian that she might free us from our curse."

Jillian relayed the story as best as she could recall it, then assumed the role of medium so Candace could make further inquiries, delighting Anne and Mary with Candace's desire for intricate details. Satisfied at last, Candace agreed to facilitate the breaking of the curse.

"*That a vestal heart,*" she quoted, "*descended by thine blood in vein, shall provide reasonable sanity for thy sins resolve.* I believe this means the spirits must provide Miss Miller with justifiable reason for forgiveness."

While Jillian attempted to absorb the meaning of what Candace had said, the surface of the stream behind her suddenly erupted and Ozzie Teach emerged, gasping for air and clutching Whitt's flaccid arm. "Take cover," he sputtered, "*Hide.*"

A Bitter Encounter

Alexander watched the half-headed man emerge onto the banks of the stream, and reached behind his back in search of a blade no longer there because Sheriff Teach had confiscated it, leaving him defenseless. The others rushed toward the Teach kid and helped drag the other boy to safety. They had already begun to work the Miller boy over with mouth-to-mouth, leaving Alexander face-to-face with the gruesome beast.

Caution evident, the half-headed man slowly stepped nearer, left side forward so that he might see, his half face draped by unhindered hair growth, eyeballs dangling on his cheek, one of them seeming to hold a steadied gaze. Tall and bone thin, a walking skeleton if Alexander had ever seen one, his clothing frayed at the edges, worn away until little remained but an ornate belt buckle screaming for Alexander's attention. Tarnished by water and time, the buckle was identical to the one Alexander wore, a commemorative issued only to the crew of the *Atlantic Whaler*, the fishing vessel that had devoured the better part of Alexander's youth.

Gaze locked on the belt buckle, Alexander felt his heart and stomach sink both at once, as he recognized the creature advancing upon him as none other than the only man he had ever called friend. Nicholas Targos had not died thirty years ago, nor had anyone stolen his body away. He'd been alive all this time, here inside the grotto, perhaps too brain damaged to find his way out. Who would believe a man could survive such an excruciating injury?

Knees bent in a warrior's crouch, Nicholas inched toward Alexander, his white knuckles clutching a rock he surely meant to use.

Alexander raised his hands, slowly dropped his stones, and backed away; hoping Nicholas might harbor some remembrance of their long-held friendship. Whatever happened, Alexander wouldn't raise a hand against Nick.

Nicholas paused, perhaps puzzled by Alexander's sudden surrender, but seemed to sense vulnerable prey. Raising his rock, he hurled it with extreme accuracy, hitting Alexander on the base of the chin, sending him reeling to the ground.

The gunshot came from behind. Alexander raised his head in time to see Nicholas fall, a jagged hole ripped into his bare chest, blood spurting from the mortal wound.

The Betrayal

The pained expression on Digger's face seemed both strange and powerful as he grimaced over the fallen man, tears streaming over his cheek, his hands pressed tightly over the chest wound, as if that pressure might provide the necessary force to return life.

Jillian attempted to wrap her mind around the idea that Digger had ever felt anything but contempt for his fellow man, when Mrs. Drummond stepped quietly to her side and whispered, "Remember, you got more than one gift at your disposal."

Jillian sighed and rolled her eyes at the cryptic message. Was it completely beyond Mrs. Drummond to spit out what she had on her mind? Apparently.

One gift Jillian did not possess was that of necromancy; Digger's friend would remain dead. She turned her face from the tragic scene, more concerned with Whitt's condition, and made her way toward the pool to tend to her brother.

Emerging from behind a large boulder, a dark arm reached for Jillian's throat and pulled her into a locked embrace, cold metal firmly pressed to her temple, the pressure on her throat so intense the only sound she could produce was a strained gurgle.

The air had hung hot and heavy before, but now with crushing pressure compacting the tender cartilage in her throat, Jillian grappled for life's basic medium, her lungs burning for their due.

When Maurine inadvertently stepped near enough to catch sight of Jillian clamped in her assailant's suffocating grasp, she began to honk loudly, the offensive yaup resounding like a flock of geese caught in a nasty tail wind. Candace burst around the corner to inspect the commotion, her eyes growing wide, first with recognition, then heavy with shock and confusion.

"Lavender?" Candace wailed, the betrayal written so clearly on her face, it was as if someone had painted it there in large red letters.

"Oh get over it," Lavender groaned, her voice thick with contempt.

Candace continued to gape, her hand covering nauseous lips as she realized Lavender had set fire to the library.

Just then, the sheriff rounded the corner and stopped short, gun poised and ready, his face registering disappointment as he must have realized he couldn't fire without risking the possibility of hitting Jillian.

"Get back!" Lavender demanded, her arm squeezing tighter over Jillian's throat, the hammer on the gun pulling back with a sickening click.

The sheriff raised his hands in a defensive gesture and backed away as instructed.

Jillian's face began to burn with broiling wrath; once again, Mrs. Drummond had prior knowledge of a life-threatening event and had done nothing to prevent it.

Obviously, Lavender meant to keep the entourage from their attempt to break the curse. Whatever her motivation, she seemed as serious as a psychopath jacked up on meth; a psychopath who understood Jillian was the only one capable of freeing the spirits confined to the grotto, a psychopath hell bent on keeping that event from transpiring. A shiver ran over Jillian's skin as she suffered an immediate knowing, a concrete awareness that Lavender would not hesitate to pull the trigger; in fact, only brief seconds remained before she did exactly that.

Lavender's vice-like grip pinned Jillian's arms to her side, but her legs were free; her right thigh still scorched and throbbing from the flesh wound Duncan's bullet had left behind. If she could manage just one precise high kick, she might catch Lavender off guard. With some luck, she might even knock her unconscious. Her chances of hitting the mark weren't exactly good with a healthy leg and nearly impossible with a fresh wound, but her options were few.

Her foot left the ground with a short bounce and a hop as she willed her leg over her head with all the force and focus she could rally. Her last conscious sensation was the sound of a freakishly loud explosion. All went dark and quiet.

Coming Around

The scent of ammonia and whispered brandy woke Jillian from her faint, her sight blurry as she focused first on Mrs. Drummond's smiling face and then on to the ghost-like appearance of Lavender's bloodied face and shackled hands. Maurine had torn a strip of fabric from her shirt and busied herself bandaging Jillian's leg.

"You ripped your stitches," she explained consolingly, her eyes bright with admiration. "That was freakin' *awesome*," she added.

Forgive me

Whitt coughed up a gallon of water, but came around nicely. Digger wept quietly over the half-headed man's corpse, which he and the Sheriff had dragged near the treasure chest where Digger continued to beat at the chest's rusted lock, more determined than ever to sever its grip.

Mrs. Drummond suggested getting on with the breaking of the curse so she might return home for a hot cup of tea. Jillian doubted the old woman craved tea, but said nothing. She, too, wanted nothing more than to escape the grotto, to wipe this bizarre chapter of her life off the slate and begin a search for some semblance of normalcy.

"The spirits must present a reason for forgiveness," Candace repeated. "I assume if the reason is favorable and Miss Miller agrees to bestow said forgiveness, the curse will be broken."

"I forgive you," Jillian blurted, her patience completely expired. Anne Bonny and Mary Read, hands folded sternly across their chests, did not fade away in the following moments. Running her fingertips through her short locks, Jillian grunted with exasperation.

"You can't cheat a curse," Candace said curtly.

Expelling a sigh of resignation, Jillian turned to face the spirits and asked, "If you had your lives to live over again, would you change anything?"

"Aye," Mary said, "and entrust slaves to Dutchmen."

Anne beamed at Mary. "Clever as always, Mary. Then no curse there would ever be."

Jillian sighed.

"What are they saying?" Candace begged. Jillian relayed the details of the conversation through terse lips.

"Remorse," Candace said. "Regret for what they did to Fujo. That's what you need to drive at."

Nodding, Jillian determined to try again.

"You're sorry, aren't you," she asked, "for killing people?"

"Nay," Anne protested, "T'was the best part."

Slowly blowing out a mouthful of air, Jillian lowered her head and repeated Anne's answer for all to hear. Maurine laughed jovially until Candace fired off a glare of disapproval.

Jillian strained to hear as Mary took Anne aside.

A Courageous Coward

"Did ye not understand, Annie, our curse can only be broken by forgiveness. We are not likely to gain such a gift if ye continue to brag about slicing throats."

"Black as my soul may be, Mary, it is not in my nature to lie, and I speak the truth when I say I adored every moment of my life and would change nothing but its end."

Mary parked her hands on her hips and jutted her chin toward Anne, "Are ye daft? Content to spend another three hundred years in this rat lair, are ye? No one has asked ye to lie, only to search for some sliver of remorse."

Anne released an indignant grunt. "It wasn't I who bestowed outrageous gifts to Blackbeard. We have Jack Rackham to thank for this curse and none other. Why, then, are all eyes cast upon me?"

Lifting her shoulders in an exaggerated shrug, Mary declared, "Perhaps because ye consider shedding blood the merriest of all adventures."

"Well it was," Anne shouted. "And who can say what lies beyond? At least here we have each other."

Mary's jaw dropped. Repulsed, she backed away from Anne and then rushed back, drawing in nose-to-nose.

"I would not have believed it of ye, Annie, not if mine own ears had not heard. The bravest woman I have ever known cowers within her soul! Never would I have believed it of ye, not ever."

Anne drew and raised her cutlass, her face suddenly flushed with a lava glow. It was the third time Jillian sensed murderous intent today; first Jared Duncan, then Lavender, and now, Anne Bonny. Maybe it was something in the water.

"How dare ye accuse the mighty Anne Bonny of cowardice," Anne bellowed, jabbing her cutlass toward Mary's midsection.

Mary rushed forward, impaling herself on Anne's sword, then stepped away unscathed, her eyes glaring with indignation. "I, too, am inclined toward truth and see it all too clearly. The great Anne Bonny is afeared of the unknown, and rather than face her fear she would settle for an eternity in an accursed cave."

Anne's sword fell at her feet without making the slightest sound. Turning away, she pumped her fists in sheer frustration.

Mary firmly held her ground, and when Jack Rackham moved toward Anne in an apparent attempt to have a word with her, Mary's razor sharp glower and tightly pressed lips seemed sufficient to keep him at bay.

Candace tugged on the hem of Jillian's shirt, demanding to know what the spirits were saying. Annoyed, Jillian shushed the overanxious librarian, saying only there were unresolved issues.

Anne turned toward Mary once again, a telltale trickle of saline escaping the corner of her left eye, streaking over her cheek. Slapping her hands to her head, she roared, "I cannot battle what I cannot see! By the power and wisdom of Athena, how can we know we will not evaporate into nothingness, or that Hades might steal our souls away to the fiery pit they so readily deserve? Is it not wise to remain content with what we have?"

Jillian tried to absorb the enormity of the situation; it would take some delicate cunning to find a suitable solution to this dilemma. Anne obviously held deep-seeded religious convictions but also had an ego the size of the entire Northern Hemisphere. Jillian spent a few moments concocting her strategy.

"Who in all of Hades," she loudly proposed, "could possibly match wits or sword with the great Anne Bonny and Mary Read?"

Anne turned sharply toward Jillian, the lines on her face drawn with concern, "It is true then, our souls be bound for eternal damnation. Is that what ye believe?"

"No," Jillian said matter-of-factly, "I don't believe in Hell at all. I believe good and evil are inherent in the human soul; but if there were such a place, I doubt a soul resides within its walls that could stand toe-to-toe with Anne Bonny and walk away to tell the tale."

"She be right, Annie," Mary said, "Ye breathed to fight and fought to breathe, it is not in ye to lay arms down now, or to settle for another hundred years of the rat head stomp."

Anne stared blankly at Mary for a few moments, and then stooped to pick up her sword, sheathing it with conviction.

"I suppose," she reluctantly confessed, "I could find some regret for killing Young Webster, though he most certainly would have hung anyway."

"Understood," Jillian said, "but what about Fujo and her sister, Catti? Did you mean to do them harm?"

"Neither one," Anne proclaimed with a firm tone. "T'was Rackham what traded the kitten to Blackbeard, not I, and that only because he be an idiot through and through."

Jack raised himself before Jillian's eyes and spoke softly. "Aye, an idiot then and yet I be. I meant the lass no harm, but simply fell faint to fear. This, I truly regret. If given the chance to live once again, I would take up a profession of honor, leaving skullduggery to those with the truest talent."

Jillian relayed Jack's remarks and asked Candace to tell the spirits what happened to Fujo after she left Port Royal. Happy to oblige, Candace went into a long oratory explaining the order of events, spinning around slowly as she spoke, attempting to make eye contact even though she clearly had no hope for success. As she spoke, Jillian watched for signs of remorse on the spirit's faces. Surprisingly, Anne Bonny seemed most grieved by the story of Fujo's bereavements, her chin dropping lower as Candace chronicled each successive event.

The moment had come; its arrival instantly recognized as Jillian's gaze locked with Anne's eyes, behind which, a wall of tears had appeared. Before a fresh tear could fall upon Anne's cheek, Jillian whispered, "I forgive you," and the spirits remained no more.

Devil's Edge

Double Damn

The rich smell of garlic lollygagged long after dinner concluded. Dixie Teach stood at the kitchen sink, scrubbing caked-on spaghetti sauce from the bottom of her favorite pot, listening to the chatter ensuing behind her. Excited blither, most of which she would forever refuse to believe; ghosts, curses, and monsters lurking in the grotto. The embellishments nothing more than satanic tales gone mad, if anyone required a truthful opinion. The water ran from the spigot hot enough to sting and Dixie adjusted the tap. It wouldn't come as much of a surprise if someone suddenly threw a mermaid into the saga. Two months had gone by since the alleged events took place, and it seemed as though someone added another trinket to the pile of stewing dung each time they told the story. Well, no one would persuade Dixie Teach. Legends and myths aplenty were born exactly this way. Frankly, *The National Enquirer* wouldn't swallow this pile of bunk. She held her tongue, unwilling to offer an immediate reprimand, too tired to deal with the resulting arguments. Her children were all safe at home, that meant more than setting the record straight.

She had known exactly what to expect from an evening spent in the company of the Miller family, long tales for long hours over a game of *30 Bones*, not exactly the way she would prefer to spend her evening, but the children had whined and pled until she finally gave in. She would suffer their outlandish fables for a few more hours before throwing herself on the mercy of her pillow.

Finishing the dishes, she cleared the counter, packing away a few magazines and the daily edition of *The Coastal Review*, its headlines screaming about the murder and attempted murder charges filed against Velma and Lavender Sinclair. Attending church on a regular basis would have done those ladies a world of good. Too late now, they'd done the devil's work and would pay dearly for it: twenty years to life each, almost guaranteed. Good riddance.

Dixie flicked off the light switch in the kitchen and parked on the living room sofa, a *Reader's Digest* in one hand, a hot cup of tea in the other.

Ozzie complained Jillian's psychic powers gave her an unfair advantage with *30 Bones*.

"No such thing as psychic power, Ozzie. Let the girl play," Dixie said, opening her Digest to a story about a woman who had used her faith to lift the front end of a pickup off a six-month-old Welsh corgi pup: *Praise God*.

"We've been playing for half an hour and she hasn't missed yet," Ozzie insisted, his nose crinkled in frustration. Dixie ignored him and stared at the photograph of the middle-aged woman who had saved her puppy from imminent death. Who can imagine lifting a big old truck up off the pavement with one hand? Only by the power of God could a body ever dream of doing such a thing.

Whitt's rack was the only one Dixie could see straight on, and he took his time setting three bones up on the hooks. "Are you really giving up science to be a doctor?" he asked. Ozzie answered without the slightest hesitation, "That's the plan."
Imagine, Dixie mused, *my son, an honest-to-god doctor.*
"I'm thinking I might have a future in archaeology," Whitt said, his expression serious as black on night.

Ted took Professor Miller out on the patio for a couple beers. After all these long, hard years, Dixie had yet to break Ted of his penchant for alcohol. No reason to stop trying now, she would eventually wear him down. For now, she took satisfaction in knowing what he was up to. Against her best advice, he'd decided to offer Professor Miller a permanent position at the UAB. Nothing she said in protest stood the slightest chance of changing his mind. No surprise, Ted had always been his own man. If he wanted Miller at the UAB, he would sweeten the deal until he had the man wrapped around his finger. Still, that wouldn't change Dixie's perception of the matter. Devil's Edge would be better off without the likes of Professor Miller and his hell-spawned offspring.

Maurine had finally aroused the courage to confess to Tourette's and had launched into a longwinded explanation of the condition for Jillian's benefit. Dixie sensed a certain tension in Maurine's tone. Obviously, this could possibly ruin their budding friendship. As hurtful as that might be, sooner or later Maurine would get over it. Dixie would definitely sleep better knowing her daughter wasn't running with the number-one delinquent in Devil's Edge.

"I hope," Maurine concluded, "we can be friends anyway."

Jillian took on a surprised expression, the kind people use when something suddenly makes all the sense in the world, laughed, and said, "Elephants doing the backstroke through the Lord's turkey gravy, I wouldn't have it any other way."

Damn, damn, double damn, Dixie bemoaned.

Ted and Professor Miller sauntered in off the patio and stood by the game laid out on the carpet, over the circle of children desperately vying for victory.

"Who's winning?" Ted said, as if he didn't have eyes to see Jillian had nearly all the bones stacked up at her right elbow.

"I don't care what Mom says, Dad. I hereby institute a lifetime ban on Jillian!" Ozzie's tone had gone dead serious, his glare plainly expressing his belief Jillian Miller constituted the world's worst sort of shyster.

"I'm not trying to cheat," she complained, a bit of a giggle escaping her throat.

"Listen kids," Professor Miller said. "Mr. Teach has been kind enough to offer me a permanent position at the UAB. What do you think?"

Jillian and Whitt stood to their feet as if discharged from a slingshot, sheer exasperation painted over their faces, "No!"

Professor Miller's cheeks flushed pink. "I guess we'll have to talk it over," he told Ted, who smirked and graciously nodded.

"Jillian, I've got something for you," Professor Miller said, pulling an envelope from the pocket in his jacket. "It's a registration badge for the National Dance Finals. If you think your leg is healthy enough to compete, I'll be front and center."

Without a word, she flung her arms around his neck and clung to him.

"Did y'all hear what the government did to old Digger today?" Ted said, plopping down on the sofa next to Dixie. "Took that treasure chest and everything in it and labeled it government property." Ted let out a tickled chortle, "Thirty years of searching and the feds walk in like they own Mother Earth and everything on her back. Old Digger's fit to be tied."

A Fitting End

Agaritha never saw a man look so puzzled as Digger Spotswood had when she slipped an emerald viper into his pocket and explained its abundant worth. "This," she winked, "might be a secret worth keepin'."

That was half an hour ago. Now she turned the key in the back door of the Sinclair cottage.

Velma had left a spotless kitchen behind. The cockatiels, unimpressed, seemed to be swearing up a storm, as they hadn't eaten for nearly a week, their chirping evolving into an earsplitting crescendo. Agaritha would eventually have to find them a new home. For now, she opened drawers and doors until she located a container filled with birdseed.

Things had settled down quite a bit over the last few weeks and Agaritha felt grateful for that, but couldn't help but wonder if Ebby would ever return from his excursions through time. In truth, she understood she would require help in gaining an answer to that question and knew of only one person who might possibly assist: Ozzie Teach. She couldn't say exactly what the boy knew, but she sensed he possessed vital morsels of information. Convincing the lad to offer his aid postured another challenge altogether.

Removing the plastic dishes from the birdcage posed no problem and Agaritha replaced them, filled to the brim with fresh food and water. She slid the bottom compartment of the cage out, emptying the soiled contents into a nearby garbage can.

On the brighter side of things, Candace Flute had set up an appointment for laser eye surgery, touting the date and time around town like a child eager to let the world in on her most coveted secrets, and she planned to attend flight school once Carla Ballencroft recovered well enough to join her. Goes to show, it ain't never too late to start livin'.

The Miller family would soon return to Rhode Island, but all things rarely being what they seem, Agaritha suspected Devil's Edge hadn't seen the last of Jillian Miller. Yes, Aggy's relationship with the talented young girl had turned to Chop Suey, but that, like everything else in life, was subject to change. Once the child understood that avoiding confrontation is not always the best course of action, the tide would turn.

Pulling a fresh copy of *The Coastal Review* from beneath her armpit, Agaritha tore off the front page, and placed it on the bottom of the cage. Wide eyed, slack jawed, and handcuffed, the photographs of Velma Sinclair and her rogue daughter seemed rather life-like.

A box of birdseed marked, 'Extra Fiber' called to Agaritha from the far side of the room.

Artwork compliments of Lianne Anderson © 2013

Another Title by BK Crawford:

The Future Queen

Patience is not one of Farrin Lockwood's strong suits
and that fact is about to plunge her headfirst into grave danger.
Hoping to outwit a menacing sorcerer, she also faces
the white dragon, attempts to rescue her best friend from an unthinkable marriage,
enlists the help of a shape-shifter,
and teams up with the infamous Merlin as he seeks to prepare
her for battle against the bloodthirsty
Morgana le Fay.
Farrin must survive it all if she is to become the future queen.

http://www.facebook.com/authorBKCrawford

Devil's Edge